The Mistress of Auschwitz

A Historical Fiction by Terrance D Williamson

"I don't think of all the misery, but of the beauty that remains."

Anne Frank

Dedicated to:
My eternal son,
My loving daughter,
And my patient wife.

Based on the life of
Eleonore Hodys

Introduction

There are times in our lives when we come across a story that captivates us to the point where we struggle to think about anything else. The life of Eleonore Hodys is one such tale that has enraptured me.

I hope I have done some justice for her life and the lives of the many souls who endured barbarisms that we shall never understand. While creative liberties have been employed – as in all works of historical fiction – I have attempted to retain as much accuracy as possible. This remains the true story of Eleonore Hodys: The Mistress of Auschwitz.

Only one character who makes an appearance in this novel is fictional, the others are all based on real men and women who are extraordinary human beings that deserve your attention if you can take the time to do so.

DISCLAIMER: This book is a work of fiction. References to real people, events, establishments, organizations, or locales are intended only to provide a sense of authenticity, and are used fictitiously. All other characters, and all incidents and dialogue, are drawn from the author's imagination and are not to be construed as real.

Chapter One:
La Venezia

"The cardinal error of the Germans who opposed Nazism was their failure to unite against it."

William I Shirer

Berlin

Staring blankly at the stucco ceiling above her bed, Eleonore lay with her hands folded neatly across her stomach. Despite the hours spent in solitude and the darkness of the night, sleep had evaded her, again.

Not that her bed was all that disagreeable, nor was her little apartment devoid of comfort, but her worries kept her mind affixed to consciousness. As was becoming her nocturnal custom, Eleonore had scarcely attempted to lure sleep. Instead, she remained clothed in the same plain, navy blue dress she wore the day before and lay on top of her sheets, ready for the day's demands.

She listened to her breathing in and out and felt the rising and falling of her belly against her hands. She timed her breathing with the patient ticking of her little silver watch spread out on the table stand next to the bed, reminding her of the inevitable: she would endure another day absent of the rest granted to countless others. She glanced over at the persistent watch, sitting oblivious to the anguish it was causing her and sighed when she discerned the hands in the dim light of dawn: 6:30.

Realizing her efforts to enter slumber were futile, she sat up slowly as the blood rushed to her head and her eyes tracked stars bouncing about the room. She ran her hand across the bedsheet, feeling the smoothness of the linen in her hands. She looked longingly at the patterns of stitched roses, like a lover mourning the absence of their partner. The bed had not offered the sweet solace she coveted, but instead operated as an instrument of taunting enticement; lacking fulfillment yet still desired – a true romance.

Not that she could blame the inanimate for withholding rest as her recent trepidations seemed fit enough for the challenge. Despite her concerns, she forced herself to her feet, sliding into her awaiting slippers, and walked to the stove which was a mere ten feet from the bed.

How she loved her humble apartment. It was a meagre one-room flat that suited her needs adequately with the bathroom, kitchen, and bed all within two strides of each other. For an unwed, childless woman approaching forty, it suited her perfectly.

Yet the minimalism seemed to scream what her late parents somehow still found a way to communicate: she was alone. Her defense, which she had perfected with each fresh argument, lay within her career; she was married to her seamstress shop. She smiled as she recalled her father's chuckle at the justification and her mother's scowl of disapproval.

As any child of a stubborn, Austrian mother can attest, Eleonore found herself in a losing battle of wills. Yet when arranging courtship failed by Eleonore's boredom of the suitors paraded, her mother resorted to demanding grandchildren; it was no longer a request. It was only with the passing of her parents did she regret failing them in that regard. Otherwise, a life spent rearing children with an inattentive husband was left undesired.

Providence, in its wisdom, had risen her to a station above that of an ordinary housewife. Not that she detested the thought of having children, but her attention was stolen by her entrepreneurial pursuits and there was little, if anything, that could break the spell. A husband, too, would certainly suffer the sting of her prioritization, and she could not, in good conscience, bestow that on anyone.

The kettle screeched and, returning her mind to the present, Eleonore poured herself a cup of tea. With the warmth spreading through her fingers, she took her drink to the main attraction of her living quarters: the balcony. Opening the double French doors, she walked out to the crisp winter air and leaned over the steel railing. Raising the cup to her nose, she let the fragrance fill her lungs as she observed the city crawling to a start.

While she loved this little routine, Eleonore found her enjoyment fading with the troubling thought that such peaceful mornings were numbered. To an extent, she was thankful she was not isolated in these uncertainties as she watched the passersby in the street below. The usual smiles and waves of greeting were growing absent as each looked at the pavement before their feet, only offering a tip of the hat to their closest confidants as they hurried along.

Weariness from war attrition was burning its mark on society. While many were beginning to understand Hitler's intentions as malicious, those in positions of privilege didn't perceive his objectives as vindictive in nature. Still, the Socialist Democrat Party – of which Eleonore was a respected patron – sought to harness the Fuhrer's ambitions.

But who could challenge the almighty savior of Germany? To defy him was to betray the fatherland, and most who adhered to an 'incorrect' political party paid a hefty price. Some were shot as traitors of the state; others were taken for forced labor. Rumors had been circulating as to the terrors within the concentration camps, but Eleonore found the descriptions so horrific that she assumed they were exaggerated pieces of American propaganda.

Despite the potential consequences, and thanks to Eleonore's ingenuity, the party had thrived as an underground resistance group. Her shop, *La Venezia* – named after her love of Italian design – was situated in the very heart of Berlin. It provided the ideal location for secret meetings with inconsequential members who had avoided state detection, such as herself.

But the numbers had been reduced of late. One by one, those who had attended on a regular basis were beginning to disappear. More disturbing was that none could account for where they had vanished. Eleonore found herself questioning reality when all traces of an acquaintance were erased. Some she assumed to have been murdered; others were taken prisoner.

Still, the location of their meetings had gone undiscovered. Whether this was by chance or by design, Eleonore didn't know, but she resolved to continue despite the dwindling turnout. Now, however, a new development had been implemented which would likely make her shop a target for Nazi inspection and was the cause for her sleepless nights. The Nuremburg Race Laws had issued another decree to the swelling list of edicts: Jews were to be eliminated from commerce and employment.

While they had already been removed from public office, ordered to abstain from schools, and levied with insufferable taxes, they could no longer be employed. While most employers had dismissed their Jewish staff, Eleonore had maintained two in her employment at the shop.

In fact, they were her only employees. Further obstructing the issue, they were an elderly couple with no children to depend on for finances and she could not simply dismiss them. The husband, Alexander, manned the counter and greeted each guest warmly while his wife, Ruth, worked with Eleonore mending the dresses or designing new ones for their wealthy clientele.

Due to respect for Alexander – who preferred to be called Alex – many of the customers did not report his race to the authorities, but instead refrained from using their services any longer. With the decline in business came an increasing financial strain that was difficult for Eleonore to bear. Maintaining their salary was possible, though scarcely, yet she was determined to not abandon them in their hour of need.

The bond of companionship, too, added to her dilemma as Ruth and Alex had taken upon the role of her late parents while she, in return, had filled the void of their barrenness. She helped them with daily chores while they provided her warm meals and Alex repaired more than a handful of busted pipes in the apartment – free of charge, of course. Expedience, she understood, drew upon the logic of survival, but she was burdened with a conscience which refused to sacrifice upon the altar of convenience.

And, while she was not a Jew herself, she felt disgust at their treatment. After all, Alex and Ruth were more Germanic than she was – born and raised in Berlin as seventh, possibly eighth, generation Jews. They were even apostates from Judaism and their parents had converted to the Protestant faith. It was at church that Ruth and Alex met, were wed, and spent their Sundays in dedicated worship. But what did piety count for in Nazi Germany if it wasn't devoted to racial purity? The Nazis relinquished no clemency upon religious groups, even those who adhered to Christianity. Race was their only concern.

With a final sip, Eleonore took a deep breath before leaving the balcony and returned into her apartment. Gathering her purse, black felt hat, and slipping into her heels, Eleonore opened her apartment door, but couldn't bring herself to step out. Lingering, she glanced back into the apartment, unwilling to trade the tranquility for the precariousness of what likely lay ahead.

She wondered if it was foolish to continue in her path with the understanding that the consequences may be grave. Or was it bravery, then, to endure in her striving to bring Germany out of Hitler's shadow? She was certain that a socialist democratic government was the dream of many even though they dared not express it. So, for their sake, for the silent majority, for those too afraid to speak, she would suffer the penalties of her resistance.

Closing the door behind her, Eleonore locked up and half-jogged down two flights of stairs until she came to the foyer. Entering the street, Eleonore walked briskly along her way towards *La Venezia*. Keeping her gaze low, as was now the custom, Eleonore passed by a square with a pile of black ash and burnt logs in the center.

Another book-burning, she thought as she held her hand over her nose to block out the remaining stench of burnt leather and wood. She strained to resist the temptation of inspection to determine if any literature had survived the flames. *What a terrible shame,* she watched as others mirrored her repulsion of the smell yet, like she, none dared venture closer than necessary for fear of reprisal.

Keeping her eyes locked on the pavement in front of her, Eleonore passed by the all too familiar streets. The bakery on the corner with the once cheerful baker whose disposition had soured after his sons had been drafted. The coffee shop opposite the bakery where Eleonore had occasionally purchased tea when her supplies ran short. Except now the business was closing as none would gather for concern of the Nazis suspecting them of treasonous plotting. 'Where two or more were gathered, there Hitler is,' had swiftly become a favorite saying amongst those brave enough to voice their dissent.

Eventually, Eleonore rounded the corner to her quaint shop. While situated in the center of Berlin, *La Venezia* had been tucked away down a side street that seemed to her a haven from the hustle and bustle of daily life. Only a handful of other shops populated the narrow street, and the foot traffic was nothing compared to some of the main strips.

While unfavorable for business operations, the seclusion was to Eleonore's preference as she could hardly tolerate the crowds. The cramming of busy people going about their own pursuits in quite possibly the rudest fashion; bumping, pushing, and squeezing past to get ahead of the next person. On the occasions she was required to venture down such detestable passageways, she made certain to attempt the mission when the least amount of people were expected.

Rummaging through her purse for her keys, Eleonore cursed the poor lighting of the street: the one blemish in an otherwise ideal environment. Not only was the street narrow, but it also faced north, meaning the sun blessed them with its warmth for a mere couple hours per day. This, of course, was not of much concern to Eleonore, as she was usually buried in her windowless room at the back of the shop. Still, some natural light would help the place seem a tad more welcoming which, on the surface, was rather bland.

The forest green windowsills and frames were ill matched against the grey bricks and each summer Eleonore swore she would paint it a bright red. But each summer came and went – along with all the hectic demands of being an entrepreneur – and the right time never arrived.

"Aha!" Eleonore pulled out her keys in victory and placed them to the door only to realize the handle had been broken.

Stepping back, Eleonore gasped as she read the black graffiti plastered above the shattered glass window: "JEWS ARE NOT WELCOME."

Glancing inside, she noticed the floor was covered with broken glass and littered with Nazi propaganda pamphlets. Her little shop, her source of pride, had been offered over to the madness of anti-Semitism.

Paralyzed, Eleonore stood before the one thing that had provided her with direction and given her hope for a brighter future. Her dwindling clientele would surely cease altogether should news of this escape – which it certainly would. Berlin was a large city, but gossip traveled fast. Not to mention that this had been the last haven for the political meetings and without the venue the party would disintegrate.

"Oh!" a voice called from behind her and Eleonore turned to see Ruth clasping a hand over her mouth in shock.

Her large, purple purse had fallen, and lipstick and a compact lay scattered on the pavement. With his hands on his wife's shoulders, Alex's eyes welled as he was lost for words to convey his shock.

The three stood in stunned silence. The only sound came from the wind rushing through the narrow street and a crumpled newspaper rolling by. Eleonore felt her cheeks turning crimson from embarrassment, but also felt a rage unlike any she had experienced before.

This was her shop, her pride and joy and it had been ruined because of some ill-begotten and senseless Nazis. She squeezed her hands into fists as she plotted a fictional revenge.

"Such ignorance," Eleonore shook her head as she fumed.

Still, Ruth and Alex stared at the graffiti, frozen in terror by the warning. Anyone would be frightened, but they were an elderly couple and escaping the country was not an option afforded by their age.

They were an odd couple to have been paired together, and not simply because of their mismatched physiques. Ruth was a rather plump, yet tall woman who carried her weight in the upper half of her body while her scrawny legs seemed to have been snatched from someone else. Adding to her imbalance, she conveyed a vibrant and sometimes overpowering demeanor with a boisterous voice to match.

Alex, on the other hand, was a slouched, slender man nearly half a foot shorter than his wife. He wore the same outfit each day which Eleonore was amused to learn he had multiples of the same clothes: a white, button-up shirt underneath a grey suit jacket with grey pants held in place by suspenders that were so loose that they had lost much of their purpose.

Yet for the mismatch in appearance, they were complimentary in spirit. Though tall in stature, Ruth was short in temper while Alex was patient, kind, and a little too subservient. Somehow, this combination worked, and when they smiled together they brought a light into Eleonore's world. On the other hand, their feuds were entertaining and the outcome predictable: Ruth was the undefeated champion.

"I thought I had given you the weekend off?" Eleonore spoke quietly as she looked at them awkwardly, unsure of how to react. She was a sensitive woman, but she often failed to articulate her feelings adequately. Besides, her embarrassment was radiant, and she couldn't find the sentiment that she wished to convey.

"We couldn't leave you to do the order by yourself," Alex bent down, slowly, to collect his wife's items and place them back in her purse. Straightening with a groan, he held out the purse for his wife, but Ruth was unable to break her gaze from the vandalism. Shrugging, Alex threw it over his shoulder.

"Well, I suppose none of us are able to finish the job now," Eleonore stood back and inspected the damage.

"A broken window won't stop me," Ruth seized the purse from Alex as if he had stolen it, and marched forward. Realizing the door handle had been busted, Ruth improvised and, taking a rock left from the vandals, smashed through the door window and unlocked it from the inside.

"What on earth are you doing?!" Alex frowned.

"Oh, don't look at me like that," Ruth growled at her husband. "Sweep this glass up so we can return the store to its proper form."

"Yes, dear," Alex's shoulders fell as he obeyed and walked obediently into the shop. At the best of times, Ruth was not of the disposition to handle defiance and Alex knew his place well enough.

Eleonore remained reserved as she watched them deal with this outrage in their own chaotic manner. However uncomfortable she had been to have them witness this hatred, Eleonore was pleased to have their guided company.

"Should I call the officials?" Alex kicked the shards around with his feet, unsure of where to begin.

"Are you mad?" Ruth threw her hands onto her hips as her cheeks burned red. "For all they know we aren't Jews, and how long do you think that will last with them poking their heads around here?"

"Well someone found out," Alex pointed to the graffiti.

"And you best get that cleaned up before the Fuhrer himself wonders what Jews are doing in Berlin," Ruth huffed as she stormed into the backroom to begin her work.

"Thank you," Eleonore touched Alex on his shoulder who shook his head, relinquishing the credit; he had no choice in his designation.

Joining Ruth in the backroom, Eleonore sat on the bench opposite the old Jewess and began stitching away. The two worked in silence with the machines sewing in their blissful ignorance. The dress in question was for the wife of a Nazi officer, and she demanded perfection. Eleonore was determined to deliver on that promise and was thankful Ruth's skillful hands would be helping. Though, she wondered how the official's wife would react should she discover that a Jew created the dress.

The truth was, though Eleonore didn't admit it, half her success was due to Ruth. Yet Ruth refused pay raises despite Eleonore's relentless attempts. Still, Eleonore would slip in an extra bill or two into Ruth's purse when she wasn't looking or pay for meals when they ventured out on the town.

"How's your portion coming along?" Eleonore paused to look over at Ruth, but she didn't reply.

With tears streaming, Ruth covered her face to hide her shame. She was a durable woman, and this display of vulnerability was not afforded with much ease.

"Ruth?" Eleonore asked sympathetically, yet quietly to provide some semblance of dignity.

"Sorry," Ruth shook her head as she blew her nose into a handkerchief. "I tend to cry when I'm angry."

"Nothing to forgive," Eleonore gave a limp smile to try and relieve the tension.

"This is the end for us, isn't it?" Ruth collected herself and wiped the tears from her eyes.

"They can't stop me from employing you," Eleonore tried to cheer Ruth up but failed to even convince herself.

"They can," Ruth sniffled, "and they will."

"I'll pay you in private, off the books," Eleonore smiled.

"We can't ask you to do such a thing," Ruth waved her handkerchief in dismissal and returned to her work.

Walking over to her employee's bench, Eleonore placed her hand on Ruth's, "I'm unable to continue without you. I need you. We're in this together, to the bitter end."

"But they'll send us to the camps," Ruth chocked. "All our friends and relations, they have been taken and never heard from again. I should think starving in our own home would be preferable to forced labor. I'll be of no service at such unforgiving work."

"It won't come to that," Eleonore sighed. She knew the realities and how unlikely it was that they would escape the consequences.

"Excuse me," Alex knocked before poking his head through the door, "an officer would like to speak with you."

"I told you not to call the authorities!" Ruth's eyes bulged with incredulity.

"I didn't!" Alex half-shouted back in defense.

"Then who did?" Ruth asked sarcastically. "None around these parts care much for our misfortunes."

"I don't believe it's about the windows," Alex glanced at Eleonore.

"It's alright," Eleonore nodded at Alex. "I'll be right there."

"Do you suppose it's about party business?" Ruth spoke quietly as she fiddled with her machine, trying to distract her nerves.

"Possibly," Eleonore frowned, wondering how Ruth knew.

"I found a pamphlet left on the floor a while back," Ruth offered a quick smile. "Don't worry, I discarded it."

"I appreciate your discretion," Eleonore smiled back, but internally she was petrified her secret had not been as hidden as she supposed.

"Miss Hodys, open up immediately!" an aggressive knock rattled against the door.

With a deep breath, Eleonore walked over to the door and, opening it quickly, stood tall before an officer, who, she was surprised to discover, was a childhood acquaintance.

"Horst?" Eleonore couldn't believe her fortune. "Is that really you?"

"This isn't the time for pleasantries," Horst held his hands firmly behind his back and stuck his chin in the air, though he failed to hide the subtle gratification at seeing her.

Eleonore was beautiful, after all, with striking blue eyes, high cheekbones, and curly, brown hair: the Aryan dream. If not for her height, or lack thereof, and her advanced age, she would have been selected by the propaganda machine as a display of perfection. During their younger years, Horst had endeavored to secure her affection on a few occasions, but with no success.

For his part, Horst was a smaller man, often bullied during adolescence for his stature. This mistreatment burdened Horst to the extent where he eventually attempted suicide, but the rope failed and he escaped with a broken leg. At least, that's how Eleonore remembered the rumors that were circulated to account for his absence from studies.

"Then say what you've come to say, though I am delighted to see a familiar face," Eleonore motioned for him to enter.

"Thank you," Horst withdrew from his previous aggression, but remained guarded. Stepping into the shop room, he removed his hat and was about to continue but then spotted Ruth sitting at the bench.

"I trust her with my life," Eleonore noticed the officer's hesitation.

"You shouldn't," Horst studied Ruth as if looking for something hidden.

When it was apparent the officer would not continue, Eleonore turned her gaze to her assistant and politely indicated for some privacy. Though indignant at the removal, Ruth submitted and left the room, but not before offering Horst an unapologetic glare.

"Now that you've kept me in suspense," Eleonore spoke quietly, "what is so urgent?"

"You've been placed on a list," Horst whispered.

"A list?" Eleonore swallowed as her eyes grew large. "What kind of list?"

"The kind that are handed down to me," Horst looked away, ashamed of his duty. While some would look upon his station as an honorable service to the state, rounding up the 'undesirables' required a callous disposition.

"I see," Eleonore's heart pounded violently within her chest, "but I don't understand what I've done that deserves such a designation?"

Scoffing, Horst raised his eyebrows, "You know perfectly well."

"I'm afraid I don't," Eleonore shrugged and persisted in feigning innocence.

"I came here at the risk of my life," Horst returned to whispering. "You must leave Berlin, now."

"And where should I go?" Eleonore looked around at her shop full of fabrics, threads, and half-finished dresses hanging on mannequins. The idea of leaving behind her life's work, when she had sacrificed marriage and children to obtain her dreams, was near impossible.

"England? The Americas?" Horst scratched the back of his neck. "Anywhere that isn't in Nazi hands."

"Why are you helping me?" Eleonore squinted. "I haven't spoken to you in years. You owe me no favors."

Horst thought for a moment, trying to articulate what he desired to say, and fumbled with the hat in his hand, "There are only a few people, that I can recall, who were kind to me. You didn't join in with the heckling or the practical jokes, and you certainly didn't make me wish that I were dead."

"They were rather mean spirited," Eleonore bit her cheek, "but I don't remember us being all that close."

"Oh, we weren't," Horst glanced away. He had a rather nervous nature which opened the door for ridicule from those of an unkind disposition. "But you were never cruel. You refused to engage with their behavior and came to my defense on occasion. I owe you a kindness in return."

"Horst," Eleonore shook her head, "I appreciate your forewarning, but I've done nothing to place myself on a 'list'. This must be some sort of mistake."

"You're a member of the Socialist Democratic Party that is seeking to undermine the Fuhrer and sacred Germany!" Horst gritted his teeth. "Adding to your sins, you've not only harbored Jews, but you've employed them in direct violation of the Racial Laws."

"I'm not leaving," Eleonore stood tall in defiance.

"You have twenty-four hours until I return," Horst put his cap firmly back on his head. "I've offered you the charity of a warning. It's up to you how to respond to this information. I wish you the best, I really do."

With that, Horst stormed out of the room and left a shocked Eleonore to mull on the consequences of her actions. Leaning against the wall, Eleonore placed her hand to her chest as her breathing labored.

"What did he want?" Ruth burst back into the room with Alex following closely behind, their concern painted across their faces.

"He's not after you," Eleonore squeezed her own shoulder which was stiffening from the tension.

"Then what?" Ruth persisted and studied Eleonore.

"He informed me that..." Eleonore paused, somehow speaking the truth would shatter whatever disbelief she clung to. "He informed me that my name is on a list."

"Oh, my child," Ruth embraced Eleonore who didn't know quite how to respond to the affection.

"I'm not sure what the best course of action would be," Eleonore patted Ruth on her back who broke off the embrace.

"We must leave," Ruth shrugged as if the answer was obvious. "Tonight!"

"Think, Ruth," Eleonore gazed upon her with hopelessness. "If my name is on a list, I will be stopped at the border."

"Then get a different name," Alex winked.

"What do you mean?" Eleonore frowned.

"We have a friend," Ruth placed her hands on Eleonore's arms and rubbed up and down like a mother warming her child from the cold, "a man that we trust who has helped many Jews escape."

"Is this true?" Eleonore looked to Alex who nodded as he held his hands behind his back. "Then why haven't you taken this avenue?"

"We're too old to travel," Alex shrugged, "but we have no choice now."

"At midnight," Ruth continued. "Meet us here at the shop. We will go together."

"You're in no condition to take this venture," Eleonore shook her head. "I can't ask you to do that."

"If they're coming for you, they're coming for all of us," Ruth put her hands into fists, ready for the fight.

"This will not be easy," Eleonore sighed.

"No," Alex shook his head, "but we have no other option."

"At midnight?" Eleonore looked again at Ruth.

"Midnight," Ruth gave a large nod. "Go home and pack."

Chapter Two:
Duplicity

"For somehow this is tyranny's disease; to trust no friends."
Socrates

Hunting again through her faded blue suitcase that sat on her bed, Eleonore made sure nothing essential had been forgotten. Her watch struck 11:30pm and Eleonore grasped that she would endure another night without sleep, but she persevered with the hope that she might take refuge in another country.

Straightening her back as it cracked, Eleonore tried to clear her mind as she closed her eyes and checked off her mental list. She had her clothes, money, toiletries, an extra pair of shoes, and a picture of her parents. Still, she was certain there was something vital hiding from her.

Regardless, she couldn't reason correctly as apprehension scattered her mind, and her stomach tightened with each passing hour. Although born in Austria, Eleonore had spent her life in Berlin without any longing for travel. Everything she could possibly desire revolved around her little flat and her quaint shop.

Besides, going to another country, England perhaps, was enough to hold her captive to anxiety. She knew a few words of English, an impressive deal of Italian, but relying entirely on a different language would be difficult enough, especially for someone who was locked into a rigid routine that had been perfected over decades. The culture on the British Isles, though suited to her reserved nature, would be contrary to the society that she was accustomed to and she considered full assimilation to be impossible.

The food, too, would be an adjustment. She had sampled English brands of tea to find them weak when evaluated against her imports from East Asia. The war had challenged her acquisition of such goods, but fortunately she carried enough foresight to stockpile should her 'supply lines' be cut.

Adding to her worries was the fact that she would be a German in Allied lands. Who would trust her enough to employ her? There were promising stories from other successful migrants, but Eleonore was not ignorant of the plight of some who were not welcomed.

Sitting again on the bed, Eleonore folded her hands neatly on her lap and took measured breaths to calm herself. Her hands were beginning to tingle like little pinpricks running across her fingertips. She didn't carry the instincts required for these precarious circumstances and even those in more perilous situations seemed to fare better, or so she assumed.

Such apprehension about change was another reason for abstaining from marriage and raising children. Plenty of suitors had attempted to court her, some with a measure of success thanks to her mother's influence, but none had enraptured what she considered romance. At least not in the sense where she felt the need to abandon *La Venezia*. That was her first love, and even now, with her eyes pressed shut, it brought her serenity as she visualized herself in the shop.

There was no end of pleasure to be found in her sewing machine as the little motor puttered and purred, creating the finest designs which she had imagined and brought to life. Time seemed to be suspended when she put herself to the task, and she lost hundreds of hours, often forgetting to eat as she followed the carefully sketched patterns.

Hold your attention to that blessed seclusion, Eleonore reminded herself as she grinned, *and all will be well. No one can hurt you there.* The shop was her palace of tranquility, where she could escape from the crowds, from the business of life, and from the loneliness and absence of family.

"Focus," Eleonore whispered to herself as she strained to think of what else she needed to pack.

Tick, tick, tick, tick, her watch continued indifferently, again reminding her of the inevitable. The hours had slipped by and Eleonore regretted that the memory of her would be erased from the apartment with her departure. She had none to call her own which would inherit the property, causing her to lament the paths not taken.

She could've married, settled down and raised children while dismissing politics as a man's game. But as soon as the thought entered her mind another arose in contention like a whisper of confirmation. What if she had chosen that life only to have her sons sent off to war? What if her husband had joined the Nazi party and she had no say in the matter? She had followed her aspirations and that conviction was not to be disregarded so lightly.

Reminding herself of her charge – to do her part in allowing Germans to have a say in who leads their country – Eleonore jutted out her chin and filled herself again with the determination that had become her closest companion.

Pressing the suitcase shut, she clasped the locks and, standing before the door, took two deep breaths and plunged into the unknown. But as she stepped outside and turned to lock the door, she understood this would the last time she walked down the steps of her apartment building. The last time she would smell that familiar dampness which preluded the warmth behind the door. How could she tear herself from such security and bliss?

Don't reflect on such sadness or you'll never leave, Eleonore reminded herself. *Just lock the door and climb down the stairs like you've done a thousand and one times before. This is your only chance.*

With that, Eleonore obeyed and soon found herself walking down the dark streets of Berlin. Lit only by the occasional lamp, the streets were entirely deserted. Only the distant barking of a dog or the alarm of an emergency vehicle could be heard amongst her footsteps echoing against the concrete. Rounding the corner to her shop, she was disappointed to see that Alex and Ruth were nowhere to be seen.

I suppose I'm a little early, Eleonore checked her watch, which read 11:55pm, and looked both ways down the street, seeing if they were only hiding in the shadows. Shuffling back, Eleonore stood against the wall of *La Venezia,* just out of the street lamp's illumination.

The next five minutes passed without a single soul traversing the street. Eleonore stood patiently while gripping her suitcase with both hands, watching her breath against the cold midnight air and attempting every sort of mental distraction to pacify her worries.

Her watch read 12:00am. *Something is wrong,* Eleonore felt a pit form in her stomach. Her heart began to pound, and the tingling returned to her hands. *I'll have to find another way,* Eleonore nodded and resolved to return to the apartment.

But before Eleonore had the opportunity to leave, she heard footsteps nearing the shop, coming from deeper within the street where no lamps shone. She strained to see who it was, but the light of the streetlamp was between her and the potential assailant, blinding her from identifying who was approaching.

"Alex?" she called out in desperation when she saw the bobbing of a hat but regretted the outburst the moment it left her tongue.

"Shhh," came a harsh whisper from a man as he stepped into the light. "Do you want to be caught?"

"Who are you?" Eleonore studied him, but glanced over her shoulder, frantically searching for any sign of Alex or Ruth.

"You are Eleonore Hodys?" the man asked while remaining under the light and squinting to see her better. He was a shorter man, about the height of Alex, and held his hands firmly in his pockets as if they were responsible for keeping his trousers up.

"I…" Eleonore paused as she wondered about the correct course of action. One misstep could spell disaster. She considered running, but that would only arouse suspicion. Fighting was not an option as she was a petite woman and not capable of much harm. Then she recalled that none were aware of the time set by Alex and Ruth except the three of them. This must be their confidant.

"I need an answer," the man grew impatient.

"I am," Eleonore swallowed as she waited with wide eyes.

"Good," the man said with a cheerful note and walked past her. "Follow me."

"Where are we going?" Eleonore checked over her shoulder again as she followed, but he didn't reply.

"Where are Ruth and Alex?" she asked while watching him carefully to see if he would give a telling reaction.

"They were early and are already on their way," he answered in such a manner that convinced Eleonore he was telling the truth.

"I appreciate your service," Eleonore exhaled as she felt peace from this strange man. "I understand the risk you are taking."

"I'm not doing this out of the goodness of my heart," the man scoffed. "You brought money, yes?"

"Of course," Eleonore patted her suitcase as it bounced against her leg. She found it odd that he had not extended the courtesy of carrying such a heavy item, but her present concerns outweighed the dismissal of chivalry.

They walked in silence for what seemed like an hour, taking back streets and alleys which, the man explained, was to throw off any who may be following them. Then, finally, they came to a plaza with a tall fountain in the middle and, beyond, an imposing government building. Eleonore had seen this building countless times before, but her only impression had been its lack of aesthetics and she cared not for its purpose.

With high, straight walls that stretched out on either side of a tall, rectangular slab of concrete, anyone would feel the intimidation and Eleonore was not immune. The only visual appeal of the building was in the red Nazi flags, ten in front of each wall, that waved gently in the cold night breeze. Lights were fastened below the flags and shone brightly upwards to give a rather despotic illusion.

Passing through the stone courtyard, they hurried up the flight of wide, stone steps and Eleonore noticed the man huffing with his hands still affixed to his pockets.

"Where are we?" Eleonore glanced up at the building as they passed into the rectangular slab guarded by marble pillars supporting the entrance.

Again, the man didn't reply, but dug out a set of keys from his pockets to reveal that his hands were deformed. Only two fingers had grown on his right hand, while his left had three. This didn't seem to impede him in the slightest and soon the door was unlocked. He motioned for Eleonore to enter as he looked back at the marble pillars, making sure no one had followed.

"Sir, I cannot," Eleonore shook her head as an overwhelming sense of dread came over her.

"This is the same path Ruth and Alex took," the man raised his eyebrows, advising time was of the essence.

"And where are they now?" Eleonore swallowed as her heart could be seen beating in her neck and the man took notice.

"I'll never tell you," the man gave a comforting smile. "Just as I will never tell a soul where I have sent you."

Don't trust him, Eleonore closed her eyes as she sighed. The silly thing was, above all her concerns, she was mostly worried about appearing impolite. She detested confrontation and this aversion produced in her an amiable characteristic. Others that were of a less agreeable nature, however, generally exploited this quality in her for their own advantage. Even now she drew upon her reserved upbringing, and the questions burning on her mind would remain silent for fear of retaliation.

"You're smart not to trust anyone," the man read her thoughts, "but now you've seen me, and you've seen my operation. For my safety, and that of my family, you no longer have a choice."

Eleonore understood the veiled threat and, motioning for the man to continue, followed him into the building. The heavy wooden door slammed behind them, echoing throughout the marble chambers.

Even in the darkness, Eleonore was stunned by the splendor within. She was led into a hall with black and white checkered tile floors that housed nearly a dozen dark, wooden tables surrounded by cheap, metal chairs. Papers and pamphlets were spread out on the tables and ashtrays littered the hall with the smell of stale smoke.

A crystal chandelier suspended above the center of the room and it drew Eleonore's eye to a winding staircase at the far end of the room leading to a balcony. On the balcony hung rolls upon rolls of paper that had been typed out and taped together. Names blanketed each paper and Eleonore wondered if her name had appeared on one of these very lists that Horst had warned her about.

"Through here," the man led her to the back of the hall where he opened a door to a little office no bigger than a closet. He turned on the small lamp on the desk to reveal blank passports piled on top of each other, spread open and ready to be imprinted.

At the back of the office hung a small portrait of Hitler and his omnipresent gaze seemed to follow Eleonore with immense disapproval for her treachery.

"Please, sit," he motioned to the chair in front of the desk and returned to hiding his hands in his pockets.

Taking a seat, Eleonore set her suitcase down by the door in such a way to be ready for flight should the need arise. Folding her hands gently in front of her, Eleonore waited patiently while the man stared at her.

"You're rather pretty," he began, and Eleonore felt her skin crawling with disgust.

I'm a damn fool, Eleonore cursed inwardly. *Men only want one thing and I've come alone, willingly, into a secluded place.*

"No husband?" the man tilted his head as he leaned back in his chair.

Eleonore shook her head quickly and looked away.

"Interesting," he threw his eyebrows up quickly. Then, inhaling as he sat forward, "Let's get to work."

Opening a drawer at his desk, the man took out a large stamp, a pad of ink, and two pens. Taking a blank passport, he began to write, again with no impediment by his disability. Eleonore watched with mesmerization at the way the man moved his arms when, suddenly, she felt a pain in her stomach.

Food! Eleonore rolled her eyes at her stupidity. *That's what I forgot to pack.* She had been so focused on the distant future that she failed to consider the immediate.

"What are you writing?" Eleonore cleared her throat.

"What do you think goes in a passport?" the man replied sarcastically.

"Not my name, surely," Eleonore grew cross at his reaction.

"Your name, your date of birth, your country of origin, and your official status in the Nazi party."

"They'll know that I'm not a party member," Eleonore frowned, but continued in a hushed tone. "I was told I'm on some sort of 'list'. I'll be stopped at the border if my real name is used."

"That's why you are Anna Thatcher. Born in England but raised in Berlin with your German cousins," the man took his stamp and slammed it down on the passport in such a manner that startled Eleonore.

"And this," he took another stamp out of the drawer, "is your official status as a member of the esteemed National Socialist Party," he stamped the Prussian seal on the passport and slid it across the table. DEUTSCHES REICH the stamp read in bold, black ink.

"Sign under your new name," he tapped the passport.

"Why have you labeled me as a party member?" Eleonore frowned. "Won't that attract attention?"

"On the contrary," the man shook his head and threw his lips upside down. "That designation turns the German border patrols into frightened boys. It's likely their questions will be brief, if at all."

"When I'm questioned about my party responsibilities?" Eleonore asked as an unease crept in. Even feigning a Nazi label made her a traitor unto herself and her ideals.

"What would you like to be?" the man pushed his chair back and crossed his legs like he was conducting an interview.

Rubbing the back of her neck as the stress seized her, Eleonore looked about the room for any inspiration, but her mind was blank. Instead, Eleonore noticed a picture on the desk of the man and two children. There was no woman in the photograph and Eleonore grew pity for him, risking his life for his children, or so she assumed.

"Something clerical, I presume," Eleonore shrugged. "That way I'm not important enough to be suspected."

"Smart," the man again threw his lips upside down. "One last thing," he began slowly. "You understand that what you have done is illegal? Should you be caught you will give no mention of me."

"If you've done this before, and none have been caught previously, then I assume your work is indisputable and there will be no need for deception on my part."

"Right," the man nodded and then stood. "Please sign."

With a deep breath, Eleonore took the pen in hand and signed away her fate.

"Good," the man ripped the passport off the desk and began to leave the room.

"Where are you going?" Eleonore grew flustered as she called after him.

"To make a phone call," he replied over his shoulder and closed the door.

Phone call? Eleonore frowned and wondered who he would be contacting and for what purpose. *I hate not knowing. Why would he have to withhold information? I don't like that, not one bit,* Eleonore huffed. Then, her suspicions rose when she spotted a phone on the man's desk. *Why couldn't he use that one?*

"Alright," the man burst back into the room with a sort of excited, yet reserved smile. Sitting back behind the desk, the man lit a cigarette and stared at her pensively.

"What happens now?" Eleonore folded up the passport and clutched it tightly.

"Where are my manners?" the man ignored her as he reached into his shirt pocket and retrieved a pack of cigarettes. "I should've offered you one."

"I don't smoke," Eleonore waved her dismissal.

"Shame," the man looked disappointed but picked his ear up when the sound of an engine hummed from outside the building. "The truck is here."

"What truck?" Eleonore shot him look of confusion.

"The one which will escort you to liberation," the man stood and half-ran out of the room.

Scrambling to catch up, Eleonore snatched her suitcase and walked briskly after him, confused as to how the truck arrived so quickly. Leading her to the back of the building, the man kept his pace as they sped into a large kitchen which had a supply door at the rear.

But as she hustled, something stole Eleonore's attention. On one of the kitchen tables was an ashtray, which was not unusual, but in the tray was a cigarette put out in haste. If not for the moonlight pouring in from the window above the sink, she would have missed it entirely.

"What's wrong?" the man turned towards her with his hand on the door handle.

Staring wide-eyed at him, Eleonore dropped her suitcase and bolted towards the main doors.

"Stop her!" the man opened the supply door and Eleonore could hear boots giving chase.

Her legs became like lead as she ran through the marble hall with the sound of her assailants closing in. Somehow, she had managed to reach the main doors before being overrun.

Locked! She panicked as she yanked and pulled with all her might, but it was of no use. Soon, a strong hand gripped her arm and tried to pull her away, but she screamed and held tight to the door. Eventually, another hand took hold of her and with the combined strength of the two she was pried from her near escape. The men dragged her back to the kitchen as she yelled and kicked wildly but with no avail.

An engine revved outside, and Eleonore felt her strength waning as the men hurried her out the supply door and lifted her to the awaiting arms of other men who dragged Eleonore into the truck. Without discrimination for her sex, they threw her onto the cold, metal truck bed and she held her sides as she gasped for air.

Unconcerned with any harm which befell her, a man stood over her and shouted so loudly that Eleonore flinched with each 'bark'.

"I...what...I," Eleonore crawled backwards as she caught the symbol on the man's cap and knew she was doomed: he was a Gestapo officer.

"Get up!" a soldier grabbed her and pulled Eleonore upright before slamming her down onto a bench lining the inside of the truck.

"Ah!" she screamed in pain and held her back, but no one cared.

Seated between two soldiers, Eleonore glanced at her captors who stared directly ahead and held their guns casually by their sides. She was in a transport vehicle with an overhead tarp to protect them from the elements, but still, the cold of the night leaked through and Eleonore shivered.

"I'm sorry," the disabled man stood at the rear of the truck as he looked at Eleonore with genuine regret.

"Where are you sending me?" Eleonore asked the man as her neck began to seize from the shock.

"How dare you address him in that manner, you seditious witch!" the Gestapo officer spit as he spewed his venom. "You're worse than the Jews for betraying your own country."

"Seditious?" Eleonore grew enraged at the accusation. "I am a loyal German citizen!"

"This document proves otherwise," the officer climbed off the truck and held up the freshly signed passport.

Eleonore slunk back in despair as she recognized the entrapment which had been orchestrated against her. The Nazis, though malicious, justified their lack of social morality through the guise of legality.

If I had done nothing and just stayed in my flat, maybe they wouldn't have had enough to substantiate my custody, Eleonore thought as depression took hold. *I've doomed myself.*

"Great work," the Gestapo officer handed the man a neatly wrapped stack of bills.

"Why?" Eleonore shook her head as she studied the man.

"You're far too trusting, Miss Hodys," the man tapped the back of the truck, signaling for it to depart and stuck his hands back into his pockets while he watched them leave.

What a wicked creature! Eleonore glared at the man as the truck began its hateful journey. Too angry to allow tears, all she could afford was a scowl of disgust. She understood why he had undertaken this scheme as she remembered the photograph on his desk. He was a single father and a cripple: there was little honest work for a man of his circumstance and tyranny had opened the door for him to become a monster. The man looked back with remorse, but then returned into the building as Eleonore disappeared from his sight.

Again, Eleonore shivered as the truck sped down streets and alleys she had known all her life: the bakery on the corner with the once cheerful baker, the now deserted coffee shop, and the square which still held the ashes of the burnt books.

Then, almost as a last reminder, her flat came into view. Her heart shattered as she leaned over slightly to catch it disappearing in the distance. Like a dear friend passing away, her apartment drifted off into the distance until disappearing entirely.

Keep that image in your mind, she pressed her eyes shut to solidify the picture. *No matter what comes to pass, that quiet and isolated haven will by my mental diversion. If, that is, they will imprison me. Maybe they will simply shoot me. I'm not sure which I prefer. Both fates sound terrible. Whatever happens, the only certainty is that life will never be the same again.*

Chapter Three:
The Final Solution

"From the deepest desires often comes the deadliest hate."
Socrates

Eleonore awoke with a start as the jostling and bouncing of the truck stirred her back to consciousness. The sun was beginning to rise, and for a brief moment Eleonore forgot where she was and why.

Peeking out the back of the vehicle, Eleonore noticed that they were in the country but was clueless as to their location or for how long they had been traveling. A part of her wished she had remained awake so that she could've tracked their movements.

Then, Eleonore heard a snore and, looking to the guard at her left noticed he was fast asleep. Slowly, she looked to her right to find the other guard was also resting. Her heart leapt to realize she had not been bound – whether by some oversight or by their ill regard for her as a physical threat – and Eleonore seized upon the opportunity for flight.

Quietly, she moved to the end of the truck and, timing herself for the speed of the vehicle, prepared to jump. But the damning tune of a train's horn blared from an engine hidden by the front of the vehicle and woke the sleeping guards.

"Get back here!" the guard grabbed his weapon firmly when he found her in the compromising position, threatening violence should she try anything rash.

"I just wanted to see where we were," Eleonore raised her hands to prove her innocence.

"I don't care," the guard motioned for her to return to the spot beside him.

Obediently, she moved over and resumed her position. *If only I had awoken five minutes earlier,* she hung her head at her misfortune. *But,* another thought popped into her head, *if there is a train then I doubt I'll be shot after all. Maybe they'll even exile me, and I can begin life anew somewhere far removed.*

While the thought was kind, it was optimistic in the extreme and, when the truck came to a halt parallel to the train, Eleonore shuddered at the cruelest site she had ever witnessed. Train cars – the kind designated for livestock – were being packed to the brim with men, women, and children. Rows upon rows of people were lined up in single file before their designated car. But what startled Eleonore the most was the absence of resistance: even vocal discontent was silent as the people, mostly Jews, were being led up ramps into the cars. It was horrendous to behold such mass dehumanization, and Eleonore felt as if she was already dead and being delivered into hell.

"Out!" the guard beside her kicked down the truck's gate and waved for her to exit.

Paralyzed with fear, Eleonore couldn't move. These train cars could only mean one thing: the camps were real, and their horrors had not been exaggerated.

"Move!" the guard from behind her gave a generous shove.

"Shoot me here," Eleonore grabbed his rifle and pointed it at her chest.

"I'm not allowed," the guard refused.

His reply was so quick that Eleonore grasped he had grown accustomed to denying such requests.

"C'mon, you filth," the first guard reached in and, grabbing her roughly by the arm, yanked her out of the truck as she fell to the earth.

"Get up," he groaned as if speaking to a child who had overreacted.

Standing to her feet, Eleonore brushed off her dress and glared at the guard with a mixed sense of dread and rage. She wanted to retaliate but knew that would only be met with the butt of the gun to her face or stomach, and not the death she craved.

"She's all yours," the guard handed a large envelope to an officer who had appeared from behind her.

"Eleonore Hodys?" the officer glanced quickly at the documents and then at Eleonore, scarcely reading anything other than her name.

"What are my charges? I don't understand what I've been accused of. I deserve a fair trial," Eleonore trembled as she spoke, but prayed that her reasoning would shine through.

"I see that you're not a Jew, did you swear the oath to the Fuhrer?" the officer tilted his head as he squinted at her, offering a lustful glance that no woman would appreciate.

"I'm loyal to Germany," she glared back at him. "If that's what you are asking."

"I thought as much," the officer nodded and began to walk away, but spoke over his shoulder to the guards. "Place her in car twelve."

"Wait, wait! Please!" Eleonore protested as the guards gripped her and dragged her along. She dug her heels into the dirt but the guards had little trouble with overpowering her resistance.

Accepting that any opposition from the realm of physical prowess was useless, though courageous, Eleonore abandoned her struggle and continued upright. As she was led past the train cars, Eleonore assumed there were thousands of people being transported. In its entirety, the train was immense in length and, if the enormity was not enough to terrify her, Eleonore grew aware of the absence of opposition: the men and women were skin and bones, half-starved.

Is this to be my fate? Eleonore wondered as she noticed their blank, thoughtless expressions.

"Eleonore Hodys for car twelve," the guards dropped her in the line as another officer grabbed the envelope.

"Horst?!" Eleonore couldn't believe her fortune.

Looking at the envelope briefly, but ignoring Eleonore, Horst threw her documents onto a growing pile atop a small table. A shell-shocked, young clerk hurriedly wrote down the details as he glanced nervously at Horst for direction.

"Horst, it's me, Eleonore!" she called and tried to draw near to him, but the guards held her back.

Still, Horst ignored her and waved for the guards to continue.

"Horst!" Eleonore wrung herself free from the guards and grabbed onto the officer's jacket. "Remember what you said: you owed me a kindness!"

"Get off me!" he broke her grip.

"How can you be part of this?!" Eleonore yelled as the guards pulled her away by force.

"I have a family," Horst spoke over his shoulder as he turned his back on her.

"Coward! Hiding behind your children!" Eleonore screamed as the guards put her in line forcibly.

There was now no chance of escape or appeal as a guard was stationed every five feet on each side of the line. But Eleonore took note of their casual manner: they smoked cigarettes as their guns were slung over their shoulders, not concerned in the slightest that they should have to use them. Their victims had already been defeated, utterly.

A pain began to form again in her stomach and all Eleonore could think about was where she could find food. She looked over her shoulder, back at Horst, but he was still ignoring her, pretending to busy himself in checking the papers.

"Is there anything to eat?" Eleonore cleared her throat as she spoke to one of the guards who frowned and shook his head, annoyed that she would dare speak to him.

"Water? Anything?" she persisted.

"Don't you animals drink your own piss?" another guard chimed in as he took a swig from his flask and the rest roared with laughter.

Overlooking the insult, Eleonore could think only on the dryness in her mouth and her stomach began to gurgle with wrath. Still, the line continued onwards with its disconcerting inhumanity, and Eleonore found herself nearing her appointed car. By now the sun had risen substantially and it was nearing midday, but still, the cold was almost unbearable.

Glancing at her destination, Eleonore's skin crawled at the thought of being packed into the car with so many people. Even at the cost of her life, Eleonore resolved to not be included in whatever wicked scheme this was. Yet for all her noble intentions, she found herself locked into the path before her. It felt dreamlike with the birds chirping cheerfully, the sun beating on her skin, and her famishment increasing. Worst of all was the absence of God's comfort. The spiritual seemed to have abandoned the world and with it went any semblance of humanity.

"In!" a guard pushed a man two places in front of her up the ramp and Eleonore began to shake, knowing her time was approaching.

"In!" he said again, this time to the woman in front of Eleonore, but the woman didn't move. Instead, she stayed in place with her head hunched over.

"Now!" the guard shouted and gave a slight push with his rifle which caused the woman to fall over.

Startled, Eleonore let a brief cry escape as she clasped her hand over her mouth. With none interested in helping the poor woman, Eleonore bent down and rolled her onto her back, asking if she was alright, but she was unresponsive.

For a fleeting moment, Eleonore saw her mother in the lady lying before her. She had been at her mother's death bed and seen the familiar labored breathing, the vacant expression, and knew that death was ready to collect her soul. A tear rolled off her cheek as Eleonore was transported to her mother's side. She found it odd – almost out of body – to relive a memory as if it were only now being experienced for the first time. She straddled two worlds: one beside her mother and the other beside this lady. Holding her hand, Eleonore gave a comforting squeeze to let her know she was not alone in these final minutes.

"She needs attention," Eleonore looked up at the guard who, for a moment, showed his regret.

"Leave her," another guard ordered.

"I think her breathing has stopped," Eleonore placed her fingers to the woman's neck to check for a pulse.

"Then she's no longer anyone's concern," the guard forced Eleonore to her feet and pushed her on her way up the ramp.

Turning sharply, Eleonore drew her hands into fists, but the guard took his rifle off his shoulder and pointed it at her chest.

"Now!" he motioned with his gun for her to move.

Even though she wished for death, Eleonore's survival instincts overpowered her and she obeyed the order. Slowly, Eleonore climbed the ramp into the car, but as she entered an overwhelming stench struck her. Placing a hand over her nose was not adequate to block out the stench and she gagged. Embarrassed at her reaction, Eleonore turned away only to grasp the origin of the smell.

Human feces and urine surrounded her feet, soaking through her shoes. With that, she vomited, adding to the pile of waste. She looked for a better position to stand but the whole car was littered.

Disgusted, she closed her eyes and thought back to her apartment with the kettle screeching happily, letting her know that the tea was ready for savoring out on the balcony. But even such a pleasant contemplation was not enough to drown out the unbearable.

Time itself stood still as more and more people were carted in, leaving Eleonore to wonder how another soul could fit into the crowded car. Still, they crammed in until Eleonore was nearly crushed by the weight of bodies pressing against her. Raising her chin, she tried to breathe above their heads but, being rather petite, all she could inhale was the warmth of their breath.

Finally, a whistle blew and the door was slammed shut and locked, blocking out the light of the sun. Save for some little slits in the wooden panels, there was no observing the outside world and Eleonore, being surrounded, was left in darkness.

A horn bellowed from the engine and the train crawled to a start. Again, Eleonore pleaded with her mind to provide some distraction and turned to the recollection of her first train ride.

She was only a little girl at the time, but she remembered her parents using the last of their savings to purchase three train tickets to Berlin, their new home. While Eleonore was ecstatic about the adventure, she recalled the tears in her mother's eyes and the worried expression of her father as they said goodbye to their homeland. Due to her age, Eleonore couldn't quite grasp the gravity of the situation, so she played and bounced on the train seats only for her father to lash out in anger. He shouted for her to sit and a shocked little Eleonore obeyed instantly. Her father was a patient, kind man and never before or after did he behave in that fashion towards her.

Wondering what she had done wrong, Eleonore spent the rest of that train ride to Berlin in silence with a lump in her throat and a sting in her heart. As age matured her, she grew to understand that her father was overwhelmed, and she was able to pardon the outburst, but she still hadn't forgiven trains.

And now Eleonore's affinity for trains was waning even further. Exhausted, Eleonore rested her head on the shoulder of the man in front of her who didn't seem to notice. She had been placed into a dehumanized environment and the spirit was contagious.

The train chugged along as hour after hour passed by, unaware of the disservice it was rendering to its passengers. Eleonore wondered how long the journey was and shuddered at the thought of the eventual destination. But such concerns were drowned out by her present tribulations of famishment, thirst and, oddly enough, loneliness.

Fear and shock had taken control, and however discouraged she may have been she was certain she was not alone in these concerns. Looking around the car, she studied the faces of those who were trapped with her. While their oppressors saw animals, she saw fathers and mothers, brothers and sisters. There were bakers, bankers, cops, government officials, mailmen, pilots, soldiers, typists, clerks, and all variety of people who had lives, plans, and hopes.

If she was going to survive whatever was coming, she understood that it was her humanity that she needed to retain. She could not, would not, allow herself to be devolved into this animalistic state. She would remain Eleonore Hodys, the seamstress of *La Venezia*. That would never be taken from her.

<u>Chapter Four:</u>
<u>The Gates of Hades</u>

"I do not see why man should not be just as cruel as nature."
Adolph Hitler

Eleonore awoke with a start as her drool lay strewn across the man's shirt in front of her. He wasn't bothered in the slightest as he stared blankly like the rest of the prisoners in this 'ghost train'. They seemed to Eleonore as if they were having some out of body experience, like their consciousness was active on another dimension.

Peeking her head around the shoulder of the man in front of her, Eleonore was struck by sunlight pouring in through the wooden panels on the side of the car, briefly interrupted by the passing vegetation. Whether it was morning or late afternoon she couldn't decipher as she had lost sense of direction. She assumed she had only slept for a couple of hours, but it was midday when she had entered the car and now the sun was either setting or rising.

Ow! she winced as a pain shot up her foot and into her thigh. *I need to move,* Eleonore searched for an avenue with which to get the blood flowing again, but it was of no use with everyone being so packed together. Looking around the train car, Eleonore locked eyes with a younger woman to her right. Desperate for some connection, Eleonore smiled slightly but the woman returned a foul glare.

"I'm Eleonore," she whispered.

The woman studied Eleonore's mouth like she had uttered vulgarities and, refusing to acknowledge her further, turned away.

Sighing, Eleonore looked to her left, hoping to find someone willing to speak with her, but was shocked to find the man next to her was dead! He had expired while standing upright and was so frail his skeleton was showing through his sunken cheeks.

Initially, Eleonore reacted as one might expect and shuddered with revulsion while she squirmed to move away. But then something grabbed hold of her spirit, like a whisper reminding her of compassion. The man beside her had died much in the same situation she found herself: alone.

Slowly, she looked at him again as her disgust was drowned by rising sympathy. Lifting her hand, she placed it over his eyes and closed them, although with some struggle. Then, clearing her throat, she quietly recited a prayer.

Yet when she was about halfway through, a man behind the deceased gentleman joined in with his own prayer, and then another, and another, until four or five of them had offered up a supplication for the dead man's soul.

Tears streamed down Eleonore's cheeks, moved by the event. They were isolated from their loved ones, terrified, but there was still a flicker of compassion. Their enemy could destroy their body, but Eleonore would be damned if she let them take her spirit.

Glancing at the man behind her, Eleonore offered a sympathetic look, but he didn't return the sentiment. He simply stared at her for a moment before bursting into tears and sobbed uncontrollably without shame for his outpouring.

"Quiet!" another beside him whispered harshly. "We're almost there. You'll be shot first if they hear you."

"They don't shoot people here," the man sniffled and wiped his nose on the cuff of his shirt.

While Eleonore was not naturally optimistic, her mind was laboring for anything positive and she clung to the false hope that wherever 'here' was meant the horror would soon pass.

With the blast of a whistle, the train began to slow down, signaling that they had arrived and suddenly the whole car burst to life. Those whom had been without expression turned to peer out the wooden panels with a curiosity Eleonore didn't believe they could produce.

Clunking awkwardly, the train jarred to an abrupt stop as the wooden cars creaked and groaned under the strain. The moment the train halted, whistles blew from outside as officers shouted orders, dogs barked, ramps were put into place at the train cars, and the doors were thrown open.

"Out, out, out!!" the soldiers yelled as they began to grab their captives.

But the noise disoriented the passengers, and after being forced to stand for hours on end their legs were stiff. This was not a concern to the soldiers who only barked louder than their dogs for the prisoners to keep pace.

Eventually, the car was half-emptied, and Eleonore's time was approaching. Her heart beat within her chest and the tingling returned to her fingers. She began to look for a way to escape and wondered if she could slip to the back and hide somewhere in the car. But the prisoners kept etching forward and pushing Eleonore along with them.

"My name is Ella," a woman whispered to Eleonore and grabbed her hand with a tight, reassuring squeeze.

Surprised, Eleonore shot the woman a startled glance and noticed it was the same person who had reacted so foully to her earlier.

Eleonore looked down at her hand in shock at the sudden affection but, regardless, clung tight. A warmth grew within her at this softness, and Eleonore felt like a child who had found a friend. There was a beauty about this Ella: the kind that drives women senseless with jealousy and men weak with desire. While the Nazis had tried to extinguish it, the allure remained within her bright, brown eyes. To Eleonore, this Ella seemed like the women she saw in pictures or on posters: the kind you don't believe exist outside fiction.

Nearing the ramp, Ella released her grip before the soldiers could see, and was pushed on her way. Eleonore, for some reason, was exempt from this physical mistreatment, and walked down the ramp untouched. Large, black dogs awaited at the bottom, barking wildly as their masters held them back with chain leashes. With sharp teeth and drool hanging out their hungry mouths, they could intimidate even the bravest of men and each clasp of their jaw sent shivers down Eleonore's spine.

"Hurry! Keep in line!" a female guard snapped her leather whip and pointed impatiently towards a gate to an enclosed camp.

Jostling and swaying, the people were herded onwards. Eleonore rose on her tiptoes to get a glance of what was coming but her disadvantaged height kept the truth concealed. She did, however, witness a man at the gate wearing a doctor's lab coat and holding a clipboard while splitting the group into two. She wondered what conditions governed this division and prayed that she possessed the qualities to place her in the more advantageous of the two.

Now, this gate in which the doctor stood was little more than a chain-link fence, but Eleonore counted nearly twenty SS soldiers guarding with fully automatic weapons capable of destroying any who attempted escape.

Still, a daring thought entered Eleonore's mind as she contemplated the possibilities. *We outnumber them one hundred to one. All we need is some organization and a dash of courage.* But, like her, none could summon this valor she imagined. The starved, sick, and downtrodden continued to limp forward.

"Remain calm. Place any luggage beside the gate," a voice called over a loudspeaker. "Write your name and address on the luggage and remember where you left it for collection at a later time. A better life awaits you after you have finished work in the camp. To eliminate the spread of disease, you will be sent to quarantine. Men will be joined to one camp; women to another. Remain calm. Place your luggage beside the gate. A better life awaits you after you have finished work in the camp," the voice from the loudspeaker repeated the script.

The voice was encouraging, and Eleonore assumed that if their belongings were to be collected later, then maybe she could allow herself to hope. She could work off her 'crimes' and return to her shop and her life.

As she grew closer to the gate, Eleonore was able to get a better view of her surroundings. While wide enough for a large vehicle to pass through, the gate was crowned with jagged iron to prevent prisoners from climbing over. Even if one could scale over, they would be met immediately by a double barbed-wire fence stretching nearly ten feet high.

Inside the enclosure were imposing two-story brick buildings but Eleonore was ignorant as to their purpose and assumed they were for housing the soldiers. Maybe, she shuddered, they were for a more sinister purpose but, by any means, their effectiveness was striking with their plain brick walls and dark wooden roofs.

Looking again towards the entrance, Eleonore caught an unusual sign that stretched over the gate which read: "Work Sets You Free." Carrying the sting of irony, the motto was placed as a permanent reminder to those who were being led against their will.

"Name?" the doctor with the clipboard asked a prisoner a few places in front of Eleonore.

"Ella Gartner," came the reply and Eleonore's ears perked up.

She didn't know why, but Eleonore felt a connection with this Ella. Though, she supposed, in an environment as grim as this, the soul is drawn to any light.

Seeing that her turn was approaching, Eleonore's heart began to beat even stronger as she prepared to give an answer. *What if I reply incorrectly and I'm sent to some horrible part of the camp? Or what if they inquire as to my political leanings?*

"And who do we have here?" the doctor spoke warmly as he knelt and came face to face with two children about the age of six.

Can't believe I didn't notice them, Eleonore frowned. She had been looking ahead, over everyone's shoulders, and failed to notice twins – a boy and a girl – standing a few places in front of her.

Clinging to her dirty teddy bear, the girl refused to answer and hid her face in her mother's torn dress while the boy held his chin to his chest timidly.

"Shy," the doctor smiled and looked up at the mother reassuringly. "I've got just the remedy," he dug into his coat pocket and produced two red candies.

Smiling, the girl grabbed it and, unwrapping it faster than Eleonore thought possible, she threw it into her mouth while the boy clung to his for later use, untrusting of the doctor.

"Place the children in my lab," the doctor stood and ordered.

"No!" the mother screamed. "You can't separate them from me!"

"They'll be fine," the doctor spoke tenderly. "I assure you, my lab has a kindergarten, a swimming pool, and plenty enough for them to eat. In fact, they will be better looked after with me than anywhere else."

"I don't care!" the mother pleaded. "They belong with me."

"Take them," the doctor's empathy vanished as the guards ripped the children away from their mother amidst screams and outstretched arms.

"Name?" the doctor nearly shouted with his eyes fastened on the sheet in front of him.

Unsure of whom he was speaking to, Eleonore didn't reply as the people were packed tightly in near the gate.

"Name!" the doctor looked up at her but was stunned to see she that was beautiful and felt embarrassed for his outburst.

"Eleonore Hodys," she replied proudly, enjoying his discomfort.

"Medical issues?" the doctor returned to looking at his sheet and checked off a little mark beside her name which Eleonore found curious.

"None," Eleonore shook her head but was surprised that such a personal question would be asked so indiscreetly.

"Valuables?" the doctor looked at the next item on his list, going down the sheet as he had surely done countless times previously.

"None," she shook her head, remembering the suitcase she had abandoned when she forged the Nazi passport.

"Her watch," a clerk sitting at a nearby desk pointed.

"What would you need with my watch?" Eleonore covered her wrist.

"Everything helps," the doctor held out his hand. "We all pitch in for the good of the community."

We all? Eleonore scoffed as she looked at his silver watch, his gold wedding ring, his adorned Nazi bracelet barely hidden under his white lab coat, and a silver ring adorning his other finger.

"What's the delay Dr. Mengele?" a man called out from opposite the doctor and Eleonore turned to see a decorated officer approaching.

With his hands held firmly behind his back, the officer took long, fast strides in his black, knee-high boots that were splattered with mud. His grey uniform had been pressed to perfection with medallions pinned on the upper left of his chest. Some of which Eleonore recognized from the first great war: the same her father had received for acts of bravery.

Yet the man who walked past her was not much older than herself, and Eleonore speculated that he must've been rather young during the first war. While slightly shorter than average, the officer carried a stern face of disapproval accompanied by rough stubble under a pointy nose and little eyes. If not for his position, there would be little in the way of intimidation, yet the other officers looked at him with a peculiar sense of awe and terror.

"My apologies, Commandant Hoess," Dr. Mengele saluted.

"Eleonore Hodys?" Commandant Hoess grabbed the clipboard and glanced at her but absent of the same twinge of lust offered by the others. He seemed to ignore her physical attributes altogether, and her attractiveness held no sway over him.

"They demanded my watch," Eleonore held her chin high, though felt slightly adolescent in her refusal, especially when considering the mother whose children had been taken. Yet, this was her last piece of home, and her first purchase with the money she made from *La Venezia*. Only on the rarest of occasions would she part with it.

"You're not Jewish," Hoess squinted as he clicked his tongue thoughtfully, "which means you're a political prisoner. I assume you're a communist, yet you don't want to be rid of your possessions. Isn't materialism the disease of capitalism? Remove her ailment and any other valuables you may find," he spoke to the guards. "Prepare her for processing in Birkenau."

Without reservation, the soldiers grabbed her arm and ripped the watch off. Then, another soldier patted her down, checking for items of worth and lingering in certain areas that flushed her face crimson with humiliation. Especially since this occurred publicly, and everyone noticed the assault but were incapable of assisting.

"C'mon!" the guard stood and grabbed her by the arm as he led her away.

"You're hurting me," Eleonore winced at the rough grip on her forearm, but the guard didn't care.

"Where are we going?" Eleonore asked, her eyes wide with fear, but she was met with silence.

Instead, the guard pushed Eleonore along to follow a group down a path which was protected by barbed wire fencing on either side. A light hung above each third post and on each side of the fence stood brick buildings, towering above their new inhabitants with ominous gazes.

"Keep in line!" Eleonore heard a guard shout from a distance and looked to her right to see other prisoners, about fifty yards away, funneling down a path which led to another portion of the camp.

Where are they going? Eleonore wondered and noticed that they consisted mostly of the old, the sick, and the young. *Maybe they are being chosen for less physical labor or being sent to Dr. Mengele's laboratory?*

Then, suddenly, Eleonore crashed into the back of a woman who had stopped in the middle of the tunnel. Spinning around, the woman grabbed Eleonore's arms and looked at her with complete terror. She was young, nearly half the age of Eleonore, and carried the wild, energetic expression of one just discovering life. But to Eleonore, this woman seemed spooked, like a prey animal cornered and ready to make a daring leap to safety.

"It's alright," Eleonore spoke calmly, but the desired impact fell flat as the woman only squeezed tighter.

"Keep moving!" a guard shouted.

Looking back towards the gates, the woman's eyes scanned for a clear path. Then, instinctively, the woman pushed Eleonore aside and bolted away. She was quick and evasive and would have escaped the guard's grasp had she not tripped and fallen into the fence.

Sparks flew and the crackling of electricity coursed through the prisoner's body as she died within seconds. Finally, her hands loosened their grip from the fence and the foul aroma of burnt flesh rose and filled Eleonore's nostrils. Stunned, Eleonore stood in a state of disbelief as to what she had just witnessed. There were no signs that this was an electric fence and no warnings or words of caution from the guards. Anyone could have reached out in ignorance of its danger.

"Damn!" the guard cursed as he spat on his deceased prisoner and Eleonore perceived that his concern lay within the realm of convenience rather than tragedy.

"Move!" a guard shoved Eleonore on her way, but she couldn't take her eyes off the dead woman lying in the mud; her vibrancy and energy extinguished in an instant.

With another generous push, Eleonore was forced to traverse deeper into the camp. Yet an odd thought pricked the back of Eleonore's mind: *what an easy escape. I can reach out, grab hold of the fence, and this horror would be over.*

But this morbid thought vanished as soon as it arrived when Eleonore passed through the tunnel and came to an open enclosure. Her breath was stolen when she saw rows upon rows of barracks for housing the prisoners stretched out across the camp. The immensity was overwhelming and Eleonore felt sick with terror.

But what struck Eleonore as most surprising was a little amphitheater in the middle of the enclosure. With a small, wooden platform and a curved concrete wall behind, the stage was lined with orchestral pieces: cellos, violins, trumpets, flutes, and even a grand piano.

This, unfortunately, was not their immediate destination and the group of women were pushed onwards towards a brick building on the opposite end of the camp. The guards were so adamant to get the women there in good time, that Eleonore wasn't afforded the opportunity to inspect her surroundings further as she was forced to run, despite her extreme exhaustion and sore feet.

Eventually, when they had closed proximity to the building, Eleonore noticed a sign nailed above the doorway which read 'Sauna'. One didn't need to be perceptive to understand this was not a house of leisure such as in Berlin, and the designation of the building was named out of cruel irony.

The malevolent design was confirmed when Eleonore spotted a group of female officials waiting outside the entrance. Though not as decorated as the guards, they carried the same authority and offered a sinister smile while brandishing their batons and whips, threatening those being rushed towards them.

Most curious, Eleonore noticed, was a band on their upper right sleeve which read 'Kapo'. She was clueless as to what this designation meant, but the sadistic look in their eyes promised nothing kind. There was an air about them which wished to prove their mettle as equal to their male counterparts and Eleonore feared that she would bear the brunt of their attestations.

"Inside!" one of the Kapo's blew a whistle and the Sauna's double doors were thrown open as the prisoners were pushed inward, terrified of what fate awaited.

Eleonore's heart pounded as she was crammed in along with the other prisoners; each struggling towards the center of the group where it was safest. While the lighting in the 'Sauna' was poor, Eleonore spotted blood and hair splattered out across a square, empty room. Her stomach seized from panic and she grew envious of the prisoner who fell on the electric fence and avoided whatever torture had been arranged.

A yellow, ceramic tile lined the floor which highlighted the rust from the drains in the center of the room. Implanted in the walls hung crudely constructed showers whose upkeep had been neglected as rust warned of prolonged use without care. The building seemed to Eleonore as if it had been designed for a sort of quarantine but now carried a darker purpose.

"Stop!" the head Kapo blew her whistle which echoed off the tile and gave a deafening ring in the ears.

Panting their exhaustion, the women, about fifty in all, huddled together in an awkward circle in the center of the room. The Kapos from outside filed in behind and surrounded them, batons at the ready.

"Undress!" the head Kapo shouted, but the women looked at her and each other in confusion.

"Undress!" she yelled louder as her eyes bulged with rage.

Still, no one moved, and Eleonore was thankful at least that she was not alone in a desperate state of uncertainty.

"I'm not to be defied," the head Kapo grabbed a woman by the hair and pulled her away from the group. The woman cried and slapped the Kapo's hand, but her pleas were disregarded. Raising her baton, the Kapo brought it down repeatedly against the woman's head and arms as she screamed from the blows. Blood flowed from her nose and gushed from her scalp, falling onto the floor and trickling towards the drain.

"You're a Jew?" the woman looked up at the Kapo, struggling to talk through a swelling lip. "Why would you do this to your own people?"

This, unfortunately, struck a nerve with the Kapo and she gritted her teeth as she struck the woman until the victim's arms fell limp by her side and the blood was a steady stream.

"Who else?" the Kapo pointed her baton at the group as her breathing labored from the excursion.

Immediately, the women undressed, and Eleonore followed suit as the murdered woman was dragged away. In the heartless cold, they stood naked and in disbelief at what they had witnessed. Next, they were ordered to put their clothes on the opposite side of the room, against what looked like a feeding trough and, again, told to remember where they had placed their items for future recovery.

Then, Eleonore watched as ten chairs were brought in and placed facing the women while razors, clippers, and other instruments Eleonore didn't recognize were set beside each chair. The intent was clear, but Eleonore was of the opinion that she had missed some pertinent detail. She remembered the loudspeaker at the gates advising of quarantine, but were such measures necessary?

Still, none dared to question the Kapo's lethal authority and they huddled together for warmth while the female guards prepared to enact their eradication of 'disease'. To each chair was assigned a stern Kapo who looked upon their prey with a sort of joyful anticipation.

"Sit," the head Kapo went through the women, picking them at random and allocating them to a chair.

"Sit," the Kapo tapped Eleonore's shoulder and pointed to the chair on the end.

Petrified, Eleonore pretended that she hadn't noticed her selection, but the Kapo was familiar with the 'games' her victims played. With a swift strike of the baton against the back of her thigh, Eleonore gasped for air and held her wound as the pain surged without promise of cessation.

"Now!" the Kapo ordered, threatening another blow.

"I'm going!" Eleonore winced at the raised baton and appeased the Kapo as she joined the others selected for the chairs.

Eleonore shook from fear and cold as she sat on the unbalanced wooden chair, wondering what cruelty was about to be committed. Unconcerned with exposing her nakedness, Eleonore gripped the sides of her chair so hard that her knuckles turned a pale white.

Without warning, the Kapo assigned to her put a heavy hand on Eleonore's shoulder to keep her steady. Suddenly, the buzz of a razor pressed against Eleonore's skull and clumps of hair fell onto her shoulder and lap. Eleonore stared in shock before bursting into sobs.

"Keep straight!" the Kapo shouted as she grabbed what remained of Eleonore's hair to keep her head level.

Shaking as she wept, Eleonore scarcely noticed when another Kapo grabbed her arm and strapped it to the chair. With the jingling of buckles, her arm was bound tightly and Eleonore winced at the pull on her flesh.

"Ow!" Eleonore barked after a sudden sting surged from her forearm.

Opening her eyes, Eleonore was alarmed to witness a Kapo kneeling before her with a crude tattooing needle against her skin. The Kapo's hands had been stained with ink and appeared to Eleonore as if they could never be cleansed.

"Wait, wait!" Eleonore begged the Kapo who looked up at her reluctantly.

"You don't need to do this," Eleonore said quietly, but failed to hide her panic.

Rolling her eyes, the Kapo returned the needle to her arm. Screaming from the pain, Eleonore tried to squirm away, but the grip was firm. With tears, all Eleonore could do was kick her feet in frustration as the final clumps of her hair fell onto the yellow tile.

"Next," the Kapo pushed Eleonore off the chair and ordered her to rejoin the group.

Shivering, Eleonore couldn't recall a time she had felt so cold, so alone, or so degraded. She hated the looks of disgust she received from the other prisoners who knew their time was approaching and they, too, would appear like her.

The burning in her forearm lingered as Eleonore wiped away the tears and read the number 75,693. *What does this mean?* Eleonore wondered and was desperate for an answer but knew she wouldn't receive a reply with much sympathy – if at all.

Eventually, everyone had been shaved and piles of hair surrounded the chairs. With large bags, other Kapos went around the room, collecting the hair and Eleonore was dumfounded as to what purpose that would serve.

It was then that Eleonore looked at the others and noticed something peculiar: she couldn't tell herself apart from them. With numbers on their arms, naked and bald, the women had become nothing more than an item for the Nazis. They had been stripped of everything they owned, sheered like animals, and reduced to primitive fear.

Frightened and freezing, Eleonore wished for death or that she had been strong enough to have touched the fence, or taken a bullet to the chest when it had been offered. Still, there was a primal drive of survival. This was undoubtedly a death camp, and she would do whatever it took to stay alive. But what did she have to live for? A shop? She had no family, none to call her own. What could she possibly cling to?

But such worries were drowned out when Eleonore caught a single pair of eyes staring at her through the crowd. A bright, brown shine illuminated under the faintest smile, one that Eleonore had seen before in the train car: it was Ella. With every fiber of her being, Eleonore clung to that brightness.

"Against the wall!" the head Kapo blew her whistle.

With the hair collected, and the chairs taken away in haste, hoses were then brought in and Eleonore's heart dropped into her stomach, grasping the next torture that was about to befall them.

With their backs turned to the Kapos, the women huddled together as they were sprayed with high pressure, ice-cold water. They screamed and yelled for mercy, but none was given.

Eleonore didn't believe that she could've have been any colder, but the water sprayed on them with such a sharp bite that she couldn't breathe. Yet, through all the chaos was a moment of warmth: a hand slipped through the crowd and grabbed onto hers. Though she couldn't see, Eleonore knew it was Ella and she squeezed back with all her might.

Finally, the hose stopped spraying, and all that could be heard was the exhausted weeping of the prisoners, wishing the agony would stop. It was difficult enough to be separated from their families, wondering as to their fate, but then to be subjugated to this torture was evil in its purest form.

"Your regulation clothes and shoes," the head Kapo pointed to a pile near the exit. "Collect them on your way out. If you are spotted wearing clothes other than those assigned, you will be punished severely."

Desperate for warmth, the women rushed to the exit and grabbed the clothes. A coarse, brown dress; the material was light and hastily made, offering little protection against the crisp winter air. The shoes, too, were wooden clogs, the kind she had seen depicted on Dutch women, and entirely uncomfortable.

"Move!" the Kapo shouted for the women to keep pace.

Again, they were ushered outside where the male guards were awaiting. The coldness struck Eleonore's now bald head and she felt each wisp of wind, however slight, reminding her of what once had been. With all the women accounted for, the guards rushed them back to the center of the camp, straight for the amphitheater.

"Ah!" Eleonore stumbled when her wooden shoe had become stuck in the mud.

"Up!" a guard grabbed her by the arm.

"My shoe!" Eleonore looked over her shoulder as the guard dragged her away.

"Leave it!" he barked and pushed her along.

Limping with only one shoe, Eleonore felt the sting of the icy, unforgiving earth against her naked foot. But she was not alone in these troubles as many others stumbled in much the same way and were also ordered to continue.

The dispersed groups had been herded to the amphitheater and the women and men were re-joined as husbands and wives searched for their partners. Most couldn't recognize each other and, worse still, many more grasped that their partner was missing. Some wept at this bitter realization; others remained in a state of shock.

"Sit!" the guards filed the prisoners in front of the amphitheater where old, wooden chairs were set before the stage.

Springing to life, the prisoners each rushed to grab a seat and rest their weary feet. Half-startled to see they had enough energy, Eleonore was pushed and jostled by the mob. Noticing that she might miss out on electing a chair, she threw an elbow or two to get ahead of the crowd to find an open spot. She ignored the laughing of the guards as they enjoyed the sport of their victims squabbling over something as trivial as a place to sit.

There's one, an open chair popped into the corner of her eye, but a prisoner set themselves down before she could arrive. *Another,* she spotted but it, too, was taken. *Finally,* she smiled as she laid claim to a chair with a firm grip and gave a warning glance to an approaching man with an envious air.

Sitting on the splintered, wooden chair, Eleonore felt, in that moment, that nothing could be more comfortable. The relief from her tender feet rushed up her calves and into her thighs. Wiggling her frozen toes with delight, Eleonore wondered if she could ever feel such relief again.

It was curious, she thought, to experience such release in something so small. Yet the turmoil she had undergone over the last few days had enabled her to enjoy comforts that had previously been taken for granted. She swore to never again complain of sore feet.

A whistle blew once the prisoners were all seated, and Eleonore sat up straight. She wanted answers as to where they were and for what purpose, and hoped they were about to be instructed.

Onto the platform stepped Commandant Hoess as he walked briskly with his hands behind his back until he reached the middle of the stage. Turning to address the new prisoners, Commandant Hoess paused to give a quick survey of those who were now under his charge.

"Work sets you free," he began with a half-shout. "Remember this and you shall be saved. Your life is no longer your own. Your existence now revolves around the sound of this gong," he pointed to the large, silver gong on stage. "By it, you shall awake, eat, wash, and prepare for your labor details. The rules at Auschwitz are simple: obedience will be met with just reward while punishment for insubordination will be harsh."

Auschwitz! the color left Eleonore's cheeks as the name of the camp formed a pit in her stomach.

"The severity of the punishment will be met in accordance with the crime," Hoess continued, enjoying the sound of his own voice. "Attempting to flee, acquiring additional food, shirking or completing work in an unsatisfactory manner, behaving out of order with the gong, wearing non-regulation clothing, relations with the opposite or same sex, or attempting to commit suicide will all be disciplined accordingly. Obey these, and you and I shall have no difficulties," he clicked his heels together, relishing in the unyielding organization of his camp.

I'll have to remember those, Eleonore panicked. *Abide by the rules, and you'll be alright,* she tried to calm herself.

"You will be on to a better life once you have completed your duties here. Remember: work sets you free," he raised his fist in passion, imitating Hitler. "Repeat."

"Work sets you free," the group spoke in chaotic unison.

"Again," Hoess threw his hands behind his back.

"Work sets you free," the group replied but with greater timing than before.

Nodding to a nearby officer, Hoess left the stage and marched back to his detail with two SS guards in his train.

"I will recite the quarters you were assigned at the gates," the officer held a clipboard in front of him. "When I advise of your number, turn and organize outside your assigned block."

Beginning at the front, the officer read out each number that the prisoner had tattooed on their forearm and assigned a corresponding block number.

Eleonore watched with nervous anticipation as he came down the line towards her. Desperate to escape the elements, Eleonore was content to receive whatever block was assigned. Looking down at her hands, she noticed her fingertips turning a pale white and tucked her hands under her arms for warmth.

"Seven Five Six Nine Three!" the officer shouted while his eyes remained fixed on his list.

None answered.

"Seven Five Six Nine Three!" the officer shouted again as he dropped the clipboard by his side and scanned the crowd.

With wide eyes, Eleonore wondered what the officer was shouting, then she spotted the other prisoners checking the tattoos on their arms. *Right,* Eleonore panicked and looked at her forearm: 75,693.

"Yes," Eleonore raised a timid hand.

"Birkenau," the officer pointed behind her. "Stand at the back with the other women."

Walking to the back, Elenore passed the rows of those awaiting their assigned barracks as they stared at their feet, ignoring anyone and everyone as they were lost in their own misery or concerned with the suffering of their loved ones.

Birkenau, Eleonore reminded herself as she crossed her arms and huddled with the other women waiting. While in 'normal' circumstances this proximity with a stranger would've sent Eleonore into a near panic, she now carried a strong attachment to these women. They understood the longing for home, the humiliation of being naked and then shaved, and the chill that set in the bones from exposure to the elements.

The snow fell gently on Eleonore's shoulders as she waited for what seemed like an eternity. Each flake which fell on her bald head reminded her of the shame to which she had been reduced. Closing her eyes, she envisioned her flat – that image of serenity and security – and wished she had never left.

Out of the corner of her eye, Eleonore caught Ella limping towards her group: her number had been called. While unable to offer much enthusiasm as she froze in the cold, inwardly Eleonore was overjoyed.

"You're limping?" Eleonore spoke through the shivers.

"My toes are frozen," Ella shook her head and glanced down to inspect her bare feet. She, like Eleonore, had lost her shoes after being stuck in the mud.

"It's so cold," Eleonore looked at Ella with woeful eyes.

Then, almost instinctively, Eleonore stepped forward and leaned her head on Ella's shoulder who returned the gesture. Amongst the gentle, falling snow the two stood as close as sisters. Neither knew each other apart from a name, but neither cared.

Eventually, the guard signaled for the women to move and the miserable group hobbled along as they followed their escort. Passing back through the tunnel with the electric fence, Eleonore was surprised to see that the dead prisoner still lay in her spot. With her arms a pale shade of blue and her skin tightened, the prisoner seemed rather like a sculpture that was being hidden by the mounting snow.

"Seven Five Six Nine Three and Seven Five Six Nine Nine," the guard read off his sheet when they had stopped in front of a barrack and Ella and Eleonore stepped forward.

"You will be assigned duties in the morning," the guard spoke quickly then continued deeper into the camp with the rest of the group.

In silence, Eleonore and Ella held hands as they stood outside their barrack and, without a word, knew each other's thoughts. One didn't require a prestigious background to comprehend the sting of absolute poverty, which both women were now forced to absorb.

With missing shingles and cracked paint, the barrack looked decades old, though Eleonore knew it was the same age as the camp. There were two entrances and neither had a door but were exposed to the willful passing of the bitter wind.

Glancing at each other, the women nodded and approached the hollow doorway where Eleonore gave a slight knock on the doorframe and peeked inside. She had heard a few voices chatting away but was stunned to see hundreds of women lying in seemingly endless rows of bunks. Except for a designated portion – which was occupied by a handful of buckets – the barracks was well over capacity. Two chimney stoves were poised on either end and joined together by a short, brick wall running down the center of the barrack where a handful of women were sitting to warm themselves.

"What do you want?" a woman, whom Eleonore assumed was about her age, threw her hands onto her hips as she studied the newcomers. She had all the makings of a mother and, by her stance, Eleonore perceived a nurturing, yet punitive nature.

"We were assigned here," Eleonore cleared her throat.

"Assigned for what?" the woman squinted, then pointed at Ella. "I know why she's here, but you?"

"I believe these are to be our barracks," Eleonore winced as she brushed against the burning tattoo on her forearm.

"Ah," the woman nodded without any enthusiasm. "Alright, come with me."

The two followed the woman inside the barracks and Eleonore's mouth turned down slightly as she looked around. While it was tidy, and the smell was not all that repugnant, the mass of people living within one, tight space without any privacy spurred Eleonore to pull her shoulders together and wish she could shrink away.

"The newest arrivals sleep on the bunks nearest the entrance," the woman spoke begrudgingly as she noticed Eleonore's revulsion.

Bunk? Eleonore scoffed inwardly, *the resemblance is more like tombs in a catacomb.*

Eleonore and Ella were led past the rows while most of the prisoners ignored them as they were just another temporary face. Some of the 'fresher' ones studied her and Ella with wide, curious eyes. For the most part, they looked too weak to move, too hungry to lift but a finger.

"Here we are, you can squeeze in here," the woman turned and patted a wooden bunk which already housed four other women on a single bed; the bunks above and below held eight or nine women, depending on the age and size of the occupants.

"This one seems occupied," Eleonore frowned. She was not one to complain, but she was certain there was a more advantageous solution.

"It's important to keep warm, especially during the night," the woman explained, but with a little embarrassment. To her, this had become normal, but Eleonore's surprise reminded her of how unusual this was.

"How can anyone stand for this?" Eleonore looked at the woman with incredulity.

"There are some that haven't," the woman replied while biting the inside of her cheek.

"And?" Eleonore wanted to know their fate.

"And they are no longer with us," the woman raised her eyebrows, not relishing in explaining what, to her, was obvious and uncomfortable.

"Well, we appreciate your helpfulness," Eleonore nodded and glanced at Ella, curious at her quietness.

"What's your name?" Ella asked the woman.

"We don't use names here," the woman blurted.

"Why ever not?" Eleonore shot her head back in surprise.

"Just call me 'Em', alright?" Em gave a harsh pat on Eleonore's shoulder and brushed passed.

Glancing at her bunkmates, Eleonore saw all sorts of women. Some were weak, close to death; others that were new like herself were crying, weeping for their fate, for their sorrows.

Climbing into their bunk, Eleonore and Ella squeezed in with the other four women, and even without blankets it wasn't long before the body heat began to warm them. Eleonore was glad to have someone like Ella but, studying her for a moment, knew that now was not a proper time for an interrogation.

"Give us your hand," demanded an elderly woman beside Eleonore.

"Sorry?" Eleonore glanced at her, surprised at the request.

"Give us your hand," she repeated.

Examining the elderly woman, who smiled warmly at her with a sort of disconnect from reality, Eleonore assumed she was a gypsy and wondered what price she would demand. She had seen enough street performers in Berlin to be wary of their tricks, but this woman's pursuit seemed to be genuine novelty. Supposing that she had already seen the worst, and nothing was left to be taken, Eleonore offered up her hand.

"That's interesting," the woman spread Eleonore's palm roughly.

"I don't have money to give," Eleonore glanced awkwardly at the gypsy.

"The only use money has here is for toilet paper," the gypsy continued reading.

"I have nothing to give for your reading," Eleonore tried to withdraw her hand.

"Not all worth is bound in material," the woman replied as she released Eleonore. "You're going to survive this, you know. You're going to get out."

"Where did you read that?" Eleonore studied her own hand, wondering what lines prophesied which, but the woman didn't reply. She simply turned her back towards Eleonore and began to sleep.

Confounded, Eleonore lay on her back and looked up at the wooden plank above her head. The names of the previous occupants had been etched into the wood and she ran her fingers over them, memorizing each name, wondering if they had received a similar prophecy from this woman.

Her charge here, she reminded herself, should be no different than her charge in Berlin. She would continue in her struggle against the Nazi regime by any means necessary. She would remain Eleonore Hodys, the seamstress of *La Venezia* no matter the cost. She would not forget her humanity.

Chapter Five:
Baptism of Fire

"Tame the savageness of man and make gentle the life of this world." Aeschylus.

"Get up," a hand reached over and shook Eleonore.

Opening her eyes slightly, Eleonore peered through the darkness but saw no one. Disorientated, she could hear movement all around her, but couldn't remember where she was.

"I won't say it again," the voice grew harsh, and Eleonore leaned over the edge of the bunk to see Em had shaken her awake and Ella was gone.

"What's happening?" Eleonore whispered as the recollection of the past few days flooded back, hoping the commotion meant some sort escape was in the works.

"The first gong has rung," Em answered as she wrapped her head in a shawl. "It's time to begin the day."

"I believe both the sun and I disagree," Eleonore rubbed her head which was now throbbing.

"The first gong rings at 4:30. You only have a few minutes to tidy your quarters and wash before coffee and tea are served."

Coffee and tea? Eleonore frowned at a phrase that seemed so foreign to this environment.

Nearly forgetting that she was on the middle bunk, Eleonore threw her feet off the side and jerked awake when she couldn't feel the ground.

You nearly killed and embarrassed yourself in one swift movement, Eleonore thought as she collected herself. Feeling for the ladder attached to the bunk, Eleonore stepped down the rungs as the stoves were lit to allow for some light and to heat the tea. Noticing the other ladies lined up for the toilets – which were small, rusty buckets on the floor – Eleonore politely stepped in line, wondering if she could even use the facilities. She hadn't eaten a crumb or drank a drop; there was nothing to void. Still, she stood patiently and awaited her turn.

Tired yawns and sighs passed down the line and Eleonore was relieved to see that most were 'appreciating' the early morning as well as she was. Some of the ladies, those of a more anxious disposition, inspected the progress of the line, ensuring none were taking an extended 'visit'. Others offered the familiar empty expressions Eleonore knew as the hallmark of Auschwitz.

As she grew aware of her surroundings, Eleonore noticed some of the ladies had leather shoes and bowls while she remained barefoot and empty-handed. Feeling silly for being ill-equipped, Eleonore rubbed her hand over her bald head. It still surprised her to feel the absence of curly locks, and she doubted she would ever get used to the prickly buzz-cut.

"Here," Em gave a gentle tap on her shoulder, and held out a pair of brown, tattered shoes.

"Where'd you get these?" Eleonore held the shoes in pleasant surprise and then slipped them over her feet.

Em cleared her throat before answering, "The lady that died in your bunk last night."

"What?!" Eleonore's eyes shot wide with shock. How could she have not known? How long was she laying next to a dead body? And where was Ella? *God*, she prayed, *please don't let it be her.*

"I took the liberty of taking her shoes for you," Em ignored Eleonore's incredulity.

"Who was she?" Eleonore remained perplexed.

"Some gypsy," Em replied with a shrug. "It's best not to get attached. She was elderly, anyways."

"I can't wear these," Eleonore looked down at her feet, remembering the woman who had prophesied to her last night.

"Then you'll die," Em said bluntly.

"What do you mean?" Eleonore frowned.

"You need three things here at Auschwitz: a pair of shoes, a bowl and, most importantly, work. Without the first, your feet will become infected and then you won't be able to work. Without the second, you won't eat, and you'll have nowhere to shit."

"You," Eleonore couldn't believe what she was hearing and resumed with a whisper, "you use the washroom and eat in the same bowl?"

"It's illegal to go in the open. They'll kill you," Em continued.

"I'm not an animal!" Eleonore shook her head vibrantly.

"In their eyes," Em spoke softly, "you'll never be anything else."

I wish Dr. Mengele had selected me for his laboratory, Eleonore mused in her ignorance. *Sounded like they are treated rather well. Maybe I should've been placed in the other camp.*

"Oh, Em, I saw something yesterday that I didn't quite understand," Eleonore spoke quietly over her shoulder.

"What's that?"

"When I arrived, our group was split into two. Why would that be?"

Em didn't reply. After a few seconds, Eleonore turned to check if she had been heard only to see tears streaming down Em's cheeks.

"What is it?" Eleonore panicked, horrified that she had caused such a reaction. She wished she could adopt a more affectionate temperament and give Em a hug or put an arm around her shoulder, but still, she refrained.

With the line continuing to inch forward, Eleonore returned to facing the front, but all she could think about was Em. Glancing again over her shoulder, she saw Em with her eyes closed and lips quivering.

"I apologize if I—"

"Quiet!" Em nearly shouted and the whole barracks turned in curiosity at the disturbance.

"I—"

"Never speak of it again," Em removed herself from the line and walked briskly to the rear.

Confused, Eleonore watched Em storm off until the other prisoners began threatening to boot her from the line if she didn't use the services. Eleonore, for all her she knew, had inadvertently made an enemy.

Uncertain as to what use she had for the toilets, Eleonore squatted over a large, close-to-full-bucket and nearly gagged at the smell and the image. Even with a decent attempt, Eleonore couldn't bring herself to use the facilities with an abundance of eyes watching her in their desperation to 'go'. Placing her head in her hands, Eleonore tried to ignore their gazes, but nothing would suffice.

"C'mon!" the woman next in line barked. "That's long enough now!"

"I'm done, I'm done," Eleonore growled as she pulled her dress back down.

"Where are you going?" the woman glared at Eleonore.

"I'm finished," Eleonore shrugged, wondering what the trouble was about.

"And now the bucket is full," the woman raised her eyebrows and threw her hands onto her hips.

"Pardon?" Eleonore studied her, pondering if this was some sort of trick.

"The last person to fill it up takes it out," the woman pointed to the door with her thumb.

"I didn't even go," Eleonore glanced again at the bucket with disgust.

"You're not above the rules," the woman pointed again at the door.

"Fine," Eleonore bent down and grabbed the handle.

Lifting the bucket slowly, Elenore gagged as she waddled with it between her knees, careful not to spill on herself. She doubted there would be an opportunity to clean any mess should the unthinkable occur. Walking out the doors, Eleonore dumped the bucket and closed her eyes as she held her breath, trying desperately to think of something more pleasant; anything.

"There," Eleonore grumbled as she set the bucket back inside without the appreciation of the demanding woman.

Instead, Eleonore received glares from those desperate for relief who now had to wait an extra couple minutes because of someone ignorant of the 'rules'. Their irritation caused Eleonore to return to her reclusiveness, and she studied the path in front of her feet, nothing else.

Taking the opportunity to examine the camp, Eleonore leaned on the doorpost at the opposite end of the barracks and looked out over the immensity. It was a sight she was sure to never forget as the efficiency of the totalitarian state was being enacted to its full degree at Auschwitz: not a soul was resisting the fate decreed for them.

They need but one leader, Eleonore felt her spirit rising with rage against the cruelty. Hundreds of thousands of Jews, Communists, Jehovah's Witnesses, and other political prisoners had been herded into their 'pens'. Yet the guards were drastically outnumbered. All it would take was one spark to ignite the fire. If only some charismatic frontrunner would resist and stand firm against the oppression no matter the personal costs. Then, surely, others would be inspired to do likewise.

Maybe, she pondered, *I've been guided throughout my existence for this very purpose. What if I've spurned children or marriage not from any decision on my part, but from providence electing me for a grander role? Children! That's why Em reacted so strongly,* Eleonore crossed her arms and sighed. *Her children have been taken to the other camp, or to Dr. Mengele's lab. Still, there was no need for her to shout at me.*

A kettle screeched, and Eleonore spun, her heart skipping a beat with excitement. She had been parted from her favorite beverage for a few days and, quite honestly, wondered how she hadn't fallen into a serious withdrawal. Of course, the tea was probably a cheap brand like the ones she had sampled in the Berlin shops, but tea was tea and Eleonore's stomach growled with anticipation.

Again, a line formed at either end of the barracks and one of the prisoners stood by the chimney stove as a large kettle, more of a pot really, chimed away in its cheerful tune. This prisoner, though elderly, had been assigned to scoop out the tea with a ladle and quickly fill the cracked and brittle porcelain cups before handing them to the other inmates.

Nearly vibrating with excitement, Eleonore held the warm cup and brought it up to her nose, like she had done so many times on her balcony in Berlin. Yet the cheerful feeling evaporated as she struggled to detect any scent. Walking back to the doorway, Eleonore inspected the tea in the dim light of dawn. Making certain it was safe, she dared to take a sip and, bringing the cup to her lips, took that craved first gulp.

In an instant, her lips turned upside down as the bitter taste lingered. Even with her burning hunger, Eleonore found it difficult to convince herself to persist. Still, she knew this would be her only supplement until lunch. If, that is, her captives were humane enough to provide one. *They must feed us at some time,* Eleonore figured, but glanced back at the ladies within the barracks and took note of their skinny legs and arms and slender faces. *Chances are you've had your last decent meal,* Eleonore sighed.

The gong rang again, and the ladies started to file with haste to a square beside the amphitheater. Hurrying along, Eleonore set her cup back near the chimney stove and kept pace with the others, unsure of what to expect. She glanced out at the rest of the camp as the other blocks began to empty and assemble in their allocated spots. In silence and in good order, tens of thousands fell under the tyrannical thumb of only a few hundred. The absurdity was overwhelming, but she, like the others, was terrified to behave rashly.

Sure, they could believe in the wild fantasy that if they employed their numbers in an organized fashion then they could have a measure of success, but the cost of life would be great, and who should be asked to make the first sacrifice? Mothers had been torn from their children, husbands separated from their wives, and friends – let alone acquaintances – were scarce. The Nazi machine had effectively isolated the masses of their enemies but to what end? Mass murder? Slave labor? Eleonore couldn't seem to understand the exact purpose of the camp, but something sinister was at play here at Auschwitz. Of that, she was certain.

Arriving at 'the square', Eleonore learned its name was derived not from any aesthetics, but rather, it was a slab of concrete built in a square – nothing else. No fountains or mosaic flooring and nothing to be proud of from the workman's point of view. Not that Eleonore was expecting grandiose in a camp such as this, but a part of her was disappointed. Her creative mind was begging to behold the beautiful. Yet the grey, winter sky above, and the plain architecture of the camp seemed to have combined their efforts in driving beauty into oblivion.

Lining up in rows of ten, the ladies who had been through this procedure before formed up in their assigned ranks. Eleonore, and those new to the whole process, seemed to be at a loss. Spotting an opening, namely the eighth position in line, Eleonore filed in and mirrored the other ladies with their hands held neatly in front and staring straight ahead as if they were Royal Prussian guards themselves.

A small, wooden podium was placed at the front of the group which Commandant Hoess climbed to stand well above those of this barrack. Eleonore found it odd that such a high-ranking officer would be engaging in such a simple capacity, but possibly his presence was due to the majority of the block being 'new' prisoners. While most were fresh to Auschwitz, Eleonore felt alone in the realm of the truly inexperienced.

Further perplexing Eleonore was Hoess' purpose at this roll call. He simply stood in his smart uniform watching over the group as an officer called out each assigned number and was met with the expected response. To Eleonore, the Commandant seemed to be looking over the group like a farmer inspecting the yield of his crop rather than a warden concerned with those under his care.

"Seven Five Six Nine Nine?" the call came from the officer and Eleonore recognized the number as Ella's. Yet there was no answer.

Curious, Eleonore peeked over the shoulder in front of her and spotted Ella standing in her 'assigned' position. With her chin high and her hands nervously forming and deforming a fist, Ella refused to answer the call.

How did she slip by without me noticing? Eleonore wondered. *And why isn't she answering?*

"Seven Five Six Nine Nine?!" the officer shouted, warning that he would not make the request again.

Still, Ella remained silent.

"What are you doing?" a harsh whisper from a nearby prisoner begged Ella to speak up.

"You'll see," Ella spoke quickly.

She's starting a revolt, Eleonore felt her heart beating within her chest. How she wanted to join, to commence the domino effect that would shake the very foundations of Auschwitz.

Storming down the line, the officer, who was a tall, handsome man with dark hair slicked back under his fitted officer's cap, stopped just short of running Ella over. Towering above, he glared at Ella who returned a defiant stare.

"I'll give you one more chance," the officer breathed heavily out his nostrils and Eleonore saw the eyes of a man gone mad with power. He was not accustomed to insubordination, and his aggressiveness indicated to Eleonore that he had exacted his dominance before and would do so again.

"What are my charges?" Ella demanded, and everyone looked upon the officer, awaiting his reply in desperation. Many had been detained against their will without so much as an explanation. Yet, for fear of punishment none dared to ask. Now, however, Ella was showing her mettle in the face of overwhelming tyranny.

"In fact," Ella continued when it was clear the officer couldn't devise a fabrication when caught off guard, "what are anyone's charges besides the coincidence of their birth?"

"You are enemies of the state!" the officer screamed and, raising his hand to strike, Ella didn't flinch as the blow came across her face, flinging her to her backside.

Standing over her, the officer raised his fist and with all the hateful malice in his heart, he unleashed his rage. Again and again, he struck her face as she lay on her back. She tried to block the blows, but each one that landed sent her further into disorientation and the officer, filled with blood lust, would only be satisfied with a brutal death.

Eleonore's spirit surged as each merciless blow stirred her to action. Still, like the others, she stood in place: hands neatly tucked in front and eyes low.

"No," the sound escaped Eleonore's mouth, and all turned in surprise.

"No!" She said louder and stepped out of line.

"Get back!" The officer wiped the sweat off his brow as he panted while hovering over Ella. "Or you'll be next!"

"She deserves due process," Eleonore cleared her throat, almost in disbelief that she would dare utter such defiance, but if Ella died, then who did she have?

Swiftly, the officer stood and slapped Eleonore across the cheek with the back of his bloodied hand. With rage, Eleonore punched the officer back to gasps of shock and horror from the cloud of witnesses.

"I'm so sorry," Eleonore spoke quickly and with regret. Here she stood in full view of the culmination of her life's choices. As a single woman living in Berlin, she had to be prepared to react violently against men of ill wishes. Yet she had not prepared for circumstances leveling this degree of depravation and the officer towered over her, ready to increase sorrow for her instinctual backlash.

"You will be," the officer offered a cruel smile but, noticing that Hoess was coming down the line to inspect the disturbance, stepped aside and stood at attention.

"Lieutenant Jung, why are you failing to keep the prisoners in line?" Hoess looked up at the officer as he belittled him.

"Miss Hodys struck an officer in Hitler's army," Jung pressed his tongue against his cheek where Eleonore's open palm had planted itself.

"She was defending a woman whom you have rendered senseless," Hoess helped Ella to her feet as she stumbled like a drunk. "This is an admirable quality, not to be diminished by the primitive use of your fists."

"Ella Gartner was defiant," Jung continued to defend himself, "and Eleonore Hodys assaulted an officer. The penalty is death."

"And what should be the penalty for your stupidity?" Hoess fumed. "What would it accomplish to deal out such a sentence on these ladies? Let me show you how to deal with insubordination. You're dismissed."

"Sir," Jung saluted and marched off, but not before offering Eleonore a malicious glare and glancing down at his bloodied fists, promising vengeance.

"I remember you," Hoess studied Eleonore and flinched with seething rage. "The esteemed member of the Socialist Democratic Party."

"My apologies, Commandant," Eleonore held her gaze low as her breathing labored. She didn't know what other excuse she could provide. Her bravery in defence of her friend, a woman she had no familiarity with apart from a brief hand-holding in the train car, had stirred her to react rashly. Now that her inevitable punishment was held in the judgement of this Hoess, Eleonore trembled, wishing she had refused her conscience.

"Lieutenant Jung is correct," Hoess looked at Eleonore without a hint of emotion, calculated.

Eleonore felt her stomach churning and her hands shook uncontrollably to the extent she could not hold them in place.

"But I am fair," Hoess sighed, "and I will spare you from punishment...if," he paused and studied Eleonore pensively.

"If what?" Eleonore's throat closed.

"Renounce your allegiance to the party that desires the downfall of Hitler and swear the oath."

For an infinitesimal point in time, the earth stood still as Eleonore watched Hoess. She was certain he would follow through with his threat, but were her ideals worth the cost? She weighed her options carefully, but her mind had been thrown into survival mode and everything within her was screaming to submit. Yet surrendering her beliefs to save her skin would damn her soul, or so she was convinced. Though she was not necessarily religious, she understood that if the divine did exist, He would not hold lightly to the breaking of one's convictions for the sake of convenience. Scores of men and women had forfeited their lives for what they believed was right and, at such a time as this, should principles continue to be abandoned? Such laying down of one's morality, individual by individual, had ultimately thrown Germany, and Europe, into the chaos of war under Hitler.

With her legs weak, Eleonore shook her head, "I can't abandon what I believe to be the right future for sacred Germany."

"You don't understand what you are doing," Hoess glared at her.

"Didn't you advise your officer that my actions were admirable?" Eleonore's face flared with courage. "I ask what Ella demanded: what are my charges?! What are anyone's charges?! You have taken loyal German subjects and made them enemies of the state. You are sacrificing your own people for some mad man's delusions."

"Enough!" Hoess shook with fury. "Take them!" he pointed to the entire line of ten women.

"Them?" Eleonore panicked. "What have they done?"

"I gave you a chance," Hoess clenched his jaw. "Now, you will learn how things are handled at Auschwitz."

At gunpoint, the ten women were marched to the front and made to kneel before the entire block. Eleonore stared at the concrete in front of her, considering it may well be the last thing she sees. She wondered if they would be shot all at once or one by one. *I hope they start with me*, Eleonore found herself wishing. *I don't think I can stand being last.*

"Bring those two here to stand with me," Hoess waved for the guards to collect Eleonore and Ella.

Terrified, Eleonore needed assistance to stand as her legs had locked into place and she was unable to move. Ella, too, needed to lean on a guard as she was wavering in and out of consciousness, barely able to appreciate the gravity of the situation. The Commandant then nodded to the remaining guards who grabbed long, thin sticks from beside the square.

"You will watch with me," Hoess seized Eleonore by the arm as he signaled to the guards to begin the flogging. "Twenty lashes," he ordered, and the women looked up at him in terror as they began pleading.

Their begging was met by deaf ears as the soldiers began the count. Eleonore winced as each strike sent screams, terrible shrieks echoing across the courtyard. The women fell on their faces and rolled around on the concrete in desperation for relief, but none was given. It was then that Eleonore spotted Em amongst those being brutalized and caught the look of hatred she bore for Eleonore as she endured the lashes.

"Stop! Please!" Eleonore looked up at the Commandant who was still gripping her arm. She could sense the beatings were disturbing him as well as his hand twitched with each strike.

"You did this!" Hoess turned and squeezed both of her arms firmly. "Every fresh shipment of criminals there is someone like you and Seventy Five Six Nine Nine. Do you think you two are unique? Do you suppose you're the first to defy the order of my camp? Everyone like you is silenced. Watch what you have done to them!" he spun her and forced her to observe the guards continuing with relentless brutality.

Finally, the count arrived at twenty, and the guards ceased. Still, the screaming continued as the pain lingered and the women writhed on the ground, holding their sides and their limbs.

"This better not interfere with your labors," Hoess released Eleonore and spoke to the assembly. "Any work shirked or completed incorrectly shall be punished accordingly."

Chapter Six:
Work Sets You Free

"Never in the field of human conflict has so much been owed by so many to so few." Winston Churchill

"And…one, two, three," the conductor counted in the orchestra. In sync, though Eleonore winced at the sharp introduction, the musicians played a disjointed selection to help the prisoners march in unison to their assignments. It was an upbeat, cheerful foxtrot which most would have recognized entitled, "The Most Beautiful Time of Life."

It was close to the saddest sight Eleonore had ever seen. The conductor, a fellow inmate, had been stripped of his glory as he directed the accompaniment in his regulation outfit. The musicians, too, looked half-dead as they played their out-of-tune violin or blasted their wind instruments with whatever breath they could afford. No doubt they had been great in their prime, but now their lips trembled as the music reminded them of brighter days.

Not that Eleonore could pay much attention to the music anyways, with the glares from the other prisoners; none more poignant than Em's. Eleonore and Ella had been assigned to work in the hospital alongside the eight other ladies who had been beaten. With tears staining their faces, and some limping, the inmates looked more like patients than laborers.

That's how they control us, Eleonore thought, but didn't dare voice her opinion for fear of retribution. *They don't punish the one that retaliates, but those closest to them. For the sake of their comrades, one submits to Auschwitz. Hoess didn't need to put a bullet through my head to stop me or Ella, he only needed to turn the camp against us: pit us as the real enemy.*

Ella, scarcely conscious, leaned on Eleonore while the group walked in silence. Guided by three guards, they were taken to a hospital near the entrance of the camp. An ominous, two-story brick building towered above them and, apart from the sign above the door, none would have guessed its purpose.

Like most of the women, Eleonore had been assigned to such designations while the men were sent to labor in the fields or construction within the camp. Yet if a choice were given, Eleonore would have elected for the demanding labor as the steely glares from her compatriots ran her blood cold. Though, she supposed, she wouldn't have survived long in those harsh conditions and at least here she stood a chance.

Reaching for the handle, the guard opened the door and stepped back for the ladies to enter, which Eleonore thought was a rather abnormal display of chivalry. The societal norms with which these men had been raised carried over even into the darkest of circumstances such as a death camp.

Entering in single file, the ladies lined up shoulder to shoulder in the foyer which, as expected for the size of the building, was just enough space for all ten. Eleonore's heart sank into her stomach as she stood in the dank, unwelcoming lobby with the only light streaming from a dirty window to their right. The grey light from the circular window illuminated the immensity of dust stirring about in the air, giving one the sense that hygiene was not a concern at this hospital.

But what Eleonore found most shocking was not the unsanitary conditions but the overwhelming sorrow. Across from them were two large, brown push doors that failed to filter out the groans and moans from patients just beyond. And the smell - a wretched stench of filth – washed over them, coating their clothes and reminding Eleonore of the train car. *I hate this,* Eleonore closed her eyes. *This must be hell.*

With hands folded neatly in front, and heels clicked together, the ladies waited, seemingly unaware or unconcerned by what lay beyond. Whatever it was they were waiting for, Eleonore didn't know, but glanced at Ella who could barely lift her own head out of exhaustion and pain.

"You're late!" huffed a deep voice from atop a staircase to their left which led to the second floor. Hurrying down the winding, wooden staircase with almost comical creaks and squeaks, a heavyset woman with a round, red face came to stand before them with the most disappointing scowl.

She, too, wore the designated armband of the Kapos with a white nurse's uniform and a little cap carrying the standard red cross insignia of the medical profession. Yet her demeanor suggested to Eleonore that this woman's credentials fell far outside the realm of the medicinal. Anyone in that field who carried even a mediocre record had been drafted to serve the soldiers at the front. Those who were left behind were often met with an apprehensiveness, and rightfully so. They were the half-trained, unschooled, the worst of the worst.

The guard cleared his throat before explaining, "There was an incid—"

"Did I ask you?" the woman rushed over to the soldier and came within inches as she pointed a sharp finger. With a voice deeper than half the men Eleonore knew, this woman carried the familiar sign of one who had spent her life savings on cartons of cigarettes.

"No," the guard swallowed and looked straight ahead. "No, ma'am."

"You stink," the woman furled her nose and one of the prisoners couldn't help a laugh escape. The guard was among those who had dealt their 'punishment' with the whipping and this justice, even in the slightest of fashions, was enough to satisfy a temporary craving for revenge.

"Who laughed?!" the woman shot her head in their direction, her face flushed a bright red.

"I did, ma'am," the prisoner raised her hand timidly, and her sleeve fell down to reveal a cut on her arm from where she had been struck.

"Good," the woman's expression turned to sudden humor, realizing that each of the women had been beaten. Although harsh, Eleonore sensed that this Kapo carried a measure of compassion. "They deserve a little humbling now and then. If any guard gives you trouble, let me know and I'll sort them out," she looked at each woman with reassurance.

"Will that be all, ma'am?" the soldier requested but with a tone of disdain.

"No, it will not," the woman stepped even closer to the soldier. "Go throw your useless, black heart off a cliff."

At this, all the prisoners chuckled. All except Eleonore that is, as she was still disturbed from the events of the morning. She stood, staring blankly at the floor in front of her, unwilling to utter a sound out of order lest the others be punished for her transgression.

"Alright, calm down," the Kapo stood in front of the prisoners and studied each of them, mentally assigning them the daily tasks.

"For those of you who are new, I'm to be addressed as ma'am, nothing else. Is that understood?"

"Yes, ma'am," the group responded.

"You will be given duties, tasks that I have carefully selected for the unimpeded operation of this hospital. Perform them with diligence, and you will be rewarded. If you shirk your work, or I find it unsatisfactory," ma'am began to pace in front of the ladies, taking pleasure in the dominion of this little kingdom where even SS guards trembled, "you will find in me an enemy without parallel. Is that understood?" she spoke each word carefully, making sure to drive home the point and looking down her nose as if she were wearing glasses.

"Yes, ma'am," they again replied in unison.

"I've not heard your voice amongst the others," ma'am stepped in front of Ella and looked at her with a measure of pity. "No doubt the day has already been unkind?"

But Ella gave no response, scarcely able to even open her eye that was now swelling and turning purple.

"Yours neither," ma'am examined Eleonore with suspicion.

"She's not one of us," Em hissed with resentment.

"Whatever do you mean?" ma'am frowned.

"Her ideals are more valuable than those around her," a prisoner spoke with sarcasm. The age-old strategy of divide and conquer had been implemented once again as Hoess had effectively pitted the camp against Eleonore and Ella. They had become the easy enemy, the convenient avenue with which to outpour frustration.

"That's not what I intended," Eleonore leaned over and glared at Em.

"But it's what happened," ma'am curled her lips pensively. "You're not Jewish which leaves me to assume you're a political prisoner. No doubt a communist?"

"I'm," Eleonore glanced at the others who were staring at her. "I'm a member of the Socialist Democratic Party."

"Is that right?" ma'am seemed genuinely interested. "Their ideology is noble, but when put into practice it leads to inequality," she shrugged as if it were an unfortunate fact.

"I believe in the rule of the people," Eleonore trembled as she spoke, her words falling flat.

"And what if the people rule against you?" ma'am stepped back and threw her hands onto her hips as she addressed the group. "Every morning, noon, and evening, the bedpans must be emptied and replaced with fresh ones. Would you like to exercise democratic liberties and elect one amongst you to undertake this duty?"

Immediately, the prisoners pointed at Eleonore and she felt herself wishing for death. If only Hoess had ordered the guards in the square to shoot her then she could be saved from this disgrace.

"That's bullying, not democracy," Eleonore said under her breath but loud enough to be heard.

"The people have spoken," ma'am rumbled with a deep smoker's cough as she covered her mouth, "and now you've witnessed your worshipped philosophy at work within Hitler's Reich. Hopefully, this gives you an inkling into the perils with which you wish to throw the whole of Germany."

Baffled by the inaccuracy, Eleonore wanted to defend further but was silenced by ma'am's stern look of warning.

"Basement floor, third door on the left," ma'am pointed to the staircase opposite the one she descended. And you," she pointed at Em. "You will supervise. Advise me if these two offer any difficulties."

Grudgingly, Eleonore obeyed and, putting Ella's arm around her shoulder, walked to the staircase as Em trailed, though at a distance. Standing at the top of a winding, metal flight of stairs, Eleonore drew a deep breath before plunging into the unknown.

She descended slowly, helping Ella with each step. Faint, orange bulbs hung from the concrete ceiling of a basement which shunned every form of natural light. There was a thick dampness in the air and Eleonore could smell the mold thriving in this environment.

But Eleonore's attention was drawn to a heart-shattering site. The basement, which stretched for hundreds of yards and was much longer than the building above, was full of clothes, suitcases, shoes, documents, and other items that belonged to the prisoners. The amount was staggering, and Eleonore wondered where all the items had been collected from as they far outnumbered the prisoners in the camp.

"We can't delay," Em barked and brushed passed Eleonore as they came to the bottom of the staircase.

Speeding towards a small office that had been cut into the cement, Em left Eleonore and Ella alone in the vastness.

Spying a seemingly out of place bench against the cement wall, Eleonore lay Ella down. Kneeling beside her friend, Eleonore noticed that the bench had been bolted into the ground, but for what purpose, she didn't know. In fact, the whole basement seemed to be out of line with reason. There was an eeriness to the belongings left untouched: the suitcases unopened with fabric sticking out their sides, and the unwashed clothes which were piled into heaps and mounds that stretched hundreds of yards.

Then, a smile caught the corner of her mouth as she was distracted by a small, brown leather suitcase that seemed identical to her fathers. She knew it wasn't his, but still, she loved the reminder. Not that her father had used his suitcase on more than a handful of occasions, but on the train from Austria to Berlin she had been awarded the special privilege of ensuring its safe travel.

She recalled holding it close to her chest as they boarded, then checking on it from time to time as it rested above their heads in the overhead storage. It was the first time she remembered that extraordinary feeling of responsibility; that weight which provided a world of worry but somehow issued her into maturity.

Her father had been so proud of her dedication, that he purchased her a small chocolate when they arrived in Berlin. Growing up in the country, Eleonore had never experienced the delicacy before and remembered her father laughing at her disapproving scrunch of the nose as she could barely stand the bitterness. But all was not lost as he procured another flavor; a milk chocolate that enraptured her taste buds and sent her on a never-ending venture to relive such a pure experience.

She even gambled with the idea of opening a sweet shop instead of *La Venezia,* but she couldn't abandon her talent for design. It was her first love, and sweets would have to remain her ever desired mistress. *What I'd do now for a sweet,* Eleonore felt her stomach begging for relief.

"Oh, come on!" Em's frustrated shout from within the office broke Eleonore's trance.

"Rest here. I'll pick up the shift for both of us. You need to regain your strength," Eleonore tapped Ella's arm as she stood. The statement struck a chord of irony as faintness from hunger washed over her. Still, her condition was nothing in comparison with Ella's agony.

"You shouldn't..." Ella mumbled something unintelligible.

"Don't speak," Eleonore glanced at her swollen lips which only enlarged with each passing moment.

"You shouldn't have saved me," a tear escaped Ella's closed eye.

"Of course I should've," Eleonore spoke with unusual determination and almost felt embarrassed by her own demeanor. "What's surprising is that I'm the only one who did anything."

"I was trying to die," Ella shook her head, "and Lieutenant Jung was more than content to oblige."

Eleonore didn't know how to reply but looked at Ella with the greatest pity. She was beautiful and came from a position of privilege, or so her conduct projected, yet her deepest wish was to die. Had she lost family? Friends? A lover? Eleonore knew there was a story to be told and she wouldn't allow Ella to succumb to her own depression.

"I'll find you some bandages," Eleonore stood with a groan. "This is a hospital after all."

"You'll do no such thing," Em growled as she grabbed a trolley full of bedpans which Eleonore was disgusted to note that 'fresh' meant cleaned and not unused. They were stained by the usage of their previous masters and, in a hospital environment, were rife of disease.

"Your little stunt at roll call this morning made us all late," Em continued. "If you think what she experienced was brutal you haven't seen anything yet," Em pointed at Ella. "Death is the penalty for improper work. You've put us all in jeopardy."

"I'll double my workload to account for Ella's absence," Eleonore drew upon her courage. She was used to hard work, after all. Why should this be any different?

"Is that right?" Em raised an unimpressed and skeptical brow.

"Yes," Eleonore gave a reaffirming nod.

"Fine," Em tapped the handle of the trolley. "Then let's be on with it. Use the pulley to take the trolley up to the 2nd floor," she pointed to an iron cage behind the staircase. "Usually the job is split up between you and the other, but since you've elected for double the work, well…" Em waved her hand and began muttering to herself in a bitter tone.

Grasping the handle to the trolley, Eleonore glanced down at the bedpans and nearly gagged.

Calm down, Eleonore talked to herself. *This is the job you've been assigned, and you'll not fail me in this regard. This is for poor Ella, for Em, and for…I don't know. Why am I here? What have I done to deserve such a cruel fate? Maybe I should just let them kill me. Oh, you can't allow those types of thoughts. You challenged the state; you knew this would be the consequence for discovery. Just keep your head down, do the work as hard as you can, and survive. Just survive.*

Chapter Seven:
The Quick & The Dead

"Day by day, what you choose, what you think, and what you do is who you become." Heraclitus.

The wheels of the trolley rattled against the iron cage as Eleonore placed it on the pulley. Closing the outer 'gate', Eleonore heaved down on the rope to take the trolley to the top floor as fast as possible. Fastening the rope to a metal hook against the wall, Eleonore tried to catch her breath as she hurried back up the stairs.

To her relief, she spotted Em assisting Ella with a glass of water and wiping the blood from her face. Ella would be taken care of, and Eleonore would do everything possible to keep her out of harm's way. She would have to work fast and efficiently, but she was happy to labor for the sake of another.

Returning to the foyer, Eleonore witnessed a scene of utter chaos as the push doors were now wide open and she could peer into the 'hospital'. The entire floor was one open room without curtains or dividers between the patients for privacy. Guessing that there were nearly fifty beds in the room, Eleonore shuddered at the site as the patients were crammed together with some being forced to share a bed. Only a handful had hospital gowns while the rest were still in their regulation outfits and some were even naked. Most seemed to be suffering either from malnutrition or some sort of an injury. Still, it was evident from the conduct of the nurses that there was no real effort made to restore those entrusted in their care back to good health.

"What are you doing?!" Ma'am barked at one of the prisoners under her watch and Eleonore noticed the others hustling about with the Kapo clapping and shouting directions that must be met with unwavering dedication. Although Eleonore's designation held all the promises of an uncivilized duty, she was pleased to be working in solitude.

But she had lingered too long and caught the glare from Ma'am who didn't take kindly to her hospital being gawked at. Regaining her composure, Eleonore hurried to the stairs leading to the second floor, but still sensed the locked gaze from the Kapo.

Arriving on the second floor, Eleonore opened the iron cage and pushed the trolley out into what she could only describe, in comparison with the first floor, as Olympus. She had left this world and entered rooms designated for the gods as every need and desire was accounted for. Spacious, single rooms with large windows allowed for natural light and a quiet, restful area for the patients.

It was of little surprise, then, when she discovered that these privileges had been reserved for the Nazis own. SS guards who had been injured or fallen ill were being pampered to bring them back to working condition as soon as possible. Without them, the camp would fall in to ruin and be overrun by a potential revolt.

In total, there were about eight rooms, and each was under the careful watch of a nurse who, at hourly intervals, checked the clipboard that was hanging outside the room. Blood levels, temperature, blood pressure, and degree of pain were all reviewed at the regulated time and marked accordingly on the sheet.

While peaceful, the floor was a hive of activity with nurses walking briskly to and from their assigned rooms, grabbing supplies from cabinets hung in the hallway and talking breathlessly to one another. It was a measure of pride to achieve perfection in their craft, and they hustled to meet, and anticipate, the demands of their patients.

Apart from their conduct, Eleonore noticed another stark contrast between these nurses and the ones below: their apparel. On the first floor, the nurses wore dirty uniforms that were seldom washed while here, before Eleonore, walked bright ladies with fresh, white uniforms and dainty aprons tied with lace around their waists.

Then, Eleonore froze when a nurse walked past her carrying a bedpan to be disposed of, and Eleonore realized she had made a terrible mistake. Glancing into another room, her suspicions were confirmed as a nurse was placing a bedpan under the bed and a pit grew in her stomach: there was no need for her to be on the second floor. *Why did I come to the top?* Eleonore wondered as she began to reverse back to the pulley. *Em didn't say anything about the second floor. I guess I just assumed.*

But like a whisper from providence, a thought entered her mind, hinting at the medical provisions on this floor that were absent otherwise. If she could get her hands on some bandages and medicine, she could nurse Ella back to health.

Looking around, she noticed that she had remained invisible to the nurses. Not only was she a prisoner, but she was also pushing a tray of bedpans. She was the lowest of the low and Eleonore was amused with the rare opportunity to be unseen while so out in the open.

Working up the courage, Eleonore pushed the trolley down the hallway, peeking into the rooms to see if they were empty. The first was crowded with a bloodied soldier lamenting his wounds to a nurse who changed his bandages with indifference. Passing by the next room, Eleonore broke into a cold sweat when she spotted Dr. Mengele studying his clipboard over a soldier who appeared as pale as the walls.

You're making a mistake, Eleonore thought as the palms of her hands became saturated with sweat. She was certain that success was not attainable, but something in her spirit stirred her on against the odds and she was determined to collect whatever was necessary for Ella.

Finally, Eleonore came to the end of the hall and spotted an empty room with a door half-opened. Knocking lightly, Eleonore peeked in though kept her gaze low for privacy in the event she had misjudged and the room was occupied. With no response, she pushed the heavy door open as it swung gently on its hinges without so much as a sound. Stepping as lightly as she was able, Eleonore left the trolley in the hallway and closed the door behind her as she took a deep breath to calm her nerves.

Find some bandages and get out, Eleonore reminded herself. *Then you can see if the nurse's station has any medicine to be lifted.*

Suddenly, the toilet in the room flushed and the curtain surrounding the little washroom flew open, startling Eleonore and revealing an equally surprised Lieutenant Jung; the same man who had beaten Ella mere hours ago.

"Are you lost?" Jung asked as he regained his composure.

Eleonore didn't reply as she stared in horror at the Lieutenant while he snapped his suspenders into place. Yet for a moment she wasn't entirely certain that this was indeed Mr. Jung. There was pleasantness to him and an air of innocence behind soft, light brown eyes. The transformation was so striking that if not for the bruising on his fists, Eleonore wouldn't have believed it to be the same man.

"I was admiring your handiwork," Jung turned his cheek and pointed to where Eleonore had struck him, further confirming his identity.

A lump grew in Eleonore's throat as she was at a loss for the appropriate course of action. Should she leave and ignore the brute who was behaving so uncharacteristically civil? If she did, he may report her, then Em and Ella would be punished as well.

"I apologize for my conduct this morning," Jung spoke softly and sat on the edge of the bed as he leaned back casually. "Us officers are expected, required I should say, to carry a level of ruthlessness to control the masses. I hope you understand. I tend to get carried away in the role and I shouldn't have hit you."

Still, Eleonore remained silent; something was amiss. The officer was apologizing for striking her? Had he forgotten about how he nearly beat Ella to death?

"I promise, you have nothing to fear from me," Jung let a chuckle escape to ease her concern. "I see you've been assigned to the bedpan duty."

Eleonore nodded.

"And I assume you have no idea what you're doing?" the officer continued.

Confirming the officer's assumptions, Eleonore shook her head, but refused to look at him as she spoke, "I...I must've misunderstood my instructions. I'll return to the first floor at once."

"Well since you're here," Jung spoke cheerfully, "they haven't changed the one under my bed yet."

"I should leave that duty for the nurses," Eleonore turned to leave.

"The hospital is at full capacity," Jung spoke quickly, and she paused to listen. "The nurses appreciate all the assistance that is offered. They carry an unusual amount of persuasion in the camp and can alleviate a burden or two should they find you beneficial."

Makes sense, I suppose, Eleonore frowned, but watched Jung for guidance.

"I assume you left the trolley out in the hall, correct?"

Eleonore nodded as she brightened a bit. The helpfulness was unexpected, but she wasn't sure if he was to be trusted. How can a man behave like a brute one moment and then a perfect gentleman the next?

"Then put the used bedpan on the trolley and replace it with a new one," Jung waved the directions as he stood beside the bed to get out of her way.

"Oh," Eleonore grinned, though maintained her reservations. "That's easy enough. And do you know where I empty them?"

"That I'm not familiar with," Jung shrugged.

Warily, Eleonore moved closer to the bed while still suspicious of Jung's intentions. Following his instructions, Eleonore knelt and looked under the bed, but saw nothing. Instead, she heard footsteps close in behind her and looked up to see Jung with his finger held over his mouth to quiet her.

"What are you doing?!" Eleonore stood quickly.

"Quiet," Jung grabbed her by the wrists. "You'll get in all sorts of trouble if they hear you."

"Stop," she tried to escape, but was powerless against him.

"I told you to be quiet," Jung clasped her mouth with a firm grip as he pinned her to the bed.

She grabbed his hand, trying to remove it, but he was too strong. She looked at him with terror-stricken eyes, but this only amused his desires and a disgusting smile etched across his lips. With his free hand, he moved it down to her leg and began pulling up her dress.

Suddenly, Jung stopped and looked at the door as he listened closely. Voices could be heard from outside, voices that Jung recognized and sent him into a terrible fright.

"Hide under the bed," he whispered to Eleonore as he released his grip.

"If you think for one moment that I'll protect you," Eleonore waved a finger in his face as she spoke with bold indignation.

"Relations between personnel and inmates is punishable by death," Jung pushed her to go under the bed, but she held her ground.

"You deserve worse than death," Eleonore fumed.

"The punishment is for both the inmate and the soldier," Jung pointed desperately for Eleonore to obey.

He's lying again, isn't he, Eleonore squinted as she studied him for any insincerity, *but is it worth the risk to find out?*

"Please," Jung looked at her again with sweet, innocent eyes and Eleonore wondered how he was able to change his appearance so suddenly to suit his needs.

"You'll let me go afterwards?" Eleonore bartered.

"On my word," Jung raised his hands in defence.

Like that amounts to anything, Eleonore paused as she again searched Jung's eyes.

"For both our sakes," Jung begged with raised eyebrows. "I'd be in your debt."

Grudgingly, Eleonore agreed and slipped under the bed just before the door opened.

"Lieutenant Jung, I see that you're out of bed," spoke a condescending voice. "You must be making a stunning recovery."

Dr. Mengele! Eleonore thought as she could see his white lab coat from under the bed. The sheets stopped just short of touching the ground, and she was able to track the doctor's movement, ensuring she stayed out of his sight.

"I may have broken my hand," Jung defended his admission to the hospital. "I believe it's best to be on the safe side."

"On the contrary," the doctor answered dryly, "you've convinced yourself of the necessity to waste my valuable time as a cover for your laziness and inability to control a group of women. I don't have the time to tend to the needs of the most incompetent officers in the entire Third Reich. I could be running important experiments which will further the evolution of our species, but instead I'm looking over the charts of a man who will use any excuse to avoid work."

Eleonore could barely contain her pleasure as the doctor berated Jung. This officer, who had appeared so formidable, was exposed as cowardly and feeble.

"Thank you, Dr. Mengele," Jung ended the conversation and opened the door, painfully aware of Eleonore's presence.

"I'll sign the discharge papers," Dr. Mengele tapped his pen against the clipboard and hurried out of the room.

With the door closed, Eleonore awaited Jung's confirmation that it was safe to exit, but the room remained silent. The officer's black boots came into view in front of Eleonore and she prayed, desperately, that she had not made some terrible misjudgment.

"You're fortunate," Jung lifted the bedsheet and reached for Eleonore's hand as he pulled her out.

"So are you," Eleonore stood to her feet as she brushed herself off. Looking up at the officer, Eleonore wondered if he would make good on his word. Thankfully, the near discovery of his sins had rattled him and any desire he once felt had subsided.

"Leave," he waved her over to the door, "before anyone sees."

"You're a cruel man," Eleonore studied him as pity mixed with loathing. "How can you take advantage of my ignorance and retain any semblance of dignity?"

"Get out!" Jung flinched as he clenched his jaw.

Peeking out into the hallway, Eleonore saw that it was clear and rushed over to the trolley that was still stationed just outside Jung's room. With her heart pounding and her hands tingling, Eleonore reversed the trolley back through the hallway and into the pulley.

Shaking as she shut the iron cage, Eleonore began the gradual descent back into Hades. *That was foolish,* Eleonore rubbed her hands together, trying to stop the tingling. Returning to the first floor, Eleonore was met with a damning glare as Ma'am awaited with crossed arms. *Please don't let that be for me,* Eleonore held her breath.

Opening the iron cage, Eleonore pulled the trolley out to the first floor and was struck, again, by the chaos. She was able to get a better view of the inmates' wing and felt as if she had been planted within a horror novel. Bodies of the dead and dying lined the large, open room while groans filled the air as those suffering went untreated. To say the medical staff were apathetic to the patients' difficulties would be a generous understatement and Eleonore's heart shattered for those whose final hours were met with cold disregard.

"Where on earth have you been?" Ma'am bellowed as she offered Eleonore a foul expression.

"I believe I was misled," Eleonore replied plainly, forgetting any connotations of station and did not address the Kapo by her preferred title.

"I'm not known as a tolerant woman," Ma'am pinched her lips together as she grew red with indignation, "and I especially don't take kindly to blatant fabrications."

"I was only acting as advised," Eleonore nodded to the pulley, indicating where her orders had come from. "Ma'am," she threw in the title like an afterthought.

"You look like one of us, but you're not, are you?" Ma'am tilted her head as she studied Eleonore. In her arrogance, Ma'am had judged the once-proud shopkeeper and left her feeling like she was undeserving of the very air the madam breathed. Eleonore had held independence and her own flat – a measure that only a handful of women could've boasted – and was now humbled to a station of which she had never foreseen.

"The bedpans are nearly overflowing!" Ma'am waved for her to follow as they walked deeper into the hospital. "You've hours of work to catch up on."

In haste, Eleonore heaved as she pushed the trolley behind Ma'am, making sure to keep pace and being careful as to not run into the many protruding patients' feet.

"Empty the bedpans into here," the Kapo pointed to a closet-like room which had a rubber covering over a square opening in the floor leading to a make-shift sewer.

Why would they not just install a toilet right here? Eleonore wondered. *At least these poor souls could retain a measure of decency.*

"When you're done, take the old pans downstairs to be rinsed."

"Rinsed? Not sanitized?" Eleonore was beside herself with disbelief. "How on earth would you stave off disease?"

"We are at war," Ma'am spoke with special attention to pronouncing 'war' as if she had thought of the word herself. "I needn't remind you of the scarcity of resources."

"Yes, Ma'am," Eleonore nodded, not wishing to further upset her.

Setting her mind to work, Eleonore went as fast as she was able, careful not to spill the contents of the bedpans. Gagging as she went, Eleonore tried her best to think of something worthier of her attention. She thought of her little shop and her sewing machine and all the designs she had made and the ones that were still burning within her mind, waiting to be articulated on a dress.

But as Eleonore was trying to afford the patients with as much privacy as possible, she couldn't help from noticing a pregnant woman lying on the bed in front of her. The woman didn't seem sick or in any discomfort, and Eleonore assumed that maybe she was close to giving birth.

While her own maternal instincts had effectively been chased away by undeserving men or by her own ambitions, Eleonore couldn't refrain from sharing in the joy with others. And, in contradiction with her reserved nature, she found it relatively easy to strike up a conversation with pregnant women and live vicariously through their experience.

"How far along?" Eleonore smiled at the woman.

"What did you say?!" the woman turned and looked at her with shock.

"Your baby," Eleonore nodded to her belly. She had made the awkward mistake of assuming once or twice before, but she was certain of a pregnancy in this instance.

At that, the woman burst into tears.

"You are not to speak to the patients!" ma'am belted from behind Eleonore.

"I'm sorry, I—"

"You're falling behind!" Ma'am shouted as she rounded the corner to find Eleonore talking. "Think of your absent comrade."

"Yes, Ma'am," Eleonore continued with the stain of embarrassment on her cheeks. *But why did she react like that?* Eleonore pondered. *Unless she lost the baby,* she shrugged. *Still, the way she looked at me begs for another explanation, and one much more sinister at that.*

With diligence, Eleonore forgot her disgust in light of her shame and, not caring anymore about spillage or the smell, nearly finished the entire first floor. Only a handful of beds remained when Eleonore made a shocking discovery: she had blocked out the cries of suffering. Her motives, though not entirely selfish, had obstructed her sensibilities. Here she stood amidst a dreadful scene of misery and her only thought was completing her task within the allotted time.

"Water," a dry voice called out from the corner bed and Eleonore's heart perked. She knew that voice, even while harsh and disguised by thirst.

"Ruth?!" Eleonore laughed and cried when she rushed over to her bedside. "Of all the familiar faces I didn't think to see again," Eleonore held Ruth's hand up to her face as she kneeled beside the bed.

"Eleonore?" Ruth squinted and looked at her as if she were dreaming.

"You're skin and bones," Eleonore welled up seeing her friend in such a state. The once-mighty Ruth who was spritely and eccentric now appeared half-starved, frail, and bald like herself.

"Where's Alex?" Eleonore looked around at the other beds.

"Alex?" Ruth spoke faintly, trying to remember.

"Yes, your husband. Where is he?" Eleonore studied her friend.

"Ah, Alex," Ruth nodded as her memory returned.

"Yes," Eleonore peered as she wondered what had happened to them. "Ruth?"

"They tortured us for days," Ruth spoke plainly as if she was discussing the weather. "They thought we knew where more Jews were hiding."

"I'm so sorry," Eleonore rested her head against Ruth's hand.

"Aren't you affectionate today," Ruth smiled at Eleonore.

"I've changed a little," Eleonore gave a chuckle. "Not entirely for the better though."

"You look skinny," Ruth tried to stand. "I'll make you a little something to eat."

"Really?" Eleonore's eyes lit up.

"Oh, yes dearie," Ruth patted the bed, looking for something. "Our fridge is never empty. Just wake up Alex. He's probably asleep on the couch again."

"What couch?" Eleonore's smile faded as she watched Ruth enter a state of delusion.

"Ruth?" Eleonore spoke with solemnity. "Where's Alex?"

"If he's not on the couch then he's probably still at the shop, love," Ruth glanced at an imaginary watch on her wrist. "Though he's running a little late."

"Ruth?" Eleonore squeezed her friend's hand as her eyes welled. "Where is Alex?!"

"Ow!" Ruth winced. "Not so hard. I need that hand to sew," she chuckled.

Just then, Eleonore heard nurses coming down the corridor and she returned to her trolley, pretending to be busy at work.

"Come to think of it," Ruth frowned. "There was a train."

"Good, a train, and then what?" Eleonore whispered as she bent down to grab a fresh bedpan.

"They have terrible service in here, don't they?" Ruth pinched her lips together. "I haven't once been asked if I'd like a refill of my water."

A tear rolled down Eleonore's cheek as she watched the degeneration a woman who had been a mother to her. Someone who had fed her, watched out for her, and cared for her as her own child for decades. But her grief would have to wait as the gong rang out for the evening roll call.

"I'll come back," Eleonore patted Ruth's leg as she left. "I promise."

But as she was leaving, Eleonore noticed an odd mark at the foot of her bed: a white 'x' was placed crudely on the wooden frame with chalk. She didn't know what it meant, but understood it was likely for an unholy purpose. *Ruth will pull through,* she nodded. *They'll see.*

Chapter Eight:
Shadows of Intrigue

"There is no witness so dreadful, no accuser so terrible as the conscience that dwells in the heart of every man." Polybius.

Eleonore listened to the silence of the world around her as she lay in her bunk during the early morning hours. Nature itself seemed to have retreated from the camp and the birds found nothing cheerful of which to sing; even the dogs withheld their howls as their grievances paled in comparison. Apart from the occasional pitter-patter of rats and a sporadic cough from another inmate, the only sound was the wind battering against the frail roof.

The one incidental piece of tranquility she acquired during these dark mornings was that her tattoo was veiled. Staring at her raised arm, Eleonore ran her fingers across the itching, burning flesh but those hateful numbers were concealed in the haze of dawn.

What's this? Eleonore felt a small lump near her feet. Investigating, she procured a small, sharpened stone. Smiling, Eleonore looked at the names carved above her: Estella, Valy, Hana, Rosette, Lea, Hertha, and Ala. *There will do*, Eleonore thought after spotting an opening and began etching in her name in between Estella and Lea. She wondered what connection she had to these women and if there was some purpose to her sharing the same bunk. *Maybe meaning is absent*, a gloomy thought arose, *and the divine really is indifferent.*

Still, she was thankful for the distraction as her insomnia had returned, and not from any want of anxiety, but by the birth pains of starvation. She figured it had to have been three, possibly four days without the required sustenance. Despite her hunger, she had worked through lunch yesterday to complete the job on time. Not that she was used to large meals or was ignorant of the trials of fasting, but to go this long without anything was torture.

She winced as the pain returned and she pressed her hands to her stomach while the throbbing sprang up and reached into her esophagus. Turning onto her side, she tried to alleviate the problem and watched Ella sleeping peacefully. But when that failed, she turned again to her back and felt the pain subsiding, for now. She knew it was only a matter of time before her anguish launched another assault and she closed her eyes, trying to hurry sleep before the 'resurgence'.

But just as sleep was stretching out its merciful arms, the gong rang. Eleonore couldn't believe her misfortune.

They warn you about hell's fire and brimstone, she attempted to cheer herself up with a bit of dark humor, *but they omit the sleeplessness and hunger. At this point, I'd exchange a good beating for a full stomach.*

Pouncing into action, Eleonore was determined to be the first in line for the buckets. Jumping down from her bunk, she scurried along in the dim light of dawn to get a prime position.

But insomnia was evidently not privy to Eleonore. Many restless eyes offered dirty glances when they spotted Eleonore closely behind them in line. The blackening of her and Ella's name had spread like a plague throughout the block, and the two had inadvertently become the enemy within. None were willing to stand too close for fear that retribution would extend to them as well.

"How dare you?!" a voice bellowed near the middle of the line and Eleonore turned to see a woman scolding Ella.

"She's injured," another woman defended.

"I don't care!" the first woman nearly shouted. "I was beaten yesterday because of her. She goes to the back of the line."

"That goes for you too," a woman behind Eleonore pushed her out of place.

Readying herself for protest, Eleonore was about to defend her position but then spotted Ella walking to the end of the line and decided it would be better if she were amongst friends.

Joining Ella, Eleonore offered a quick smile but was met with a blank, exhausted glance. It was obvious that Ella was suffering from her injuries and Eleonore felt an immense pity for her. *If only I could've laid my hands on some medicine yesterday.*

The two waited patiently and in silence as the line progressed gradually. For Eleonore's part, she was more than comfortable without conversation, and merely enjoyed the presence of someone she felt a kinship with.

"Thank you," Ella whispered over her shoulder and, in the rising light of dawn, Eleonore could see her bruises were turning an unsightly shade of purple. "I shouldn't have reprimanded you for your kindness yesterday. It was generous of you to risk yourself and save my life."

"You would've done the same," Eleonore rolled off the compliment.

"They hate us now," Ella indicated to the rest of the ladies, some of which were still scowling at them.

"I wish that they valued our determination," Eleonore whispered back, "but I find myself in the unusual position of understanding their dislike. Popularity and I were often at odds anyways, and I see no reason why that should suddenly change."

Ella chuckled and glanced again at Eleonore with brighter eyes, "We share that much in common. Why should life in Hades be all that different? There are still cliques, social hierarchies, 'bad blood,' and no place for women of our temperament."

Eleonore bit her cheek to contain her smile from growing too large. She had found a companion, one who could relate to her and not just within the confines of a concentration camp, but also within the shattering fabric of society at large.

"Though," Ella rubbed her sore jaw, "I wish you had found your courage a few blows sooner."

"Speaking of beatings!" Eleonore grabbed Ella's arm in excitement. "You'll never guess what happened at the hospital."

"What's that?" Ella leaned in, enjoying the intrigue.

"The officer that beat you, that brute Lieutenant Jung, had admitted himself thinking that he had broken his hand from hitting you too hard."

"No!" Ella's mouth fell open. "That coward!"

"What's more," Eleonore relished in the gossip, "Dr. Mengele stopped just shy of verbal abuse for Mr. Jung wasting his time."

"Dr. Mengele?" Ella's smile faded, and she looked at Eleonore with the deepest concern. "You were near him? How did you hear all this?"

"Well," Eleonore paused as she realized sharing the details of Jung's attempted assault would be humiliating.

"I need to know," Ella squeezed Eleonore's shoulder, anxious for a reply.

"I was working in the room when Dr. Mengele attended," Eleonore left out the damning specifics. She doubted Ella would betray her, especially after all Eleonore had done, but she recalled Berlin with the disabled man and how she had failed to use her better judgement. *Trust no one,* she reminded herself, *at least not entirely.*

"How could you tolerate his presence?" Ella grew infuriated.

"I'm sorry he hurt you, but I wasn't in the position to enact vengeance, nor am I strong enough," Eleonore defended, surprised by Ella's sudden change of behavior.

"I don't care about Jung," Ella threw her hand in the air, dismissing the lieutenant.

"Dr. Mengele?" Eleonore frowned. "Why are you so interested in him?"

"His death would save millions of lives."

"He seems so nice," Eleonore held her conclusion in reserve. "He even offered candy to some of the children when we first arrived."

"Yes," Ella rubbed her sore jaw again, the stimulation had inflamed the muscles, "he poses as their friend and then takes them to his laboratory where he performs wicked experiments."

"Experiments?" Eleonore frowned in surprise.

"Don't speak of such things," a woman in front of them turned around sharply with tears streaming down her face.

Ella and Eleonore glanced at each other and gave a knowing nod that they would speak further when they were alone. But Eleonore could scarcely contain her curiosity and waited anxiously in line as Ella's condemnation of the doctor ran through her mind.

Finally, their turn arrived and after 'tea' the second gong rang. As the ladies lined up for roll call, Eleonore noticed that the atmosphere had shifted, and not for the better. If she had considered the previous temperament as draconian, she didn't know what to label the soldiers' demeanor today. Unbridled rage was the thought that came to her mind. The officers' tolerance had dissolved entirely and anything out of line would be punished severely. With red faces, they screamed and hollered and held their guns at the ready.

Then, Eleonore noticed black smoke rising from the large chimneys in the 'other camp' and covered her nose at the awful smell. *Maybe that's Dr. Mengele's laboratory?* Eleonore pondered as a chill ran down her spine. *But what could they be burning this early in the morning?*

"I won't be beaten for your sake," a voice whispered behind Eleonore and she felt a sharp object press against her back. "Understand?"

Nodding quickly, Eleonore didn't dare turn her head, but knew that it was Em threatening to stab her if she was insubordinate to these devils.

"Seven Five Six Nine Nine?" the call came from Lieutenant Jung, who Eleonore noticed had returned to his severity, and all glanced out of the corner of their eye, begging to be spared the rod.

"Here," Ella raised her hand to her fellow prisoners' relief.

"Hospital," Jung shouted the assignment without any hint of remorse for his previous brutality.

"Seven Five Six Nine Three?" Jung called out, but his voice shook slightly.

"Here," Eleonore replied.

"Hospital," Jung replied quickly without looking up from his paper.

"Selections!" another officer called out, and Eleonore saw a shudder amongst the women as they all looked at one another in panic.

"What are selections?" Eleonore whispered to someone beside her, but they shook their head, not willing to speak a word.

Just then, Dr. Mengele arrived with his armed escort and stood on the small, wooden podium as he looked out over the women, examining each with a discerning glare. Then he began walking down the line, inspecting each prisoner carefully. Pointing to an elderly woman, the guards dragged her out of line as she sobbed, begging something in Polish that Eleonore couldn't understand.

"Hey, hey," Dr. Mengele stopped the guards and then spoke warmly to the woman as he held her hand. "It's going to be just fine."

"Please, I've done nothing wrong," the woman pleaded in broken German.

"You're going to block twenty-five. You'll be fed well and there is also a bed for you to rest," the doctor nodded but the woman only sobbed harder. She knew what this signified and Eleonore's mind was running wild with curiosity. Seeing that his attempt for calm had failed, the doctor's sympathy vanished and he nodded for the guards to continue.

Moving down the line, Dr. Mengele paused to inspect Ella with her bruised face and limbs. Standing back, he looked her up and down with some sort of internal measurement. With a huff, he moved on to the next woman but passed by her and came to a stop beside Eleonore.

Her heart raced as she stared straight ahead. She didn't know what criteria the doctor was using for his selections, or what block twenty-five meant, but she was damn certain she would not be parted from Ella. She was desperately hungry and wished for nothing more than a comfortable bed, but the woman's reaction petrified her. Eventually, the doctor came to his conclusion and moved on to select another elderly woman.

"That's all for today," Dr. Mengele spoke to the guards and they gave the signal for the women to march towards their respective assignments.

To the melancholic rhythm of the orchestra in the cold winter air, the group commenced again for the day but, as they made their approach, Eleonore found herself falling faint. Her hunger and exhaustion were combining their forces and threatening to punish her with unconsciousness for her dismissal of their needs.

Slowly, the world around her grew dark, and Eleonore fell to her knees. Desperate to stabilize herself, Eleonore stared at her hands planted on the earth in front of her, covered in the snow.

"Get her up!" a guard threatened Em with his baton.

"Stop drawing attention," Em grabbed Eleonore by the arm and forced her to her feet.

"Thank you," Eleonore looked gratefully at Em who shot her a dismissing glare.

Em was merely protecting her own back from the guard's violence but, regardless of the intention, Eleonore couldn't help feeling the warmth in a helping hand.

Arriving at the hospital, the guards, again with the most unusual display of courtesy, opened the doors for the ladies. They filed into the foyer where Ma'am was awaiting with hands held firmly behind her back.

"On time this morning," the Kapo looked down her nose at her 'subjects'.

"Will that be all, Ma'am?" the soldier asked while staring straight ahead.

"Am I that disgusting you can't even look me in the eye?" Ma'am walked over to the soldier who couldn't contain his nervousness. "You're sweating like a frightened little brat," Ma'am sniffed with revulsion. "Get out of my sight."

"Yes, Ma'am," the soldier saluted and clicked his heels before turning to leave.

"Did he bother any of you yesterday?" Ma'am looked over the ladies like a collector, affectionate yet distant; interested primarily in the return on investment.

"No, Ma'am," the ladies replied in unison.

"Good," Ma'am breathed a deep sigh of relief.

"Now," the Kapo turned her attention to Ella and Eleonore and rumbled in a deep voice of dissatisfaction, "have our troublemakers changed their wanton ways?"

"No, Ma'am," the group replied, still resentful from the previous day's errors.

"That is most unfortunate," Ma'am tilted her head and seemed to Eleonore to be rather pleased with the disheartening news. "You know your duties then," Ma'am clapped and marshalled some dormant energy as she resumed her character. Eleonore didn't exactly know Ma'am's station at the hospital, and she didn't dare question the woman on her authority when even soldiers broke into a sweat by her gaze.

Eleonore, Ella, and Em returned to the basement by the staircase that wound down to the concrete floor beneath. But when they arrived, Eleonore was startled to see that the piles of shoes and clothes had nearly doubled from yesterday.

"Where did all these come from?" Eleonore walked over to a table and inspected a worn, leather shoe from the top of a pile. She was surprised that the other ladies didn't show the same interest and seemed to ignore the peculiarity.

"Am I the only one concerned about this?" Eleonore looked back at her comrades.

"We've greater things to discuss," Ella sat on the bench fastened to the wall, resting her weary head in her hands. "And keep away from the belongings. They're going to Canada."

"Canada?" Eleonore frowned. "Why are they being shipped there?"

"Not the country," Ella waved her hand in frustration. "It's a place in the camp here where the items are sorted."

Odd, Eleonore tossed the shoe back onto the pile, and again winced at the sudden pain in her stomach. Even the leather in front of her was starting to become appealing. She had heard of people, in desperate times, staying alive with a bite or two in their stomachs.

"Take all the time you need," Em patted Ella on the back, but Eleonore noticed that Em's lips were trembling.

"Are you alright?" Eleonore studied Em.

"Oh! You just have to pry!" Em stomped away into the office.

"Meddling is not something I'm commonly accused of," Eleonore spoke under her breath to Ella who was not concerned in the slightest at Eleonore's embarrassment.

"We only have a few minutes," Ella tapped the open spot on the bench beside her for Eleonore to sit.

Without hesitation, Eleonore obeyed and sat beside her friend. It was seldom that others appreciated Eleonore's company as her reserved temperament only allowed for a handful of others into her sphere. She was enclosed, withdrawn, and these 'sharp edges' posed too great of a risk for potential companions. This personality defect, however, provided her value in the realm of courtship as the undesirable suitors abandoned their pursuits from the sense of hopelessness.

"Dr. Mengele," Ella leaned forward for hushed secrecy and Eleonore mirrored her. "Do you believe you can get close to him again, privately?"

"I believe he makes his rounds daily," Eleonore shrugged, "but there's no reason for either of us to be on the second floor."

"Can you sneak up there?" Ella persisted.

"It's possible," Eleonore nodded reluctantly, "but if I'm caught, then what?"

"Do you know who Dr. Mengele is?" Ella sighed.

Eleonore shook her head.

"He's the devil incarnate," Ella stared into Eleonore's eyes. "I don't give much credence to the supernatural, but he's the very manifestation of evil. You wouldn't believe me if I told you about some of his experiments."

"I don't understand," Eleonore frowned.

"Don't you realize where all these shoes come from?" Ella indicated to the piles.

"But," Eleonore paused as she thought, "I've not heard any shots from firing squads, or people begging for their lives, or seen bodies buried."

"You saw the smoke this morning," Ella's countenance fell as she was saddened to be breaking the harsh reality to Eleonore, an innocent amongst this hell.

"No," Eleonore put her hand over her mouth. "The smell? That was the bodies? But...how?"

"Gas," Ella gazed at the pile of shoes. "They separate the newcomers into groups, selecting the weak, the diseased, the old, and the young to be sent to the gas chambers. The Nazis tell the victims to remove their clothes as they need to be showered to eliminate any diseases. You've heard the loudspeakers, telling the prisoners to remember where they placed the items so that they can reclaim them afterwards, removing any hint that once they enter, they'll never return. But when they are within the chambers the doors are locked and gas is dropped in from the roof. Within minutes hundreds are dead," Ella chocked.

"I don't believe you," Eleonore studied Ella with skepticism. "How did you come by this knowledge if they are all murdered?"

Ella checked over her shoulder to make sure Em was still out of earshot before continuing, "I'm part of the resistance."

"What resistance?" Eleonore whispered back.

"The one that will overthrow these camps," Ella's voice swelled with passion. "We were about to deploy our plan at Dachau when we were betrayed by one of our own. Fortunately, my name remained off the Nazis' list, so I was sent out, as scheduled, to be killed here at Auschwitz with the rest of my people."

"I still don't understand how you came to know of the gas chambers?" Eleonore rested her chin on her palm.

"A soldier who was aware of our resistance defected and told us everything," Ella began to grow annoyed at defending herself.

"One soldier's story doesn't amount to much," Eleonore shrugged.

"He hung himself afterwards," Ella blurted. "It troubled him enough to take his own life."

"Well," Eleonore took a deep breath and then waved her hands in the air, "let's say this is true and the Nazis are murdering in the thousands, then how are we, two women, going to stop it?"

"The resistance is alive and well in Auschwitz," Ella smiled. "I promise you that we're not alone."

"But I haven't seen one confrontation apart from your display yesterday," Eleonore grew perplexed. "How can you say it's alive and well?"

"If you haven't noticed then that means the Nazis haven't either, and that gives me courage," Ella took Eleonore's hand in hers.

"I'm not known for being observant," Eleonore let a chuckle escape. "I wouldn't take my word as gospel that others haven't grown suspicious of a thing or two."

"Regardless, can we count on you to gain intel on Dr. Mengele?"

"C'mon!" a shout arose from the office as Em was struggling with the trolley.

"I'll see what that's about," Eleonore let go of Ella's hand and stood, "but I will think about what you've asked me to do."

"I need an answer," Ella pleaded as she looked up at Eleonore with a swollen, purple eye.

There was something charismatic about Ella that Eleonore found difficult to disregard. Still, she questioned whether her 'allegiance' to this resistance member would bring her greater suffering. Would it be worth taking matters into her own hands, even at the cost of her life?

Without replying, Eleonore ventured into the office to see Em nearing the end of whatever patience remained. The front wheel of the trolley had been caught on the leg of a shelf and the narrow space was not convenient to maneuver within. Shelves lined either side of the office, which was more of closet than anything, and carried toiletry supplies as well as bedpans. In fact, the only affiliation this room carried with an office was the standing desk just by the door where records could be kept for the inventory.

"Let me help," Eleonore squeezed in beside Em.

"I've got it," Em raised a frustrated hand and Eleonor believed that each interaction they shared only further soured Em's attitude towards her.

Stepping back, Eleonore was about to leave Em alone with her troubles when she spotted two pairs of shoes set neatly on the standing desk.

"What are these?" Eleonore picked up a little, light blue pair for a child no older than about five or six.

"What's wha—hey! Put that down!" Em pointed wildly for Eleonore to replace them. "What were you thinking?" Em rushed over and straightened them out on the desk, making sure they had returned to the exact place.

"I'm sorry," Eleonore looked at Em with wide, frightened eyes.

"Just get out," Em waved towards the door, but Eleonore didn't move, finally understanding.

"I reminded you of what you try to forget," Eleonore's eyes welled as she studied Em with the greatest pity.

"I said to—" Em paused as she collected herself and then stared at her feet. She tried to hide her sorrow as she walked aimlessly before Eleonore and put her hand to her chest as the tears streamed.

Eleonore didn't know how to respond and simply held her hands in front of her as she waited patiently for Em to elaborate.

"These were my son's," Em collected herself and moved over to the desk. Picking up the little, blue shoes she held them in her hands as she offered a bittersweet smile of reminiscence.

"They didn't fit him when we arrived, but he still clung to them," she continued. "We were humble farmers once, feels like ages ago now, and we didn't have much. My son was small for his age, you see, and most assumed he was sick or diseased, but I knew that he was just of smaller stature and that he'd grow into himself one day. Still, when he was nearly six, a preacher came through our village and thinking my boy was one of the misfortunates, bought him these shoes. My boy was so pleased that he took care of them to the best of his ability and wore them three or four times at most. 'I'll do the same for others' he used to tell me," Em wiped the tears from her eyes, but more continued and all she could do was weep.

"I'm sorry Em," Eleonore didn't know what else to say. She wished she had the words to dispel the burden of mourning. Yet in the same breath, she recalled the loss of her parents and the bitterness she endured through grieving and how she would've never wished it away, as odd as that sounds. The pain allowed her to be present with her parents after they had passed and she could endure anything if it meant being close to them again, even if for a moment.

"He was so sweet, that little man of mine," Em shook as she smiled. "But when we came to Auschwitz, the Nazis didn't perceive the strength within his character. All they saw was a frail Jew undeserving of the life God gave him."

Moving closer to Em, Eleonore rejected her own reserved nature and, putting an arm around the woman, held her as they sobbed together.

"May I ask what happened?" Eleonore released her embrace.

"What do you mean?" Em took out a handkerchief and gave a blow.

"What happened to him," Eleonore nodded to the shoes.

"Well, the gas, of course," Em frowned.

Eleonore went pale as she studied Em.

"Oh," Em tilted her head sympathetically. "Oh, you didn't know."

"Ella was telling the truth?! I thought it was propaganda!" Eleonore put her hands to her knees as she began to hyperventilate.

"I'm afraid not," Em took her turn being unsure of how to behave.

"Those piles of shoes?" Eleonore straightened and looked at the piles. "There must be thousands upon thousands!"

"Those are just from this week," Em stood beside Eleonore as the two looked out upon the vastness.

"How could I have been so blind?" Eleonore shook her head in bewilderment.

"They hide it well," Em sniffled. "That way the camp isn't in a constant state of panic. Most believe the fabrication that, if they work hard enough, they will eventually be set free."

"I can't believe this is real," Eleonore shook her head.

"Most can't," Em shrugged and teared up again. "Even when they're selected to be sent to the gas chambers, they can't comprehend what is happening."

"We have to stop this!" Eleonore looked intensely into Em's eyes.

"Don't you think we've tried?" Em frowned.

Rubbing her eyes, Eleonore sighed and then looked again at the boy's shoes, "What was your son's name?"

"I...I can't tell you," Em fought off the tears again. "Not because it's difficult, which it is, but because he's mine. His sweet spirit was impossible to refuse and any who saw him or knew him found it irresistible to leave his presence. In life, he was the world's, but in death, he's mine and mine alone."

Eleonore stood in silence as she processed both the grand destruction and the personal loss. *What a wicked, wicked regime,* Eleonore's rage rose at the crime. *Who are they to determine who is fit or unfit for life?*

"But," Em bit her cheek thoughtfully, "I will tell you my name. It's Julia."

"Julia?" Eleonore frowned and then smiled curiously. "Then why Em?"

"My husband called me 'Em' and the boy caught on. Never called me mom, not once. He wasn't slow or anything, just lazy," Em chuckled. "Both of them: slothful, useless men. Don't get me wrong, they were charming and loving, but there were times I wondered how our farm ever survived," Em scoffed and shook her head. "They'd sit for hours in front of a little brook talking about Lord knows what, and I'd get so wound up and frustrated with their lack of ambition, but they'd somehow find a way to get the chores done and the animals fed. Sadly, my time here has given me the perspective that I wish I had carried when they were alive."

"How so?"

"I used to worry about all sorts of trivial things, but now I'd give everything to have their sorry asses back sitting by the brook. Maybe I would've joined them, and thrown the occasional rock into the brook, instead of stressing."

Eleonore studied Em for a moment as she was lost in her reminiscing, "I should still like to call you Em."

"I'd like that very much, but we must get back to it," Em clapped and motioned for Eleonore to exit. "I'll have this out in a minute."

Leaving the office, Eleonore saw Ella slouched with her chin resting on her chest and her eyes closed. Carefully, she sat beside Ella and in her heart determined to do what was right. For Em's son and husband, for Ruth and Alex, and for the multitudes destined for this hell, she would join the resistance.

"So," Ella opened her eyes when she noticed Eleonore beside her, "are you with us?"

"We need a more elegant plan than elimination," Eleonore nodded her compliance. "If Dr. Mengele is removed, they'll only replace him."

"That's already in motion," Ella waved her hand with a slight air of arrogance as if she had everything under her control. "All we need from you is espionage: his routine, habits, what he likes to eat or drink, if he fraternizes with any of the soldiers, if he takes any of the female prisoners, and--"

"I understand," Eleonore crossed her arms as she thought. "The only problem now is how I'll get to the second floor undetected. It's a miracle I survived yesterday's 'adventure'"

"You'll find a way," Ella tucked her chin back to her chest and closed her eyes.

Chapter Nine:
The Plans of Men

"Most powerful is he who has himself in his own power."
Seneca.

With a deep breath, Eleonore plunged into the unknown and closed the cage to the pulley as she began her duties. Though not yet equipped with an alibi for why she would be on the second floor, Eleonore decided to start with the first floor to allow her some time to concoct a believable explanation.

She walked briskly with the trolley out onto the first floor. She had a mission; a task of the highest priority and she would not fail Ella. Today, however, she started with the back of the hospital where she had seen Ruth. She remembered her promise to return and was anxious to assess if Ruth had reclaimed some of her mental stability. If Alex was still alive, Ruth would know.

Passing quickly through the crowded hospital, Eleonore almost brandished a smile in anticipation. She was starving, exhausted, cold, and alone, but she couldn't wait to speak with Ruth. Although her friend was delirious, Eleonore was sure Ruth would pull through, being a tough woman after all. Besides, it was cruel for her to be left without Alex. While the two were often at odds – as most couples of opposing dispositions typically are – they were undoubtedly in love and relied on each other heavily.

But Eleonore's brief smile began to fade when she neared the end of the hospital to find Ruth's bed was vacant. Checking the other beds, Eleonore began to panic when she couldn't spot Ruth. In fact, the whole back section of the room had been cleared. Not one soul remained, and the white 'x' marked on the beds had been wiped off.

"Excuse me," Eleonore reached out and grabbed a passing nurse by the arm.

"What do you want?" the nurse wrenched her arm free and scowled at Eleonore for the interruption.

"Where is Ruth?"

"Who?" The nurse frowned and shook her head.

"The woman who was in this bed yesterday," Eleonore nodded.

"She died," the nurse answered abruptly and brushed passed a stunned Eleonore.

Standing in place, Eleonore didn't know how to react. She had lost loved ones before and knew what grief was, but for some reason she didn't feel anything. The nurse's pronouncement was akin to hearing another language; the words carried no meaning.

Absentmindedly, Eleonore returned to her duties. In her shock, she became numb to the filth and seemed to be disconnected from her senses. She wanted to cry, to scream in rage, but there was nothing to draw upon, and this only upset her more. Ruth had been to her as a mother, a close confidant with which she had shared many years side by side in *La Venezia.*

I've got no choice now, Eleonore rallied her courage. *If Ruth is gone then it's safe to assume Alex is dead as well. If anything, I should do this for them. They didn't deserve such a fate and the world truly has been robbed of their wonderful souls. Go up to the second floor, look busy and maybe no one will bother you. If you're caught, tell them Dr. Mengele has requested you. That should work. I hope.*

"I can't go on," a man further down the hall lamented, but Eleonore pretended not to notice.

"Don't give up," a nurse replied vigorously as she sat at the foot of the man's bed.

Caught off guard by this unexpected inspiration, Eleonore was transfixed by the scene and couldn't bring herself to look away. She watched the woman, who was a little younger than Ruth, take the man's hand in hers and smile brightly at him. She didn't view him through the lens of misfortune, but rather, from a determination in her eyes that spurred the soul onwards.

"Who've I got to live for now?" the man wept loudly and without shame.

"One more day," the woman pressed. "That's all I ask."

"I don't think I can," the man spoke through sobs.

"I promise you this," the woman leaned in, "life will be difficult from here on out. You will know this sorrow for the rest of your days, but I'm not asking you to take on the challenge of years and decades. I'm asking you, for my sake, to take on the challenge of today. Can you not do that for me? Just one more day?"

"I can't," the man wiped away his tears. "They might as well put the 'x' at the end of my bed."

"Can you give me an hour?" the woman clutched his hand tighter.

"That…that I can do," he glanced at her with red, swollen eyes.

"Good," she sighed. "Sleep for a bit. I'll come back in an hour."

Retrieving a pad of paper from her apron, the nurse was about to scribble down her thoughts but was startled to see Eleonore staring at her. Eleonore, too, was shocked at being discovered, but continued to examine the woman, intrigued by her demeanor. She was well-spoken, not necessarily in terms of sophistication but in the manner which she spoke, and carried herself with an air of importance; not in arrogance, but in kindness.

"I see that you're new," the woman folded her hands in front of her as she smiled warmly, yet sternly at Eleonore.

"How can you tell?" Eleonore frowned.

Pointing at Eleonore's head, the woman reminded Eleonore of her baldness which she was surprised she had forgotten.

"Right," Eleonore ran her hand over her head.

"Where's your bowl?" the woman nodded to Eleonore's waist.

"My bowl?" Eleonore glanced down in confusion.

"How else do you eat?" she shrugged.

"I haven't eaten yet," Eleonore patted her stomach.

"Not uncommon," the woman turned and rummaged through a desk beside an empty bed. "Shock takes over and one forgets to eat, or you become too busy with your assigned task. Here," she handed a bowl to Elenore.

"Thank you," Eleonore took it, but watched her warily.

"Put it in your pocket," the woman pointed to Eleonore's regulation outfit.

"Ah, yes," Eleonore obeyed, and returned to watching the woman while full of awe.

"When the gong rings for lunch, tell the one who is dishing out the food that Mrs. Felix sent you. Also, aim for the middle of the line. If you are at the front all you'll get is warm water, and if you're at the back then you may not get anything at all," Mrs. Felix nodded.

"Why are you being so kind?" Eleonore shook her head in disbelief.

"That's the wrong question," Mrs. Felix tilted her head, yet maintained an austere gaze. "The question is why am I the only one?"

"Who are you?" Eleonore remained lost to incredulity.

"No one," Mrs. Felix shrugged. "A school teacher from Berlin."

"That explains why you're so articulate," Eleonore smiled and took note of the Kapo band around her arm. "What is your position here?"

"I took some nursing before I entered education," Mrs. Felix looked about the hospital room. "I employed my previous training to secure a better position for myself and my daughter, Kitty. She's working in Canada now, actually."

"I wouldn't mind something like that," Eleonore pondered. "Why do they call it Canada?"

"I never thought to ask," Mrs. Felix threw her lips upside down. "I see that you've been assigned to the bedpan duty."

"Rather disgusting," Eleonore turned her nose up.

"Yes, but it means you're not working in the cold. Also, if you're doing a job like this then you'll like be left alone which is rather invaluable."

"Can you find the positive in everything?" Eleonore became annoyed.

"When it comes to survival, yes," Mrs. Felix nodded. "I should continue. Remember, when you go to eat, tell them that Mrs. Felix sent you."

In mesmerization, Eleonore watched Mrs. Felix leave the room, walking briskly and with purpose. How she wished to be a woman of her quality: someone who could mold the immensity of the hell around her.

With a deep breath, Eleonore resolved to complete her assignment from Ella. Glancing around the room, Eleonore noticed that the nurses were either busy with the other patients or tasks and ignored her entirely. Leaving the trolley, Eleonore grabbed a blank clipboard hanging on the wall. It was dated from three months ago and not a single box had been checked off; its absence would not be noticed. Tucking it against her chest, Eleonore forced a determined expression and stood tall as she headed towards the stairs.

As she returned to the foyer, Eleonore was curious to find no trace of Ma'am. In fact, none of the Kapos or guards were present, and it was eerily quiet without their barks dominating the spirits of those under their charge.

Climbing the staircase to the second floor, Eleonore took measured steps to limit the creaking of the wood. She squeezed through the narrow stairway, wondering how Ma'am, being rather plump, managed to make it seem effortless. Rounding the corner to the top of the stairs, Eleonore grew suspicious with the apparent lack of nurses: only two were present on the floor.

With another deep breath, Eleonore burst out from the staircase and walked swiftly onto the second floor. Though her demeanor gave the illusion of some objective, Eleonore had no inclination of where she should start or what excuse she'd offer should she discovered.

Still, she was determined to follow through with finding out whatever she could on Dr. Mengele. Employing her peripheral vision, Eleonore checked for the doctor as she passed by each room while moving towards an imaginary destination. If the door to a room happened to be closed, she listened for voices inside, trying to decipher if they belonged to the doctor.

Nearing the end of the hall, she began to doubt her mission would produce much fruit. The nurses that were on the floor walked passed her without a second thought and Eleonore blended into the business of the hospital environment.

Finally, she arrived at the last room on the ward to find its door had been left slightly open. Peering in, Eleonore noticed it was empty and stepped inside. Closing the door behind her, she shut her eyes and felt the weight of her hunger and exhaustion. Desperate for the gong to ring for lunch, she patted her large pocket, feeling the bowl and remembering Mrs. Felix.

She needed a moment to strategize on how to track down the doctor, but the obsession of hunger was burning within her belly. Sustenance, however, would again have to wait as she heard a damning tune that sent shivers down her spine. A train whistle blew, and Eleonore walked warily over to the window which overlooked the gates of Auschwitz. She knew it was ill-advised to linger in the room any longer than necessary, but her curiosity stole her attention; she had to see the event for herself.

Even though she had been one of those packed into the train cars, she was still ill-prepared for the enormity. Thousands upon thousands of men, women, and children were herded towards the gates by soldiers holding back vicious dogs and female Kapos brandishing thick leather whips. Again, she was baffled that only a few hundred could control so many, but she figured that they, like her, were just as ignorant to the malevolent intention of the camp.

There! Eleonore moved closer to the window when she spotted Dr. Mengele standing at the gate a mere twenty yards from her position. With his clipboard in hand, the doctor ran his wicked eye over the multitude as he instructed the soldiers on which prisoners were useful and which should be destined for destruction.

She watched as he grabbed candy from his pockets and handed them to children, rustling their hair and smiling like he was their favorite uncle. Hatred swelled in her heart for such an evil human, though to count him amongst the same species was charitable. With her perfect vantage point, Eleonore wished she could take a rifle, aim and squeeze the trigger. It would be suicide, but to see him dead would be worth the price.

Though she had been raised in Berlin, her father had not forgotten their humble country origins and refused to allow Eleonore to be without the instruction he himself had received as a boy. Her mother had forbidden Eleonore to join in the annual hunting trip, but her father had utilized methods of either sneaking Eleonore along or boldly disobeying. While it led to some household tension and conflicts, Eleonore looked forward to each expedition.

While her mother could only see a tragic accident waiting to happen, the truth was that these trips were not as harsh as she was imagining. In fact, they were rather tame. Quiet, stationary waiting enveloped the day as they hunted timid game while the nights were lost to the tranquility of sitting in silence by the fire. Still, Eleonore was grateful to be educated on how to use a gun, skin the prey, prepare and eat the kill, build a fire, and to endure days while patiently waiting for the moment to strike.

Only now she wished to employ the harsher nature of hunting against Dr. Mengele. But her loathing had set her into an unwitting trap. She had lingered too long and she froze as, out of the corner of her eye, she could feel the unwavering gaze of an officer just below the window.

Glancing quickly, her breath was robbed when she locked eyes with Lieutenant Jung. He had been watching her with a sinister curiosity, hands held firmly behind his back, and brandishing a triumphant grin.

Don't make any sudden movements, she recalled her father's training. Jung was the predator, and she was the prey. Pretending she had nothing to fear, Eleonore returned to staring at the masses as her heart pounded in her chest and her face flushed crimson. Eventually, she worked up the courage to move slowly away from the window, but not before she caught Jung waiving to some soldiers and pointing up at her.

Placing the clipboard against her chest, Eleonore rushed back to the stairs. Her fingers began to tingle, and her legs went limp as she bounded for her escape.

Take the back stairwell, the thought arrived and, deviating sharply, Eleonore began to descend the staircase. But as she wound downwards, she caught the bobbing grey helmets of soldiers ascending.

Why'd I do that?! Eleonore panicked as she hurried back up the stairs only to realize that she had cornered herself.

Standing before her was an out of breath and red-faced Ma'am, looking down at her with a disapproving scowl.

"Are we boring you Miss Hodys?" came the shrill voice of Ma'am.

"No, Ma'am," Eleonore forced a polite, subservient smile but didn't dare offer an excuse as she stood a couple of steps below the madam.

"I decide who comes to this hospital," Ma'am pointed to her chest. "You wouldn't last a minute in the labor fields. I gave you a golden opportunity and you squandered it."

Eleonore didn't know how to respond as the soldiers, with Mr. Jung in their trail, continued their ascent. Suddenly, the defense which she had considered solid now fell flat and she could scarcely remember what it was.

"Now," Ma'am raised her eyebrows, "I hesitate to rush to conclusions, so I'll give you this one chance to give me a damn good reason as to why I again find you on the second floor shirking your work."

"Dr. Mengele..." Eleonore's breathing began to labor as she spoke softly.

"Speak up!" Ma'am barked.

"Dr. Mengele requested my assistance," Eleonore swallowed, praying that Ma'am would somehow believe her fabrication.

With a heavy foot, Ma'am walked down a step and stood tall over the petite Eleonore. She reeked of sweat and body odor and Eleonore could barely contain her disgust. Droplets fell from Ma'am's forehead while her neck seized from outrage.

"Come up here," Ma'am gritted her teeth and turned sharply as she climbed back up the stairs and onto the second floor.

Following with wide, terrified eyes, Eleonore was shadowed by the soldiers and Mr. Jung who filed out from behind her. Again, she felt her legs trembling as she was surrounded by tall, fierce soldiers who would unleash the cruelest of tortures without any hesitation should Ma'am but give the order.

"Search her," she commanded while keeping her eyes locked on Eleonore's.

Patting her down generously, the guard found the bowl that Mrs. Felix had given her.

"Here," the guard handed it to Ma'am.

"Those things are riddled with disease," Ma'am swatted the guard's hand away.

"I didn't steal it," Eleonore defended. "If that's what you're thinking."

"That is what I'm thinking," Ma'am fumed. "Shirking your work and stealing…"

"I've comple—"

"Not another word," Ma'am held up a hand to silence her. "I believe solitary confinement is in order. Cell block eleven," she nodded to Jung.

"Eleven?" Jung paused, and Eleonore caught the trepidation in his tone. "Is that necessary?"

Ma'am darted her bulging eyes at the lieutenant, making her resolve clear that she was not to be questioned.

"Yes, Ma'am," Jung gripped Eleonore's arm and led her away as she looked back at Ma'am, her eyes pleading for mercy.

"What's in block eleven?" Eleonore asked Jung as he and another guard led her away by force back through the camp, but he refused to acknowledge her gaze.

"Please! You owe me, remember?" Eleonore whispered, and the other guard glanced curiously at Jung, wondering what Eleonore could possibly be referring to.

"You're delirious," Jung chuckled and offered a warning squeeze on her arm.

Despite any further protest from Eleonore, they arrived at a building which didn't appear to house anything more malicious than the rest. Yet even in her state of terror, Eleonore recognized the bars across the windows and the extra guards stationed at the doors or patrolling. Further intimidating its prey, the building itself seemed to moan and groan from within as it attempted to stifle the tormented screams from its unseen victims.

A small staircase led up to the doors of cell block eleven, but Eleonore was so petrified she couldn't climb the steps by herself. Instead, she was handed to two guards at the door who were more than cordial towards her. They were young – too young to be in such an environment – and they still bore that natural fear towards the opposite sex which accompanies the innocence of adolescence.

Ordering the young guards to open the metal door, Jung placed his grip back on Eleonore's arm and signaled to his comrade that he was able to handle processing her by himself. At least, that's what she thought he said as the world around her had shriveled into a narrow tunnel where all she could focus on was what dread awaited her. She assumed that if she wasn't about to be shot, then she was undoubtedly going to be tortured and she couldn't bear the thought.

Besides, now that Jung had isolated her he would be free to finish what he intended back in the hospital room. While it was only slight, Eleonore detected the pleasure he was experiencing with her under his control: a sharp, yet momentary drop of his eye that lingered longer than acceptable, the pressing of her against his body, and the firm but affectionate squeeze of her arm.

But such concerns evaporated as the guards opened the metal door with a terrible, heavy growl. At once, the screams and wailing which had been muffled now soared up the stairs from a dark, lightless basement. The clunking of metal against metal echoed from the inmates trapped within their cells and a fear gripped Eleonore's chest so that she was unable to speak.

Forcing Eleonore forward, Jung led her down into the darkness where the only light available came from the open door behind them. The suffering of others didn't bother him in the slightest, and he proceeded as if this experience was normal.

As her eyes adjusted, Eleonore saw four windowless, concrete cells with thick, iron doors. The bitter wailing of the inmates swelled with the echoing throughout the whole bunker. *This is hell,* Eleonore panicked. *This is hell.*

"I beg you," Eleonore panted as her legs went limp. "I'll do anything."

Ignoring her plea, Jung clicked on his flashlight and dragged Eleonore to an open cell. The metal door had been left ajar and Eleonore saw that the inner door, which was made of iron bars, had remained shut.

"Help!" a cry came from one of the cells.

"We can't breathe," another cry arose, but Jung had hardened his heart and their cries fell upon his deaf ears.

"In," Jung nodded after he had unlocked and opened the inner door.

"I can't," Eleonore shook her head as she inspected the tiny cell, introducing her to a terror she didn't believe possible.

"Now!" Jung shouted as his voice echoed in the darkness.

"State my crime!" Eleonore raised her chin defiantly, though she trembled. "I've done nothing worthy of this torture."

Removing the club attached to his belt, Jung threatened violence if she continued in disobedience.

"I'd rather you beat me senseless then go in there willingly," Eleonore closed her eyes in preparation for the blow. She understood there was nothing she could exchange for her release, at least not materially, but to give Jung what he desired so cheaply was as impossible as what was ordered.

"In!" Jung pushed Eleonore towards the cell, but she refused to budge.

"Don't make this difficult," Jung warned with his raised club, "or I'll make sure that you'll never leave here."

"Veiled threats," Eleonore called his bluff in her rising rage. "You're no more than a glorified escort. What authority do you have?"

Seething in rage, Jung gripped Eleonore's shoulders and spun her towards the cell. Yet Eleonore stood her ground as she placed her hands against the doorpost. Jung, however, was accustomed to such struggle and, wrapping his arms around her, squeezed her arms down to her sides and lifted her. Still, Eleonore refused and threw her feet against the doorpost, but Jung wrestled her to the ground and pinned her down with his knees on her arms.

"You can enter the cell with your wits, or I can send you in with half your senses knocked out," Jung warned, but Eleonore spit at him in defiance.

"Have it your way then," Jung tightened his fist and readied himself to strike, but something stopped him. He looked at Eleonore with all the hatred he could muster, but still couldn't bring himself to harm her in such a helpless state.

Shouting in frustration, Jung stood Eleonore to her feet and rushed her into the cell but, just before he could get her inside, his uniform ripped on the half-opened door and the crude, jagged metal cut his skin.

"Look what you've done!" he held his arm as he shut the iron bars behind Eleonore.

Baffled at the accusation, Eleonore panted as she leaned against the cell, exhausted and bruised. Her outfit had become disheveled and her first instinct was to check if her hair had been ruined but, again, she was provided with the disheartening reminder of her baldness.

"Damn it!" Jung drew his pistol in rage and aimed at Eleonore.

"I can fix it," Eleonore raised her hand to shield her face.

"What?" Jung frowned and lowered the gun slightly.

"I can fix it," Eleonore pointed at his uniform.

"How?"

"I was a seamstress," Eleonore reached through the iron bars, dismissing her fear of his firearm, and gently put her hand to the torn fabric. "It would only take a few minutes."

"You're all liars," Jung scoffed and pushed her hand away.

With that, the door was slammed shut and Eleonore was left in complete darkness. She listened as his footsteps paced away quickly and the moans of her fellow inmates returned. They had still been there, of course, but her struggle had drowned out their sorrows. Now, however, they flooded back, reverberating through this dungeon of death and despair.

Feeling around in her new surroundings, Eleonore practiced breathing to calm herself as the walls began to close in, threatening to crush her. If she stood with her back against the wall, she could touch the door with her hands, and if she so much as moved her elbows outwards she bumped into the surrounding walls.

Why didn't he hit me? the thought ran through Eleonore's mind. *He had nearly killed Ella without reservation, so why did he hold back with me? Maybe he's not the cruel creature he wants to be, and without an audience to prove himself his true nature is revealed. Not that this would absolve him of his sins, but maybe I can play upon his conscience; bring whatever light is within him to the surface. If, that is, I get another chance. For all I know that was the last I'll see of him, or anyone for that matter.*

Feeling around with her feet, Eleonore judged how much space was available for her to try and sit or kneel. Startled when her foot hit against something that rolled, Eleonore thought it was a dead animal, but then a smell arose from the item being disturbed and Eleonore gagged as she realized it was feces.

What a cruel thing, Eleonore began to sob and was lost to self-pity thinking about her previous existence. She was a self-employed, respectable woman with independence and a perfected, safe routine. *Maybe I should've just sided with the Nazis. Did I do the wrong thing? Oh Ruth,* Eleonore cried as she finally felt the sting of her friend's loss and the tears rolled down unimpeded, *if only I had known that would be the last time I saw you. I would've told you how much you meant to me. How after the passing of my mother you took her place in caring for me like the child you never had. I'll forever miss your determination.*

"*I'll never be far, dearie,*" Eleonore heard Ruth's voice in her head.

"But I failed you," Eleonore spoke aloud. "I should've terminated your employment and paid you in secret."

"*You know we wouldn't have let you,*" Alex spoke and, in her mind's eye, she could see him standing beside his wife with the typical, comforting smile that lifted her spirits.

"*At least here you're away from all who hate you,*" Alex continued in his compassionate voice. "*The guards, the dreadful Lieutenant Jung, Ma'am, and Commandant Hoess can't touch you while you're locked in isolation.*"

"I want to go home," Eleonore wept bitterly as she knelt. "I'm so hungry. I'm so tired."

Although far from comfortable, the position at least alleviated the strain on her feet. Leaning her head against the cold concrete, she looked up through tear-stained eyes to see the dullest glow of light from a slit, about half an inch wide, cut into the top of the cell.

A shooting pain ran up her stomach, and she grabbed her side in anguish as her mind delved into a singular focus: nourishment. She struggled to think upon anything else, but every distraction failed. She patted her uniform, wondering if she still had the bowl Mrs. Felix had so kindly given, but then remembered the guards had stripped it from her. Not that it would do her any good: what was a bowl with nothing to fill it?

Closing her eyes, she eventually found a departure from her anguish with the thought of Ella. She hoped that Em was still taking care of her and began to marvel at the recent events. Less than a week ago she was in her flat, drinking tea and preparing herself for the day's work. Not even amongst her darkest nightmares could she imagine a fate such as this. *I must get out,* Eleonore shook her head. *Somehow, someway, I need to procure my release. I'm not strong enough to endure this.*

Chapter Ten: Rebirth

"Tame the savageness of man and make gentle the life of this world." Aeschylus.

The hours passed by as Eleonore's hunger pains waxed and waned. There were moments where the anguish was so fierce that she thought about smashing her head against the concrete. Adding to the cruelty, the torture of the isolation slowed the passage of time. She tried to amuse herself by pretending that she had her sketchbook in front of her, designing the finest dresses to be worn by the most fashionable clientele of Berlin.

A door slammed, and footsteps echoed in their approach towards her cell. Her heart began to beat, imagining who was coming and for what purpose. She wondered how long she had been in this tomb and looked at the slit above which still gave a faint glow, making it impossible to get an accurate reading on the time of day or night.

The door unlocked and swung open while Eleonore shielded her eyes from the blinding glare of a flashlight. She tried to peer through her fingers to identify her observer but could only determine a shadowy figure with a baton at the ready.

"What do you need?" Jung whispered.

"Lieutenant?" Eleonore was surprised to hear his voice.

"We don't have much time," he shone his flashlight back at the entrance to make sure they were alone.

"For what?" Eleonore grew confused.

"To fix my uniform," he replied and turned the flashlight back on her.

Eleonore thought for a moment, not of what she needed, but of how to barter an alleviation from the affliction of prison. This was her one and only chance and she couldn't afford to falter.

"Well?" Jung grew impatient.

"I have some demands," she whispered eventually.

"Demands?!" Jung couldn't believe what he was hearing. "You're in no position to make demands of me!"

"Then enjoy explaining to your superiors why your uniform is ripped. My father fought in the first war; I'm well aware of the penalties for a torn uniform," Eleonore swallowed. She was not one for confrontation and was often poor at negotiations – including when she had owned her shop. She had convinced herself that she was not in her vocation for advancement, but for the privilege of doing what she loved. Compromises had been made, the likes of which confused many shrewd businessmen and they mocked her openly for her poor decisions. In the end, however, Eleonore had retained customers while the others were losing them in waves. Her clientele knew Eleonore's ambitions wouldn't revolve around simply turning a profit, and they respected her immensely.

A speechless Lieutenant remained bewildered as he shone his light on Eleonore, blocking her from measuring his reaction. She perceived only what she assumed: she was sealing her fate, but it was necessary to try.

"Please close the door on your way out," Eleonore continued, wondering if she was making a terrible mistake.

"If that's your wish," Jung grabbed the door, but stopped himself short of slamming it shut.

Pondering and weighing his options, he surrendered his pride and asked, "What…what are your requests?"

"For a start, take the flashlight out of my eyes," Eleonore huffed in her annoyance. "Then, I want my immediate release…and food. I'm desperate for anything. Even just a bite."

"I won't be able to release you till the morning," Jung clicked his tongue as he thought, but lowered his flashlight. "The proper paperwork will need to be filed. As for food, I won't be able to get you anything now, but I have an idea."

"And when I'm released, you'll have your uniform," Eleonore leaned upon her courage.

"The uniform must be done tonight," Jung shook his head.

"Then we have no deal," Eleonore waved for him to close the door.

"Look, look," he raised his hand. "I'll give you my word that in the morning you'll be returned to your regular quarters."

"Your word?" Eleonore scoffed. "What's that worth?"

"Not much," Jung shrugged as he reflected. "But can you afford the risk of refusing me?"

"I could ask you the same thing," Eleonore tilted her head as she countered.

"Then we are at a standstill," Jung leaned against the iron bars.

"Give me your gun," Eleonore nodded to his weapon.

"Whatever for?" Jung frowned.

"A refundable deposit, of sorts," Eleonore gave a faint grin remembering how often she took such credits at *La Venezia*. Not guns, of course, but ladies would leave their purses or husbands would grudgingly hand over their wallets if their funds were not readily available.

"Absolutely not," Jung scoffed at the absurdity. "You'll just shoot me."

"What good would that serve? I'd still be locked in this dungeon. Besides, when the next guards find you dead with me holding the pistol I'll be hung, or worse. Take the bullets out if I make you so nervous," Eleonore persisted.

"It's out of the question," Jung shook his head.

"Then provide me with something of value. I need assurance; collateral if you will."

Tapping his hands against the bars, Jung took a deep breath before grumbling and, digging into the inside of his jacket, produced a faded gold pocket watch. It was of simple design, but it carried an antique quality that Eleonore was drawn to with little scratches and marks that screamed character.

"This was my father's," Jung handed Eleonore his pocket watch, but wouldn't release his grip as he stared at her with a warning gaze.

"What do you need?" he asked with his hand still firmly on the pocket watch.

"A needle and some grey thread," Eleonore replied.

"Good," Jung released his grip and reached again into his pocket. "I anticipated correctly then."

"Hand me your jacket," Eleonore reached through the bar and held out her hand.

Undressing, Jung passed his ripped uniform to Eleonore who cleared her throat at the slight awkwardness. While Jung was a man that she detested, she admired his alluring form as he stood before her in his trousers and undershirt. The light of the flashlight shone off the crevasses of his muscles, exaggerating their physique. Though inexperienced with the male sex, Eleonore couldn't help an attraction develop. He was the antithesis of what she desired in a man yet, somehow, the dominance he displayed made her blush like an adolescent first discovering temptation.

"I'll need the light," Eleonore motioned for Jung to come closer.

"You weren't lying. You're a seamstress then?" Jung leaned against the bars as he held the light above her head.

"Was," Eleonore said with a hint of bitterness.

"You said you had your own shop too?" Jung continued, unfazed by Eleonore's self-pity.

"*La Venezia,*" Eleonore lifted her head as the title rolled off her tongue.

"That's the little shop on that side street near that bakery, ya?" Jung hummed.

"You know it?" Eleonore shot Jung a look of surprise.

"I've never been," Jung paused and then grew solemn. "But my late wife bought a dress or two from you."

"Really?" Eleonore mused at the odds.

"She spent ages in that square, and a fortune at your shop," he gave a slight chuckle as he reminisced.

"Do you remember what any of her dresses looked like?" Eleonore smiled. Discussing designs was her ultimate delight, but she understood that most people didn't share in her enthusiasm, so she rarely found the opportunity. When it arrived, however, there was little that could persuade her otherwise.

"Um," Jung searched his memory. "There was a white one with some sort of blue flower in the corner of, uh, the bottom of the dress."

"Yes! And it had a blue ribbon that tied around the waist?" Eleonore struggled to contain her excitement.

"Ya," Jung offered a grin at Eleonore's behavior.

"Oh, that was one of my favorites," Eleonore sighed as she closed her eyes and pictured the dress. "Not a stitch out of place and the perfect shade of blue against a bright white. Elaine...no...Evelyn is your wife's name, if I recall correctly?"

Jung didn't reply as he leaned against the bars, and Eleonore wondered if nostalgia or loneliness were playing against him.

"Sorry," Eleonore remembered what Jung had said earlier, "you mentioned 'late wife'. I wouldn't press if I hadn't known her, but may I ask how she passed?"

"Just hurry," Jung growled, and Eleonore flushed crimson with embarrassment. She knew it was wrong to ask such a personal question, especially to someone of Jung's violent disposition.

In silence, Eleonore worked as fast as she was able under the flashlight. Yet all she could think about was her awkward blunder of overstepping her bounds. *He won't help me now,* she cursed. *Why do you have to open your mouth?*

"There," Eleonore spoke softly as she finished and handed the jacket back to Jung.

"That's fine work," Jung threw the uniform back on. "Surprising, actually."

"Surprising?" Eleonore scowled.

"Considering your limited resources," Jung explained as he studied each shoulder, comparing the sides in bewilderment.

"Oh. I see," Eleonore grinned at the compliment, but her stomach seized in pain.

"Thank you," Jung looked at Eleonore and she caught a genuine thankfulness in his expression.

Nodding her acceptance of his thanks, Eleonore leaned back in her cell, unsure of how to react to this sudden change of character. Whoever this Jung was that stood before her was not the officer that had tried to take advantage of her at the hospital or beaten Ella. Instead stood the man prior to putting on the uniform: the human. The man before the war and Hitler had robbed him of his soft nature and replaced it with a brute.

Without further consideration, Jung retrieved his keys from his pocket and placed them in the second door, ready to close it.

"Wait!" Eleonore put her hand through the iron bars and pressed against the steel door.

"What?" Jung asked earnestly.

"Our deal?" Eleonore looked at Jung with pleading eyes, but he only replied with a nod to the pocket watch she was holding as he shut and locked the door. Again, Eleonore was left alone in the darkness surrounded by cold, heartless concrete.

"Is it morning yet?" Eleonore asked the empty cell as she counted the minutes to pass the time.

"You asked me that so often as a child," Eleonore's mother spoke in her mind. *"You despised sleep, keeping me awake until the bitter hours of the night, then waking me as early as possible."*

"I couldn't accomplish anything while my body was idle," Eleonore defended. "If only I knew what the absence of a soft bed felt like."

Eleonore's dad chuckled in the familiar way that seemed to make the world brighter, no matter the circumstance. There was an understanding persistent within his character, almost an insight into the future: a looking ahead to see that the way was clear and that the present troubles were nothing more than temporary afflictions. She could envision the smile he gave, telling her to cast her worries upon the Lord, and to not be burdened with the things beyond her control.

"Well if you were to ask me," Ruth chimed in with a huff, *"you've gone and squandered your one opportunity. You helped that godless officer Jung and now he won't be coming back for you. You'll be joining us soon enough."*

"He'll be back," Eleonore spoke without reassurance. Her feet had been aching to such a degree she had been unable to sleep which, as it happens, was the intent of the standing cells: a psychological terrorizing of the mind through the limits of the body.

"Maybe it's best if I just die," Eleonore leaned her head against the iron bars.

"Why would you say such a thing?" Eleonore imagined her mother would say as she placed a comforting hand on her back.

"I'm not cut out for survival," Eleonore sighed her despair.

"Nonsense," her mother brushed away the ridiculous conclusion. *"You've made us proud."*

"I have?" Eleonore's eyes welled.

"Why would I lie?" her mother slapped her arm.

"He's not coming," Eleonore felt her stomach begging for relief, but knew there was nothing that would silence the agony.

Then she heard it: a distant door open and shut. Pressing her ear against her cell, she listened for anything that would give her hope. Holding her breath, Eleonore tried to catch every sound, every utterance. But the groans of suffering from the other inmates drowned out any conclusive indication that the officer had returned.

"That must be him!" Eleonore hoped.

"How do you figure?" Alex asked innocently. He loved Eleonore's intuitive mind and took to testing her knowledge of the world like he was learning the secrets to life.

"Only one pair of boots," Eleonore replied and returned to listening, "and coming this way."

Keys rattled, and Eleonore smiled awaiting her sweet release, but then her heart sank when it was not her door that opened. Across the hall, a metal door creaked, and a muffled voice could be heard demanding what was going on.

That's not Jung's voice, Eleonore listened as two men spoke. One, she assumed, was the prisoner as he spoke with frailty; the other was an officer whose tone was gruff and raspy. Only certain words carried through the door, leaving the context of the conversation concealed, but their pitch indicated to Eleonore that they were having an argument of sorts.

A shot fired. The noise was so loud that Eleonore let out a frightened squeak and placed her hand over her mouth. A thump echoed shortly after the shot, and Eleonore guessed it was the prisoner's body hitting the floor.

There was no movement from the officer, and the shot had rendered the other prisoners silent. None dared utter a sound for fear they would be shot next. Finally, a sigh came from the officer and Eleonore heard his boots walking back towards the main door which slammed shut after him.

The hours passed by in eerie stillness as Eleonore flinched at every creak and clink, imaging the officer had returned to kill her. It was useless, she understood, to be prepared or not for his return as there was nothing at her disposal with which to defend herself. Still, she determined to not be caught unexpectedly. At least then she could minimize her panic.

Jung's not coming back, Eleonore thought as she clung to the pocket watch the lieutenant had left as a security. She felt its weight in her hands, the smoothness of the metal, and then brought it up to her ear as she listed to it tick away patiently.

I should've persisted for his gun, and at least one bullet, Eleonore closed her eyes as she imagined the pocket watch was a gun and pointed it to her temple. Squeezing the pretend trigger, a part of Elenore wondered if she had enough courage should she hold an actual gun.

A door slammed and Elenore quickly stood to her feet with the pocket watch dangling by her side, prepared to meet her death.

If it's not Jung, then whoever appears will assume I've stolen the watch, Eleonore thought and tried to piece together a fabrication. Further terrifying her nerves, the keys rattled at her door. Eleonore panicked as she thought of some escape, assuming Jung had now ordered her execution. Eleonore shook as she aimed the watch at the door, pretending it was a gun, envisioning where her killer was standing.

"You were praying for death just a few minutes ago," Ruth reminded.

"I suppose I don't have much control over my survival instincts, but I don't want to die like this," Eleonore stood tall and proud. If this was her appointed time, then she was going to die with honor and without the shame of tear-filled supplication.

The door swung open and before her stood Jung who initially startled with the watch aimed at him, but then he grinned at the sight of the small woman with an empty threat.

"Who were you talking to?" Jung asked innocently and peered curiously into her cell.

Eleonore didn't reply at first as she stared at the dead man in the cell opposite her. Blood was pooling from the bullet wound in his head, running out of his cell and into the center of the dungeon. Without trial, isolated from his family and afraid, the man had been given over to death in callous, calculated murder.

"Are you going to kill me too?" Eleonore panted as her gaze remained on the dead man.

"No," he frowned and shook his head, wondering where she had acquired such a notion. Then, glancing over his shoulder he understood the terrible fright she must've been under.

"I'm honoring my word," he opened the iron bars and waved for her to exit.

"Why did he deserve such a fate?" Eleonore remained wary.

"Orders are not to be questioned," Jung replied bluntly. "Whoever shot him had the proper paperwork."

"What was his name?" she looked at the man with such pity, curious about the life he left behind, the woman he loved, and the children he might've had.

"What does it matter?" Jung shrugged. "Come."

Still, Eleonore didn't move. Not because she remained untrusting, but her legs had been locked into place for more hours than she could account for.

"Come!" Jung grew impatient.

"I can't," Eleonore tapped her legs, unsure of how to describe her difficulty. Her famishment had impeded her ability to articulate adequately.

"Here," Jung reached out his hand.

Surprised by the chivalry, especially in comparison to the unbridled barbarity the officer previously displayed, Eleonore endured in her mistrust.

There were two men in front of her inhabiting the same body: one was chaos, passion; the other was unquestioned order, unhinged brutality, and immorality.

"You need to get to roll call before the gong rings," Jung reached in and grabbed her hand. "Otherwise all the paperwork I've forged will look suspicious and my body will be hung next to yours."

"Ow," Eleonore fell to her knees as she left the cell through Jung's forceful guidance, still holding the watch he left her with.

"Can you walk?" Jung bent down and took hold of her arm.

"It'll take a minute," Eleonore poked her foot but couldn't feel anything. She knew the encroaching 'pins and needles' would be near unbearable.

"Let me know when you're ready," Jung straightened and, reaching into his uniform, pulled out a silver case of cigarettes. Flipping it open, he motioned for her to take one.

"Can we smoke elsewhere?" she indicated to the dead man.

Jung nodded, almost surprised to see the body as if he had forgotten; entirely disconnected.

"You're unbelievably good at your job, aren't you?" Eleonore looked at him with incredulity.

"Thank you," Jung replied, still detached.

"It wasn't a compliment," Eleonore's astonishment intensified.

"This is how I survive," Jung looked at her with understanding.

Then, growing impatient and, without warning, he bent over and picked her up in his arms and began to carry her towards the door. Not in a delicate sense as if he were carrying a lover, but rather, in a gruff, uncaring manner.

"What are you doing?!" Eleonore's skin crawled with disgust at the proximity with such a monster.

Kicking the bunker door open, Jung walked outside with Eleonore still in his arms as the snow danced softly in the crisp December air. The sun had not yet risen, and the light above the door was streaming down, isolating them from the world.

"Rest here," Jung placed her down abruptly on a wooden crate beside the door.

"Careful," Eleonore winced and reached down for her feet as the nerves were awakening with a painful rebirth.

Without apology for his gruffness, Jung reached again into his coat pocket and retrieved a cigarette. Though she accepted the smoke, Eleonore turned her face sour to make a point of his rudeness.

"I'll need my watch back," Jung held out his hand.

"Right," Eleonore surrendered the watch which had nearly frozen to her hand as she gripped it so hard.

Lighting a match, Jung held the flame near Eleonore's face as she took a deep, craved breath in, letting the smoke fill her lungs with its promise of pleasure.

"Sophia," Jung spoke as if he was continuing a conversation.

"Sorry?" Eleonore frowned in confusion.

"My wife's name," Jung took a puff. "Sophia."

"Sophia…Sophia…" Eleonore scratched her head as she searched her memory. "Oh, yes, Sophia Jung. She preferred her middle name, Emily if I remember correctly. Why was I thinking Evelin?"

"I was not allowed the privilege of using that name," Jung chuckled, and Eleonore was surprised he could show such a human emotion.

"What do you mean?" Eleonore asked, but wondered why she should give this beast the time of day.

"You asked how my wife passed," Jung cleared his throat. "Truth is, she was so ashamed of my vocation in the army that she cut off all communication from me. Her aunt was a Jew – through marriage – who was, uh, taken. Sophia blamed me personally for her death and, eventually, the shame was so great that she took her own life. She knew what I had been instructed to do here at the camps. No one else believed her, some thought she was mad, and it killed her. I killed her, essentially."

Letting the cigarette burn out in her hand, Eleonore remained silent with the gravity of the conversation. She didn't overly enjoy smoking, only taking a few puffs here and there to get the effect but this, however, was certainly an occasion which a cigarette was almost as welcome as a dear friend. Yet now she remained motionless, out of respect for Jung's wife. Why, Eleonore wondered, should she care at all for this devil's sorrows when he had multiplied grief to hundreds of other families? Still, there was something crying out within the officer, she could see its light begging to escape the self-deprecating abyss.

"She didn't understand," Jung continued as he shook his head. "You go where you are ordered, and I was assigned to work in the camps. I thought she would be pleased knowing I would be safe from combat, but then I found a letter she had attempted to forge, requesting my transfer to the front lines. She wanted me dead. I don't take pleasure in this job," Jung justified his position, "but if I refuse, then I'll be shot and someone much crueler than I will take my place."

"There's always a choice," Eleonore glanced at Jung and then away, avoiding eye contact as much as possible.

"Like you?" Jung laughed. "Judge for yourself who is in a better position."

"Don't be so short-sighted. When the Allies arrive and see what you've done, what then?"

"The Allies?" Jung smirked. "What are they going to do? Everything done in the camps is legal. We aren't operating outside of any law. Besides, we have won every encounter with that feeble house."

"I've heard other reports," Eleonore whispered. "Reports of Hitler's incompetence."

"You dare speak that way of the Fuhrer?" Jung grew indignant. "The very man who is saving Germany?"

"If he's saving Germany, then why are boys as young as thirteen being called to fight?"

"To help with the labor," Jung shrugged. "Everyone must do their part in this great struggle."

"Don't you understand? The flower of sacred Germany is being trodden upon by the steel-toed boots of Stalin, Churchill, and America," Eleonore's passion permeated through her voice. "All because that demon rose to challenge the world. The righteous have responded in kind."

"Is that the narrative the Allies are propagating?" Jung glared at her with rising outrage. Then, with a swift backhand, he struck the cigarette out of her hand, and she looked at him in surprise.

"You'd be wise to remember that the only reason you and I are here is because I keep my word," Jung continued to glare at her as he tapped his chest.

"Don't hide behind honor," Eleonore delved deeper into his troubled psychosis.

"What do you mean?" Jung tossed his cigarette into the snow as it sizzled.

"You're not helping me from any sense of principle," Eleonore elaborated. She was pushing her luck berating him in this manner, but her patience with his callousness was nearing its limits. "The last time you and I were alone you tried to take advantage of me. Now you have the perfect opportunity, yet you haven't once offered me that familiar gaze of lust. You have affection for me now, but why? What changed?"

"You're reaching," Jung shook his head and shrugged but, as he looked away, Eleonore caught a measure of embarrassment in his expression; the look one gives when they've been discovered. When their secrets, which they themselves hadn't even considered, are exposed.

The gong rang and the barracks sprang to life, preparing themselves for the day.

"Let's get you back for roll call," Jung nodded, refusing to look at her.

Chapter Eleven: The Villa

"Two things fill the mind with ever new and increasing admiration and awe, the more often and steadily we reflect upon them: the starry heavens above me and the moral law within me." Immanuel Kant.

Escorted by Jung, Eleonore returned to the square just as the barracks were forming for the roll call. Met by curious eyes when the two of them appeared – alone – Eleonore wondered what impolite thoughts were plaguing their minds. Stepping in line, Eleonore ignored their gazes except for one beautiful pair of eyes resting above a relieved grin: Ella. Her swelling had reduced drastically and, although the discoloration remained, Ella was on the proper track to healing.

Seeing his captive to her position, Jung left Eleonore and strolled to the front where his subordinates were awaiting with the list of numbers for him to call out. But, as he went up the line, his eye caught Ella and the sorry state she was in. As fleeting as his conscience arrived, he had again made it subject to duty, and continued in his disregard.

Still, it was enough for Eleonore to catch the rekindling of Jung's humanity. There was hope for him yet. Maybe not for forgiveness or absolution of his sins, but Eleonore had faith that Jung would stir his soul to action when it would matter most: the darkness would not be able to keep out the light.

As usual, the roll call began with Dr. Mengele choosing those who were too weak or sickly, and sending those weeping few to Block 25. Though she appeared famished and tired, Eleonore didn't fear the selections. She had a purpose, of sorts, and a reason to live which shone in her countenance. She would continue working on Jung's conscience and then use it for an advantage to gain access to Dr. Mengele.

After the heartless selections, Jung went down the line as he called out the prisoner's numbers, assigning them to their duties. But when he arrived at Ella, he called out her number with an awkwardness; an unfamiliar shame for his previous behavior towards her. Although he was not outwardly apologetic, Eleonore could sense him doubting the ideology which he had once thought so incorruptible.

"Here," Ella replied as she raised her hand, and Eleonore thought she almost sounded glad.

She must've been worried sick about me, Eleonore smiled at the notion that the bonds of friendship were deepening.

"Hospital," Jung collected himself and moved on to the next in line.

She won't believe what happened last night, Eleonore pictured Ella's expression at her encounter with Jung.

"Seven Five Six Nine Three," Jung stood next to her.

"Here," Eleonore replied immediately.

"Villa," Jung read out the order and moved on to the next person.

All eyes turned to Eleonore with an amazement brought on by envy, but Elenore was clueless as to why. She didn't remember seeing a Villa in the camp, and her pessimism led her to believe the Villa was most likely a perverse nickname for a hovel or a concrete bunker.

"You have your assignments," Jung held the clipboard under his arm as he signaled to the orchestra to begin their procession.

Turning, the group prepared to march towards their assignments, but Eleonore was lost as to her destination, and she didn't dare ask.

"I'll take you to the hospital first," Jung spoke to Eleonore, but with a harsh tone, "and I'll explain why your services there will no longer be required."

Relieved, Eleonore nodded, and the group stepped to the beat of the slightly out of tune instruments. Yet as they headed towards the hospital, Eleonore became aware of the hushed whispers from the ladies around her.

"Whore," one of the ladies spoke under her breath.

"I would've never slept with that animal," another whispered. "No matter the reward."

Eleonore's face flushed red with embarrassment and rage at the unjust accusations. How could they believe her elevation in status came from such immorality and without any proof?! None of them knew that she had spent the night in the standing cell, but none cared. They saw what they wanted and came to their own twisted conclusions. Nothing she could say would correct their perversion of events, so Eleonore kept quiet and refused to defend herself.

"Don't listen to them," Ella whispered as she grabbed her hand. "Hunger and fear twist the mind. They don't understand what they are saying."

"Sorry we won't be able to talk," Eleonore whispered over her shoulder. "I've got so much to tell you."

"I've got news myself!" Ella whispered back, but a little too loudly.

"Quiet!" one of the guards glared at them.

With a knowing nod, Eleonore promised they would speak later. What news could Ella possibly have? She couldn't wait to hear.

Arriving at the hospital doors, a cold chill ran over Eleonore with the thought of Ma'am's reaction. Besides, for all the Kapo knew, Eleonore was still suffering in the standing cell of Block 11 and was in for a steep surprise. Eleonore hoped Jung had a proper justification for her ascent to privilege; if that's what the Villa promised.

Opening the doors, the ladies filed in as usual and were met by Ma'am waiting patiently for her arrivals. Again, the cries and moans from the patients disturbed Eleonore and she looked at a smiling Ma'am, wondering how she could find any gratification in this cruel environment.

But nothing was as troubling as witnessing the sharp gaze Ma'am adopted when Eleonore came into view. The Kapo glanced at Jung, lost to bewilderment that the woman she destined for torture was standing before her the very next morning. Yet to question the peculiarity would be to lose authority, so Ma'am didn't press the issue.

"Good morning," Ma'am spoke slowly, still stunned.

"Good morning," the ladies replied in unison.

"Now, before I separate you to your groups," Ma'am began, but was interrupted by Jung clearing his throat.

"Yes?" Ma'am gritted her teeth, enraged with the interruption.

"I regret to inform you that you'll be shorthanded today," Jung stood at attention as he addressed her, and all could sense his trepidation.

Frowning, Ma'am double-counted the ladies, "I see ten before me. Did you interrupt me to announce your stupidity?"

"Seven Five Six Nine Three has been assigned to the Villa," Jung moved behind Eleonore and gripped her arm firmly as if in punishment.

"What?!" Ma'am mirrored Jung and stood in front of Eleonore as she gripped the other arm.

"She has been assigned to--"

"I heard you!" Ma'am growled. "On who's authority?"

"Commandant Hoess," Jung blurted, pleased by the look of sheer amazement on Ma'am's face.

You didn't have to bring me to the hospital first, Eleonore glanced up at him as she thought. *This is in retribution for a petty slight, isn't it?*

"That can't be..." Ma'am was lost for words as her grip loosened.

"Her services are required. We cannot delay," Jung turned towards the door and ushered Eleonore out, but not before she caught the scowl of jealously splattered across the Kapo's face.

Led by Jung and two guards towards the main gates of the camp, Eleonore again read the damning sign held triumphantly above, *Work Sets You Free*. The guards at the gates saluted Jung and requested the proper papers, which he supplied. With the gates opening, Eleonore stared out into the 'beyond' with mesmerization. She supposed that she would never set foot outside the camp again, but now her feet were touching sacred dirt as she left the hellish perimeter.

"I'll take her from here," Jung notified the other guards and they left the Lieutenant alone with Eleonore.

"Thank you," Eleonore whispered when she was sure they were out of earshot.

Jung looked down at her with a soft expression and Eleonore almost caught a smile in the corner of his mouth. Again, Eleonore witnessed the man who existed before the Nazi regime corrupted many just like him; good men who had grown up with the Christian instruction of peace and gentleness. The cross had been replaced with the swastika, dementing the finest aspects of these young men and turning them into monsters capable of unspeakable brutality.

"What is the Villa?" Eleonore asked as they walked towards a house just outside of the camp.

"Your salvation," Jung released his grip from her arm. "This is where the Commandant and his family live."

"And what is expected of me here?" Eleonore studied the house as her anxiety took hold of her. Even in Berlin, it took her some courage to venture somewhere new as her routine rarely faltered from the set schedule.

"The same that is expected of me," Jung replied, and Eleonore shot him a confused glance to which he explained, "To do their bidding. You will report to the Commandant's wife."

"And what will she request?" Eleonore persisted.

"A seamstress," Jung grinned, and patted the repaired arm of his sleeve.

The Villa, Eleonore found, was a rustic two-story house that, although plain, exuded peacefulness. *Salvation,* Eleonore mused as Jung opened the door for her and music poured out from a gramophone. *Wagner's Tristan and Isolde,* Eleonore smiled as the strings blared in perfect harmony. *Odd music for the morning, but a welcome change.*

Stepping inside, Eleonore was struck by the warmth and coziness and felt the coldness in her bones beginning to melt away. The uninsulated barracks had caused her to forget what it truly meant to be sheltered. How she wanted to sit and read a book beside the gramophone as it projected its welcoming tune.

Creeping in along with the beautiful orchestral piece was the deadliness of nostalgia. Eleonore's spirit begged for the return of her perfect life, back to where she had obtained what so many had sought but failed to find: contentment. She wondered if she would acquire that tranquility again someday – if she survived.

Even while standing in the foyer, the first impression of the Villa left Eleonore near speechless as it screamed its overabundance. The bland, parquet floors had been covered with bright, white carpets and over the dreary windows hung curtains of royal purple. Maids were busy dusting the living room, putting the furniture in perfect order, and readying the house for its masters.

Walking briskly past the foyer was a short, spritely woman carrying a mop and bucket in one hand, and a rag and dusting wand in the other. She wore a burgundy dress with a complimentary white apron whose pockets were filled to capacity with cleaning supplies. But what stole Eleonore's attention was the woman's hair. Not only was it existent, but it was long, curly, and vibrant. The other servants, too, either had or were growing back what had been so rudely shaved off.

"What's she doing?" the servant paused and panted as she spoke to Jung, her fingers turning white under the strain of carrying a bucket full of water.

"She's been assigned to the Villa," Jung offered the servant the papers, but she didn't have a free hand.

"Not like that she's not," the woman looked Eleonore up and down with a foul expression.

Humiliated, Eleonore stared at her feet like a child shamed. Her beauty was usually quite prominent, and to have that stripped so casually was a harsh blow. In the camp, her appearance was similar to the others as they were all dirty and unkempt. Here, however, the contrast magnified each blemish.

"I…I didn't mean it like that," the woman realized her offence and Eleonore shot her a surprised glance for the unexpected apology. "I'll take her to the servant's quarters. There she can wash up and be presentable for Mrs. Hoess."

Placing her 'tools' near the door, the woman walked over to Eleonore and gave another quick inspection before stretching out her hand to grab Eleonore's wrist. But as she was led away, Eleonore glanced over her shoulder at Jung. He had risen from the depths of hatred into someone she now considered as a protector of sorts and felt vulnerable leaving his shielding presence. He was terrible, there was no doubting that, but he carried affection for Eleonore, and it was tempting to exploit that for her own comfort and well-being.

"I'll give you a brief tour as we go along," the woman slowed her pace a little to walk beside Eleonore.

"Here is the kitchen," she opened the door and at once the smell and sizzle of meats, vegetables, and fruits struck Eleonore with a yearning so powerful that she nearly fainted. She watched the cooks preparing the meals and, although the woman was speaking to her, Eleonore couldn't hear the words. All she wanted was a bite. Just one bite.

"Don't worry," the woman closed the door, realizing how cruel it was to show Eleonore her deepest desires then forbid her partaking, "I know you're hungry, but you'll be fed soon enough, and you'll be fed well."

At that, Eleonore welled up. Such words were as golden to her as if she had been handed her release from the camp altogether.

"Oh dear," the woman took pity on Eleonore and rubbed her arm. "I know it's tough. My name is Roza by the way. Roza Robota."

"Eleonore Hodys," Eleonore wiped the tears from her eye.

"Pleased to meet you, Eleonore," Roza smiled and then wrapped her arm around Eleonore's.

"Next to the kitchen we have the living room," she opened another door to reveal a sofa, three chairs, two side tables, and a standing lamp.

"Beautiful table," Eleonore looked into the dining room which was just beside the living room.

"Made by prisoners here, in Auschwitz," Roza grinned with pride.

"Really?" Eleonore was shocked as the craftsmanship was near perfection.

"Oh yes," Roza moved into the dining room and ran her hand on the elliptical table. "It even extends so that you can sit eight comfortably."

"And these chairs?" Eleonore rubbed her hand across the leather.

"Also made by prisoners."

"Fascinating," Eleonore studied the precision. "May I speak to the craftsmen? I'd love to know how they were able to get such fine detail."

"They are no longer with us," Roza's delight faded as she recalled their absence.

"I'm sorry," Eleonore straightened as she realized her blunder.

"Nothing to forgive," Roza waved her hand. "They'll be avenged. In this life or the next. Come, let's continue," Roza left the dining room followed by a curious Eleonore.

What does she mean 'in this life or the next'? Eleonore wondered. *Is she part of the resistance that Ella was talking about?*

"Oh, before I forget," Roza turned and pointed towards a door on the other side of the living room. "That is the Commandant's private office. You are never to enter."

"That won't be a problem," Eleonore shook her head.

"Good," Roza nodded. "Now, my quarters are upstairs, so we'll have to be quiet otherwise we'll wake the children. We don't want to start off on the wrong foot now do we?"

Following Roza up the stairs, Eleonore noticed elaborate paintings on the wall. *Likely stolen,* Eleonore thought as they ranged in variety and taste. Some appeared more expensive than the house itself while others were more decorative and basic, yet still pleasant.

"This one was done by Hedwig's brother," Roza pointed to a painting of the Sola River which was near to the camp.

"Hedwig?" Eleonore frowned.

"Mrs. Hoess," Roza corrected herself. "Sorry, I shouldn't have been so casual with her Christian name. She's a kind woman, but she is strict nonetheless and there are certain rules which must be obeyed at all times."

"Well it's a great painting," Eleonore was surprised.

"You should tell her that," Roza studied Eleonore as one examines a new apprentice; appreciating the merits and evaluating the flaws.

"Anyways, let's continue. On this floor, there are three bedrooms and a playroom for the children. At the end of the hall," Roza pointed, "is the master bedroom which — "

"Is not to be entered," Eleonore interrupted.

"Correct, and my quarters are in the attic," she reached up and pulled a string to let down the ladder. "Can you climb alright?"

Nodding, Eleonore looked up at the stairs and saw them swivel and sway. She was exhausted, and it was difficult to think of anything besides food and rest.

"Good," Roza began to climb, followed by Eleonore who shook while lifting her own weight, alarmed at how much strength she had lost.

"It's a little cramped," Roza ducked as she walked through the attic, "but I doubt you'll need to come up here again."

Thankful for her petite figure, Eleonore didn't have to stoop all that much as she was led to the washroom. She passed by three beds that were tidied and figured one belonged to Roza while the other two belonged to the other maids she spotted while in the foyer.

"Here we are," Roza opened the door to the washroom and Eleonore grinned as she fell in love with the little room. Painted grey, it was rather bare, but the light from the stained window shone in a serenity that reminded her of her flat. She looked at the tub longingly as she wanted to rest her weary joints and muscles in the healing, warm water.

"Unfortunately, there's no hot water," Roza shattered Eleonore's spirits as she drew the curtain, "but it's something at least."

"Ah!' Eleonore jumped when she saw a dark, gangly looking creature.

"What's wrong?" Roza looked around the room, wondering what on earth had startled Eleonore. But her heart softened and swelled with pity when she noticed that Eleonore had only caught her own reflection in the mirror.

"I remember that feeling well," Roza came to stand behind Eleonore and the two of them looked at her likeness. "You haven't seen yourself in some time, have you?"

Eleonore shook her head as she stared with mesmerization at the pathetic person before her. Her hair was growing back in patches, her face was pale with sunken, dark eyes, and she had lost so much weight she appeared only a shadow of her former self.

"C'mon," Roza said warmly as she guided Eleonore away from the mirror and turned on the shower. "Let's get you sorted. You'll feel much better after a wash."

Removing her clothes without care that Roza should see her nakedness, Eleonore stepped into the running shower. She winced as the coldness struck her feet, but she persisted and entered deeper as she drew the shower curtain. Turning her face to heaven, Eleonore closed her eyes as the grease and mud were washed away. A hidden tear rolled down her cheek, blending in with the rest of the water, as a cleansing washed over her soul.

"Are you alright in there?" Roza asked after a minute, waking Eleonore from her trance.

"Yes," Eleonore turned off the shower and withdrew the curtain.

"No kids?" Roza frowned as she handed Eleonore a towel.

"Pardon?" Eleonore asked with confusion.

"I meant you have no children."

"How'd you know?" Eleonore wrapped the towel around her, growing self-conscious under the gaze of Roza.

"No stretch marks," Roza shrugged as if the answer was obvious, "and the other parts of you are still where God intended them to be."

Eleonore chuckled and offered an appreciative grin for the compliment. She was a vain woman, which she recognized, and anything that returned the pride of her beauty was welcomed.

"I know the journey may be long," Roza stood back as Eleonore dried herself, "but you'll soon be back to normal. I'm not saying life is pleasant here," Roza bit her cheek awkwardly, "but in comparison with the camp...and with the angel of Auschwitz watching over you...well...you'll be fine. Life here will be amiable if you allow it."

"Angel?" Eleonore tilted her head in curiosity.

"Mrs. Hoess," Roza explained.

"How can you praise her so highly?" Eleonore shook her head in disbelief. "They live in the splendor that was robbed from the prisoners like you and me."

Roza thought for a moment, unsure of how to articulate her thoughts adequately, "You'll have to see for yourself," she nodded. "Now, let's do something about those poor clothes."

"I didn't mean to upset you," Eleonore continued. "By condemning her I've extended the same discourtesy towards you."

"It's nothing. The verdict has been shared by many who have passed through the Villa. Come, sit," Roza patted a chair in front of the mirror.

Eleonore hesitated, half expecting to be re-visited by the pathetic creature she witnessed earlier.

"Don't worry," Roza grinned, "you look years better already."

Cautiously, Eleonore peeked her head around the edge of the mirror and caught a brighter face staring back at her. Pleased that the shower had returned some of her former glory, Eleonore sat down as Roza withdrew some makeup from the drawer. Applying some powder under her eyes, Roza worked carefully to make Eleonore as presentable as possible.

As an only child, Eleonore assumed this is what most sisters did for each other and felt a connection to Roza for her kindness. She only wished that she had hair for her to brush or curl.

"There," Roza put her hands on Eleonore's shoulder as she studied her handy work in the mirror.

"You've done a wonderful job," Eleonore looked rather pleased with herself.

"That's very kind," Roza bent down, searching through some other drawers, "but we're not done yet."

"What do you mean?" Eleonore wondered.

"A crown," Roza drew out a curly, brown wig.

"What do you think?" Roza asked after she had placed it on Eleonore's bald head.

Employing everything at her disposal to not cry and ruin her makeup, Eleonore looked at herself in amazement. The wig was curlier than her own hair had been, but the color was a near match and the person she thought she had lost was staring back at her.

Clearing her throat to drive away the emotion, Eleonore asked, "What was your profession, before you came here?"

"A mother," Roza spoke quickly. "I wanted to enter cosmetics, but I became pregnant, and then became pregnant again, and again, and again. Fortunately, my four girls loved to be my projects."

"Oh well that's lovely," Eleonore looked up over her shoulder.

"Another hint that you're not a mother," Roza whispered cheerfully. "You didn't catch the sarcasm in my voice. My children fought me bitterly each and every time."

"Oh!" Eleonore burst into a laugh.

"What I'd give for a good fight with them about now," Roza chuckled, but then her countenance fell at the bitter thought. Reading her mind, Eleonore reached her hand up and took hold of Roza's.

"Thank you," Roza gave a squeeze and then sighed. "I think it's time we dress and prepare you for your introduction to the Commandant's wife. Hang your towel over the tub and I'll clean it later."

Eleonore stood as Roza handed her some plain undergarments and a navy-blue jumper that was pressed and clean; not at all dirty or freshly used like her regulation outfit.

"It should be your size," Roza watched anxiously as Eleonore slipped the jumper over her head.

"A little snug," Eleonore lifted her arm as the fabric tightened near her shoulder, "but I'm happy for new clothes."

"It should stretch enough with some wear," Roza produced a white apron from her pocket and gave it to Eleonore. "Put this on too."

Tying the little apron around her waist, Eleonore reviewed her new look in the mirror and grinned with surprise. With the wig, makeup, and this new outfit, the blemishes of famishment and exhaustion were softened substantially. Yet there was a miserable thought underlying the trimmings: the hunger was still present, the tiredness clung tightly, and she was still a prisoner in a death camp.

"I think you're ready to meet her," Roza put her hand to her chin as she examined Eleonore.

Chapter Twelve:
The Angel of Auschwitz

"The mind is its own place, and in itself can make a heaven of hell, a hell of heaven..." John Milton, Paradise Lost.

"Oh good, the children are awake," Roza's eyes lit up as she descended the stairs from the attic. "You'll be able to meet them."

Giggles, playful shouts, and the pounding of little feet poured out of the playroom just down the hallway and Eleonore's heart filled with contentment at the happy sound. Children were absent in the camp, apart from those that were kept in Dr. Mengele's lab. In the Nazi mindset, no usefulness equaled no productivity and, therefore, the most precious were sacrificed.

Opening the door to the playroom, Roza burst in as Eleonore trailed her to find a large room with toys, cushions, trinkets, and children running around. Five children, Eleonore counted, as two girls were sitting nicely with their dolls and teacups while two boys were wrestling and the fifth, a baby, was held by a nanny that Eleonore assumed was also a prisoner.

"Children!" Roza called over the rowdy noise but to no avail. "Children!" she called again with a clap. "I have someone I'd like you to meet."

At this, the girls glanced up to see Eleonore and abandoned their stations as they bounded towards her. The boys, lost in their typical indifference, were slower to be appreciative of the novelty. Still, they arrived shortly after the girls to inspect the newcomer.

"This is Eleonore," Roza leaned over with exaggerated emphasis. "She will be working in the house for some time."

"What are your names?" Eleonore studied them as she smiled, adoring the children.

"I have a doll," the youngest ignored Eleonore's question, and held her doll up high for her to see.

"It's beautiful," Eleonore fluffed the doll's hair.

With the children being curious yet shy – save for the youngest – Roza walked over to the oldest and put her arm around him.

"This is Klaus," she began. "Next we have Heidetraud, Inge-Briggitt, Hans-Juergen, and the little one swaddled over there is Annegret."

"Well I'm very pleased to meet you all," Eleonore smiled brightly.

"You're pretty," Heidetraud spoke plainly as she inspected Eleonore.

"Well aren't you perfect," Eleonore giggled. "I love your dress."

"I made it myself," Heidetraud boomed proudly.

"Did not!" Klaus ratted her out.

"Did too!" Heidetraud pushed out her tongue.

"I'm afraid we don't have the luxury to discover the truth," Roza moved to the door and spoke to Eleonore. "I'll take you downstairs now."

"I'll see you all shortly," Eleonore waved to the children as she left and the youngest, again the boldest, waved vibrantly as her doll dragged along the floor.

"We'll find Mrs. Hoess reading in the drawing room," Roza boasted of her knowledge of the routine.

"She won't mind the interruption?" Eleonore grew nervous for meeting this woman who had donned such an elaborate title as 'angel'.

"Not at all," Roza spoke with confidence to put Eleonore at ease as they walked down the hallway, "though her demeanor can sometimes give off that impression. She's proper you see, but underneath the hard exterior is a compassionate woman who wishes the best for all who enter under her care."

Walking down the stairs, Eleonore could hear the wonderful gramophone still blaring the tunes of Wagner. The contrast between the Villa and the camp caused Eleonore to consider if she had only imagined Auschwitz. How could so much luxury and loveliness exist only a fence away from torture, terror, and mass death? The proximity to the unbelievable gave the appearance of the camp being fictional.

When they reached the bottom of the stairs, Roza led Eleonore into the living room where they found Mrs. Hoess reading.

With a blank gaze, Mrs. Hoess lowered her book at the disturbance. Then, placing her bookmark, she set the book aside on the table and began to examine Eleonore without the slightest expression. Such judging eyes from a woman of her importance unnerved Eleonore and she again felt faint. Could she see through the makeup and the wig and spot the humble creature that she was? Or was she content with the gentle woman who stood before her? It was impossible to read her reaction and Eleonore wished she would show some sign in either direction.

Hedwig Hoess was a stern woman with small eyes and a rather plain face which shunned makeup. Yet there was a certain beauty in her simplicity; a kind of sincerity that wasn't concealed by false extravagance. She was as she was, nothing more, nothing less. But for the indulgence within the house, her austerity was almost on par with the servants. She wore a white, untailored dress that was so modest that it gave the appearance of an undergarment.

"Name?" Mrs. Hoess examined Eleonore.

"Eleonore Hodys," she cleared her throat.

"You're not Jewish?" Mrs. Hoess remained without expression and Eleonore wondered if she were capable of showing emotion.

Eleonore shook her head.

"You're the seamstress, then?"

"I am, ma'am," Eleonore fidgeted with her hands nervously.

"Don't worry," Mrs. Hoess stood and walked over to stand just to the side of Eleonore who was surprised to find they were about the same height. "You're in my care now. You'll be looked after so long as you do as commanded and do it well. Understood?"

Eleonore nodded eagerly.

"Good," Mrs. Hoess took a deep breath as she continued to study Eleonore. "I see that Roza here has washed you and brushed your hair."

"She's been very kind," Eleonore glanced at Roza, happy that Mrs. Hoess hadn't recognized it was a wig. Either that or she was being rather generous.

"Yes," Mrs. Hoess answered bluntly as if Eleonore was stating the obvious.

The tension in the room thickened as Mrs. Hoess examined Eleonore like she was investigating a piece of artwork, trying to unravel its mysteries.

"You have beautiful children," Eleonore broke the silence.

"I have loud children," Mrs. Hoess replied quickly. "But you're right," she finally broke her gaze and returned to her spot on the sofa, "they are beautiful. You're dismissed. Roza will show you what needs repairing."

"I see that you're reading *The World of Yesterday*," Eleonore spoke, and all eyes turned on her in shock for the informality: the first real emotion Eleonore could procure from the mistress.

"Yes…yes, I am," Mrs. Hoess looked curiously at Eleonore. It was a provocative piece of literature – written by a Jewish author nonetheless – and one that the wife of a Nazi Commandant shouldn't be reading so openly. It was exactly the sort of work that had been used to kindle the fires of the book burnings across the country.

"How are you enjoying the work of Stefan Zweig?" Eleonore continued.

"I've only just begun," Mrs. Hoess spoke cautiously. "I've not yet reached a conclusion. You seem familiar with his work, have you read it?"

"No," Eleonore glanced at her feet, "but I met Mr. Zweig once."

"You met him?!" Mrs. Hoess' eyes lit up and an intrigued smile crept onto the corner of her mouth.

"Oh yes," Eleonore nodded proudly yet absent of arrogance. "It was some time ago, long before he was seen as controversial."

"Someday you must tell me every detail," her faint smile retreated. Mrs. Hoess was a reserved woman who didn't let outsiders get too close. Yet underneath her detachment, Eleonore knew was a woman screaming with excitement. Still, propriety triumphed over the moving of the soul and her expression remained as unchanged as possible.

"I look forward to that," Eleonore let her smile grow larger than it should've as Mrs. Hoess' cheer faded rapidly.

"Have you eaten?" Mrs. Hoess asked.

"I have not," Eleonore replied as she felt her mouth salivate at the mention of food.

"I assume you work best on a full stomach?" Mrs. Hoess continued.

"It would help me concentrate," Eleonore nodded and struggled to withhold her eagerness.

"Roza," Mrs. Hoess leaned over to look behind Eleonore, "would you have Sophie arrange a plate for Eleonore?"

"Of course," Roza said softly.

"That'll be all," Mrs. Hoess dismissed them as she picked up her book again. "Oh, and Roza," She lifted her hand as the two began to leave.

"Yes?" Roza turned.

"Liberate a pack of cigarettes from the carton outside," She whispered over her book as her eyes remained fixed on the pages before her. "In reward for the time you spent on Eleonore."

"Gladly, ma'am," Roza gave a slight bow of the head and led Eleonore back to the kitchen.

"Why did she whisper?" Eleonore asked Roza when they were out of earshot.

"About the cigarettes?" Roza looked over her shoulder at Eleonore.

"Ya."

"Well," Roza stopped in mid-stride in the hallway and looked around to make sure none were present, and then continued in a hushed tone, "it's a little-known secret that you will be privy to rewards here that are technically forbidden."

"How so?" Eleonore whispered back, enjoying the intrigue and wondering what rewards awaited. Yet part of her wished she had not stopped to ask the question. The kitchen, and the end to her famishment, was a mere few feet away.

"The Commandant has forbidden the use of illicit work and payment. Still, Mrs. Hoess employs a hairdresser, cooks, extra rations, servants like myself, and now a seamstress," she pointed at Eleonore. "She pays us in cigarettes, usually."

"The Commandant hasn't noticed these luxuries present within his own house?" Eleonore glanced at the extravagant paintings.

"Oh, he has," Roza bit her lip to hide a smile, "but to pacify his wife he turns a blind eye."

"What about the other SS officers? Haven't they noticed?"

"They're cruel, not stupid," Roza shrugged, "but Mrs. Hoess supplies their wives with their own personal slaves, so everyone keeps quiet. If their spouses are happy, the men don't dare disturb the balance. It's corrupt, but it provides people like you and me with a life outside the camp. Still, it can't last forever."

What are you planning? Eleonore squinted as she watched Roza. *She must be part of the resistance.*

"Anyways," Roza tapped Eleonore's elbow. "Let's get you fed."

The magnificent smell again flooded Eleonore's senses as Roza opened the door to the kitchen and led her through a paradise for the hungry. Fruits, entrees, pastries, fish, shellfish, chicken, beef, and vegetables were being prepared for the day.

"Sophie," Roza called to the chef who was a tall, lanky blonde girl with a strong jaw and harsh eyes. Yet behind her contrasting features lay a sweet, charming expression of one who found encouragement from challenge and opportunity from trials. The kind who drove Eleonore insane with their optimism when she wished to remain in her defeatism. But now that life had devolved into this chaos, Sophie's enthusiasm was like a beacon to Eleonore.

"Yep?" Sophie said casually as she crossed her arms awkwardly and held them in what seemed a rather uncomfortable position.

Unrefined and forthright, Sophie was a gentle girl about the age of fifteen, and Eleonore assumed she probably came from some of the cruder areas of society. As it happens, this worked to her benefit as she was genuine and one could trust her word: an undeniable benefit in a chef. She wouldn't place the Hoess family in jeopardy, at least not without some indication of insincerity.

"Mrs. Hoess has ordered Eleonore here to be fed," Roza put her arm around Eleonore as if they were the closest of friends.

"What do you want?" Sophie looked at Eleonore without much excitement.

"Excuse me?" Eleonore was confused with the plainness of Sophie's language.

"To eat," Sophie explained. "What do you want to eat?"

"Oh…um…uh," Eleonore thought as she looked over the meats and the fruits and the vegetables, desiring them all.

"Everything?" Sophie asked as she caught the bouncing eyes of Eleonore.

"I believe that would be presumptuous of me," Eleonore found herself in the awkward position of being polite. Even while near starvation, she couldn't dare ask to eat more than what was acceptable.

"What?" Sophie frowned, not understanding.

"She'll have it all," Roza nodded and, with her arm still around Eleonore, led her to a back room where the servants ate.

It was a musky, dark and windowless room with a dull, orange lightbulb hanging from the ceiling. Sitting on a rustic chair at a flimsy table, Eleonore bounced her leg anxiously as she kept glancing at the door waiting for the food to be brought in.

Finally, Sophie burst through the door and slapped a bowl of fruit down on the table in front of her. There were apples, bananas, kiwis, strawberries, raspberries, blueberries, and grapes arranged in an elegant manner.

"There's more coming," Sophie spoke over her shoulder as she returned to the kitchen.

Taking a grape, Eleonore took a bite as her jaw seized from the rush of saliva and the fruit gushed its flavor throughout her mouth.

"Oh, c'mon!" Roza laughed. "Don't be polite. You're hungry. Eat!"

Taking the instruction to heart, Elenore grabbed a handful of grapes and shoveled them into her mouth like a savage animal. She cried tears of joy as she satisfied her primal instinct, yet guilt laid its heavy hand as she thought of Ella still starving in the camp. How could she enjoy such delights knowing most others would never experience such pleasures again?

But her conscience was drowned out with the crisp smell of fried meat as Sophie returned with a plateful of eggs, sausages, and toast. They were salted and sprinkled with spices, herbs, peppers, and infused with seasonings, and Eleonore felt she was dining at a four-star restaurant.

"She's fantastic," Roza smiled. "Isn't she?"

Eleonore nodded as she chewed away, her eyes almost rolling back in bliss. She knew she had to slow down, otherwise the agony of hunger would be replaced with the ache of overeating, but how could she? Despite the simplicity Sophie had shown in her social skills, she more than compensated in her extravagant cooking. The presentation, the texture, and flavor were all faultless, and Eleonore wondered what Sophie could attain with a real, full kitchen at her disposal.

"I'm guessing you're having the same thoughts as I did?" Roza continued. "Is the food this good or does it just taste this incredible because I haven't eaten in so long?"

Eleonore threw her eyebrows up in confirmation and paused from chewing to await the answer. Could she really eat this well every day that she worked at the villa?

"You'll be happy to know that Sophie was training to be a master chef," Roza tilted her head as she boasted. "Odd for a woman, but as you can tell she has a gift. In fact, you're eating the same dish that the Commandant himself eats."

"What'd she do?" Eleonore abandoned all sense of decorum as she spoke with her mouth full.

"She's a Jehovah's Witness," Roza whispered.

"Hm," Eleonore returned to chewing, uncaring what religion, race, or other Nazi designated 'blemish' was feeding her such phenomenal food.

A rather telling metaphor, Eleonore thought. *They group us into our subcategories or 'tribes', but they've forgotten to account for the individual qualities that stand in opposition to the group designation. A Jehovah's Witness can make a fantastic cook, a Jew can make the closest of friends, and a loving couple can make a lonely girl feel like she's not so isolated in the world.*

"What are you thinking?" Roza peered thoughtfully at Eleonore.

"Oh," Eleonore came back to reality. "Nothing. Just taking in the experience. It feels surreal to be here, knowing what my existence was like only a few short hours ago."

"That's life I suppose," Roza shrugged.

"I can't seem to wrap my mind around the destruction that's happening here," Eleonore paused from eating.

"Don't attempt to reconcile it either," Roza shook her head. "Otherwise you'll spend morning till night in tears. Only the hardest and fittest survive. There is no room for weakness. Remember that."

Guilt soared back as Eleonore ignored Roza's advice and thought again on what she had witnessed in her time at the camp: the train car packed with near-dead passengers, the smoke rising from the 'other camp', and the hundreds of thousands who had been killed for the coincidence of their birth.

"Finish up," Roza spoke softly, feeling the heaviness herself, "and I'll show you to your assignment. It's best if you get as much time to work so that you can do a masterful job and ensure you return."

Taking one last bite of sausage, Eleonore took a moment to appreciate the women she had met in the camp and at the Villa. Where would she be without Ella? Would Mrs. Hoess have accepted her if not for Roza's dedication? Despite all that had happened, Eleonore counted herself as fortunate; not from circumstance, but from companionship. As long as she had Ella and Roza by her side, Eleonore surmised that she could endure whatever came to pass, however awful.

Chapter Thirteen:
Viva La Villa

"Better to reign in Hell than serve in Heaven." John Milton,
Paradise Lost.

"Here we are," Roza threw her hands onto her hips when they arrived at a storage room in the Villa.

Chairs, folded tables, paintings of lesser value, desks, boxes of items awaiting to be sorted, curtains, cloths, and decorative plates lay organized in the room. But Eleonore's focus was stolen by a rich, red carpet that had been torn at the top right corner and was likely what the mistress required repairing. From the angle of the tear, Eleonore assumed it was some sort of vandalism as even poor craftsmanship wouldn't have split it in that fashion.

If it was an act of defacement, then the deed was understandable as the red carpet carried a gold embroidered Prussian phoenix clasping the swastika in its talons. While Eleonore could appreciate its aesthetics, the symbol was unforgivable and it made her happy to see it torn: a hoped-for prophecy.

"How long will this take you?" Roza watched as Eleonore bent down to inspect.

"Probably a day," Eleonore rubbed her jaw as she pieced the order together in her mind, like she had done thousands of times in her shop. "With the right materials, that is."

"Make it two days," Roza whispered and winked.

Eleonore smiled at the gesture, but then, her cheer evaporated with the sudden tightening of her stomach and a sharp pain developed in the lower left side.

"You alright?" Roza noticed her discomfort.

"I..." Eleonore didn't dare say another word as any strain on her stomach would be sure to make her sick.

"Oh, you ate too fast," Roza grabbed a stool from the corner of the room and placed it against the wall.

Thankful, though she couldn't show it, Eleonore sat on the stool as her forehead broke out into a cold sweat and she began to panic.

"Just take a minute," Roza patted Eleonore's back. "You'll feel bett—."

Eleonore interrupted with the loudest involuntary hiccup that echoed out into the hallway. Roza jumped back in surprise that such a sharp sound could be produced by one so petite.

"I'm sorry," Eleonore glanced up at Roza with alarm.

But to Eleonore's relief, Roza wasn't offended by the impropriety in the slightest. Instead, she was covering her mouth to stifle her laughter.

Eleonore, however, was not at all amused and continued in her embarrassment. At least at first, as Roza's amusement was so contagious that Eleonore eventually allowed a chuckle or two until she was also bursting with laughter.

"I thought," Eleonore tried to breathe through her giggling. "I thought I was about to have a heart attack. I thought I was dying!"

"I needed that," Roza put her hand against her chest and wiped the tears of joy away.

"Glad I could be of service," Eleonore massaged her cheeks as the muscles grew sore.

"I thought I was dying!" Roza quoted Eleonore and again burst into laughter at Eleonore's troubles.

"My goodness," Eleonore laughed again at her own expense.

"If only for this moment," Roza sighed as she calmed, "I'm glad I met you."

"Feels good to laugh," Eleonore mused.

"That is does," Roza grew solemn and Eleonore read her thoughts.

"Also gives one a sense of guilt," Eleonore peered into Roza.

"We can't think like that," Roza shook her head as she welled up. "You won't survive long clinging to sentimentalism."

"But that's what keeps us human," Eleonore persisted.

"Not in their eyes," Roza nodded. "And until the Allies start winning the war, their opinion is the only one that matters."

"Do you have everything you need?" Mrs. Hoess appeared suddenly in the doorway behind them, dressed for an outing.

"Yes, ma'am," Roza stood quickly to her feet and Eleonore followed suit.

"Good," Mrs. Hoess nodded as she fastened her gloves.

A startling, high pitched scream burst out from behind Mrs. Hoess, and Eleonore grabbed her chest in surprise. Mrs. Hoess, however, was well accustomed to the screech and she rolled her eyes with annoyance as the youngest boy raced past her and towards the door, followed closely by the three other children who were equally as enthusiastic for some planned activity.

"I get to go in the front," Klaus wrestled his way to the head of the group.

"You went in the front last time," came the infuriated reply from Heidetraud.

"That's 'cause I'm the oldest," Klaus reminded.

"Walk! Don't run!" Mrs. Hoess commanded, and the children obeyed immediately, though continued their aim briskly.

"They seem rather thrilled," Eleonore spoke to Mrs. Hoess and Roza glanced at her in astonishment for the casualness in her tone.

"Where are they going?" Eleonore continued when she didn't pick up on the hint from Roza.

Turning toward Eleonore with an air of indignation, Mrs. Hoess narrowed her brow slightly, "I like you, Miss Hodys, but be careful of becoming too familiar."

"Yes, ma'am," Eleonore shot her eyes down at her feet, feeling the shame of her transgression.

"I'll leave you to your work," Mrs. Hoess left the two women alone.

"Don't let it concern you," Roza tapped Eleonore on the arm. "As I said before: she's strict but kind. Keep to yourself, though, as I doubt she'll forgive another breach."

"I should best get to work then," Eleonore felt the anxiety of having accomplished next to nothing.

"The supplies are in that box," Roza pointed to a little, wooden toolbox and Eleonore opened it up to reveal matching thread and needles of various sizes and purposes.

"Do you need anything else?" Roza asked as she watched Eleonore with curiosity.

"I'll just need to know where the washroom is," Eleonore said quietly. Her stomach was still reeling from eating too quickly and she assumed she would need the facilities sooner or later.

"You'll be restricted to the washroom in the attic," Roza pointed back out into the house. "I'll be off to resume my duties."

"Thank you," Eleonore straightened.

"For what?" Roza crossed her arms.

"For your guidance," Eleonore tilted her head.

"I, for one, hope there will be some more jobs for you after this," Roza grinned. "I might just 'accidentally' tear up a carpet or two in the living room."

"It'll be me they suspect," Eleonore giggled.

"You're too sweet for that," Roza shook her head. "Anyways, I'll check up on you in a bit. Oh, they were going off to school."

"Pardon?" Eleonore frowned.

"The children. They were going to school," Roza smiled quickly and then left.

"Ah," Eleonore's frown soured as she thought about the peculiarity while Roza departed from view.

Rather odd, Eleonore thought. *The world has been handed over to death, yet the devil still finds time for his children's education. I wonder if they know what is happening here? I wonder if Mrs. Hoess knows?*

The grandfather clock from the living room ticked impatiently, reminding Eleonore that time was against her. She sat on her knees in the small storage room as the sunlight poured in through the window, warming her skin. *It's only a piece of carpet,* she tried to pacify her guilt as she stared at the Nazi symbol. *It's unlikely if I leave it that Hitler's empire will fall. I will fall, that's for sure, and no one will care to remember me or write songs of my valiance for refusing to fix a carpet.*

Focusing on her project, Eleonore moved over to the torn section and, heaving the heavy carpet onto her lap, took out the needle and thread and prepared her supplies. There was little that could shake Eleonore's concentration now that she had become locked into her momentum.

How close she felt to home at that moment yet, in the same breath, so far away. All she wanted was to rewind and retrace her steps to make the choices that would've enabled her to carry on her perfect life. But such reflections would have to wait as Eleonore's mind delved into the void, shutting out all thought apart from the motions of the needle and thread.

This thoughtless chasm had been her ever-present escape from troubles. On birthdays, with the absence of friends, she would sit at her table in her flat and create new, wondrous designs and forget her loneliness. At Christmas, she would sew something for herself as a gift, shunning the hideous thought that she had no family apart from her adopted Ruth and Alex.

To her discredit, Eleonore often became so lost in her work that her other senses fell obsolete. Time stood still yet the day passed within minutes, her ears fell deaf, and the only thing which mattered was the fabric in front of her.

Some mistook this preoccupied behavior, which plagued her since she was a little girl, as self-absorption. To an extent, they were correct, but it was more of a self-drowning out of consciousness than a selfish pursuit. When she had taken it upon herself to reflect on her behavior, Eleonore believed that her isolation stemmed from her experiences as a child, or rather, witnessing her parents' struggle with the challenges of life.

While she was mostly sheltered by her mother, the harsh whispers or the sudden rage from her father could not be filtered out and Eleonore was aware of something inauspicious. To the present day, Eleonore didn't know exactly what had transpired or why, but she knew enough to understand whatever harrowing situation they fled in Austria had followed them to Berlin.

During her father's spouts of anger, Eleonore's mother would give her a toy, put her in a room, and wait until it was safe for Eleonore to rejoin them. In her ignorance, Eleonore would play contently with her toys, drowning out the foul cursing of her father and the sobs of her mother. She learned to avoid challenges, ignore them until they passed, instead of facing them properly.

This evasion spilt out into the social arena where a young Eleonore had difficulty making friends. She recalled a trip to a beach with her parents one summer, and while the other children splashed in the waves or created sandcastles, Eleonore was off by herself digging through the rocks, seeking ancient and beautiful gems. She had heard of arrowheads being found in rural areas, and while she doubted she would be fortunate enough to find any, she was devoted to trying nonetheless.

In her adolescence, too, this avoidance continued, and she was often teased for her reclusiveness. While she detested the bullying, she preferred the isolation, so she tolerated the vilifications with grace. While her parents were concerned, and her teachers saw a child failing with socialization, such a temperament allowed her to be kind to others of a similar disposition. Such as the officer Horst who had warned her in Berlin that her name was on a list.

Then, snapping her out of recollection was a creak on the floor from the hallway. Her heart stopped, and she ceased breathing to listen closely as she watched with wide eyes. The creaking had stopped, almost as if the host was aware their presence had been noticed. Then, the stench of thick cologne invaded her senses, betraying the culprit as an officer. While she had hoped it was Jung, the scent was not the harsh, severe smell he wore, but rather, a light fragrance mixed with sweat.

Eventually, the steps continued, and the black boots of an officer came into view and then stopped in the doorway and turned towards Eleonore. Looking up, Eleonore saw the intimidating figure of Commandant Hoess staring back at her with a restrained, but building, anger.

"You're Seven Five Six Nine Three?" Hoess asked as he squeezed his hand into a fist.

Eleonore nodded. *Does he not recognize me?* Eleonore wondered. *Did a shower and new clothes change my appearance that drastically?*

Throwing his hands behind his back to stifle any outburst, Hoess peered into Eleonore with all the hatefulness in his heart, "As a political prisoner, you should not be in my home. How dare you come anywhere near my wife and children."

Eleonore's heart pounded as she waited for Hoess to raise his fist or kick her with his boot, but he only stared at her with menace. She wanted to explain how little choice she had in her assigned station, but she knew that would only produce ill fruit. *You are what they deem. Nothing will change that,* she reminded herself and kept quiet.

Hoess huffed and drew a deep breath before continuing with the humbling statement, "My wife has expressed her desire to keep you employed. You can thank her for her misplaced mercies."

With that, he marched out of the room, leaving Eleonore in a state of shock. She tried to focus again at the task, but her mind was reeling with dreadful imaginations. The Commandant had the look of one who was absent: a deranged psychopath removed from reality.

But another thought arose in contest as a comforting notion: Mrs. Hoess had saved Eleonore. Why, she didn't know, but was pleased at least that she had one of the most powerful people in her 'world' as a sort of protector. She assumed to have lost her standing with the 'angel' of Auschwitz when she had been too familiar, but was glad to see she was incorrect.

Keep your head down and do a good job. Maybe then Mrs. Hoess will find me a different assignment and I can stay here, away from the terror of the camp. God do I ever want to go home.

Chapter Fourteen: Duplicity

"Then out spoke brave Horatius,
The captain of the gate:
To every man upon this earth
Death cometh soon or late.
And how can a man die better
Than facing fearful odds,
For the ashes of his fathers,
And the temples of his gods."
Thomas Babington Macaulay,
Lays of Ancient Rome.

"Oh, is that ever nice," Roza rounded the corner, astonished with the progress Eleonore had made with the carpet.

"Well," Eleonore was made bashful with the praise and pinched her lips together. Though she was aware of her talents, her parents had instilled into her the necessity of humility which made compliments difficult to acknowledge.

"I suppose you'll have to come back tomorrow," Roza leaned against the door frame.

"What time is it?" Eleonore glanced at the window to find the sun had already set.

"Late. But don't worry, you can eat supper here," Roza nodded for her to follow and they walked back towards the kitchen, "then you'll need to return to the camp. An escort should arrive shortly."

"An escort? Just for me?" Eleonore beamed proudly.

"Well for everyone who works in the Villa," Roza squinted, wondering how Eleonore had misunderstood.

"Of course," Eleonore shook her head, feeling silly. "Today was rather liberating, and my good spirits have caused me to be somewhat erratic."

"You were in your own little world for hours on end," Roza grinned, "oblivious to the chaos around you."

"Chaos?" Elenore frowned, curious as to what she missed.

"Oh, just the children in their natural state," Roza spoke over her shoulder as she led Eleonore to the kitchen.

"I see," Eleonore nodded, but became distracted by a wonderful smell spilling down the hallway.

"Roast chicken tonight," Roza wafted the air towards her face as she inhaled.

Returning to the back room, Eleonore and Roza sat expectantly as Sophie brought them and herself a plate of food. Digging into the chicken, potatoes, corn, peas, and gravy, the three didn't speak a word until finished. Eleonore relished in their company and in the satisfaction of filling her belly twice in a single day, something she never thought to take as a measure of success.

"You have a gift, Sophie, a real gift," Eleonore wiped her face with a silk napkin. "I didn't think I could eat any more after that extraordinary breakfast, yet here you've ensnared my senses to indulgence."

Staring at Eleonore with a blank expression, Sophie turned to Roza for an interpretation.

"She means you're amazing," Roza patted Sophie on her arm.

"Then why didn't you just say that?" Sophie looked at Eleonore with slight annoyance for the pretension.

"Do you simply throw the chicken in the oven? No, you take your time perfecting it with the correct spices and herbs until it's the most delicious piece of poultry anyone has ever had the pleasure of tasting," Eleonore defended as she swelled with passion. The assignment and the refined rations were rejuvenating her spirit. "So it is with language, though I'm not as eloquent as I prefer, but what good is communication if all we impart is what animals can convey to one another? Why not push our minds and intellect to the edge of poetry to extract that which separates man from beast and raises us to a pinnacle before untouched by previous species?"

"I never knew you were so zealous," Roza studied Eleonore as her mind hinted at hidden designs.

"They're here," a servant girl burst into the backroom.

"Who's here?" Eleonore wondered as the others stood quickly.

"The guards to take you and a couple of others back," Roza brushed herself off and motioned for Eleonore to stand.

"Already?" Eleonore panicked as she shoveled some more corn into her mouth.

"They must be a little early," Roza held out her hand, signaling for Eleonore to hand her something.

"What?" Eleonore shrugged and looked about her person in confusion.

"The wig," Sophie removed her golden locks to reveal a head of short, greasy brown hair which had been flattened. Then, with a sympathetic smile, returned the wig snuggly on her head, being one of the fortunate souls permitted to live within the Hoess Villa.

"The clock has struck midnight," Eleonore gave a sad chuckle as she removed her crown of hair. "I suppose the fiction must end at some time."

"Don't worry," Roza collected the wig from Eleonore, "You'll return. I promise. Now, come with me and we'll collect your old clothes."

Venturing back through the tranquil Villa, Eleonore returned to the attic with Roza where they found her old, regulation outfit where it had been left in the washroom. But as Roza went to collect the clothes, Eleonore stood in the middle of the room and looked longingly at the beds. Resting on iron bars, the thin mattresses didn't invoke a sense of luxury, but in comparison to a cramped, eight-person bunk, they seduced her to covet.

"I remember that feeling," Roza understood the longing in Eleonore's gaze and handed over the old clothes.

"How did you secure such a privilege?" Eleonore grabbed her outfit, grudgingly.

"That's a long story," Roza cleared her throat as she brushed away her unease.

"I'm desperate to hear it," Eleonore pleaded as she changed back into her camp outfit, unconcerned that Roza should watch.

Studying Eleonore for a moment, Roza hesitated but then began, "Not everything at the Villa is delivered solely upon merit. I've done things of which I'm not proud."

"I see," Eleonore gathered Roza's discomfort. "I won't ask you to elaborate."

With a quick smile, Roza held out her hand to the stairs behind Eleonore, indicating politely that time was of the essence.

"I hate these," Eleonore scratched an itch on her shoulder as she descended out of the attic, feeling the stiffness of the poorly made fabric. As one who had spent her life with textiles, the scant craftsmanship was only adding insult to the discomfort.

"Well you can shed them tomorrow when you return," Roza replied as she followed behind Eleonore. "And we'll get you back into that wig as well."

"That would be splendid," Eleonore spoke with longing and ran her hand over her bald head, feeling the prick of her tiny hairs.

"Oh, I forgot to mention earlier," Roza grabbed Eleonore's arm as they climbed down the stairs, "but I overheard the mistress talking."

"And?" Eleonore leaned in with baited-breath.

"Well, it turns out there may be more work for you after this carpet is mended."

"Really?!" Eleonore beamed with excitement.

"I can't promise anything," Roza held up her hand to dilute the excitement, "but I heard Mrs. Hoess talking to the Commandant about keeping you employed for other projects."

"That's...that's..." Elenore was lost for words as she felt immense relief. "...amazing."

I hope Jung is here, so I can tell him the good news, Eleonore smiled but then felt the horror of such a statement. *What?! How could I think such a thing? He's a monster! Besides, if things proceed as I hope they do here, then I won't need his protection for much longer.*

Still, her heart leapt when she returned to the foyer to find that Jung had been dispatched, along with two other guards, to collect the ladies returning to the camp. Lining up neatly before their escort, Eleonore and the ladies waited patiently as Jung looked over his clipboard and then at each lady, three in total, and checked off their numbers.

But Eleonore's high spirits sunk when Jung wouldn't so much as offer her a glance. Whatever affection Jung may have held previously had now faded, or he was simply disguising it well. Not even twelve hours ago he had been watching her as a hopeful lover, leaving Eleonore to wonder what had happened.

"Let's go," Jung opened the door and the ladies marched out in silence to the cold of winter, followed closely by the guards.

Last in line to leave the warmth of the house, Eleonore stepped passed Jung as he gave a pat on her back. Anyone else would have assumed he was only hurrying her along, but there was a tenderness in his touch that convinced Eleonore it was meant with care. Maybe, after all, his concern for her was genuine.

Are those sleigh bells? Eleonore wondered at the distant jingling and, just as they had stepped outside the house, the Hoess family arrived laughing away in the pinnacle of giddiness. Even Hedwig had forsaken her reserved temperament and was cackling with wild abandon.

"Keep moving," Jung ordered the women who had paused to watch.

Usually, such cheerfulness would be contagious, but none who watched were smiling, understanding the stark inequality between this family and the hundreds of thousands just across a barb-wired, electric fence.

"Up we go," Hoess called out, and Eleonore watched as the Commandant picked up his children off the sleigh with a kiss on their cheek as any loving father would.

They were a happy family, and this disgusted Eleonore. She was repulsed by the Commandant's ability to enjoy such pleasures while simultaneously suppressing guilt for removing countless others of the same opportunity. The Hoess family continued in their gaiety by throwing snowballs at each other and screaming in delight.

The cries of joy echoed across the snow and bounced into the camp, reminding so many families of what had once been. The winter celebrations with their loved ones who were now dead or dying, the songs of cheer which had now fallen silent, and the happiness to which they could never return. Eventually, the Hoess family migrated their amusement indoors, shutting out the world from experiencing their pleasure vicariously.

Continuing in silence, the women approached the camp but, as they drew near, Eleonore noticed a train was stopped near the gates. No steam rose from the engine and with the lights off, she assumed it had been there for some time. Which was curious as the procedure, from what she could tell, was to have the 'shipments' work endlessly, meaning the trains left as soon as their cargo had been dropped. Still surprising was that there were only a handful of cars attached to the engine and the prisoners were just now being taken out.

Something's different, Eleonore watched as these prisoners didn't behave in the mindless manner that Eleonore had been packed in with. Instead, they looked savage; deranged. The guards, also, behaved oddly as they weren't shouting orders, no dogs were barking, and the victims seemed almost desperate to get into the camp like it was some sort of haven.

"Quickly!" Jung moved to position himself between the women and the train, and Eleonore caught the look of horror in his eyes as he spurred the women onwards.

"Help them!" Jung ordered the two guards with him and pointed towards the train, but they pretended not to hear.

"Help them!" Jung grabbed a guard's shoulder, but he shook his head in terror, refusing the order.

Wrapping their shawls over their heads, the other women with Eleonore cried and covered their eyes while running towards the gates. All except Eleonore seemed to understand what was happening, and she was driven mad with curiosity and dread as they hurried along.

It was only when she beheld what they all feared did she wish to persist in her ignorance, but it was too late. She had become aware of one of the most horrific images she had ever seen. For as they ran towards the gate, the last train car that was closest to the engine was opened to reveal a scene so disgusting that not even her most depraved imaginations could conjure.

Stunned, Eleonore stopped in her tracks as she saw dead, naked bodies lying in the car with their noses, fingers, genitals, and various limbs missing. One body was missing a whole half while another had become unrecognizable with bits of their face torn. Bite marks could be seen on the bodies, and Eleonore at once knew the truth: cannibalism. The prisoners had been pushed to the brink of starvation and their fallen brothers and sisters had been used to keep them alive.

Reeling with revulsion, Eleonore vomited, tasting again the once-proud meal she had eaten only moments ago. How could she ever indulge again after witnessing this horror? In despair, she fell to her knees, unable to take her eyes away from the awfulness.

"Stand up!" Jung stood in front of her, his back towards the train and panic dominating his spirit.

But Eleonore couldn't move, and she stared past him at the hellish scene. She knew how easily that could've been her, and she wondered how long those unfortunate souls had been traveling, left unattended with their own dead. Only in the extreme would hunger move someone to behave in such a depraved manner.

A gun fired.

Startled, Jung drew his pistol as he crouched down and put his arm out to shield Eleonore.

With a ringing in her ears, Eleonore looked in the direction of the shot – a mere few feet from her – and saw a soldier lying on his back. Blood was flowing from his head, creating a crimson puddle in the snow, with his hand still grasping the smoking pistol.

"Not again," Jung sighed and holstered his weapon. Signaling to the two other guards, Jung took out a notepad and tried to make a note, but his hand shook. Slapping his hand against his leg in frustration, Jung attempted the note again with more success.

The dead guard stared blankly at Eleonore, and she spotted stains on his face where tears had fallen. She felt immense pity for him: a man's whose conscience had spoken and he, unlike the others, couldn't drown it out any longer. He had elected to take his life instead of facing another day in his post, being responsible for the most horrendous events known to man.

Even the guards, who were used to making fun of the prisoner's misfortunes, found the image too much to bear. They kept quiet with their eyes lowered and remained distant.

"I'll take you from here," Jung rounded up the women and guided them towards the gates.

As they approached, Eleonore doubted they would be able to get past the fresh passengers with much success as they were clamoring around the gates, begging to be let in. They were shouting in Polish but from their tone, Eleonore assumed they viewed Auschwitz as some sort of refuge.

"Move!" Jung ordered the crowd, but they didn't listen.

"Now!" he shouted and drew his pistol.

Still, they disregarded the officer and directed their attention to the guards on the other side of the fence who were clueless as to how to react. Ignorant hollering occurred on both sides as the young guards aimed their rifles at the prisoners, threatening violence in German while the inmates continued their demands in Polish. With their hands stretched out, the prisoners were nearly touching the electric fence, unaware of its potential harm, all while looking over their shoulders at the train, half-expecting something sinister to appear.

Seeing that reason had abandoned them, Jung resolved to use force and, removing his baton, began striking at them to move out of the way. Escorting Eleonore and the other two women, Jung was able to clear a momentary path through the thicket of frail bodies.

Yet Eleonore felt herself close to fainting as she squeezed through the crowd. Witnessing the event was traumatic enough, but to be plunged into its depths was hellish. And the smell, that stench of urine, feces, and blood, was enough to drive a person mad.

"Open up!" Jung shouted to the guards on the other side of the gate.

"I can't! Lieutenant, I can't," the guard refused while bouncing the aim of his rifle between inmates.

"That's an order!" Jung grew enraged.

"What about them?!" the guard indicated with his rifle to the crowd.

"Shoot any that give you trouble," Jung threw his hand into the air as if the answer was obvious.

Cold sweat ran down the panicked guard's face as he struggled to contemplate the right course of action, but finally he relented and, lowering his rifle, opened the gates.

Like water bursting from a pipe, the crowd surged forward into the camp, and Jung pulled Eleonore and the other ladies to the side, saving them from being trampled.

"Stop!" The guard aimed his rifle but there was little he could do against so many.

Not resolved to kill, the guard began striking people with his gun, but still, they pressed forward in a maddened craze. Their reckless abandon was not entirely without reason, Eleonore understood. She watched as they glanced over their shoulders, running as fast and as far as they could from a terror beyond words.

Eventually, more guards arrived at the scene with large, black dogs which only generated further disorder. Forming a perimeter around the Polish Jews, the Nazis shouted in German for them to stop and, thankfully, they submitted at last. Tired, cold, and traumatized, the Poles slunk down to their knees and wept for their misfortunes. Even their oppressors took pity on them and Eleonore watched as a guard or two helped the inmates to their feet. Most guards, however, remained in their wickedness and cared not for their sorrows.

"Let's go," Jung waved to Eleonore and the other two to proceed.

Led back through the camp, they walked through the tunnel with the electric fence and, again, Eleonore thought of her first day at Auschwitz, witnessing the other inmate drop dead from brushing against the fence.

It's incredible how much has transpired in so short a time, Eleonore thought as she rolled up her sleeve and inspected her almost forgotten tattoo. *Those poor people,* she thought back to the events at the gates, *they're about to be shaved and marked, just like I was. Though, I suppose most of my experiences would pale in comparison to theirs. Odd to think that it could get any worse and there are still things to be thankful for.*

In silence, the group continued through the camp until they came to the first set of barracks and, as fortune saw fit, Eleonore's lodgings were last. Discharging himself from their care, Jung left the other women at their assigned barracks and continued alone with Eleonore.

"Here," Jung handed Eleonore a cigarette as they walked at a more casual pace.

"I'm not allowed," Eleonore shook her head. Besides, she didn't think she could stomach anything at the moment.

"Didn't stop you last time I offered," Jung persisted.

"It's too open here. Someone will see and report me."

"So be it," Jung closed the silver case.

As he returned the cigarettes to his jacket, Eleonore noticed a slight shaking of his hand, betraying the lingering effects of the trauma. She remembered the look in his eyes when he knew what awaited on the train and his inability to write steady notes. Despite the callousness he tried to convey, these events still troubled him deeply.

Yet her concern with Jung faded as her mind retreated into the harrowing memory, and all she could see was the half-eaten body, the naked dead, and the deranged, psychotic passengers.

"Just one puff," Eleonore broke and snatched the cigarette from his mouth.

With a deep inhale, she thrust the cigarette back into his hand. It was strange being so nonchalant with her guard when she had just witnessed the greatest of horrors, but there was something that craved normality; a counteraction between two humans that fit within the common sphere.

"Earlier you said, 'not again,'" Eleonore spoke candidly to Jung as the recollection of the suicide jumped back into her mind.

Jung looked at her but didn't answer. Instead, he took another puff and began to quicken his pace, sensing Eleonore would not relent in her interrogation.

"Answer me," Eleonore tugged on Jung's jacket, forcing him to stop and look at her.

"What good will it serve?" Jung tossed his dwindling smoke into the snow and produced another from his silver casing.

"What do you mean?" Eleonore frowned.

"Is it correct that you have no children?" Jung paused as he awaited Eleonore's response.

"That's right, but what does that have—"

"If you had children then you'd understand that some troubling details of life are best kept hidden."

"Such as?" Eleonore frowned, unsure of where this conversation was heading.

"Things they shouldn't know," Jung replied with a puff of his cigarette, letting the smoke rise and conceal his face.

"Are you saying I'm a child?" Eleonore fumed.

"I'm saying that you're innocent," Jung sighed. "It's evident in your innocent eyes. Is it so wrong for me to admire that about you?"

How could such a detestable man also seem of such excellent character? Eleonore thought as she was left speechless by his blunt flattery.

Then, Jung gently squeezed Eleonore's shoulder with his free hand and offered her a charming smile. Her heart pounded in her chest as she didn't refuse this advance. She knew what he wanted and whether it was lustful or affectionate didn't matter as she craved that physical touch. She needed to feel whole and protected. She hated herself for not pushing him away, but she was willing to ignore his barbarity for the sake of her own gratification.

With a final puff, Jung threw his cigarette away and inched closer to Eleonore. This proximity, however, stirred Eleonore's defensiveness and, finally, conscientiousness won the battle over her longing for safety.

"What are you doing?!" Eleonore slapped his hand away and stepped back.

"I thought you wanted this?" Jung shrugged, but respected her distance.

"How could you say such a thing?!" Eleonore grew indignant.

"Keep your voice down!" Jung looked around at the barracks, making sure none had spotted them.

"After what we just witnessed," Eleonore whispered harshly, "how could you even consider something so indulgent?"

"Don't you understand," Jung raised a defensive finger, "we need each other. Do you think it's easy for me to carry out my duty? You think I enjoy seeing that?"

"You're part of this whole wicked scheme," Eleonore pleaded with Jung's sensibilities. "You are perpetrating these events."

"I didn't put them in that train," Jung threw his hands into the air. "I didn't ask them to be sent here. I didn't starve them for days on end. How could you accuse me of this?"

"The sins of Auschwitz are on you," Eleonore moved within inches of Jung and grabbed his collar, "because you sacrificed your conscience on the altar of duty."

"What would you have me do?" Jung looked back at Eleonore with understanding eyes. He knew she was right, and it was tearing him apart.

"Help," Eleonore shrugged and backed away. "And not just me, but all of us."

"I can't," Jung shook his head.

"You're a coward," Eleonore spoke coldly and watched as her words sunk into his heart.

"I need you," Jung spoke after a minute of reflection, "and you need me."

"Help us and I'm yours," Eleonore nodded.

"I can't," Jung shrugged.

"Then I bid you a good night," Eleonore turned to enter her barracks.

"Do you enjoy working at the Villa?" Jung called after her and she stopped. "I arranged for that, you know, and I can take it away."

"If that's what you feel is right," Eleonore looked over her shoulder and walked briskly towards her barracks, wondering if she had permanently sealed her fate.

Lesser women would have given in to Jung, being that he was tall and handsome, but Eleonore knew that if he had his prize then she would be discarded altogether. He would have his pleasure, then dismiss her and she would be left for dead. The line between chaos and order would be a tight walk, but she must not falter, not at such a critical hour.

Chapter Fifteen: Perversion

"What is a friend? A single soul inhabiting two bodies."
Aristotle

"You're back!" Ella wrapped Eleonore in a giddy embrace when she had returned to the barracks. "I have so much to tell you."

"As do I," Eleonore broke off, still uncomfortable with such familiarity.

"Come, come," Ella grabbed Eleonore's hand and led her back to their bunk. "On second thought, let's talk outside," she grabbed Eleonore's shoulders and spun her towards the door with a glance at the watchful eyes.

Leading Eleonor back outside the barracks, Ella stopped when they were a few yards away and crossed her arms as she leaned in, "the resistance is growing, and we have a plan."

"Really?" Eleonore mirrored her, enjoying the intrigue.

"Yes," Ella nodded excitedly. "Soon we will all be free."

"How?" Eleonore shook her head.

"Well," Ella checked over her shoulder, "I've been reassigned. Thanks to some clever bribery, I 'm now 'employed' manufacturing weapons in the armory."

"I don't understand how constructing bombs for the Nazis helps the resistance?" Eleonore was thoroughly confused.

"Slight defects here and there which go unnoticed to the untrained eye," Ella winked.

"Genius," Eleonore nodded.

"But that's not the main purpose," Ella lowered her voice even further. "I've been sneaking small portions of dynamite. The men are going to construct some rudimentary explosives to destroy the crematoriums."

"That's ambitious," Eleonore threw her eyebrows up, enthralled but wary.

"What's wrong?" Ella stood back, catching Eleonore's lack of enthusiasm.

"Nothing," Eleonore shook her head, but knew she had failed to keep Ella off the trail.

"Tell me," Ella tilted her head.

"Even if the plan works," Eleonore sighed, "what then?"

"What do you mean?"

"What happens when the explosives go off and the buildings crumble? That won't stop them."

"It's a rather elaborate plan," Ella defended, "and I've only imparted the highlights to you."

"I didn't mean to offend," Eleonore raised her hand. "I'm just concerned is all."

"I know," Ella relaxed, "but even if we can destroy the production of death and bide some time for the Allies, wouldn't that be enough?"

"I hate not knowing what's happening out in the world," Eleonore crossed her arms as she shivered. "Even at the Villa there's no gossip to pick up on."

"Oh, yes," Ella's eyes lit up, "tell me all about the Villa."

"Well," Eleonore paused as she pondered what would be worth telling. She certainly was not going to indulge on how well she was fed, not to someone as hungry as she had been. "The Commandant's family live quite comfortably, enjoying the fruits of plunder. They are a happy bunch, and I doubt anyone besides Commandant Hoess knows what the real business of Auschwitz entails."

"Did you see him?" Ella peered at Eleonore who was beginning to wonder if their friendship went any deeper than Ella's ambitions.

"Hoess?"

"Who else?" Ella shrugged.

"Yes," Eleonore nodded cautiously, curious as to what request was going to follow.

"Excellent," Ella's eyes bounced as her mind ran wild with scheming. "We can use that."

"You mean you can use me," Eleonore grew impatient.

"Don't be petty," Ella lowered her gaze. "This goes beyond either of us. There's no room for sentiment."

"Our enemy believes the same thing."

"How dare you liken me to one of them!" Ella fumed. "I thought you'd be excited about this."

"The potential excites me," Eleonore offered a limp smile to try and pacify her friend, "but I believe you're too angry to see clearly and your attempt at revenge will only increase sorrow."

"I don't believe that's possible," Ella sighed.

"Who'd you lose?" Eleonore continued, tenderly.

"I haven't the heart to tell you," Ella's lips trembled as she looked away. "And I don't want your pity either. I don't want to be included in the list of the poor, unfortunate souls. That's not how I'm going to remember him and that's not how the world will remember me. I'm not some injured creature waiting for the world's charity and compassion."

"Then how do you want to be remembered?"

"As the one who brought down Auschwitz," Ella stood tall with passion swelling in her voice.

"How?"

"By any means necessary," Ella gritted her teeth.

"I fear you'll become like the enemy you're trying to destroy," Eleonore watched her friend.

"No," Ella clenched her jaw and wiped away a tear before it had a chance to form. "I'll become much worse."

Eleonore looked at Ella somberly and wondered if her advantage should run dry, would Ella treat her with expedience like the Nazis? Was it wise to make friends with someone so vengeful?

"It's cold. Let's go back inside," Eleonore shivered.

"Just a few minutes," Ella reached out and grabbed Eleonore's hand.

"I'm freezing," Eleonore pleaded.

"It's not much warmer inside," Ella glanced at Eleonore who agreed with a nod. "You've gone soft on me already."

"What do you mean?" Eleonore frowned.

"You're working inside an insulated home. You've forgotten what it's like to be permanently cold," Ella waved for Eleonore to come close and she rubbed her hand across her back.

"Patrols," Eleonore tapped Ella's leg when she spotted flashlights bouncing at a distance.

In haste, the two bounded up and slipped inside the barracks just before the light landed on them. Quietly, they made their way to their bunk and warmed themselves as best they could against the body heat of their bunkmates. With a smile at Ella, Eleonore gave a yawn and closed her eyes, ready to receive what little sleep would be afforded her.

"Hurry up!" Jung barked as he led Eleonore and the other two ladies back to the Villa after the morning selections and roll call.

Despite his previous threats about removing her from the Villa, Eleonore assumed that he either overstepped his authority, or his threat had been merely idle.

His temperament was more impatient than usual, and Eleonore wondered what part she played in his distasteful behavior. Dark circles underlined his eyes, and he had the look of one approaching the madness brought on by exhaustion. Not that he deserved sympathy, but Eleonore recognized that she should remain wary of any interactions with him in such a volatile state.

The snow had fallen thick last night and the troop of three guards and three women were having difficulty traversing the open terrain towards the Villa. *At least no trains will be coming through today,* Eleonore looked at the empty tracks, lamenting their existence and remembering the events of last night with a shudder.

Finally arriving at the Villa, Jung opened the door and the ladies filed in with the hems of their dresses plastered with snow. They were thankful, at least, for the warmth of the house, and Eleonore breathed a sigh of relief as she left the cold outdoors. The guards, too, tried to warm their hands as much as possible while holding them close to their face and puffing hot air.

Jung, however, seemed unconcerned as he simply gripped the strap of his gun with his hands red from the cold and stared at the floor. His mind was elsewhere, and Eleonore wondered if he was lingering on some distant memory or their recent altercation.

"Late!" Roza rushed around the corner and waved for the ladies to follow.

Obeying, the ladies marched behind Roza as they were taken to the attic to dress in the assigned garb. Eleonore was quick to notice that no showers were offered this morning and no private sessions in front of the mirror. Still, being returned to the cover of her wig was enough to rejuvenate Eleonore.

"You'll have to skip morning rations," Roza ordered and pulled out a piece of paper from her dress with a scribbled list of tasks. "I'll need you to get straight to your assignments without delay."

Eleonore held her stomach but, not wishing to push her luck, did as commanded. Leaving the attic, Eleonore noticed the absence of children screaming happily from the playroom and assumed they must not be awake yet. Continuing quietly down the stairs to the main floor, Eleonore wondered as to the eerie silence. There was no music blaring from the gramophone, no children running, and the only sound stemmed from the kitchen as Sophie was busy preparing for the day.

Then a thought struck her as she stood at the bottom of the stairs: she was alone and unguarded. Apart from the other maids, there was none which could block her flight. All she needed was to walk out the front door and be moments away from freedom. From her position, she could see the foyer, begging her to take the escape which was handed to her so freely.

But it was not to be. A match flickered from the drawing room, and Eleonore watched as the Commandant's face was illuminated while he lit his cigar. Remaining ignorant to her inquisitive gaze, he sat at the head of the table while puffing smoke and reading some documents spread out in front of him under the dim light of a few candles.

Then, out of Eleonore's view, the door from the kitchen opened into the drawing room, briefly flooding the room with light before it closed again. Eleonore knew she shouldn't linger, but curiosity had spurred her to remain in the hopes that she could provide some useful information to Ella.

"What are you doing?" came the puzzled voice of Hedwig.

"Good morning, my sweet mutz," Rudolph spoke dryly while he kept his gaze on the documents.

"Why aren't you in your study?" she asked.

"Too dreary for the morning," Rudolph defended. "Don't worry. I'll have this cleaned up before the children awake."

"And what is this?" Hedwig asked cautiously.

"We shouldn't ask questions we don't want answers to, dear," Rudolph polluted the air with a few puffs from the cigar.

"I can't understand how you smoke those, least of all in the morning," Hedwig shuffled along her trajectory.

Hearing her footsteps approaching, Eleonore attempted to appear as if she hadn't been eavesdropping. Yet Hedwig caught the expression on Eleonore's face and, with enthusiasm, shut the door to the dining room, leaving her and the Commandant in privacy.

She doesn't know, Eleonore frowned and, returning to the storage room, knelt in front of the carpet and lost herself in the work as time slipped on by. Eventually, she was distracted by a warmth on her back and looked over her shoulder to see the sun shining through the window. The clear blue sky was blotted with small clouds, and Eleonore grinned as she felt the sun against her face.

"Oh!" Eleonore startled when she turned back and noticed a girl was standing before her. It was Heidetraud, the oldest girl, and she was looking at her with a blank, observant expression.

"I didn't see you there," Eleonore chuckled as she put her hand to her chest.

Still, Heidetraud didn't reply as she continued to stare awkwardly at Eleonore.

"Can I help you?" Eleonore tilted her head and looked behind the girl, wondering if someone was searching for her.

"What are you doing?" Heidetraud asked innocently, though with an air of arrogance as if Eleonore was treading upon a princess' domain in her father's kingdom.

"Repairing the carpet," Eleonore nodded to her task.

"Why?" the girl came and sat beside her.

"Someone ruined it," Eleonore pointed to the tear.

"Why would they do that?" Heidetraud looked up at Eleonore.

"I suppose there are a few reasons," Eleonore glanced at the Nazi insignia, "but I don't know who it was, so I can't tell you with a great deal of certainty."

"Can I watch you?" Heidetraud folded her legs under her and positioned herself for a long stay.

"I don't mind if you do," Eleonore returned slowly to her work, "but shouldn't you be getting ready for school?"

"Not today," Heidetraud grinned proudly.

"And why is that?" Eleonore took her turn interrogating.

"It's Saturday," Heidetraud continued and with such a happy expression that Eleonore couldn't help smiling back at her. "Besides, it's Christmas Eve."

"It's what?!" Eleonore's smile faded as quickly as it arrived, and she shook her head in disbelief.

"The day before Christmas," Heidetraud enlightened Eleonore. "Tonight, papa is going to read to us, and we get to go on another sleigh ride," she bragged, but in the manner which children are permitted.

"That sounds lovely," Eleonore smiled, but her voice broke as her eyes welled.

Christmas had been a favorite holiday of hers growing up and, after her parents had passed on, Alex and Ruth insisted she joined them. Though Jewish, Alex and Ruth were proud protestants and Eleonore seldom felt she was overstepping her welcome with such charming and gentle people.

"Maybe you can join us," the girl spoke with empathy when she had noticed the tears in Eleonore's eyes.

"Well," Eleonore chuckled, "I doubt anyone would want me invading a special moment with their family."

"Where are your parents?" the girl asked naively, and Eleonore was surprised by her caring nature.

Heidetraud was not at all cruel like her father, or a traditionalist like her reserved mother. Ironically, this was the greatest testament against the pseudoscience of eugenics the Nazis employed in their 'final solution'. Genetics were not solely responsible for a person's behavior and the accident of one's birth did not determine their character.

"They passed away many years ago," Eleonore spoke quietly.

"Does that make you sad?" she asked.

"Would it make you sad if you were all alone?" Eleonore threw the question back.

"I'd get all the toys to myself," Heidetraud's eyes lit up with possibilities.

Eleonore burst into a laugh but calmed herself before continuing, "but wouldn't you miss your siblings or your parents?"

"I wouldn't miss Klaus," Heidetraud stuck her nose into the air. "He's a bully."

"You would too," Eleonore leaned forward. "Believe me. He might be a bully to you now, but when the two of you are older, he will protect you from anything or anyone that might harm you."

"I don't need protection," she drew her hands into fists, demonstrating her strength.

"Of course you do," Eleonore reprimanded. "Sweet girls like you need it the most."

"No," Heidetraud stuck her chin even higher. "I'm the queen."

"Of what kingdom?" Eleonore raised her eyebrows, but then looked at the abundance of wealth the two of them were surrounded by.

"They call me the Nazi Queen," Heidetraud stood and raised her arm with a sort of royal pretension.

"Who's they?" Eleonore frowned.

"All the kids at school, and my teachers," Heidetraud replied as her pride continued to swell.

Probably for fear of your father, Eleonore thought but bit her tongue.

"There you are," Roza came around the corner and half-jogged towards Heidetraud. "I've been looking all over."

"I've been right here," Heidetraud defended.

"That's the problem," Roza held firmly, yet respectfully, on Heidetraud's wrist.

"Does mother want me?" she asked with fear dominating her voice.

"That she does," Roza nodded with the same sort of trepidation. "You're going into town to see the Christmas play and sing carols."

"Really?!" Heidetraud's eyes beamed with joy. "Can Eleonore come too?"

"That's very kind," Eleonore looked longingly at Roza, hoping against hope the answer would be 'yes'. She would do anything to hear the carols and see a tree lit in all its glory.

"I'm afraid she needs to finish this up," Roza nodded to the carpet. "And finish it quickly."

"Why the urgency?" Eleonore began to panic. She had taken her time, as Roza had hinted, to do an efficient job and keep herself from the camp work.

"The mistress wants to have some sort of family gathering this evening and the rug will pair well with her decorations. Will that be a problem?"

"No," Eleonore shook her head and returned immediately to the task at hand. "Just a couple more hours at most."

"Good," Roza breathed again. "Heidetraud, why don't you run along to your mother. She has your dress picked out. I'll be right behind."

Without a word, the girl obeyed as she skipped out of the room humming a song she had likely learned at school. Roza followed behind slowly as she cleaned and walked, picking up toys and trinkets along the way.

With that Eleonore again set herself to her work, forgetting time and being lost in what she loved. Only now Eleonore couldn't seem to shake her hunger. It persisted, previously expecting to be satisfied, yet enduring in emptiness.

It was just such a pricking of the senses that allowed her to continue in her awareness of the world around her. The smells from the kitchen, the cries and laughter from the children, the business of the maids ensuring the house stayed in perfect condition, and the sudden note of music from the dining room.

Someone had started up the gramophone and a delicate pianist played out Wagner's *Song to the Evening Star*. It was so gentle that Eleonore had difficulty concentrating and closed her eyes as the melody reached into her soul. *Such a lonely tune, singing out to the empty sky.*

Is that a cigar? Eleonore sniffed and opened her eyes, although she wished she hadn't. Before her was Rudolph, smoking and studying her with a sort of marvel, not at all the look of disdain which he had displayed earlier.

"Herr Hoess," Eleonore addressed him informally and felt her heart beating.

Yet the Commandant continued staring at her as if she was an inanimate thing. Taking another puff of his cigar he pointed, "Did you notice the tear in the carpet?"

"Uh," Eleonore looked down at the carpet drawn over her lap and then back up at the Commandant to see him smiling.

Did he make a joke? Eleonore frowned in her confusion and didn't know how to respond.

"Papa!" a voice cried out and Heidetraud came slamming into his legs with a hug. "We are going into town!"

"I know," Rudolph smiled lovingly, and Eleonore felt as if she was looking at another man entirely. "I'm the one who is taking you."

"I asked Roza if my friend Eleonore can come but she said no," she pointed at Eleonore who panicked at the drawn attention. Rudolph had been so cross with her yesterday for existing within the same four walls of his family, that she didn't know how he would react knowing the two had spoken.

"I'll have to chat with Roza then, won't I?" Rudolph pretended to be rather serious.

"I need to finish the carpet," Eleonore interjected as she pointed.

"That's the mentality I want you to have," Rudolph knelt and put his hands on his daughter's arms. "Put your mind to your work and don't let anything come in the way of accomplishing your task. No matter the cost," he looked over at Eleonore with a slight smile, "do your duty to your utmost."

"Yes papa," Heidetraud smiled.

"Now," Rudolph put the cigar to his lips, "let's get you bundled up for our journey."

"Rudolph," Mrs. Hoess walked around the corner as well and Eleonore immediately returned to her work, trying to focus.

"Do you not suppose someone will need this?" Mrs. Hoess continued, and Eleonore peeked up quickly to see a fancy dress slung over her arm.

"Another donation," Rudolph kissed her cheek.

"But," Hedwig looked at him full of confusion.

"It's best not to ask questions, dear," Rudolph insisted but Eleonore caught his glance, wondering how much she herself understood.

How can she not know what is happening here? Eleonore wondered. *It's not possible to be this willfully ignorant. Though, I suppose I didn't realize the full extent at first. But does she really believe this is all from donations?*

"Lovely," Mrs. Hoess spoke plainly, and Eleonore raised her head to catch an unimpressed stare from the mistress inspecting what work Eleonore completed.

Conscious of the glares from Mr. and Mrs. Hoess, Eleonore returned to her work as the couple watched her labor in awkward silence, apart from the occasional puff of a cigar.

"We should be off," Rudolph finally spoke and put his hand on his wife's back as he kindly ushered her in front of him, but not before offering Eleonore another admiring glance.

Chapter Sixteen: Christmas

"Give sorrow words; the grief that does not speak knits up the o'er wrought heart and bids it break." William Shakespeare

A bird chirped, and then another. Prying her eyes open, Eleonore saw two birds sitting in the doorway of the barracks, pecking away at something they hoped was food. *To be a bird,* Eleonore grinned at the thought of flying away. *It's so cold,* she rubbed her arms and noticed a chill emitting from the bunkmate beside her.

She's dead, Eleonore thought plainly, growing callous to another loss. She looked at the pale face of the woman, wondering if she was now reunited with her family. The light of dawn was striking her blank, peaceful expression and a part of Eleonore envied the end of sorrows.

It's light out! Eleonore sat up with a start. *I've missed the gong,* she panicked and jumped out of the bunk. *Why did no one wake me?* she grew annoyed, but then paused when she noticed that all the bunks were full. In ghostly stillness, the ladies stared blankly at the ceiling or the bunks above; others were sitting up, fidgeting with their dresses or blankets.

"It's Christmas," Ella explained as she arrived from outside, though absent of the melancholy the others seemed to share.

"That's right," Eleonore leaned her head against the bedpost and closed her eyes.

"Never cared much for the holiday myself," Ella shrugged.

"How can you dismiss such a perfect thing?" Eleonore spoke with a hint of resentment. She didn't want to carry a grudge against her, but Ella's willingness to use Eleonore had left her feeling disposable.

"Want to take a walk?" Ella cleared her throat as she glanced away.

"We're allowed?" Eleonore looked around at the rest of the women remaining stationary.

"The day is ours for the taking," Ella raised her fist in sarcastic triumph.

"Alright," Eleonore wrapped herself in a shawl and followed behind Ella.

"Where are we going?" she asked as Ella led her outside.

"Um," Ella looked around with no real target in mind, "let's go this way."

"Sure," Eleonore perked up and put her arm through Ella's as the two walked aimlessly.

"I've been thinking about our conversation the other evening, and I'm sorry if I upset you," Ella spoke softly. "You've been kind to me, kinder than I deserve, and I returned that thoughtfulness by being rather inconsiderate."

"There's nothing to forgive," Eleonore patted Ella's arm.

"How is the Villa?" Ella continued. "And before you reply, please know that I'm genuinely interested in you, not the Commandant."

"Well," Eleonore checked over her shoulder to make sure none were within earshot. "as it happens, the Commandant is acting rather odd around me."

"How so?"

"The first day he was hostile and not impressed that I should be in his house. Then, yesterday, he seemed happy to have me there. I'm not sure how to read into his behavior."

"Well he is the Commandant of an extermination camp," Ella raised her eyebrows. "It takes a certain type of imbalanced lunacy."

"That's the thing," Eleonore continued. "He doesn't seem unhinged. Quite the opposite in fact. If not for the war, I believe he would have been content to be a farmer or live quietly in the country. It's remarkable that someone can be so merciless yet so genial. Makes him appear all that more malevolent that he can silence his conscience when it suits him."

"Interesting," Ella mused.

The two continued in silence for a while as they walked through the stagnant camp. If Eleonore perceived Auschwitz as lacking joy earlier, Christmas was a new level of miserable. Even the guards seemed to be just short of homesick tears. None dared to speak or take pleasure in the break from their labors as if any added weight to their despair would summon an inescapable chaos.

For most, work and survival had been their only thought. From morning until night, they labored without rest. Now that they were without the day's demands, they were forced to contemplate on the severity of their losses. To Eleonore, this compulsion of idleness seemed crueler and she wondered if it was done by intention.

"Eleonore," Ella tapped her shoulder and pointed towards the gates.

"What?" Eleonore skimmed her eyes along the direction but couldn't detect what Ella had spotted.

"Officer Jung," she pointed again.

"Oh," Eleonore was surprised that she hadn't noticed him, smoking and talking with some other guards. "What about him?"

"Oh come on," Ella rolled her eyes. "Everyone knows."

"Knows what?" Eleonore stopped and looked at Ella crossly.

"Don't worry," Ella laughed. "You're not the first inmate with a secret and you won't be the last."

"But nothing's happened," Eleonore protested.

"Doesn't matter," Ella shrugged. "What matters is what is perceived, and the other inmates believe that you and Jung are having an affair which has elevated you to working in the Villa."

"It's not true!" Eleonore's panic intensified.

"I know," Ella gave a reassuring nod and then watched Jung. "He looks at you with yearning, not the way a man does after a conquest."

"How could they think such a thing without a shred of evidence?"

"Well," Ella shrugged. "The two of you have been seen alone on more than one occasion. Plus, you're beautiful which makes all the others jealous, naturally."

"I suppose that's flattering," Eleonore frowned, "but if it gets me killed then I'd rather be plain."

"You should just be thankful that you're not both Jewish and beautiful; otherwise you'd be working in the brothel," Ella whispered.

"Can this place get any more hellish?" Eleonore grew disgusted. "I don't remember seeing such an appalling establishment."

"It's near the crematoriums," Ella pointed. "I'll show you."

Stopping near the electric fence, the two looked out over the chimney stacks rising from the crematoriums. Their stillness seemed to magnify their malice; waiting like hungry beasts desperate to devour the next victims.

"Do you have feelings for him?" Ella turned towards Eleonore suddenly. "Jung, that is."

"That's what I can't understand," Eleonore refused to look at Ella, feeling rather foolish and selfish for even thinking about herself in the face of such overwhelming hatred as the crematoriums. "I think I see him as a sort of protector, but I don't have affection for him. Who could appreciate a man like that? He's a wild beast, ready to enact whatever punishment, however severe, in the name of duty."

"When the time comes," Ella looked back at the crematorium, "will you choose him over us?"

"Oh Ella," Eleonore looked at her with disappointment. "How could you even ask? You know where my heart lies."

"I suppose one doesn't really know until they are in that situation. No matter how prepared you are, the temptation to take the easy route will present itself, and that will be the real test."

Eleonore didn't respond as she watched Ella looking out over the camp, her mind running rampant with plans of revolution. How she wanted a glimpse of her designs, but Eleonore knew better than to ask.

Then, Eleonore was distracted by the beautiful melody of 'Silent Night' coming from the amphitheater. Turning her attention to the stage, Eleonore watched with amusement as the familiar song echoed throughout the camp from a lonely violinist. The rest of the orchestra sat patiently, waiting for their time to join in. The inmates, too, appreciated the momentary diversion from their sorrows and came trudging out of the barracks and filed in front of the amphitheater.

"Let's go listen," Eleonore grabbed Ella's hand, but she didn't budge.

"I'd rather not," Ella withdrew and crossed her arms.

"I know the memories can be painful," Eleonore studied Ella.

"I have a husband," Ella sighed as she lowered her guard.

"Really?" Eleonore glanced at Ella's hand and saw no ring but, of course, the Nazis had taken her jewelry as well.

"Had a husband, I suppose would be more accurate," Ella shook her head. "We were separated before being placed in the train, where I met you, and I haven't seen him since."

"I'm sure he's in the men's camp," Eleonore tried to encourage her. "You never know, he might be sitting in front of the orchestra right now."

Ella fiddled with her hands as the tears began to well, "He was sick."

"I see," Eleonore slouched, understanding the implication.

"That's why I behaved so rashly during the first roll call," Ella wiped her eyes and cleared her throat, drawing upon her strength.

"My Bernhard," Ella drew a sad, reminiscent smile. "Stupid thing is I wrote a letter to a friend, the day before we were taken from the other camp and sent here. I told her that our spirits were high and that she shouldn't be afraid, everything will be alright," Ella held her hand over her mouth as the tears streamed.

"I'm sorry," Eleonore didn't know what else to say.

"He used to hum Christmas carols," Ella chuckled. "All year round. And always off-key. I hated it," Ella's smile faded as she thought. "It was tormenting, but I'd give anything to hear him humming again."

Eleonore studied Ella's lips trembling and shaking hands as she struggled to comprehend her loss. How Eleonore wished she could take away her pain, yet she knew it was the fuel to Ella's ambition. She would destroy this Nazi kingdom if she could, and such an objective was driven purely from a desire for revenge.

"I can't wait," Ella's countenance fell into bitterness as she gritted her teeth while looking at the crematoriums. "I can't wait to make them taste death and to see their glorious flag and leader trampled."

"When will it happen?" Eleonore spoke softly.

"Not soon enough," Ella glanced at Eleonore. "I'm sorry. This is why I don't speak of my husband. I become resentful which makes for poor company. But they took him from me," she began to cry again. "I'm so very angry. All I want to do is scream. Still, I know Bernhard would want me to be happy," Ella spoke as her lips trembled. "He was one of those annoying people who could find the positive in any circumstance. Whenever I grumbled or complained, he'd find a way to lower my defenses and procure a smirk."

"And what would he want you to do now?"

"He'd want me to help as many people as I could," Ella grew bold as she stood up straight.

"Are you going to destroy the crematoriums today?"

"No," Ella glanced at Eleonore, curious as to her direction.

"Then how can you help them today?" Eleonore pressed, but when Ella didn't answer, she continued, "I know the memories are difficult to bear, but make some new ones with me."

"There is no memory of this place I want to carry away," Ella shook her head. "I'm sorry, but I can't."

"You want to help them, don't you?" Eleonore nodded back towards the camp.

"Of course," Ella shrugged.

"Then come with me. Sit, smile, and enjoy the music."

"What good will that do?" Ella grew cross. "They'll still all be killed."

"And wouldn't some joy be beneficial in one's final hours? You can't protect them from the sins of the Nazis. Not yet, at least. But what you can do is help them rise out of the psychological terror imposed by this camp. Stir them to remember what happiness felt like, what joy could mean for the soul. Then, maybe then, you will encourage the masses to remember what is worth fighting for. If not for themselves, then for each other."

"Are you a medium?" Ella studied Eleonore.

"Pardon?"

"I do believe that you're channeling my Bernhard," a smile grew in the corner of Ella's mouth and Eleonore smiled back.

"Just one song," Eleonore persisted.

"Alright," Ella nodded, and held up her finger, "but just one."

"Agreed," Eleonore extended her hand. "Then you can return to your misery."

Together, the two walked back into the heart of the camp towards the amphitheater. A crowd was beginning to form and soon the chairs placed in front of the orchestra were filled with solemn and expressionless creatures.

Men and women sat beside each other – something strictly forbidden but allowed on this special occasion – and old acquaintances passed little waves while dear friends embraced. Wives and husbands wept as they were reunited and saw the sorry state in which their loved ones had devolved.

"Why do they get to hold their husbands again?" Ella spoke under her breath. Her resentment was returning under the pangs of jealousy and made the bittersweet reunions something to be detested. She wished she could delight in families being rejoined, but they were only a painful reminder that she should never again embrace her Bernhard.

And Ella was not alone in her resentfulness. Many were left without surviving family members. Their children had been taken and their elderly parents transported to the hospital, never to be seen again. They, like Ella, remained isolated in their fear, wondering when their number would be called in the selections.

The orchestra, too, was weeping as they played the Christmas carols of peace, love, and forgiveness reverberating across a camp filled with fear, hatred, and death. The meaning fell on deaf ears as the survivors had been stripped of the 'fruits of the Spirit' and given over to a tyrannical regime. The old world had been driven out, and these songs had no implications here, except maybe for forgiveness. But who could forgive this?

As they came closer to the amphitheater, Eleonore noticed that even some of the guards were trying to hide their tears without success and were quickly removed from their post. They, too, felt the conviction from the strings of the violin and cello, reminding them of their humanity, of their time spent with a loving family or how they had robbed so many of the opportunity.

Only those absent of emotion survive here, Eleonore observed. *Even amongst our enemy; only the hardest soldiers can survive. If they disobey their orders they are shot – or worse – and if they carry out their duty, they cannot live with themselves. Not that they are guiltless,* Eleonore spotted Jung as he joined a group of soldiers listening to the orchestra, smoking but quiet and respectful.

"There," Ella pointed at two empty seats and the two sat near the aisle at the back.

Grasping Ella's hand, Eleonore sat with a heavy heart as she listened to her favorite carols. A voice or two could be heard from the crowd, singing half-heartedly along with the stringed instruments. Part of her wanted to belt out the words, to sing them as loud as she was able, but she refrained and listened quietly. There was no telling if this would be her last Christmas, and she wanted to soak in every detail. If she survived, she wanted to remember what this terror felt like, and if she died, then she wanted to go with at least one more happy memory.

Yet Eleonore couldn't help feeling the loneliness of being without her mother and father or Alex and Ruth. She thought of all the years they had spent together around a simple table exchanging sentimental gifts. That was Alex's rule: the gifts could be any price, but they must mean something; otherwise Christmas was lost to consumerism.

But a creeping feeling arose from her peripheral vision as a pair of watchful eyes distracted Eleonore from reminiscing further. Turning slowly, Elenore locked gaze with a grinning Jung. He was staring at her with that arrogant smile men offer when they have convinced themselves the attraction is mutual.

Tossing his cigarette into the snow, Jung took a deep breath and began walking towards her. With her heart beating, Eleonore shifted in her chair, unsure of his intentions. But suddenly Jung stopped in his tracks, and Eleonore studied him with curiosity. Then the scent of a sweet cologne wafted around her and Eleonore's breathing ceased.

Looking up slowly, Eleonore's dread was confirmed when she saw the Commandant standing over her with a blank, observing expression.

"Commandant Hoess?" Eleonore asked and glanced back towards Jung, catching his disappointed gaze. "How can I help you?"

"You can't," Hoess looked up at the orchestra and seemed to be rather unsure of himself and fumbled awkwardly with his hand on her chair. "Come with me."

"Have I done anything wrong?" Eleonore began to panic but tried to hide her concern.

"I just want to talk," Hoess tapped the back of her chair before walking away, indicating that Eleonore should follow.

"Alright," Eleonore gave a worried look to Ella who seemed to share the concern with a quick squeeze on her hand.

Swallowing, Eleonore followed Hoess about a half step behind with her hands held politely, yet nervously in front of her. She caught the curious glances from the other inmates and guards, wondering what connection Eleonore had with the Commandant.

"There," he turned when they had walked about twenty yards away from the chairs, "now you don't have to sit with all those Jews."

Eleonore shot him a surprised glance at the dismissal. *Is he not aware of my affiliation with Ella?* She wondered.

"Unless you prefer the company of degenerates?" Hoess leaned in with an interrogative gaze as if trying to uncover her true leanings.

"No," Eleonore shook her head, disgusted that she had blurted out the denial so quickly. Looking back at Ella, she saw her worried expression and Eleonore gave a brief smile to show that she was alright.

How could I have forsaken them so quickly? Eleonore wondered. *I abandoned Ruth and Alex with almost no hesitation. Which, I suppose, will keep me alive, but at what cost?*

"Here," Hoess took out a cigarette and handed one to Eleonore.

"I'm not allowed," Eleonore put her hand up, but Hoess gave her a look which suggested her refusal would deliver a worse punishment.

"Those rules are for the Jews," he whispered and, taking his lighter, held it near her face as he ignited her cigarette.

"You did fine work with the carpet," Hoess inhaled his smoke.

"Thank you," Eleonore held her arm uneasily, trying to convey her wish to merely listen to the orchestra.

"Though," he hesitated, "I'm sorry to say I ripped it again."

You didn't! Eleonore turned to him sharply. Two days of work gone?! Despite the nature of the job, it was still her pride.

Hoess shook his head and smiled while taking another puff.

"Oh," Eleonore frowned and turned again to the front.

"I was only joking," he leaned over and explained.

"I gathered," Eleonore nodded and offered a polite smile.

"It wasn't a very good joke," Hoess leaned over again, and Eleonore looked at him with horror, wondering how to answer him.

"I know a better one," Hoess cleared his throat, desperate to redeem himself. "Would you like to hear it?"

"Uh," Eleonore glanced at him and then away. *I wish he'd just leave me alone,* she thought. "Alright."

"The setting is two men meeting at a coffee shop: One says to the other, 'I see you're free. How was the concentration camp?' 'It was great!' says the other. 'Breakfast in bed. A choice of coffee or chocolate, and for lunch we got soup, meat, and dessert. Then we played games in the afternoon before getting cake. After dinner, we took a little snooze then stayed up late watching film.' The first man, astonished, says, 'That's incredible! But I just spoke to Meyer, who was also locked up there, and he tells quite a different story.' 'Yes, well that's why they arrested him again.'"

Eleonore stared at Hoess at a complete loss for how to react. She wondered if she had gone mad and was imagining this preposterous turn of events. Despite the cold reality of the joke, it was humorous in its own merit and she did, surprisingly, obtain a guilty pleasure from dark comedy. Yet she couldn't bring herself to enjoy such a casual remark about the conditions in the camp when Hoess had everything and people like Em and Ella had lost everyone.

"You like that?" Hoess tapped his cigarette to shake off the ash.

"Sure," Eleonore shrugged.

"You'll like this one. I promise," Hoess cleared his throat and checked over his shoulder to make sure none were listening. "It may get me into some trouble, but it's clever: Hitler walks into an insane asylum where all the patients rise and offer the salute. Then, Hitler sees a man who is not partaking. 'Why didn't you greet me the same way as everyone else?' he demands. The man answers, 'My Fuhrer, I'm an orderly, not a patient.'"

At this, Eleonore burst into a laugh and covered her mouth as the back rows turned to look at the disturbance. Laughter was such a rare sound that when someone did venture the expression it was usually coupled with madness.

"Risky, I know," Hoess smiled. "Could land me here in pajamas like yourself, but it's too good to pass over."

"It's genius," Eleonore wiped the tear from her eye. "Thank you for that. I needed a good laugh."

"I can see that," Hoess returned to solemnity. "Someone of your caliber shouldn't be here."

"If only something could be done about that," Eleonore glanced at him.

"Maybe," Hoess puffed his smoke again. "In time. Maybe."

Eleonore's heart leapt at even the hint of hope. *Could I really be free?* She wondered but looked again at Ella and remembered her question from earlier. At the first chance of freedom, could she really abandon Ella?

"The Mrs. has some other projects for you at the Villa," Hoess tossed his cigarette into the snow as it sizzled. "You'll be needed first thing tomorrow morning."

"Understood, Commandant Hoess," Eleonore nodded and smiled at the thought of returning to the splendor. She had dreaded the idea of working at the hospital again and being assigned to the bedpans. Especially now that Ella had obtained 'employment' at the armory.

"Address me as Rudolph, please," Hoess grinned politely. "I'll see you tomorrow," he walked away with one hand in his pocket, leaving Eleonore entirely perplexed.

Chapter Seventeen:
Bird of Prey

"Hell is empty and all the devils are here."
William Shakespeare

Opening her eyes slowly, Eleonore looked at the wood above her bunk. As was becoming her morning tradition, she ran her fingers over the names of those who had gone before. They reminded her that, despite the terror, she was still alive and there was still hope. She realized the fortune of her birth which provided her with the potential of liberation yet wished she could trade fates with someone as deserving as Ella.

Will I have enough strength when the time comes? Eleonore wondered as she threw her feet over the edge of the bunk. Making ready for the day, she heard others rummaging around in the dark with the same intention. She looked at the bunk across from her and, in the dim light of dawn, caught the vacant eyes of an elderly woman; dead. Then, looking a few bunks down, she caught the blank eyes of another woman. Three or four died each night, or so Eleonore counted, and her heart shattered at the regularity. But none stopped to offer a prayer; tardiness was unforgivable to their masters and, if they were late for the roll call, it was likely they would be counted amongst the deceased as well.

Then, Eleonore thought of the strange absence of Ella. She had disappeared after the concert and didn't arrive until late at the barracks, well past curfew. *She probably heard me agree with Hoess that I didn't want to sit with Jews. She knows that's not true, though,* Eleonore rubbed her head in frustration. *Oh, it's too early for these types of thoughts. I need coffee, and not the disgusting brown water here, but the good, strong brands from the Villa.*

Slipping down the bunk, Eleonore was about to make for the 'toilets' when she spotted Ella sneaking back into the barracks.

"Where have you been?" Eleonore asked her friend who brushed passed her without reply.

"Ella? What are you doing?"

"Why should I tell you anything?" Ella looked at her crossly.

"Pardon?" Eleonore squinted in confusion.

"We all heard you flirting and laughing with the Commandant," Ella clenched her jaw and flinched her eye. "You two seem rather familiar."

"I thought you wanted me to get close to him?" Eleonore raised her eyebrows in confusion.

"Close, yes," Ella crossed her arms, "but I didn't ask you to become a Nazi sympathizer. I made the mistake of supposing you were one of us. You don't know our suffering."

"I'm in this camp, same as you!" Eleonore grew red with indignation.

"Same as us?" Ella scoffed. "You work in a rich house where they feed you and treat you like their maid. Do you think we don't know what happens there? You're not part of the resistance."

"How can you even begin to believe that? After everything I've done!" Eleonore threw her hands into the air.

"Your 'sacrifices' have elevated you to a position of privilege," Ella shook her head. "You're playing the game masterfully."

"Game?" Eleonore laughed. "There is no game. I want to live. That's all. That's my only motivation."

"Don't you understand? You have a chance to survive this place, I don't!" Ella tapped her chest. "You can do your work comfortably in the Villa, waiting for the day they release you."

"I didn't ask to be taken to the Villa and I especially didn't seek Rudolph's attention!" Eleonore defended as she raised her voice.

"Rudolph?" Ella laughed ironically. "You're on a first-name basis already? My you move quick."

"What do you want from me?" Eleonore sighed.

"I want you to leave us alone," Ella turned her back.

"If that's what you wish," Eleonore said softly.

With that, Eleonore left the barracks without offering another word to Ella. She was stubborn, Eleonore understood, and didn't anticipate her friend to yield with any ease, but she wasn't about to forsake Ella. Without their friendship, all Eleonore had was poverty.

Seeing that there was nowhere else to go, Eleonore made for the square and stood in her allocated spot, awaiting the roll call. She endured patiently in the cold morning air, surrounded by the crisp blanket of snow. The snowflakes danced softly down to the earth, indifferent to the ground upon which they fell. Turning her eyes to heaven, she watched the endless sheet descend without concern for any that should be locked in this wretched hell.

The dark clouds loomed overhead, making her feel small and insignificant, and promising that the bleak dawn would be met with an ugly grey sky. No birds chirped, no dogs howled, and the only sound was the gentle sighing of trees under a distant wind, prophesying an unkind breeze. But Eleonore was not disheartened by any of these miserable portents as her heart was set upon one thing only: proving herself to Ella. *She'll see,* Eleonore nodded. *She'll see.*

The gong rang, and Eleonore watched as the barracks emptied and each rushed to their allocated position in the square.

"I'm sorry," Ella whispered as she passed by Eleonore and gave a slight pinch on the back of her arm.

There's nothing to forgive, Eleonore wished to say, but Ella was already in position for the roll call and out of earshot. *Poor thing,* she studied her friend, *she's probably starving. She wants to take control of her life, to help those in need but she feels powerless.*

Then, stealing Eleonore's attention, Jung arrived at the square and began the roll call. She watched him full of curiosity, wondering what his intentions were at the Christmas 'concert'. He had wanted to speak with her, that was clear, but Eleonore was left to speculation. Their last conversation had been rather unproductive, but now that the Commandant and his wife had personally ordered her to return to the Villa, she was free from Jung's authority. *Still, what was it he wanted to discuss?* Eleonore squinted. *He seemed so determined until Rudolph arrived.*

The assignments were handed out after selections and the women were marched to their allocated stations. The familiar orchestral procession blared its uncomfortably cheerful tunes. Their luster had dissipated with the passing of Christmas, however, and they returned to their solemn, heartless attempt at the music ordered for them to play.

Leading the women through a now cleared path in the snow, Jung's agitation seemed to Eleonore to have changed directions. He wasn't fidgeting with his hands as much, but now they seemed void of energy as he held them low by his side.

Approaching the Villa, the ladies were ushered inside to find Roza waiting for them in the foyer. As it had been when Eleonore first met her, Roza was burdened with more than was reasonable, making her attempt at cleaning rather inefficient as she juggled the various instruments.

"You two with me," Roza ordered the other ladies when they had lined up in the foyer. "Eleonore, wait here. The mistress has requested to speak with you."

Whatever about? Eleonore began to panic. *Did she hear of Rudolph's behavior with me yesterday at the concert?*

"I'm required back at the camp," Jung played with his cap nervously as he looked at Eleonore. She sensed his wish to continue their conversation from earlier but didn't want to jeopardize his station in such a precarious environment.

"Ah, Eleonore, come with me," Mrs. Hoess rounded the corner and spoke in her monotone manner while offering a limp wave for her to follow.

With a sensation of dread, Eleonore followed Mrs. Hoess down the hallway and past the kitchen until they came to the living room. There was a quietness throughout the house; a sort of tranquility which follows a blissful Christmas.

"Can this be repaired?" Mrs. Hoess pointed to the dining room table. On the table was a simple, green tapestry that pictured a grassy field with a solitary hill to the right-hand corner. While it invoked a sense of solitude, there was a familiarity which gave Eleonore the impression that she herself had been to that exact spot.

Reviewing the tapestry, Eleonore inspected for tears or holes, but found it was intact. There were no rips around the corners, no odd discoloration from exposure to sunlight, and no defects that Eleonore could tell.

"Forgive me," Eleonore frowned, "but I can't tell what needs to be repaired."

"The inscription," Mrs. Hoess tapped the lower right corner.

"Oh! I didn't even notice," Eleonore was impressed with the craftsmanship.

"It eluded me as well," Mrs. Hoess sighed. "But now it can't be unseen, and it stares back at me whenever I admire the tapestry."

"It's English," Eleonore smiled.

"Do you know what it says?" Mrs. Hoess watched Eleonore curiously.

"When it comes to other languages, Italian is my first love," Eleonore leaned into the tapestry, "but I can understand a good measure of English, though it's been some time."

"Can you read it?"

"I'll give it a go," Eleonore squinted as she recalled her studies.

"It's a poem," Eleonore tilted her head, "which reads:

Into my heart an air that kills
From yon far country blows:
What are those blue remembered hills,
What farms, what spires are those?
This is the land of lost content,
I see it shining plain,
The happy highways where I went
And cannot come again," Eleonore chocked on the last line
and cleared her throat to keep the tears at bay.

"Can it be removed?" Mrs. Hoess continued, still absent of
emotion.

"Yes," Eleonore nodded, but wondered why on earth she
would want to remove such beauty.

"You think me cold?" Mrs. Hoess stared at Eleonore.

"I—"

"There's no room for sentiment here," Mrs. Hoess
continued without offering Eleonore the chance to reply. "I
cannot think about the peaceful days or of the simple country
that we left behind. It would tear me apart."

"I understand," Eleonore nodded, but wondered how Mrs.
Hoess could even begin to consider her life here as
misfortunate or inconvenient. Though none would, or should,
feel pity for her, Eleonore understood that Mrs. Hoess was not
content, despite the immensity of wealth surrounding her. She
was a modest woman who desired only a quiet family life.
And while the accruement of material had stirred her to
arrogance, she had not succumbed entirely to avarice which
was evident in her humble apparel.

"Besides," Mrs. Hoess crossed her arms. "Most of this will
be going back to the prisoners when they are released."

At this, Eleonore shot the mistress a confused look. *She
really doesn't know.*

"You mentioned," Mrs. Hoess began and cleared her
throat, uncomfortable with her next inquiry, "that you once
met Stefan Zweig."

"Yes," Eleonore smiled, remembering the book she saw the mistress reading at her first encounter, "that's right."

"Have you had coffee yet?" Mrs. Hoess asked.

"If you mean the brown water they serve in the camp, then no," Eleonore jested.

"It's off-putting to complain," Mrs. Hoess corrected sternly, almost instinctively as if she were speaking to one of her children.

"Of course," Eleonore's smile faded, and she felt the heat of her embarrassment. Yet in the same breath, it was outrageous for someone with everything to tell another with nothing that they should not complain.

"Would you care to join me?" Mrs. Hoess asked rhetorically as she moved towards a couple of chairs set about a small coffee table near the living room window.

Feeling a little out of place and mismatched, Eleonore sat across from Mrs. Hoess, still in her regulation outfit and unadorned without her wig. Thankfully, this severe modesty was appreciated by the Commandant's wife who, apart from a full head of hair, was dressed almost as plain as Eleonore.

Ringing a bell loudly, Mrs. Hoess gave a limp smile as she set it back down and waited for the response. She was an organized woman, one of routine, and conversation was not permitted to commence until the bell had been answered.

"Yes, ma'am?" Roza burst into the living room.

"Coffee, please," Mrs. Hoess ordered, almost showing off like she wanted to impress Eleonore. "And one for my guest as well."

"Of course," Roza nodded but Eleonore caught the twinge of jealousy in her eye.

"Black for me," Mrs. Hoess looked at Eleonore for her to give her order.

"Same," Eleonore glanced at Roza awkwardly.

"So," Mrs. Hoess put her hands neatly on her lap and looked at Eleonore expectantly.

"Right," Eleonore nodded as she searched her memory. "It was some time ago now, long before he was famous. Stephan was still well known, of course, but not to the degree he is now. During the summer of 1932, I walked into a book store in Berlin and saw a man at a table selling books. By the pile left on the desk, it was evident he wasn't having much success. Feeling rather sorry for him, I summoned the courage to inspect. I picked up his copy of 'Marie Antoinette' and nearly fainted when I read the author's name on the front. It was Stefan himself sitting in a pool of self-pity. I had—"

"Here we are," Roza interrupted as she returned with an elaborate pot of coffee and two cups that were equally as intricate. Placing the ornate cups on the table with their gold trim and blue flowery designs, Roza poured the hot, black liquid as the steam rose, enticing desire with its strong fragrance.

"Thank you, Roza," Eleonore looked up at her but Roza ignored eye contact.

"You were saying," Mrs. Hoess grew impatient.

"Yes," Eleonore shook her head, "well, I just happened to have read a previous work of his that…oh…now what was the title. Anyways, it was about an English widow. Ah! Twenty-four hours in the life of a woman, or something along those lines. Which, as it happens, began my interest in the English language."

"So, you met him at a book signing?" Mrs. Hoess fell into disappointment.

"Initially, yes," Eleonore smiled, "but we began talking and, seeing that his opportunity for further sales was diminishing with each passing hour, he invited me to dine with him and his wife. Being that he was Austrian, he was pleased to have a conversation with a fellow-countryman such as myself."

"I can imagine the discussion must have been lively," Mrs. Hoess returned to being impressed.

"That it was," Eleonore's eyes brightened. "We talked for hours about politics, religion, gender, and all the grand ideas that were swirling around in his head. He was rather passionate about Zionism and concerned about the state of his people," Eleonore paused as she realized her error. She had been so caught up in the memory she forgot to contain her own political leanings.

"It's alright," Mrs. Hoess whispered and offered a rare moment of openness, "you can confide in me."

"Mrs. Hoess, can I ask?" Eleonore glanced at the book lying on the coffee table. "Are you not concerned that your husband will be upset?"

"Rudolph has no jurisdiction here," Mrs. Hoess raised her chin slightly. "And please, call me Hedwig."

"It'd be my pleasure," Eleonore smiled.

"Do you know the name they have for me in the camp?" Hedwig asked.

Eleonore swallowed as she looked at Hedwig with a mixture of fear and admiration before answering, "The angel of Auschwitz."

"Do you know why?" Hedwig tilted her head as she peered thoughtfully at Eleonore.

"I've heard you're kind," Eleonore said softly.

"Kindness alone doesn't offer you the designation of 'angel,'" Hedwig stood. "I think I'd like to show you something."

"Where are we going?" Eleonore stood and followed Hedwig, although with nervous anticipation. Besides, she had yet to take a sip of her coffee and she looked at it longingly as she walked away.

"You'll see," Hedwig returned to the foyer and began dressing in her winter garb.

"You can borrow one of my jackets," Hedwig pointed to the coats hanging on the wall.

But Eleonore didn't comply. She remained stationary, watching Hedwig, wondering about her intentions. Besides, borrowing the coat of the Commandant's wife felt criminal, even though she knew the jackets were likely taken from the inmates.

"Go on," Hedwig nodded as she fitted her boots. "We don't have all day."

Reluctantly, Eleonore obeyed and slipped her arms through a heavy, navy blue winter jacket. At once the insulation warmed her and she felt an odd measure of pride. A smile grew on her face as she buttoned herself up, prepared to face the cold of winter.

"Ready?" Hedwig glanced at Eleonore, but didn't wait for a reply as she turned the door handle.

"Rudolph!" Hedwig almost fell backwards in surprise to see her husband standing outside, reaching for the door handle himself.

"Sweet mutz," he leaned in and gave her a kiss on the cheek, but Eleonore noticed his discomfort with the gesture in front of her.

"Why are you home?" Hedwig frowned.

"I, uh," he stumbled and glimpsed at Eleonore. "I forgot something."

"Well, what is it? I'll have Roza deliver it," Hedwig shook her head in confusion.

"It's too complicated to explain," he brushed her off. "Where are you two headed?"

"Why?" Hedwig squinted, but Eleonore wished she had just answered and removed the cowl of mystery, for her sake.

"Only curious," Rudolph shrugged.

"We'll be back within the hour," she nodded for Eleonore to follow along as she exited the house. But as they walked, Hedwig kept looking back at the house, stirring Eleonore's curiosity. Eventually, Eleonore herself looked but wished she hadn't engaged as she locked eyes with Rudolph. He had remained outside, smoking his cigar, and watching them.

"I worry about him," Hedwig looked at Eleonore as a friend. "He works so hard."

Eleonore couldn't believe what she had heard, but kept silent as their boots crunched the snow underneath while Hedwig led them further away from the camp. Thankful at least it was a clear path, Eleonore wondered at the level of trust both Hedwig and Rudolph were displaying. For all they knew, Eleonore could attack Hedwig and make off for freedom. But there was something stopping Eleonore from the rash reaction. Whether it was the hand of fate, or just curiosity to see what Hedwig was about to show her, Eleonore didn't know. Maybe her nature didn't allow her to betray one who had entrusted her; she wasn't fit for that sort of treachery.

"May I ask where we are going?" Eleonore spoke as she held her shawl over her head for warmth.

"Do you know why I asked you to fix the carpet?" Hedwig stopped and faced Eleonore, her nose and cheeks turning a rosy red.

"It was damaged," Eleonore shrugged.

"I have hundreds of carpets. I could care less about that one," Hedwig gave a limp smile and began walking again. "It was an interview, my dear."

Interview? Whatever for? Eleonore frowned as she returned to following behind Hedwig. *That still doesn't explain where we are going.*

"What a beautiful view," Hedwig stopped to catch her breath and pointed out into a valley where the quiet town of Auschwitz sat blissfully unaware. The snow-covered chimneys released a steady stream of smoke, the river had frozen over, and a handful of children could be seen skating on the ice. It was quaint and peaceful which revealed its willful ignorance as malevolent.

"My shop is just down this hill," Hedwig pointed to a moderately sized brick building hidden just inside some trees where two SS soldiers stood guard outside.

Shop? Eleonore glanced at Hedwig but didn't dare ask for clarification.

"I'll give you the tour," Hedwig said with an almost joyful tone and Eleonore thought she caught a skip or two in her step.

Arriving at the shop, the guards saluted and opened the door to a sound Eleonore had almost forgotten: laughter. Stepping inside, Eleonore watched in awe as twelve women worked on dresses and gowns while chatting away vibrantly and laughing so hard that they barely noticed the arrival of two new guests.

Although they were dressed in prison outfits, Eleonore didn't recognize any of them from the camp and wondered where they had come from. Regardless, her attention was stolen by the wonderful craftsmanship. Dresses of grand and exotic designs were hanging, ready for delivery while others were still being designed or sewn.

"Ladies!" Hedwig called over the clamor and at once they ceased their work and chatter and stood at attention.

"Thank you," Hedwig continued and clasped her hands together in a rare bout of excitement. "I would like to introduce you to Miss Hodys. She will be working with me in the house, but in time I hope to have her included amongst your ranks. Miss Storch, may I speak with you? The rest of you, please return to your duties."

At once the shop returned to organized chaos as the women chatted away while working at their sewing machines. Eleonore's fingers itched with eagerness as she watched them work, and she could scarcely focus as Hedwig introduced her to the head seamstress, Hermine Storch. All she desired was to sit at one of the stations and put her pencil to paper and allow the creative engine within her to produce the designs that were begging to be released.

"Isn't that right?" Hedwig turned to Eleonore and she panicked, realizing that she had failed to listen to the beginning of the conversation.

"I'm so sorry," Eleonore's face grew red with embarrassment, "I was distracted."

"I was just advising Hermine that you used to own a shop in Berlin," Hedwig explained, and Eleonore appreciated her patience.

"That's right," Eleonore smiled.

"Sounds delightful," Hermine, who was a stern, elderly woman, spoke plainly. "What was it called?"

"La Venezia," Eleonore boasted. How she missed proclaiming its name and even now she smiled as it reminded her of that perfect, little world.

"I've not heard of it," Hermine remained unimpressed.

"Would you give us a quick tour?" Hedwig asked rhetorically as she proceeded to the back of the shop followed by Hermine and Eleonore.

"There is one mission here:" Hermine began with her chin raised and her hands held firmly in front of her, "to create the most elegant evening gowns found in all of Europe."

"Rather ambitious," Eleonore nodded, "but a noble challenge."

"Indeed," Hermine's patience seemed to dwindle. "This sewing room produces not only beautiful everyday wardrobes, but also elegant evening gowns, the like of which many SS wives could scarcely imagine."

"They're beautiful," Eleonore ran her hand along the fabric of one of the dresses.

"Of course they are," Hermine frowned. "Anything else would be unacceptable."

Mindful of the disposition of the head seamstress, Eleonore refused to say another word as they continued the little tour. Yet Hermine stirred Eleonore to the greatest of jealousy as she showcased previous designs and current creations. If Auschwitz was to be her 'home' for some time, then here is where she longed to work.

But the tour was over as soon as it began, and Hedwig was anxious to return to the Villa. Yet now the return was uphill, and Eleonore's exhaustion was getting the best of her. Not that Hedwig noticed much as she herself was huffing and puffing as they climbed back up.

"I don't know why," Hedwig panted and paused for a break when they had finally reached the top of the hill, "but I tend to forget how steep this path can be. Usually one of the guards drives me, but I thought you wouldn't mind the little walk."

"You thought right," Eleonore lied as she tried to catch her breath, "but I don't think either of us are young enough to attempt that again."

Hedwig chuckled and looked warmly at Eleonore who understood the mistress was not one to offer emotion lightly. Stern, yet kind, Eleonore found Hedwig to be exactly as Roza had predicted and wondered what providence had in store for their acquaintance.

"Let's get out of the cold," Hedwig spoke after catching her breath a little and the two of them returned to the Villa.

But as they approached, they could hear the gramophone blaring from inside the house. Even with the doors and windows shut, the muffled strings of Wagner's compositions poured out.

"Oh, that husband of mine!" Hedwig picked up the pace and opened the door with a huff.

Storming inside, Hedwig muttered curses under her breath, leaving Eleonore behind, and unattended. Looking around, Eleonore saw no soldiers standing guard.

Now is the best chance I have, Eleonore glanced back down the hill which they had just ascended. *Don't hesitate – just run! But where will I go? I have no money, my clothes will be spotted as prison garb, and I don't know a soul who will help me in this part of Poland. Besides, let's say I escape successfully, my name will forever be on the Nazis' list. If, as the Commandant hinted, I can achieve my freedom, then maybe I should opt for a legal out.*

Yet the choice was stripped from her as quickly as it was offered when Hedwig returned to the foyer, "Come in before you freeze," she waved.

Entering the Villa, Eleonor caught the strong, yet sweet scent of a cigar and noticed a haze wafting about from the living room.

"You might as well get straight to the tapestry," Hedwig took a deep breath as she unwrapped herself from the winter apparel. "There are a couple of other projects I have around the house for you, but once those are completed I can get you designing dresses in the workshop."

"Nothing would make me happier," Eleonore stopped a tear from forming.

"Get to it then," Hedwig's friendliness dissipated as she returned to her regal authority in this little kingdom.

Entering the living room, Eleonore spotted Rudolph sitting in a chair directly in front of the gramophone with a cigar hanging out of his mouth. The attempt at impressing her was so obvious that Eleonore had to control her eyes from rolling to the back of her head.

Yet whatever amusement she felt at his blatant behavior, it soon evaporated into disgust with the Commandant's lingering stare. There was the glimmer of desire in his gaze, but it was rather like a distant admiration, as if Eleonore was incapable of reading his intent.

Standing slowly, Rudolph took the cigar out of his mouth and held it down by his side as he walked over to Eleonore. He tilted his head while studying his subject, inspecting every aspect of her being, uncaring that he should make her uncomfortable.

"May I help you?" Eleonore asked politely but alluded to his invasion of personal space.

Still, he did not answer and remained in place, watching her. The record reached its end and the needle played out it's static, hitting a bump on every other rotation. Bump, bump, bump, it went until, finally, Eleonore's salvation approached with the pounding of footsteps down the hall, warning of Hedwig's imminent arrival. At the last moment, Rudolph broke off his gaze and left the living room, giving his wife a kiss on his way past.

"I hate when he leaves that on," Hedwig rushed over to the gramophone and lifted the needle. "He's going to ruin the record. Then what will he listen to?" Hedwig mumbled, and Eleonore smiled at the slight as Rudolph rarely, if ever, listened to anything other than Wagner.

"That's lovely," Hedwig came over to the table and inspected the obliteration of the beautiful poem from the tapestry. "You're returning it to its former glory," she sighed. "Like Hitler and Germany, I suppose."

Eleonore glanced at Hedwig with an uneasy smile. She couldn't quite pin her character. At first, she was arrogant and unapproachable, but now she was warm and kind as if they were the closest of friends. Eleonore also sensed that she held a strong conscience and despised the work her husband undertook or, at least, what she thought was his work. Still, she wondered how Hedwig could praise Hitler while also enjoying the work of Stefan. The doctrine of racial purity had been so ingrained within Hedwig, that she didn't understand the resulting chaos which had been birthed.

But far be it from Eleonore to correct her. This was the woman who was allowing her a chance at redemption and work away from the death camp. While flawed, Hedwig really was the angel of Auschwitz and Eleonore was thankful to be in her graces. Yet in the same breath, she was unable to shake a sense of guilt. Ella was back in the camp, working in harsh conditions and wondering if Eleonore would betray them for the promise of reward.

My sweet Ella, Eleonore sighed. *Soon you'll see where my priorities lie.*

Chapter Eighteen: Revelation

"Never interrupt your enemy when he is making a mistake."
Napoleon Bonaparte

"Out! Out! Out!" shouted some guards and Eleonore, along with the whole barracks, awoke with a start.

Shining their flashlights around the room, the guards hit their batons against the wooden bunks, making a terrible and frightful noise.

Shielding her eyes, Eleonore wondered what devilish design had been implemented. Then she heard the guards selecting women at random to head outside. Petrified, Eleonore slunk back down in her bunk, making herself as unnoticeable as possible and turned her face towards Ella.

"Pretend you're sleeping," Ella whispered and closed her eyes, trying to calm her breathing and Eleonore mirrored her attempt at deception.

"You!" a guard nearby called, but Eleonore didn't dare open her eyes.

"Out!" he grabbed a woman on the same bunk as Eleonore and dragged her to the ground. She pleaded for him to be gentle, but he ignored her.

"You!" he called again, this time closer to Eleonore. Still, she refused to move.

"I'll make an example out of you!" he grabbed the next woman and pulled her out of the bunk. Screaming, she fell to the floor and tried to get away, and Eleonore opened her eyes to watch as the guard held firmly onto her arm and began to beat her relentlessly.

"Stand up!" he wheezed when he had finished, but the woman didn't move. She lay immobile, shaking in pain. Eleonore closed her eyes again as two other guards appeared and dragged the woman out into the cold and flung her to the snowy earth.

Passing by a few bunks, the selecting guard dragged his baton against the wooden posts as everyone held their breath, praying they would be spared. He continued down the line of beds, muttering something to himself and Eleonore thought she heard him say, "Just a couple more."

Curiosity finally got the best of Eleonore but, turning her head, she made a fateful mistake. Locking eyes with the guard, Eleonore winced as he smiled and approached her. Tapping his baton against her shoulder, he whispered, "out."

A waft of alcohol poured off his breath and Eleonore's fear intensified. He was not in his right mind, whatever that was, and she was about to die because of a drunken stupor.

Clearing her throat, Eleonore began, "Commandant Hoess is expect—"

"Out!" he shouted and raised his baton.

Glancing at the other woman who had been beaten, Eleonore knew there was no hope in resistance. Still, she hesitated as she found her legs frozen from fear and glanced at Ella who was staring at her with wide, terrified eyes.

"Now!" he yelled and raised his fist, ready to strike.

"Coming! I'm coming!" Eleonore raised her hand in defense.

Grabbing onto her raised arm, the guard pulled so hard Eleonore screamed in pain as she tumbled to the ground. Thankful at least that her arm was still in place, Eleonore glared at the guard for his mistreatment.

"You've got spirit," he chuckled and ran his hand along her head, feeling her short, prickly hair.

"Stop!" Eleonore swatted his hand away as she stood.

"Easy now," the guard laughed, but then, suddenly, buckled over and vomited. The stench of his alcohol filled the barracks, and all looked at him in utter disgust. It was revolting that such a man should lord over them.

Yet it was this very revulsion that then sparked a flash of bravery within Eleonore. With the guard bent over, his pistol was protruding, tempting Eleonore to relieve it from its holster. Eyeing the gun, Eleonore's heart began to beat as she reached out. A harsh hiss stopped her from behaving rashly and Eleonore turned to see Ella shaking her head.

"Not now," Ella whispered as her lips trembled. "Trust me."

"C'mon," the ignorant guard stood, wiped his mouth, and gave a generous shove for Eleonore to proceed.

"What's the hold up?" another guard peeked into the barracks as he took a swig from his flask.

"Put this bitch with the rest," the drunk guard mumbled as he patted Eleonore's back.

"Are you pissing drunk already?" the second guard laughed.

"Alright," the first guard stumbled out of the barracks and the second guard grabbed Eleonore by the arm as he led her out.

"Move," the second guard ordered Eleonore, along with the rest which had been selected, and pointed towards the gates. "You're to be shot today."

Eleonore's heart fell into her stomach with such a damning statement spoken so casually. *Just shoot us here and be done with it,* she thought as her legs grew heavy.

In bitter silence, the prisoners were marched along the usual route, and Eleonore glanced at the amphitheater, wishing she could hear the strings one last time, even in their untuned imperfection. She looked towards the Villa with its quaint and quiet stillness and wondered if she should've bolted for freedom when she had the opportunity.

"Turn here," a guard held out his arm for the women to file along towards a concrete wall with holes peppered into its surface.

This is it, Eleonore thought when, in the darkness, she was close enough to spot the blood splattered against the wall and the ground.

"Remove your clothes," the first guard ordered and offered Eleonore a horrendous smile.

"Now!" another guard shouted and aimed his rifle when the women didn't comply.

Reluctantly, the women began to undress and shivered in the cold as they huddled near to each other for warmth. The guards shined their flashlights while they whistled and laughed as their victims covered themselves, desperate for dignity.

"Look at this one," a guard shined his light on Eleonore and she turned away, enraged at the humiliation.

"I like the back of her better anyways," another guard joked and they all burst into drunken laughter.

Just shoot already, the depressing thought entered Eleonore's mind and she closed her eyes, waiting for that blessed moment to be reunited with her parents and Ruth and Alex.

"She's peeing!" another guard snickered and pointed.

Feeling a warmth run down her leg, Eleonore glanced down in surprise. She had been so frightened that she had lost control of her bladder and, if it was possible, her humiliation intensified.

"Alright, alright," the first guard drew his pistol. "Enough games. Turn and face the wall."

In silence, the women all turned and joined Eleonore with their backs towards the soldiers. None called out or begged for mercy. None cursed their enemies or prayed for their destruction. There was a quiet, unifying opposition to the Nazis' hatred.

While most were too shocked to even speak, others offered silent tears for those they were leaving behind and for those they would soon be reunited with.

"Take aim," the guard ordered amongst snickering.

They better not be too drunk for a clean shot, Eleonore braced for impact and begged for a quick, painless death.

"Fire!" came the command.

An infinitesimal break in time snapped Eleonore into a moment which lasted seconds yet felt like an age. She had heard stories of people viewing their life's events before their departure, but what she witnessed was nothing at all what she expected. She didn't see the face of her parents or loved ones, nor the shop with its perfection, and neither did she see her awaiting flat. In fact, she didn't see anything at all, just the bloodied wall and ground before her which had accounted for countless innocent deaths.

Instead, a song played in her mind. The first song she heard when she had arrived at Auschwitz and the orchestra played the upbeat foxtrot *"The most beautiful time of your life."* It was eerie, as if life itself was making a mockery of her existence while she waited for that bullet to come ripping through her flesh.

As quickly as it arrived, this warp in time evaporated as something struck Eleonore lightly on the back of her head. Shaking, Eleonore opened her eyes, wondering if she was still alive. Looking down, she saw some charcoal at her feet and then turned to see the guards rolling on the ground in laughter.

"Do you think we'd waste bullets on you?!" the first guard cried tears of laughter as he held his side. "You stupid bitches were so scared. You even pissed yourself," he pointed at Eleonore.

"What's going on here?!" a familiar voice boomed and at once the guards stood at attention for Jung and his company.

"Just a little joke," the first guard tried to contain his drunken giggling but failed.

"You're intoxicated," Jung glared at the guard as he caught the poor state of Eleonore, though he avoided causing her further shame by staring.

"And you're not," the guard replied and handed his flask to the lieutenant.

"Get dressed," he ordered the women and turned his back to them to allow for dignity.

"Ignore that order!" the drunk guard drew his pistol and came face to face with Jung.

The drunk was a pudgy, short man and when squared against the tall lieutenant he looked ridiculous. Especially as he staggered while attempting to sober himself.

"I outrank you," the drunk gritted his teeth as he glared up at Jung.

"What you're doing is illegal," Jung remained calm and spoke with reason to his superior. "I have no qualms with reporting this behavior to Commandant Hoess when I see him later this morning."

"Are you threatening me, lieutenant?" the drunk cocked the pistol by his side, offering a threat of his own.

"Are you certain you want to play this out," Jung slowly put his hand to his own pistol. "Your reflexes are impaired."

The drunk looked at Jung as he struggled to weigh the possible outcomes, yet his consciousness had been drowned out by his liquor, and he was acting on impulse alone. Then, glancing again at the women, the drunk locked eyes with Eleonore and a smile crept across his face.

"Ah," he chuckled, "now I see why you care so much. You don't want your little whore damaged."

"And?" Jung shrugged, not defending against the slander.

"If we're…if…uh…we're talking about…uh," the drunk stumbled through his thoughts.

"If we're talking about something illegal," Jung patronized him as he helped along, knowing the direction.

"Right!" the drunk half-shouted, not appreciating Jung's tone. "Then…uh…then…"

"Then I'll make you a deal," Jung continued. "You don't tell the Commandant about my affair and I won't tell him about your mistreatment."

"Yep," the drunk stuck out his hand and Jung shook it.

"Get dressed," Jung nodded to the women. "We'll return to the barracks."

Nearly freezing in the cold and in trauma, the women dressed and followed Jung as he escorted them back to their barracks.

"Thank you," Eleonore whispered as she walked beside him, but he didn't reply. It wasn't safe yet.

Returning to the barracks, the ladies began to file in, but Jung grabbed Eleonore's arm before she could enter.

"Not you," he said with a sternness meant to divert any rumors that he knew were certainly running rampant.

"I'm freezing," Eleonore nodded to the barracks, begging to return to the little warmth it offered.

"That'll be over soon," he smiled.

"Am I being released?!" her eyes flew open wide with hope.

"I wish," he shook his head. "You're being transferred to the detention center."

"Why?" Eleonore studied him, wondering how she should feel.

"You'll see," he gave a reassuring nod. "Collect your things and we'll be off."

"I'm wearing them," Eleonore glanced down at her clothes and back up at Jung, surprised that he thought she carried possessions. *Is he really that out of touch with reality?*

"Of course," Jung seemed a little embarrassed. "Come with me then."

"What's the detention center?" Eleonore asked as they walked.

"Something more suitable for you," Jung offered her a cigarette which she gladly accepted. "You'll have your own cell with your own bed and lavatory. You'll have a desk where you can read and write and even smoke if you'd like."

"Why?" Eleonore frowned. "Why should I be offered these luxuries?"

"Well," Jung became uncomfortable and cleared his throat. "The why I don't know, but it was on the orders of Commandant Hoess."

"I see," Eleonore stared at her feet as her mind ran wild.

"As do I," Jung became cynical.

"What do you mean?" Eleonore glared at him.

"Is it true?" Jung puffed his cigarette.

"What's true?" Eleonore studied him.

"You're the Commandant's mistress. The mistress of Auschwitz."

"Is that what they call me?!" Eleonore resisted the urge to slap him. "I haven't so much as said three words to him!"

"That'll change soon," Jung looked defeated. "I'll take you to the Villa and then escort you to the detention center this evening."

"If you...if...oh..." Eleonore felt faint and put her hand to her head.

"What's wrong?" Jung held out a hand to stabilize her.

"I..." Eleonore tried to catch her breath. "I think the morning's events are catching up with me."

"It was a cruel joke," Jung shook his head. "And not all that funny either."

"Help me up," Eleonore reached out her hand.

"Can you continue in your condition?"

"If I don't work, I die," Eleonore shrugged.

"Then let's get you to the Villa," Jung nodded.

Chapter Nineteen: Spark

"But I say unto you, that whosever looketh on a woman to lust after her hath committed adultery with her already in his heart."
Matthew 5:28

"Fine work," Hedwig said plainly as she stood back to take in the full scope of the tapestry.

Although pleased with the compliment, Eleonore felt she had erred in removing the splendid poem. Someone had placed it there from a sense of reminiscent hope, and she had complied in eradicating its beauty.

Don't be so hard on yourself. If it was between your life and removing the poem, then you did the right thing, she heard Alex speak softly.

But what if it comes to burning a book to save my life? She countered. *Then removing someone from business, then removing them from their house, then moving them to a camp to be exterminated. I've become part of the process, however small.*

Shaking her from self-pity, Eleonore heard the delightful neighing of a horse just outside the front of the house. Eleonore leaned over to look out the front window to inspect but couldn't see anything from her vantage point. Hedwig, however, remained unmoved so Eleonore didn't feel it appropriate to excuse herself.

Within seconds, the floor above Eleonore vibrated with the excited pattering of four children who bounded down the stairs. Bursting into the living room, the oldest two struggled for first place as they raced along while the younger two straggled behind, ignorant as to the purpose of this exhilaration.

"It's papa!" Klaus shouted to the others and Eleonore's heart skipped a beat.

Why is he home? Eleonore wondered and hoped against hope that she was not part of his equation.

"Come outside," Rudolph's muffled cry came through the window. "It's nice out."

"Mama?" the children ran up to her and tugged on her dress. "Can we go out with papa?"

Hedwig didn't answer as she stood in front of the tapestry, ensuring perfection, then finally replied, though dryly, "Alright."

"Yay!" the kids bounced up and down.

Grabbing onto Eleonore's hand, Heidetraud looked up at her mother and asked, "Can Eleonore come too?!"

"She has work," Hedwig responded and finally broke her attention from the tapestry with a sigh. "Let's get your jackets and boots on. Eleonore, would you help me?"

"Of course," Eleonore gave a light squeeze on Heidetraud's hand as she followed the children to the foyer.

Assisting the younger two slip into their fine boots and warm winter jackets, Eleonore helped them get ready for a little adventure. With the kids all bundled and ready for the journey, Eleonore returned to the living room and spotted Hedwig watching her husband and children from the bay window. Joining her, though standing at a respectful distance behind, Eleonore watched as Rudolph dismounted and led the horse by the reins closer to his children.

"Never stand behind a horse," he warned them. "They can get spooked and kick without warning."

"Why?" Heidetraud asked innocently which made Eleonore smile. She was developing an attachment to the little girl. There was a sweetness to her, an innocent curiosity.

"Because they are prey animals. Their survival instincts are strong," Rudolph glanced up at the bay window and caught the two women watching, yet his eyes lingered on Eleonore. Noticing the peculiarity, Hedwig also looked at Eleonore who then became uncomfortable with the studying gaze.

"He's good with animals," Hedwig returned her attention to Rudolph and Eleonore breathed a sigh of relief.

"I've often thought," Hedwig continued, "that if he hadn't joined the military, my dear Rudolph would have been content farming."

"Sounds rather nice about now," Eleonore smiled at the thought.

"It does," Hedwig crossed her arms. "Though Auschwitz is a paradise for my family. They have everything they want. I don't think I should ever like to leave."

Frowning faintly, Eleonore studied Hedwig with hidden incredulity. Though, she supposed, if Hedwig was ignorant as to the extent of the of 'work' being done at Auschwitz, a little clemency could be extended. Still, she was living in the wealth stolen from other people for the coincidence of their birth. She was just as guilty as her husband.

"You mentioned you have another project for me?" Eleonore changed the subject, anxious for distraction.

"Yes," Hedwig turned and walked into the storage room. Returning with her arms full of supplies of fur, threading needles, and other assorted sewing items, Hedwig set them down on the coffee table with a huff.

"Sit," Hedwig nodded to the couch in front of her and Eleonore behaved, wondering why her demeanor had suddenly turned so stern.

Does she suspect Rudolph and I of some indiscretion? Eleonore tried to read her but found it difficult with such an expressionless face. *Should I say something? No! That would only arouse suspicion if none existed.*

"I have something rather serious to discuss with you," Hedwig looked at Elenore with a vacant stare.

"Yes?" Eleonore looked back with wide eyes, ready to defend herself. She had done nothing wrong with Rudolph. It was he that had sought her out in the camp, and she desired nothing from him.

"I need you to make a carpet for Rudolph's car," Hedwig continued as a smile crept onto the corner of her mouth. "A state official will be attending for a tour."

Returning the smile – more from relief than excitement – Eleonore's mind retreated into memory as she recalled the state motorcades in procession in Berlin. It was the first time she had seen Hitler and she, like the countless thousands, had been fighting for a position to get a glimpse of the savior of Germany. She remembered him standing as his convertible drove down the street, offering the Nazi salute to his subjects, and wearing the most solemn expression. A lush, brown fur carpet, like the one Hedwig was asking her to make, was spread over the back of his car. It invoked the idea of prominence, while he himself remained in his authoritarian uniform.

She blushed as she recalled returning the damning salute, ignorant as to its significance. If she had known what Hitler would become, what he would do to sacred Germany, then she would have fled a long time ago. Yet it was in this euphoric rapture that Eleonore discovered an inkling to the Nazi intentions which solidified her resolve to forsake the party.

She recalled a man on the other side of the street, just opposite Eleonore, and she recognized him as belonging to the dwindling Democratic Socialist Party. He was alone, clutching a black leather book, and refusing to offer the Nazi salute. Those around him shouted and spit on him, but he continued in his resolve. He simply scowled at Hitler while he drove by and, for the briefest of moments, Eleonore caught the glint of rage in the Fuhrer's eyes.

This man, this politician, was baiting Hitler to show his true colors, tempting to expose the dictator for who he was. All bore witness to this fleeting interaction, yet continued in their blind worship. It was such dedication without reason that stirred Eleonore's conscience to suspect that Germany's liberator was not the man she hoped he was.

"Am I privy to the knowledge of who is attending?" Eleonore inquired as she returned to the present.

"I'm not at liberty to say," Hedwig shook her head, but then leaned in closer and whispered, "but if you must know, it's Herr Himmler."

A cold chill ran down Eleonore's spine as the name resounded with all the hatred she had experienced. He was the grand architect for the 'final solution'. He, above all others, was responsible for the mass murder.

"So," Hedwig beamed with pride, "he will be making the inspection via Rudolph's vehicle, and the mode of transportation must appear as luxurious as possible without seeming excessive. Do you understand?"

"I do," Eleonore nodded. Regardless of the man, the station was rather prestigious, and Hedwig's request was quite the honor.

"I need you to focus," Hedwig clasped her hands together, becoming rather excited and animated, "so I will take the children to the village for some shopping and dismiss the servants for the day. Feel free to use the radio beside you and if there is anything else you require, don't hesitate to look for it. Alright?"

"That sounds lovely," Eleonore smiled at the thought of some craved solitude and pleased that she could be trusted.

With that, Hedwig nodded and left Eleonore who couldn't remember the last time she had been alone, at least not in pleasant circumstances. Closing her eyes, Eleonore breathed deeply and listened to the clock ticking patiently and relished in the privacy.

Then, out of the corner of her eye, she spied the little 'people's radio' begging to be employed. With a molded brown plastic cover, its only decoration was a Nazi eagle just below the two dials and Eleonore appreciated the simplicity of its design.

Flipping on the radio, Eleonore's grin nearly leapt off her face as Richard Strauss' *Die ägyptische Helena* blared its sweet melody. With a needle, thread, and fur in hand, Eleonore began her work and, again, lost all track of time. The hours sped by as inch by inch she created the carpet for the Commandant's car. Her senses evaporated as she focused on her work and even the serenading radio felt the cold sting of her distraction.

That is until the music suddenly halted and a crisp announcer's voice advised of the purpose of the interruption: an update on the war effort. Eleonore paused as she listened intently, begging to hear of the allies advance into Germany, signaling the end of the Third Reich and, in turn, her captivity.

The Russians will probably reach us first though, the terrible thought made her stomach sink. *Their ideology is just as genocidal as fascism. And they have no love of the Jews. Chances are I'll be given a swift death or taken to their own concentration camps. Please let me be rescued by the Americans.*

No reply was given as the announcer continued, ignorant of Eleonore's supplication. First came praise for Hitler's 'incredible genius' and 'militaristic aptitude'. Then, the announcer could be heard shuffling his papers as he prepared to read the organized statements which were carefully reviewed beforehand.

"Victory on all fronts," the announcer began strongly as he mimicked the charisma of the Fuhrer. "The Russian dogs are losing Stalingrad. That celebrated city named after the failing dictator is buckling under the unstoppable blitzkrieg and it is about to fall into the hands of our glorious Fuhrer. We have the advantage."

How does anyone fall for this? Eleonore rolled her eyes. *The propaganda is so blatant.*

"On the western front, the disgraced Allies have been held in check, abandoning their posts and forfeiting strongholds. None can withstand the unified front of Nazi strength."

Interpretation: we are losing the war, Eleonore smiled.

A sudden creak came from the hallway, and Eleonore paused as she turned down the radio and listened closely.

Must've been the wind, Eleonore rolled her shoulders as if to dislodge the creeping feeling and turned the radio back up. Again, another creak came from the hallway, this time closer to the living room.

"Hello?" Eleonore called.

Her breathing paused as she waited anxiously for someone to appear. With her heart pounding, she turned off the radio and, when nothing else disturbed her, she returned to her work while occasionally glancing towards the hallway.

"Why did you turn the radio off?" Rudolph burst into the living room and a startled Eleonore clasped her hand to her chest.

"Sorry," Eleonore caught her breath. "I thought I was alone in the house."

"Is that right?" Rudolph put a cigar to his mouth.

"What can I do for you Commandant?" Eleonore studied him warily. *He must know that Hedwig ordered the house to be emptied.*

"Nothing," Rudolph spoke casually as he sat on a leather chair not far from her, crossing his legs and holding his lit cigar in a limp hand.

"Forgive me," Eleonore picked up her threading needle as she swallowed, "but Hed…Mrs. Hoess requires this item to be completed as soon as possible for the state visit."

"Don't let me disturb you," Rudolph eyed her and gave a large puff of smoke which lingered and floated towards her.

"I believe Mrs. Hoess ordered the vicinity to be evacuated so that I could work on this project unimpeded," Eleonore couldn't believe the words had escaped her mouth, but once she had started, there was no stopping.

"Aren't you bold," Rudolph smiled as he ran his tongue across the inside of his cheek. "What makes you think a carpet is important?"

"Well, I—"

"It's not," Rudolph interrupted. "My wife is desperate for a chance to appear essential to my operation, but no man has ever thought a woman to be of any significance because of her ability to weave."

Stunned and a little embarrassed, Eleonore didn't know how to respond, but lowered her gaze in shame.

"I just remembered your previous vocation as a seamstress," Rudolph clicked his teeth upon the recollection. "I didn't mean any offence."

"None taken," Eleonore lied as she smiled quickly.

"I'll leave you to your work then," he took another puff and stood, but remained beside his chair.

Trying to ignore him, Eleonore returned to her project, but found it hard to disregard his figure standing a mere few feet from her. She cringed as she could feel his gaze and wished with all her heart he would just leave.

"You're rather beautiful," he began again, and Eleonore's skin began to craw. "How old are you?"

"Excuse me?!" Eleonore's disgust melted in the rising rage.

"Sorry," Rudolph shook his head with an embarrassed smile. "It's just that you look younger, but I'm told you're about my age."

Still, Eleonore didn't reply as she figured any answer would only invite further conversation. Besides, he had access to all her records and could simply look up her file, but she knew he was after more than information.

"Pretty name too," Rudolph continued as he was either ignorant of or willfully dismissing Eleonore's disgust. "Eleonore. Do you know where that name originated?"

Eleonore shook her head quickly.

"Well," Rudolph sat down again. "It literally means 'the other Leanor'. Eleanor of Aquitaine was the first of her namesake. Rather interesting story, actually," Rudolph leaned back in his chair and folded his hands across his chest.

Bracing for the monologue, Eleonore begged, prayed to God in heaven that Hedwig would return and Rudolph would break off the chase.

"From my readings of her life, I'd conclude that her troubles were entrenched in the misplaced hope of romance. It's interesting, don't you think, that our concept of an ideal relationship stems from this period in history? A man buying a woman flowers, or kneeling as he proposes, all came from this era and has remained unchanged since."

Nodding quickly, Eleonore returned to her work, wishing the conversation to end.

"I'm boring you," Rudolph offered an apologetic smile, but his gaze still held firm on his prize.

"No, no," Eleonore shook her head, feigning politeness.

"Maybe you'd rather discuss her progressive liberties?" Rudolph took a deep puff of his cigar and Eleonore felt herself shuddering with disgust. "She is the inspiration for the fiction of Guinevere, after all."

"I think my supplies are running dry," Eleonore stood, sensing the direction of the conversation. She had seen such displays before; little tricks that men play when they try to arouse women into devious behavior.

"Sure," Rudolph waved for her dismissal, still oblivious to her hints.

Stomping into the backroom, Eleonore found the supply closet near the kitchen and, rummaging through, found a thick piece of cloth. Pressing her face into the fabric, she let out a low growl of frustration. Gathering herself with a deep breath, Eleonore ran her hands along her stomach to calm herself and made her way back.

Turning into the living room, she was met suddenly by Rudolph standing directly in front of her. Surprised, Eleonore tired to walk around him, but he moved to step in front of her. Then, placing his hand on the back of her neck, he leaned in and kissed her on the lips. The motion had been so fluid that Eleonore didn't know how to defend against it and found herself in the awkward position of having his mouth pressed against hers.

Finally, after she offered a few limp hits against his chest, Rudolph backed off. Still, he wasn't concerned that she should have no interest, and he leaned in again. Without a word, Eleonore slipped out of his grasp, turned and fled into the bathroom, and locked the door behind her.

What do I do? What do I do? Eleonore panicked and looked around the bathroom for anything that could be used as a weapon should Rudolph force entry. Holding her breath, she watched for shadows under the door but saw none.

He didn't follow me, she began to breathe again, but her relief was stripped away by the slow turning of the doorknob. Pressing herself against the wall, she watched in frozen terror. Thankfully, the lock held true and the doorknob stopped.

"Eleonore," Rudolph knocked against the door, "may I speak with you?"

But Eleonore didn't respond and forced her mouth shut.

"I only wish to speak with you. Nothing more," he tried the door again, twisting the handle the opposite way.

"There…" Eleonore fumbled with her words. She needed to say something, but what would make him leave her alone, "there are too many obstacles barring any relations between us."

"I am the Commandant," Rudolph pressed his face to the corner of the door and spoke softly. "You needn't be afraid."

"Relations between personnel and inmates are forbidden," Eleonore persisted. "Besides, there exists the most obvious of hinderances."

"Such as?" Rudolph questioned.

"Your marriage," Eleonore frowned. How could he push the woman who bore his children aside so swiftly?

"You needn't worry about that either," Rudolph continued.

"What do you mean?" Eleonore regretted pursuing the conversation.

"She's having an affair," Rudolph sighed.

Then, saving her from further disgrace, Rudolph's children could be heard outside. Their return was not full of the boundless gayety that they had departed with, but rather, the bickering over something undoubtedly trivial. Yet, to Eleonore it was the most joyous of disagreements.

Immediately, Rudolph shuffled away from the door and, seizing the opportunity, Eleonore made her escape. Returning to the living room, she set herself again to the project, trying as best as she could to appear as if there had been no interruption.

"It was my turn!" Klaus protested as he stormed into the house.

"Which lasted an eternity!" Heidetraud countered.

"Both of you upstairs!" Hedwig clapped in frustration, nearing the end of her patience. "And take your younger brother and sister with you."

Passing by the living room and ignoring Eleonore, the children bounded up the flight of stairs, preparing to continue their competition on a new field of battle that was the playroom.

"Well," Hedwig sighed as she removed her scarf while entering the living room with rosy cheeks, "that was supposed to be a pleasant outing."

Chuckling slightly, Eleonore kept her focus on her work, but was distracted when Hedwig began sniffing.

The cigar, Eleonore panicked and noticed that Rudolph had left it in the ashtray but had failed to put it out. The smoke rose, betraying both Rudolph and her.

"Was my husband home?" Hedwig glanced at the ashtray and back at Eleonore.

Do I lie? Or will the truth get me into further trouble? Eleonore tried to think of an excuse but came up empty.

"He was," Eleonore cleared her throat, unable to hide her nervousness.

"Odd that he didn't finish his cigar," Hedwig moved over to the ashtray and put out the smoke.

"Some trouble at the camp," Eleonore was impressed she had thought of an excuse so quickly.

"I don't remember any alarms," Hedwig squinted as she studied Eleonore.

"They telephoned," Eleonore nodded to the phone sitting conveniently beside the chair where Rudolph had been smoking.

"I have five children," Hedwig held her hands tightly in front of her. "I'm an expert at detecting deception."

Staring at Hedwig with wide eyes, Eleonore didn't know where to start. Should she advise Hedwig that Rudolph had made a pass at her or should she dampen the truth to save her own skin? Surely Rudolph would deny the accusations.

"I may be outside the camp," Hedwig sat on the couch beside her, "but I'm still, on occasion, privy to some gossip. Though I despise such wanton behavior, I must admit some of the rumors are beneficial."

Still, Eleonore didn't respond as she watched Hedwig and waited for her to come to some sort of conclusion. Then she could deny or confirm whatever she supposed.

"It appears," Hedwig continued but held her head high, "that my husband has taken an interest in you."

"I—"

"It's alright," Hedwig raised her hand. She could tell the truth by Eleonore's guilty expression. "I know you're not to blame. You are rather beautiful after all and my husband needs the distraction from time to time. Still, it is a wife's duty to keep her husband faithful. I could live with his watchful gaze, but his boldness in pursuing you has transgressed a boundary I cannot accept. I'm left with no choice. Your services are no longer required."

"I must protest," Eleonore began but, again, Hedwig raised her hand to stop her.

"Even if it is untrue," Hedwig looked at Eleonore with sympathy as if she was punishing her against her will, "I cannot take that risk. I will ring for your escort. Please wait in the foyer."

Robbed of the hope which had only just been promised, Eleonore remained sitting. This was to be her path to liberation. She would work in Hedwig's shop, preparing dresses and pretending that life was suitable at Auschwitz. For the crime of another man's affections, that promise was destroyed.

"He told me of your affair," Eleonore spoke softly.

Glaring at Eleonore, Hedwig's eyes bulged with rage. Then, in a swift movement, she ripped the wig off Elenore's head.

"Get out!" Hedwig stood and pointed to the door.

"Nothing transpired between us," Eleonore pleaded.

"To think that I took you into my house," Hedwig tilted her head with her increasing anger. "That I let you near my children!"

Seeing as objection was useless, Eleonore accepted her fate and headed for the foyer as Hedwig rang for an escort. But, before she could reach the door, a pair of little arms wrapped around her leg and Eleonore looked down to see Heidetraud smiling blissfully up at her.

"Come here!" Hedwig waved to her daughter while she talked on the phone, becoming frantic.

"Go," Eleonore nodded while tearing up.

"Now!" Hedwig snapped her fingers and pointed to the floor beside her. "Yes, immediately," she spoke to the person on the other line.

Standing in the foyer, Eleonore felt an ugly pit of loneliness in her belly as she inspected the Villa one last time. She listened to the business of the kitchen just down the hall, knowing that she had likely had her last decent meal. She smiled at the children's footsteps running in the playroom above her head. In all, the time she spent at the Villa had been uplifting, but the recent events had tainted her stay. Yet here, at Auschwitz, termination from employment meant death.

"Eleonore!" Roza said warmly and stopped in her tracks as she passed by the foyer.

"Hello," Eleonore gave a limp smile, trying to hide her dismay.

"What's wrong?" Roza's cheer faded when she noticed her grim demeanor and that she wasn't wearing the wig.

"I..." Eleonore didn't know how to begin.

But even if she could explain, that opportunity was lost as footsteps could be heard crunching in the snow outside. Glancing through the window of the door, Eleonore noticed Jung was approaching. *Maybe if I explain myself, then he can put in a good word for me with Mrs. Hoess.*

"Eleonore," Roza caught her attention again and whispered with a little nod, "Soon. Just stay alive."

"What's soon?" Eleonore whispered back.

"Stay alive," Roza whispered again, and then disappeared before Jung opened the door, leaving a bewildered and perplexed Eleonore wondering if she could allow herself to hope again.

Chapter Twenty:
An Unexpected Visit

"We are more often frightened than hurt; and we suffer more from imagination than from reality." Seneca

"Your new cell," Jung unlocked and opened a thin, steel door to reveal a small, yet furnished detention cell on the second floor of Block 25.

Purposed for temporary prisoners, the cell was equipped with a bed and mattress, a writing desk with a lamp, and a functioning toilet tucked in the corner. But Eleonore's attention was stolen by the names written on the walls. In white ink, every inch of the concrete walls were plastered with the signatures of all who had visited this cell. Some of the signatures were large, while others were discreet, echoing the owner's personality.

Eventually, she pried her focus away from the walls and nearly cried when she studied the bed, wishing for nothing else than to lie down. Not that it was luxurious, but in comparison to an eight-person bunk it was a hefty improvement.

Still, Eleonore felt the sting of her falling from glory. The more she contemplated her current predicament, the more she became upset at the injustice. Firstly, Auschwitz should never have existed. Secondly, once she had a small haven within this wilderness, it had been robbed of her by the Commandant's lust.

"I ruined my chance," Eleonore confided in Jung.

"You did nothing wrong," Jung took pity on her. "The Commandant is to blame. No one else."

"We didn't partake in any illegal behavior," Eleonore defended.

"I know," Jung nodded.

"How?" Eleonore frowned.

"I saw the way Mrs. Hoess looked at you when I arrived at the Villa. You're a potential threat, not an active one."

"My freedom was close at hand," Eleonore continued to wallow. "I could feel it."

"I've seen others released before," Jung walked into her cell and placed his silver case full of cigarettes on her desk. "Don't give up hope just yet."

"How did they do it?" Eleonore became desperate and grabbed his arm.

"There's no rhyme or reason," Jung removed himself from her grasp. "Write to the Commandant and his wife and see if they will hear your case."

"What about you?" Eleonore begged as he began to leave.

"You and I both know I'm not important enough," Jung closed the cell door, but opened the little spy hole and peeked in. "If I was, you'd be far away from here."

"Maybe it's time for a promotion then?" Eleonore smiled, trying to find some humor in the bleakness.

With a slight chuckle, Jung closed the spy whole and left Eleonore to get acquainted with her new surroundings, not that there was much to discover. She stood awkwardly in the center of her quiet, secluded cell as the walls with their names began closing in.

Thankful at least to have a window – though decorated with iron bars – Eleonore tried to align herself within the camp as the sun had already set. Squinting, Eleonore was able to discern her direction and noticed that she was facing her old barrack which was about two hundred yards away.

I wonder if Ella is still alive, she thought as she looked at the barracks.

Not allowing herself to hesitate any further, Eleonore sat at the flimsy, wooden writing desk which shook back and forth on its wobbly legs. Running her hands over the surprisingly smooth surface, Eleonore noticed that there was a drawer tucked under the right-hand side. Poorly constructed, the drawer wouldn't budge, but was stuck against something hidden inside.

"You stupid thing!" Eleonore fumed as she unleashed her rage on the inanimate.

Finally jostling the drawer free, Eleonore was pleased to find a supply of paper and a pen. Turning on the lamp, Eleonore pulled out the supplies and set her mind to writing. The lamp shone down on her, isolating her from the rest of the world as she was lost to thought and recollection. In a way, it reminded her of the desk of the crippled man who betrayed her to the Nazis. How she wished she could rewind and pay greater attention to her instincts. Then, maybe, she wouldn't be in this mess.

Mrs. Hoess,

Eleonore began the letter absent of endearments. Hedwig was a woman of practicality and efficiency; there was no room for sentiment, and she needed to appeal to her sensibilities.

I implore you to reconsider my dismissal. Please don't pay attention to idle rumors by those who hate me. I have not been much welcomed into the camp by the other women and at every available opportunity they seek my reduction. Their jealousy was stirred by my elevation to working inside the Villa and they created the vilest of rumors as to their explanation for my rise in status.

"Think," Eleonore talked to herself as she placed her head in her hands. "What else can I say?"

"It won't make a difference," a familiar voice answered from the other side of the wall, startling Eleonore.

"Who's there?" Eleonore knew the voice but couldn't pinpoint from where.

"It's me, Julia," the voice replied.

"Who?" Eleonore's confusion grew.

"Em," she chuckled.

"Oh Em?!" Eleonore breathed a sigh of relief. "I knew I recognized your voice. What are you doing here?"

"Same as you," Em grew solemn.

"I don't follow," Eleonore listened intently.

"Why do you think the beds are so comfortable?" Em huffed. "Write all you want, the letters are never delivered. I suppose it's less distressing if you believe you've made peace with your outside family or friends."

"Em," Eleonore held her breath. "What is this place?"

"The last stop," Em sighed. "This is where the 'selections' are placed until the cells are full."

"And then?" Eleonore wondered what she had gotten herself into.

"I'm so afraid," Em began to weep. "And I don't know why. All I've wanted these last months is to die, yet now that the time is at hand, I'm terrified."

"How do you know they are going to kill you?" Eleonore studied the signatures on the walls with fresh eyes.

"Everyone knows it," Em calmed down a little. "Watch, they'll give you double rations this evening. I believe the officer gave you his case of smokes as well?"

"Why wouldn't Jung tell me?" Eleonore spoke quietly as her knuckles turned white from gripping the desk.

"Maybe he didn't want to upset you?" Em shrugged. "Or, maybe you will be spared after all."

"Maybe," Eleonore responded quickly, focusing more on the potential entrapment. Not that she had much of a choice, but being locked here under false pretenses was cruel.

"I didn't think my existence would be snuffed out by a bullet," Em lamented. "I thought for sure I would be sent to the gas chambers."

"That's what I don't understand," Eleonore raised her finger in protest. "Why would they shoot you?"

"They gas those that have run out of usefulness," Em explained, "but those of us who are part of the resistance are afforded a more violent death by hanging or firing squad."

"You're part of the resistance?" Eleonore shook her head. She couldn't have heard that correctly.

"Only recently, I'm afraid," Em chuckled hopelessly. "Ella can be rather charismatic. She convinced me to help."

"Help with what?" Eleonore leaned in.

"I wish I could tell you," Em whispered, "but the walls have ears."

"How were you caught?"

"They found gunpowder in my apron," Em leaned her head against the wall. "They've been torturing me for days, but I haven't offered them so much as a word. I promise. Not one word."

"I believe you," Eleonore nodded and placed her head in her hands in shock. Did the Nazis know of Eleonore's affiliation with Ella? Was that why she was brought here, to be tortured?

"But why didn't you?" Eleonore frowned.

"Pardon?"

"Why didn't you save your life? If they'll kill all of us anyways, why put yourself through the agony?"

"I wondered that myself," Em sighed. "It's the sensible thing, I suppose, to spare oneself. But I didn't refuse from a sense of duty, nor from any obligation to my fellow Jews. Half of those inmates would've ratted me out in a heartbeat."

"Then why?" Eleonore shook her head.

"My husband used to read to me," Em continued. "He loved to read history books to me by the fireplace after my sweet boy had gone to sleep. I wished for romance novels or adventure tales, but now I'm so glad he did."

A moment of silence passed as a thoroughly confused Eleonore waited for Em to elaborate on whatever tangent she had adopted.

"Anyways, he read me this incredible story of the siege at the fortress of Jotapata. During combat, one of the Jewish rebels was captured and taken to the Roman camp to be tortured for information. You see, the pagans couldn't understand how they, being heavily armored and well trained, were losing to fanatics who were armed only with their courage and had little to no experience. In their frustration, they subjugated this rebel to the cruelest forms of torment, but he refused to offer them so much as his name. In the end, they resolved to crucify him, but as they drove the nails into his flesh he smiled at them, knowing he had foiled their attempts. I don't remember much of what my husband read, but that, that I remember. Now I have become that daring soldier. I have become the one who gave them nothing and I'll smile as they put the bullet through my head."

Tears streamed down Eleonore's face as she listened to the passion stirring in Em's voice. Her death had a purpose and, although the circumstances were dreadful, she was meeting her end with all the mettle and grit she could offer.

"So," Em sighed, "finish your letter to whoever needs to hear your appeal. You never know, they may show you favor since you're not a Jew."

"Em?" Eleonore asked.

"Yes?"

"How is Ella?"

"As vengeful as ever," Em chuckled. "Even more so since you've been taken away from her."

"I find that surprising," Eleonore frowned in her bitterness.

"What makes you say that? I thought you two were rather close."

"I'm expendable to her," Eleonore shook her head. "That night when the drunken officer barged into our barracks, I had an opportunity to take his gun, but Ella stopped me. Her plan had not yet reached fruition, and she sacrificed me without a second thought."

"My dear Eleonore," Em began sympathetically, "Ella knew their intentions, and that you wouldn't be harmed. If you had taken that gun, then you would've been shot. She saved your life."

Feeling a lump in her throat, Eleonore smiled as the emotions mixed within her. There was much left unsaid between the two of them, and Eleonore was concerned that she had allowed enmity to sour their relationship. She was pleased to know that someone she considered as close as a sister still loved her.

After a minute or two of silence, Eleonore resolved to continue writing, trying to retrieve the correct combination of words which would stir Hedwig's heart to sympathy. Yet all she could withdraw was emptiness and she sat staring at the walls. She stared for so long that the signatures written in white ink appeared to be moving, like they were laughing and mocking her attempt to seek clemency. None was given to them, why should it be granted to her?

Exasperated, Eleonore signed her name furiously at the bottom of the letter and threw the pen back into the drawer. Folding her arms as she leaned back in the chair, Eleonore ran her hand across her forehead, massaging the growing headache.

Do I dare write to the Commandant? Eleonore thought. *But what if Hedwig sees and then supposes incorrectly. Then my chances will disappear altogether, if they haven't already.*

A knock came to the door and Eleonore watched as the peephole was opened quickly and a pair of light, blue eyes glanced inside.

"Stand beside the bed," he commanded, and Eleonore obeyed, holding her hands neatly in front of her.

With her compliance, the peephole was shut quickly, and keys jingled. The door was unlocked and opened abruptly as a guard entered with a tray of food and set it down on the writing desk.

"Double rations," he announced without looking at her and Eleonore's heart sunk as she remembered Em's warning.

"Wait," Eleonore asked as the guard turned to leave, and he stopped briefly, but refused to look at her.

"Please," Eleonore grabbed the letter off the desk, "can you make sure this is delivered?"

"Correspondence is attended to in the morning," the guard rushed out and locked the door behind him.

Do I even have until morning? Eleonore wondered and felt her stomach churning, promising what would occur should she indulge her hunger and eat. Not that the food provided much in the way of temptation. The potatoes were mushy to the point where they resembled soup, and the unseasoned meat was so dry she supposed it would be better suited as a blunt weapon.

Opening her eyes, Eleonore stared at the ceiling, wondering where she was. Apart from a faint, orange glow of light stemming from the hallway, the room was entirely dark. Looking at the wall, she spotted the signatures and her memory flooded back.

What time is it? Eleonore ran her hand across the back of her neck, feeling the grease from not washing for some time. *Seems too early to be morning.*

Sitting up, Eleonore squinted at the light coming from the half-opened cell door. Yawning as she stretched, Eleonore glanced out into the hallway.

The door! Eleonore's eyes flew wide open. *What happened?!*

Moving to the edge of the bed, Eleonore went to inspect but then froze when she believed she had heard someone in the room. She peered into the darkness, but her eyes were still heavy with sleep. Still, she felt the unmistakable presence of someone else in the room with her.

Holding her breath, Eleonore listened for movement. Her heart leapt as she heard the rustle of a uniform. Tucking her legs against her chest, Eleonore backed up on the bed as she struggled to identify the intruder.

"Who's...who's there?" she called out. "If this is some prank, stop it at once!"

In response to her demand, a lighter flickered but did not light, and all Eleonore caught was the direction, coming from the corner of the room. Glancing at the writing desk, Eleonore thought about the pen in the drawer that she could use as a weapon. Inching her way towards the desk, Eleonore prepared herself to make the daring attempt.

Again, the lighter flickered and Eleonore paused in terror to watch as it was finally lit and raised near the face of a smiling Rudolph Hoess.

"What are you doing here?!" Eleonore raised her voice.

"Shh," he held his finger near his mouth. "You're being released."

"What?!" Eleonore shook her head, wondering at this sudden reversal of fortune. "Now?"

"No," Rudolph chuckled. "There is quite a bit of paperwork to do before that can be arranged."

"Then what are you doing here?" Eleonore repeated while watching him warily.

"I've come to see you," he smiled and sat at the foot of her bed.

"You cannot!" Eleonore leapt off the bed, making as much noise as possible.

"Quiet," Rudolph stood and held his hand up to calm her. "Please, I just want to talk."

Looking again at the open door, Eleonore wondered how Rudolph had slipped past the guards. Also, she knew he was not allowed to wander around the camp alone and his escort must be near at hand.

"No one will disturb us," Rudolph sat down slowly and patted the bed for her to do likewise.

Slowly, Eleonore calmed down and sat on the opposite side of the bed, as far from Rudolph as possible and in such a way that she could spring for the door should the need arise.

"Sit next to me," Rudolph whispered.

"I'm fine where I am," Eleonore refused.

"Don't be silly," Rudolph moved to the foot of the bed and sat near Eleonore.

"I've written a letter," Eleonore pointed to the desk. "It's addressed to your wife. Will you deliver it for me?"

"Depending on the contents," Rudolph spoke in a low, threatening voice.

"I'm merely requesting an explanation as to my sudden detainment and removal from the Villa," Eleonore elaborated as her breathing labored and her heart pounded.

"It's unfortunate that you are here," Rudolph sighed. "But I'll do whatever I can to make your stay more comfortable."

"So, I'm not to be shot?" Eleonore watched him closely as the fire from the lighter illuminated his wandering, lustful eyes.

"No," Rudolph frowned, wondering where she had adopted such an odd thought. "You're to be released shortly."

"How shortly?"

"Do you need anything to improve your condition?" Rudolph ignored her request and inched closer.

"Nothing," Eleonore lied as she shook her head quickly. There was plenty which could alleviate a sorrow or two, but she didn't want Rudolph to gain the satisfaction. Besides, he was threatening to make another move and Eleonore was preparing to defend herself.

Placing a quick, firm grip on the back of her head, Rudolph leaned in to kiss her, but Eleonore jumped up and stomped her feet, sending echoes throughout the prison.

"What are you doing?!" Rudolph whispered harshly. "You'll wake the guards. No one knows I'm here."

"How did you get in anyways?" Eleonore demanded.

"There is a garden door at the back. I happen to have the keys."

Convenient, Eleonore scowled at him in the dark. *No wonder it was on his orders that I was placed in this cell.*

"Come," he patted the bed. "Sit."

"No," Eleonore shook her head vibrantly and felt her heart pounding.

"We must discuss the plans for your liberation," he patted the bed again.

Tempted and a little disorientated, Eleonore finally agreed but sat at a distance.

"You worked at the hospital here, correct?" Rudolph continued, and Eleonore was relieved that he would discuss liberation sincerely.

"Correct."

"Good," he nodded. "Then I will have you trained as a chemist before being released to the SS hospital."

"That's wonderful," Eleonore smiled as she felt that fateful twinge of hope.

"Yes," he nodded again. "I will discuss it with Ma'am in the morning. I will come back tomorrow night with an update."

"You're welcome to see me during the day," Eleonore hinted.

"I didn't want to disturb you," he lied, and Eleonore had to bite her tongue from responding rudely.

"Anyways," Rudolph stretched out his hand to grab hers, but she pulled away. "I'll leave you alone now. I shall see you tomorrow night."

"Please don't come back during the night," Eleonore found courage enough for a reasonable request.

Ignoring her, Rudolph procured a watch from his pocket and set it down on the desk. Then he slipped out of the cell, locked the door, and walked away quietly.

After a minute or two of sitting silently in the darkness, trying to comprehend the evening's events, Eleonore moved over to the desk to inspect the watch. Surprised to find it was the very one which had been taken from her at the gates, Eleonore held it close to her face and took a deep breath, hoping it still carried the scent of home.

Instead, she caught the strong aroma of a cigar and pulled away sharply. Rudolph had kept her watch with him, a memento of their first meeting. Now that it was tainted with these immoral sentiments, Eleonore studied it with resentment. The reunion with her possession was supposed to bring her joy, but Rudolph had deprived her of that pleasure.

What could he have possibly hoped to have gained? Eleonore scowled at the watch. Then, shaking in fury, she threw the watch onto the floor and crushed it under her heal. The glass splintered and cut her skin, causing her to curse as she withdrew abruptly and held her aching foot as she sat on the edge of the bed.

He'll pay for this, Eleonore fumed.

<u>Chapter Twenty-One:</u>
<u>Revolution</u>

"War is peace. Freedom is Slavery. Ignorance is Strength."
1984 – George Orwell

Sleep continued to evade Eleonore for the rest of the night as she was certain Rudolph would return. A creak here and there from the wind kept her assuming the worst. Finally, as the dim light of dawn flooded her cell, Eleonore felt she could relax. Drawing deep breaths, she closed her eyes and attempted to rest.

The letter! Eleonore sat up with a start, realizing it was missing. Bounding out of bed, Eleonore searched the writing desk, but it was nowhere to be found. She had placed the letter along the edge, she knew she had, but where could it have gone? *Did the Commandant take it?* Eleonore wondered. *He must've snuck it when he left the watch, but why?*

A cough came from the other side of the wall.

"Oh good, you're awake," Eleonore sighed. "I need someone to talk to."

"Of course," Em replied. "I haven't slept yet, actually."

Eleonore's heart sank as she realized that Em must've heard what transpired between her and the Commandant last night.

"Don't worry," Em gave a little tap against the wall. "I know that you acted admirably."

"Thank you," Eleonore breathed her relief.

"I'll take your secret to the grave," Em chuckled but then Eleonore thought she heard crying.

"It's alright," Eleonore didn't know what else to say but wanted to help Em as best as she was able.

"I'm afraid to die," Em calmed a little. "I keep running over my life, wondering what I did to deserve this, or what my boy did. How could God allow such a thing?"

Lost for an explanation, Eleonore shook her head as she sat with her back to the wall, feeling the vibrations as Em spoke. The walls were so thin that Eleonore could detect the heat from where Em sat on the other side. She wasn't one to crave human touch, but with this isolation Eleonore needed the comfort of a close friend.

"But you know what?" Em whispered.

"What's that?" Eleonore replied.

"It doesn't matter," Em sniffled.

"How so?" Eleonore frowned.

"Cause in the end the result is the same. I'll be taken to paradise to be reunited with my son and husband, where sorrow will have lost the day. 'Where neither rust nor moth doth corrupt, and where thieves do not break through nor steal.' They've broken our bodies, but our spirits, those belong to God."

Eleonore welled up as she listened to Em's courage. She doubted that she would draw upon the same resilience should she find herself awaiting a similar fate. As for God, she had, truthfully, forgotten Him. Not that she had been especially religious anyways, preferring to place her care into the arms of the practical. Yet in the hell of Auschwitz, Eleonore deemed the divine to have forsaken them, and prayers were wasted breath.

A vibrant and rushed knock rattled against Eleonore's cell door and the peephole opened quickly.

"Stand beside the bed," the guard instructed, and Eleonore obeyed as the peephole was again shut.

A little early for breakfast, Eleonore thought and heard the keys jingling outside. *Unless Rudolph was lying, and I will be executed today.*

Surprised to find that she had guessed wrong in both regards, the door swung open and Eleonore was startled to see three elderly women ushered inside. Exhaustion dominated their countenance and they huddled together in shell-shocked fright. Their thin, dirty jackets hung off their skinny, famished shoulders and Eleonore assumed they were country folk as they had the appearance of nomadic gypsies with shawls over their heads and dark, olive skin.

The door closed behind them before Eleonore could inquire with the guard as to the abnormality. The three women, still huddling together, turned and looked at Eleonore, awaiting direction like she was their host.

"Hello," she gave a slight wave. "My name is Eleonore Hodys."

The women didn't reply but looked at her suspiciously. They seemed to be awaiting a specific instruction, but Eleonore was just as clueless as they were.

"Uh," Eleonore scratched the back of her head. "I'm sure your feet are rather sore, but I only have the one chair to offer," she tapped the back of the chair, "but you are welcome to sit on the bed as well."

Still, the women stood clutching their handkerchiefs, the last of their belongings which they were permitted to retain. Lost for an explanation, Eleonore had no indication whether these women would become permanent residents or if they were somehow under her charge. The whole event was rather peculiar and would almost be comical if it weren't for how pitiful they looked.

"Please," Eleonore pointed to the bed and the chair, "have a seat."

Glancing at each other, the women agreed, warily, and held onto each other as the three sat on the edge of the bed. A collective sigh rose as they stretched their legs and felt the relief from rest. Eleonore assumed their journey had been similar to her experience and they had been forced to stand for longer than acceptable in a crowded train car.

Turning the chair towards them, Eleonore sat just to the side of the bed and gave a quick smile, trying to ease the tension. Unfortunately, it didn't work, and the women seemed to grow agitated.

"Che è lei?" one of the women leaned over and asked the other.

"Italiano?" Eleonore shot her head back in surprise.

"Si," the middle woman looked at her curiously, surprised that she understood them.

"So solo un po'," Eleonore advised that she only knew a little.

"Dove siamo?" the middle woman asked with a low, rumbling voice where they were. She reminded Eleonore of Ma'am back at the hospital, but with a more pleasant demeanor.

"Auschwitz," Eleonore swallowed and immediately the women looked at each other with tearful eyes and squeezed each other's hands.

Another knock came to the door and again the peephole was opened quickly.

"Stand beside the bed," the order came, and Eleonore obeyed but the ladies, not understanding German, looked at Eleonore with confusion.

Eleonore signaled for them to imitate her and the ladies, being older, struggled back up as they moved to the other side of the bed.

The door opened and in walked the guard with three trays of food. Setting them down on the floor, the guard retreated without so much as glancing at the women or Eleonore and locked the door again.

At once, the women half-ran over to the food. Starved, they didn't so much as lift the trays off the floor but shoveled the provisions into their mouths as they knelt. Unsettled by the display, Eleonore turned away to allow them some dignity.

"Scusi?" one of the women called to Eleonore.

Turning, Eleonore's revulsion melted when she saw the woman with an outstretched hand, offering her some of the bread. It was not so long ago that she herself had devoured her meal in the same fashion at the Villa. How could she judge these women for such behavior? Especially with such a kind gesture.

Declining with a polite smile, Eleonore knew she would be fed later and didn't dare take from these poor few. Besides, she noticed that they had received a double ration and wondered if it was their last meal. Cleaning her face, one of the ladies leaned back against the wall and looked at the others before breaking out into sobs.

"Perdonaci," the woman asked for forgiveness, but Eleonore waved her hand to signify there was nothing requiring absolution.

Fatigued from their journey, and only having eaten after quite some time, the women became drowsy and fell asleep after a brief conversation with each other. One leaned against the bed, while the other two leaned against each other, resting their heads on one another with their backs against the wall.

Eleonore would have been amused by the scene if their experiences had not been so harrowing. They reminded her of Ruth, in a way, with their shawls and their resilience. While frail, they still gave the impression that these were the type of women who were not to be trifled with. The kind that travel in packs and defend each other with unbridled zeal.

Taking out a cigarette from the silver case Jung had left, Eleonore lit it as she sat at the writing desk and began fumbling through the dusty books, seeing if any would be of interest. There was a bible, a dictionary, a thesaurus, and a children's adventure book. Sighing her disappointment, Eleonore leaned back and stared absentmindedly as she smoked.

But then something caught her eye. Stuck in between the pages of the thesaurus was a white paper that mismatched the faded colors of the book. Retrieving it, Eleonore was pleased to find it was a letter, probably written by a previous inmate.

Lieutenant Jung is the devil, the letter began, and Eleonore sat up straight in surprise to be reading the officer's name. *He likes to play cruel jokes. This morning he ordered me out of my cell to join a group of men designated to be shot. The other ladies in my cell, fifteen in all if you can believe it, helped me dress and prepare myself. Jung ordered us out to the place where the executions transpire and prepared the men to shoot. I awaited my death as the guns volleyed but my soul remained affixed to my body. When I opened my eyes, I saw Jung and the soldiers laughing hysterically. This was his idea of entertainment. My life is a joke to him.*

"I wonder how old this letter is," Eleonore whispered to herself.

A knock came to the door and Eleonore slipped the letter back into the book. The peephole opened quickly to reveal a pair of familiar eyes.

"Stand!" Jung ordered, but the women were fast asleep.

Cursing to himself, Jung fumbled with his keys angrily outside the door.

"Hey!" Eleonore stood and clapped her hands, but still, the women slept. Shaking their shoulders, Eleonore was finally able to wake them before Jung could unleash his wrath. This was not the same man which had kindly escorted Eleonore to her cell; this was the beast which poured out his rage on Ella, the man who had sought to take advantage of her, and the man who was not to be tampered with.

The women climbed to their feet and stood beside the bed just prior to the door opening. Seeing them in place, Jung's rage cooled slightly and, straightening his uniform, he pulled out a list from his pocket.

"You three," the officer pointed, "line up against the wall outside the cell."

Without understanding, the women didn't move but stayed in place, confused.

"Now!" Jung pointed, and the women grabbed their coats.

"No," he waved. "Leave them. You'll collect your belongings soon."

He's not even trying to cover up his lie, Eleonore felt a hateful vengeance swelling up in her heart. *What have these women done? What crime did they commit that they should be killed?*

"I said leave the coats!" Jung grabbed his baton.

"They don't speak German," Eleonore protested on their behalf.

Looking her up and down, Jung inspected Eleonore as if he had been unaware of her existence until now. Then, a softness formed in his eyes, and his gaze gave her a sort of misplaced comfort.

"What do they speak?" Jung asked, showing his discomfort that Eleonore should witness him in this vocation.

"Italian."

"I'll find an interpreter," the officer turned to leave.

"I speak a little," Eleonore stopped him.

Watching her for a moment, Jung held some sympathy and nodded, "Alright."

"Tornerai," Eleonore advised they will return and motioned for them to leave the coats by the bed.

Understanding, though hesitant, the women agreed and slowly draped their coats over the side of the bed. It was the last of their possessions, the final piece of home. Looking at Eleonore again, who offered a reassuring smile, the women left quietly with Jung under Eleonore's false assurances.

As the door shut, Eleonore broke. Falling to her knees, she wept for perpetuating the deception. Was it mercy, or was it for her own convenience that she limited the trauma? But the distress was only within its birth pangs as Eleonore heard Em's door open. Ceasing her tears, Eleonore placed her ear against the wall and listened intently.

"Come," Jung called.

"No, no, no!" Eleonore sobbed as she planted her face into her hands.

"Eleonore," Em spoke quietly.

"Yes?" Eleonore listened closely.

"I shall tell my husband and son about you," Em said calmly.

"I…" Eleonore fumbled as her eyes welled. She wanted to tell Em not to speak with such certainty about her own death, but there was no disguising what was about to happen.

"Now!" Jung became impatient.

"Watch through the window," Em spoke, and Eleonore listened as her friend shuffled away slowly and the door was eventually shut.

Running to her window, Eleonore wiped her eyes clean as she watched anxiously for any sign of Em or the three women. Eventually, they were escorted with four other male prisoners and a group of soldiers outside to a wall about twenty yards away. It was the same bullet splattered wall which the guards had threatened to murder her only a few nights ago.

The inmates were instructed to line up and, without warning, the guards opened fire. Eleonore held her hand over her mouth to stifle a startled yelp as she watched the event transpire quicker than she thought possible. There was nothing romantic about their sacrifice, nothing poetic which would endure into song. They had been murdered mechanically, methodically.

Eleonore couldn't lift her eyes from the body of her friend, slumped over with bullet wounds littering her chest. She hoped, at least, that Em had been reunited with her husband and son; that her suffering and separation had finally ended.

Then, Eleonore's heart stopped when she spotted Jung staring up at her pensively. He was looking at her with a sort of dreaded purpose like he had some task to complete and he was not of the present mind to carry out the action.

Walking back towards the bunker, he checked over the clipboard and Eleonore strained to get a glimpse of the numbers, praying hers had not been added to the list. She wondered if her refusal of Rudolph's advances had spelt certain death.

Waiting nervously, Eleonore slunk down with her back to the window and wept as she watched the cell door for Jung's return. The marching of boots down the hallway echoed in their approach and, closing her eyes, Eleonore breathed deeply to calm herself, but all she could envision was the sight of Em lying in the dirt.

The keys jingled, and Jung entered. Opening her tear-stained eyes, Eleonore caught the look of guilt dominating his expression as he stood in the doorway.

"Jung," Eleonore pleaded. "It's me. You can't do this."

With a sigh, Jung walked over to the desk and took out the clipboard with the list of numbers. Retrieving a pen from the drawer, he set it beside the clipboard.

"Sit," Jung spoke quietly and pulled out the chair for her.

Not willing to test Jung in such a state, Eleonore obeyed quickly and sat at the desk. Then, reaching into his uniform, Jung pulled out some papers and placed them beside the clipboard. They were blank death certificates, waiting to be filled in.

"Here," Jung retrieved yet another list from his jacket and set it on the desk in front of Eleonore, "this is the cause of death."

Studying the list, Eleonore noticed a scribbled note beside each name. At 8:02 am Julia, 76654, had died of typhus, 8:07 am Isabella, who had no number, had died of appendicitis.

"This letter contains the location of their last know relations," Jung pulled out another sheet. "Please address the death certificates to the families."

"And the belongings?" Eleonore glanced at the coats.

"We will dispose of them appropriately," he turned and slung each coat over his arm like a valet.

"Why me?" Eleonore asked after him as she sniffled. "Why am I being asked to do this job?"

"Your survival hinges upon your usefulness," Jung answered over his shoulder and left Eleonore alone with her sorrows.

Unable to sleep for fear that Rudolph would return, Eleonore sat at the desk with the little lamp enshrouding her in light. Unwilling to complete the death certificates, Eleonore stared at the list with Em's name, begging to be put to rest. The world needed to know what had happened, how she died, and why. But Eleonore lacked the courage to either pen the fabrication or disclose the truth.

As the hours slipped by, Eleonore's anxiety grew as she checked the clock every few minutes. Rudolph had appeared at around 11:00 pm the previous night and now the clock read 10:55 pm. She had asked him not to return, but she doubted that he would respect her wishes.

Then she heard it, that dreadful sound of footsteps approaching. Turning off the lamp, Eleonore quickly slipped into bed, hoping to convince Rudolph that she was sleeping. The ruse was childish, but she was desperate.

Yet the footsteps continued down the hallway passed her cell. Frowning at the curiosity, Eleonore hoped that this meant Rudolph would not be attending after all. Relaxing a little, Eleonore took a deep breath as she remained under the thin sheets.

Placing her hands to her stomach, she felt them rise and fall with each deep breath, but her heart would not cease its strong and rapid beat. She was afraid, terribly so. Should she be caught with the Commandant – even though it be against her will – she would be executed. Should the Commandant tire of her resisting him, she would be executed. Much like the death warrants left incomplete, her death would be covered over with 'natural causes' and justice would go unserved.

Suddenly, the jingle of keys rang from outside and Eleonore jerked upright, unable to commit to her deception. Slowly, the door opened, and Rudolph's silhouette appeared. The light from outside surrounded him and left a menacing figure staring down its prey.

"What are you doing?" Eleonore spoke loudly.

Raising his hand to silence her, Rudolph closed the door and returned the room to darkness.

Listening intently for his footsteps, Eleonore reached into her pocket and retrieved the pen she had taken from the desk. Placing it behind her back, Eleonore made ready to strike should Rudolph attempt anything rash.

A lighter flickered about five feet from her and she startled as Rudolph illuminated his face. Yet tonight he didn't carry the repulsive look of lust, but rather, the humble countenance of someone seeking friendship.

Sitting beside her on the bed, again closer than reasonable, Rudolph looked at Eleonore but didn't speak. Instead, he lightly stroked the back of her arm.

"Please don't," Eleonore shuffled away, clutching the pen tighter.

"Why are you so reserved with me?" Rudolph asked as though he were hurt.

"I respect your position," Eleonore swallowed, her heart still beating strong, "and your marriage."

"I know what I'm doing," Rudolph rumbled in a low voice. "You needn't worry."

"I'm not the sort of woman that you suppose I am!" Eleonore whispered harshly.

"I've heard otherwise," Rudolph gave a knowing look.

"Vile rumors!" Eleonore clenched her hands into fists. "Even if they had a shred of truth, someone will come in and find us."

"Will you not be my friend? You must be lonely?" Rudolph ignored her concerns about being discovered.

"My only need is to be released," Eleonore demanded.

"There is a slight hold up," Rudolph bit his cheek nervously.

"What?!" Eleonore frowned.

"The Madam that runs the hospital," Rudolph cleared his throat and Eleonore could see that even he was afraid of her, "she has refused to sign your release papers allowing you to work in the SS hospital."

"I'm surprised that she carries more authority than the Commandant?" Eleonore mocked. "Could you not overrule her?"

"I could," he shrugged, and his suggestive gaze reappeared.

"I'd rather rot," Eleonore couldn't believe the words coming out of her mouth. But the truth was she had no indication from him, no promise that if she did as he requested that she'd acquire freedom.

"There is another hold up in your papers," Rudolph continued, undeterred by her resistance.

"What now?" Eleonore sighed, realizing the game. Until Rudolph wished, she would never leave Auschwitz.

"When you arrived, there was no indication of where you're from, relations, previous employment, nothing. Almost as if you came into existence when you walked through these gates."

"There isn't much to know," Eleonore shrugged.

"I doubt that," Rudolph looked sincerely at Eleonore and she felt a genuine interest from him. Maybe, after all, he did have some affection for her beyond carnal relations. Not that it would improve his chances, however.

"Born in Austria," Eleonore began, "moved to Berlin at a young age. After my parents passed away, I opened my own seamstress shop: *La Venezia*."

"Fascinating!" Rudolph hummed.

Does he think he will win me through over-exuberance? Eleonore rolled her eyes.

"You hate me, don't you?" Rudolph tilted his head.

"Can anyone love you? You carry no pity or love for others, and I need you to leave."

Unfazed by the denouncement, Rudolph continued to study Eleonore and, taking in a deep breath, began, "I heard about what you did today," he nodded to the death certificates.

"Yes," Eleonore began with a hint of sarcasm, "I have served the Fuhrer well with perpetrating fabrications."

"I meant with the women," he smiled. "Lieutenant Jung advised how you calmed them down, let them know that they would be returning shortly."

"I still didn't keep them from the grave," Eleonore grew bitter.

"No," he shook his head. "But you had no choice whether they lived or died. You did, however, choose to give them false hope to ease their passing."

"What's your point?" Eleonore squinted.

"How are you and I so different?" Rudolph smiled, relishing in what he perceived as a triumphant, moral victory.

"Because you have a choice!" Eleonore raised her voice.

"What makes you think that?" Rudolph frowned. "I was given direction from Himmler himself to remove this threat to German civilization. If I refused, I would be killed and someone else would take the position, and someone much harsher than me as well."

"It's marvelous to watch you justify your position," Eleonore shook her head.

"The Jews that are gassed believe they are only going into de-lousing," Rudolph cleared his throat. "I did exactly what you did for those women. You had no choice if they lived or died, same as I, so you eased their worry by telling them they would be right back, same as I," he tapped his chest lightly.

"You've neglected a crucial point," Eleonore's passion began to swell.

"Go on," Rudolph shrugged.

"I refused," the tears welled up in her eyes. "I refused the call of those murdering tyrants. I refused to have any part of the Nazi party and its self-destructive methods. I refused any part of Hitler's demonic vision for Germany and Europe."

"And look where you are," Rudolph took his turn to examine her with incredulity.

"Yes," Eleonore felt like screaming her rage but held her tongue, "but in life you either pay a price with your body or with your soul, and I choose the former."

"Keep your self-righteousness," Rudolph stood as he grew enraged. "You don't have a family to provide for. Would it be right for me to allow them to starve so that I can have a clear conscience?"

"The end is coming for you," Eleonore pointed in warning. "Then you'll see, when your sins catch up with you and your family is left destitute, that you have erred. Might does not equal right. You chose convenience, but I have chosen goodness and decency and compassion."

"I chose my family!" Rudolph slammed his fist against his chest.

Watching Rudolph for a moment Eleonore understood the trap in which the Nazi regime had ensnared him. He believed that he was merely carrying out the duty which he was instructed by his superiors, thus suppressing his guilt. Still, it was beyond comprehension that he could view himself as a good man.

You're backing the beast into a corner, Eleonore thought. *Don't do anything foolish or you'll join Em soon. Yet isn't that how Rudolph and the other guards think? They believe they are doing whatever necessary to survive. Am I really all that different? If I had a family what would I do for their sake?*

"Its warm in here," Rudolph calmed down as he removed his cap.

"Its better than the freezing cold barracks," Eleonore glanced out the window.

"I don't take pleasure in this job," Rudolph dabbed the sweat off his head with a cloth he retrieved from his pocket, "but I make sure that those being killed aren't frightened."

"How do you know?" Eleonore studied him.

"Because I watch them," he said quietly, showing his shame. "Every time, I watch. With each shipment, I witness everything: the bodies being collected and then burned, teeth being broken out and the hair cut off, and I observe these horrors hour after hour. I stand in the dreadful, sinister stench, and I look through the peephole into the gas chambers and watch the criminals dying."

"Why?"

"Because my men look to me, and they must see that I not only issue the orders, but that I am willing to be present as well, just as I'm requiring them to be present."

"Look at the words you are using," Eleonore leaned in. "'Shipment', 'Criminal'. You've dehumanized your victims and you're plagued with guilt!"

"They aren't human," Rudolph replied quickly, almost instinctively. "You've seen them in the camp. They aren't like us. They come here dirty, half-starved. Some of them even eat each other. That's not human."

"They are in such a condition because of Nazi making!" Eleonore couldn't believe what she was hearing. "You've reduced them to such a state so that you can justify these degenerate designations."

"I'm beginning to regret this," Rudolph huffed.

"Well—"

Suddenly, an explosion shook the earth and Eleonore and Rudolph fell to the floor. Covering their heads, they waited for another explosion, fearing an attack, but none came. Rushing over to the window, Rudolph looked out to see the night sky aflame, reflecting the devastation of the earth below.

The camp burst into action as guards shouted, machine guns fired, dogs barked, sirens blared, and fog lights aimed in the direction of the explosion. Then, another explosion burst out, followed by yet another, and Rudolph startled away from the window with a pale expression.

"Hurry," Rudolph called out as he heard boots approaching from outside the cell, "you must hide me."

"You can die as the rat you are!" Eleonore refused.

"It's not the Allies," Rudolph pleaded.

"How do you know?" Eleonore crossed her arms as the footsteps came closer.

"The explosions came from the crematorium."

The door to the cell beside them opened and closed and Eleonore could hear a guard shouting to his comrades that it was clear. The footsteps continued until they stopped in front of Eleonore's cell and Rudolph hid behind the door.

Throwing the lights on, the guard peeked through the spyhole to see Eleonore watching out the window. Satisfied that everything was in order, the guard shut the lights off and left. Still, Eleonore didn't move as the largest grin crept onto her face while watching the flames rising.

You did it, Ella, Eleonore smiled, but her joy faded as assault rifles continued their barrage and she began to worry for the sake of her friend.

Without a word, Rudolph returned to his uniform and slipped out of the cell, leaving Eleonore alone to wonder about the fate of the camp. Should the revolution be successful, Eleonore could be on the front lines of something much worse than her current predicament. But she would endure whatever came to pass if it meant the downfall of Auschwitz.

Chapter Twenty-Two: Proposition

"Don't let us mistake necessary evils for good." C.S. Lewis

The night passed with Eleonore paying close attention to the excitement. The dogs and sirens continued into the early morning and, after they settled down, the business of the camp went on in the fashion that Eleonore came to understand as 'usual'. The Nazis were well prepared to quell this uprising, and their experience indicated to Eleonore that such an incident may have transpired before.

Eleonore remained standing at the window, watching black smoke ascend to heaven in the rising light of dawn. Only one crematorium remained, but Ella and her revolution had succeeded in carrying out their plan. While proud beyond measure, Eleonore was sick with worry for Ella. If she had avoided being killed by the Nazi suppression, then she was likely captured and being tortured. Eleonore couldn't bear to think of the terrible things being done to her sweet Ella.

But her worry would have to wait as the spyhole opened and closed on her cell door. Turning towards the door, Eleonore watched as four girls, ranging from the ages of fourteen to eighteen, were ushered inside. Two of the girls were twins with dark, black hair and beautiful, bright brown eyes. The others were blonde with blue eyes, likely unrelated, and a picture of Aryan perfection, yet the status of their birth barred them from such an honorable, fascist designation.

Sick, tired, skinny, and afraid, the four girls huddled in the corner for warmth. They were so frightened that they paid little attention to Eleonore. To them, she was just another amongst the sea of faces. Besides, she looked too healthy to be counted amongst those suffering.

"Hello," Eleonore cleared her throat as she spoke to the girls who looked at her blankly.

"What are your names?" Eleonore continued, and three of the four looked to one whom Eleonore assumed was the eldest.

"Do you have anything to drink?" the eldest asked with such a parched voice Eleonore couldn't help her face from scrunching in revulsion.

"Sorry," Eleonore shook her head.

"Where are we?" another asked.

A knock rattled against the door before Eleonore could answer and a guard ordered the women to stand beside the bed. Yet, oddly enough, the order was not abrupt and threatening like usual. Instead, the guard sounded gentle, like his order was more of a polite request. The mystery was quickly unshrouded, however, when the young guard entered the room and Eleonore understood that affection was playing a merciful hand.

With reddish cheeks, the guard brought in the trays of food and water which were pounced upon so quickly the contents almost dispersed on the floor in vain. The girls drank with heads tilted backwards, desperate for hydration with the water spilling everywhere. Still, the amount provided didn't pacify their need and they begged for more, which the guard offered a fumbled apology for the scarcity of supplies.

Then, retrieving his cigarettes, he handed them to each of the girls, but ignored Eleonore entirely. Not that she minded since she had her own case of cigarettes, but she didn't appreciate being disregarded in her own cell. Which, she mused, was rather peculiar that she would become possessive over her place of confinement. Regardless, Eleonore remained vigilant of the girls' movements.

"What is going to happen to us?" one of the blonde girls asked the guard.

"The doctor will be seeing you shortly," the guard brushed off the answer.

"Are we sick?" the girl frowned.

"No," the guard laughed uneasily. "He makes his rounds on Tuesdays."

Makes his rounds? Eleonore grew curious at the phrase. *Why would a doctor come by here?*

"Is this a hospital?" another girl asked in a panic.

"No, no," the guard reached out to touch her arm reassuringly, but she withdrew, and his embarrassment radiated.

"Here he is now," the guard cleared his throat as he looked down the hallway. "Quick, put out your smokes," he ordered, and the girls stamped them under their feet.

"Dr. Mengele," the guard left the cell and spoke to the doctor just outside the room. "The girls have arrived."

Rushing into the room, the doctor looked about with mad, wide eyes until he spotted the twins and breathed a sigh of relief like an addict indulging a craving. Stained with sweat on his forehead and armpits, the doctor panted as he collected himself from his brief sprint.

"Good morning. Welcome to Auschwitz," he smiled warmly and diverted all his attention to the twins. "I'm Dr. Mengele. I'll be taking care of you from here on out. Please, allow the guard to escort you to my laboratory where you will be well fed and looked after."

Eleonore wanted to stop them, but she was powerless in this instance. Besides, even if she warned them about the doctor's intentions, there was nothing which could be done. Instead, she watched as the guard held out his hand to guide the twins out of the cell.

"Now," Dr. Mengele looked at the two blondes before him. "You two are rather beautiful."

At this, the eldest took a slight step forward and hid the younger behind her, wary of the doctor and promising that she would be protective.

"What brings you to Auschwitz?" the doctor ignored the threat and asked the question as though the girls were on some sort of cross-country tour.

Unsure of how to respond, the girls looked nervously at each other and the eldest reached out to hold the younger's hand. The gesture reminded Eleonore of her first interaction with Ella, and a loneliness grew in her heart for her friend. Like a pressing necessity, Eleonore wished for Ella's friendship: that confidant which she could disclose the recent events with Rudolph.

She would know what to do, Eleonore turned towards the window with a shudder, wondering if her friend was being tortured for information, or if she was alive at all.

"Don't worry," he looked at his clipboard. "I have all the information here. Ah, oh my," he frowned. "You are suspected in the murder of a SS guard."

"He raped our mother," the eldest replied boldly, justifying their actions.

"What skills do you have?" Dr. Mengele continued without sympathy for their cause.

"Skills?" the girls frowned.

"Yes," he nodded. "Cooking, typing, medical experience, anything?"

"None, sir," the girls replied timidly.

"It's doctor, not sir," he corrected them as his interest faded.

"Sorry," the eldest replied.

"I think for the both of you, it would be best if you rested a little and then we can train you in some sort of skill. How does that sound?"

"Good," the girls answered, though still timid.

"Excellent," the doctor grew excited and glanced at his watch and then went back into the hallway as he called for an assistant.

Squinting, Eleonore watched the doctor warily. 'Rest' was not a word to be used at Auschwitz, and Eleonore assumed some foul play was at hand, but Dr. Mengele's compassion appeared genuine.

"Here we are," the doctor said as his assistant came into the room with a tray of needles and a vial of clear liquid.

"What's that for?" the eldest grew nervous.

"Just something to help you relax and rejuvenate," Dr. Mengele inspected the proper dosages.

"What is it?" the younger girl whispered to her companion.

"It's a new medication that the soldiers use at the front to reenergize themselves," the doctor replied and was so convincing that even Eleonore believed him.

"Please," he motioned to the bed, "sit down."

Obeying, the girls sat on the edge of the bed and looked up at him with a tense expression as he drew the liquid from the vials.

"I'll need to access your arm," he indicated to the first girl and then prepared the second needle.

"You'll feel a slight prick, and then some pressure," the doctor took a cotton swab and dabbed it in some alcohol and rubbed where he intended to place the injection.

Maybe he's telling the truth, Eleonore began to breathe a bit easier. *He wouldn't go through all that trouble otherwise.*

"Don't be nervous," the doctor smiled and withdrew two red candies from his pocket. "Here, these will set your mind at ease."

Grinning, the two girls grabbed the candy and plopped them into their mouths as they bounced excitedly at the end of the bed.

"Settle down now," the doctor laughed at the girls' delight.

"I'm going to go rather quickly," he explained. "I'll inject her arm and then I'll inject yours straight after, understood?" he looked at the girls intently who nodded nervously.

Taking the one needle, Dr. Mengele delivered on his promise as he injected the eldest quickly and then moved to the other girl and injected her as well. Replacing the needles on the assistant's tray, the doctor nodded his task was completed and the assistant left the room as the doctor washed his hands in the sink.

"I'm not feeling so well," the eldest tried to stand, but instead fell flat on her face.

"Joanna!" the younger girl called out but she, too, became faint and fell backwards on the bed.

Placing her hand over her mouth, Eleonore did all she could to stop from screaming at the horror. This madman had just murdered two girls before her very eyes. Trembling as she stared at the floor, Eleonore was left in shock.

Whistling a happy tune, Dr. Mengele inspected himself in the mirror and dried off his hands. Then, returning to the girls, he checked their pulse as he studied his watch. He behaved without shame, undaunted by Eleonore's watchful, horrified gaze as she witnessed his cruelty.

"How many more inspections today?" Dr. Mengele glanced at his assistant when he returned and the two left the cell.

The door closed behind them and Eleonore was locked in with the dead. Petrified, Eleonore couldn't move. She tried to scream, but her breath was stolen from her. Instead, she just wheezed, like something heavy was sitting on her chest.

Eventually, keys jingled outside the door and Eleonore teared up with relief at the sight of Jung's familiar face, but he did not return the sentiment. With his head down, Jung and a handful of other guards brought in a couple of stretchers and carried the two dead girls out of the cell.

Again, without so much as a glance at her, Jung closed the door and left her in isolation. In contrast with the doctor, his shame was palpable. The killing could be carried out as part of his duty if the disposition of the victims matched the narrative: degenerates, sub-human. But these two girls who matched the Aryan ideal exposed the murderers for what they were.

Falling to her knees, Eleonore broke down and sobbed. With her head against the sheets, she let out screams, muffled by the fabric.

I just want to go home, she begged. *Please, I just want to go home. I've done nothing wrong. Is this how you reward those who resist evil? I can't go on like this. It's not natural, none of it. So much hatred, so much malice. And for what? Why would they do this to all these people? To a sweet old couple like Alex and Ruth? To Em and her son? Oh Ella, please, I need to know you're alright.*

Staring out the window in the darkness of the evening, Eleonore couldn't remove the image of the two teenage girls dropping dead.

I can't survive this, she thought as she wiped away a tear.

"*Be strong,*" she heard her father speak. "*You'll make it. I know you will.*"

"Papa," she whispered as the tears streamed. "I fear that I don't have your gift of endurance."

"*Mio dolce angelo,*" her dad spoke softly, "*you're the strongest woman I know.*"

"You're too kind," Eleonore smiled, recalling how her father often spoke to her in such comforting sentiments and her confidence in entrepreneurship owed much to his encouragement.

"He's going to return tonight," Eleonore glanced at the clock which read 10:59 pm. "Last night's revolution should've scared him away for good, but I believe his character is incapable of refusing temptation."

"Keep your focus," her father reminded. *"Don't waver from the path. He's persuasive, he may sound sincere, and he may even appear to be right, but don't listen to any voice that convinces you to leave the path you've set yourself on. No matter the cost, don't stray."*

Keys jingled outside the room, and Eleonore glanced at the clock: 11:00pm. It was Rudolph again and Eleonore knew that he was not here to have another philosophical discussion about his position in the camp. If he was indulging his temptation under such a great risk, then he would not be leaving until he secured his prize.

"Hello," Rudolph spoke quietly as he stood in the doorway.

"Good evening," Eleonore returned a soft reply as she stared out the window.

Though she dared not show it, Eleonore was glad the Commandant had arrived. It was true that she despised him and abhorred his immorality, but she was desperate for information. She assumed the discussion would be short, and Rudolph would either take his desires by force, or he would leave in a rage and solidify her demise, but she needed to know about Ella.

"I'm sorry," he began, and Eleonore turned to face him in surprise.

"I'm not happy with how we left things yesterday," he continued and shut the door. "I couldn't stop thinking about what you said."

Is he sincere? Eleonore watched him cautiously.

"I think it's time I did the right thing," he walked over to the bed and sat on the edge near the window.

"Which is?" Eleonore frowned as she remained guarded.

"A woman of your caliber doesn't belong at Auschwitz," Rudolph sighed.

"Who does belong here?" Eleonore frowned. "Two girls were murdered today in this cell. Exactly where you're sitting now."

"Here?" he patted the bed. "I'll make sure they stop using your cell."

"That's not the point," Eleonore raised her eyebrows. "It's not where they carry out the deed, it's the fact it was done at all!"

"What were their crimes?" he asked.

"There was no trial," Eleonore scoffed. "So how are we to know?"

"Murder, I think," Rudolph clicked his tongue thoughtfully.

"So, you did know?" Eleonore crossed her arms. "Why didn't you do anything about it?"

"I receive the reports afterwards," he shrugged. "This is Dr. Mengele's jurisdiction."

"Stop making excuses," Eleonore clenched her jaw.

"What right do you have to judge me?" Rudolph stood in a fury.

"Leave me," Eleonore turned again to the window.

"Ah!" he flung his arms outward and took a deep breath to calm himself. "Listen, I didn't come here to fight again."

"I know what you're here for," Eleonore looked over her shoulder.

"And?"

"You're married!" she spun around. "Besides, you're the Commandant. If I'm this close to being released why would I destroy what chance I have?"

"Your greatest chance is with me," he moved closer to her and put his hand lightly on her shoulder. "I'm your only hope of leaving Auschwitz. I can even sign the papers tonight if you so wish?" he nodded towards the bed, suggestively.

Eleonore's mind screamed at her to take the chance, but her heart continued to warn her of the deception. She thought of the Italian women murdered yesterday, of the teenage girls murdered earlier, and believed that she couldn't witness any more death and retain her sanity. Either she slept with Rudolph, or she calloused her heart to the point where she didn't care about anyone's suffering. Yet it was likely that Rudolph was lying, and she would lose her dignity and sacrifice her conscience in the process.

"No," Eleonore whispered as a tear fell, knowing that she was sealing her fate.

"I thought you might still be of the position to reject me," Rudolph reached into his uniform and produced a picture.

Handing it to Eleonore, she nearly screamed her horror and placed her hand over her mouth. The photo was of Ella tied to a chair and badly beaten with bruised eyes and lips.

"You're a monster!" Eleonore threw the picture at him.

"My intention was not to upset you," he defended.

"I know exactly what you intend!" she shook as the tears fell from her face.

"I was providing you with an opportunity. We can both benefit."

"Get out!" Eleonore pushed him.

"Ok," he raised his hands and backed away. "But in case you change your mind," he picked up the picture and placed it on the writing desk.

"I won't!" Eleonore clenched her hands into fists.

"You know," Rudolph spoke as he headed towards the door, accepting the evening's defeat. "I can't stop thinking about you. If only we had met many years ago."

With that, he closed the door and Eleonore collapsed to her knees as she sobbed and held tightly onto the sheets while screaming her rage.

How dare he! She pounded her fist against the bed repeatedly. *How dare he use her against me!*

Chapter Twenty-Three:
Compromise

"Those who can make you believe absurdities can make you commit atrocities." – Voltaire

Staring out the window as she sat at her desk, Eleonore lit her cigarette and watched the sun shining from behind thick, grey clouds. She was desperate to pen her thoughts, to journal what she had witnessed these past few weeks but knew it would be lethal.

A knock came to the door and Eleonore put out her smoke before standing beside the bed. Yet, oddly enough, the peephole was not opened and neither did the door unlock. She had expected to have more 'visitors' like the last two days, but none were ushered in.

Wondering if she had imagined the knock, Eleonore studied the door. When no further sound was made, she returned to the desk and was about to re-light the cigarette when a knock came again.

"Yes?" Eleonore called out.

"It's me," Jung spoke through the door.

What's he doing here? Eleonore wondered.

"Do you have a minute to talk?" he asked.

"Um," Eleonore frowned at the strange question.

At that, the keys jingled, and the door opened as Jung walked in and removed his hat, respectfully.

"What do you need?" Eleonore said curtly, she was not in the mood to balance yet another man's brittle affections.

"I wanted to warn you," he began as he avoided eye contact.

"Warn me about what?" Eleonore turned her head as she began to worry.

"The executions will begin shortly," Jung nodded towards the window.

"Executions?!" Eleonore panicked.

"The revolutionaries from the other night are to be hung near that wall," Jung walked over to the window and pointed at the concrete wall where Em had been shot.

"That's dreadful," Eleonore shook her head, "but I fail to see how this involves me, unless I'm to be hung along with them?"

"You don't understand," Jung sighed and crossed his arms. "Rudolph is creating a cruel game, and you'll have no choice but to play along."

"I'm tired, and I'm desperate to know when I'm going to be released," Eleonore gave Jung a look of warning. "Please speak your peace and leave."

"Rudolph is promising liberty to take advantage of you," Jung looked at Eleonore with sympathy.

"So, what does that have to do with the executions?" Eleonore remained confused.

"You haven't taken the bait yet," he nodded to the picture of Ella on the table.

"No," Eleonore turned the picture upside down, unwilling to have her friend viewed in such a manner. "I have not."

"Which is why he's upping the ante," Jung again looked out the window as prisoners began to drag lumber and rope over to the wall. "He will use Ella against you, and he'll gladly kill her in the process."

"Why are you helping me?" Eleonore squinted.

"I know you don't harbor affection for me," Jung nodded and swallowed, "and I've accepted that you never will, but I'll be damned if I stand idly by."

"He hasn't forced himself upon me yet," Eleonore rubbed her forehead in exhaustion, "and he's remained respectful, to a degree, but I'm worried that time is against me."

"I share that concern," Jung shook his head in frustration.

"Not entirely," Eleonore smiled slightly. "He's not trying to sleep with you."

"Right," Jung's compassion swelled as he thought of Eleonore's plight.

"When is Ella scheduled to be executed?" Eleonore couldn't believe the words were coming out of her mouth.

"Tomorrow," Jung rubbed his chin in thought. "The rest are to be executed today. I have to say, as far as revolts go, she did a damn good job. They destroyed most of the crematoriums and killed seventy SS guards. With a bit more firepower, they would've had us. Though where they obtained the explosives or weapons is beyond me."

"Interesting," Eleonore spoke, pretending to not have any knowledge of the details.

"You must understand," Jung pressed, "Rudolph will kill your friend regardless of what you do for him."

"Thank you," Eleonore touched Jung's arm. "I appreciate the warning."

With that, Jung nodded and left her alone in the cell, but not without one last, hopeful glance. Knowing that she didn't return his love, Jung had done everything within his power to prepare her for Rudolph's deception. It was now up to Eleonore to decide whether she would play along.

The hours passed by as Eleonore watched helplessly as the Nazis forced the Jewish prisoners to build the gallows. The hammering and sawing lasted the entire morning until, fatefully, the crude gallows were completed.

As a cruel display of power, the Nazis gathered the entire camp to bear witness to the executions. All duties and labors were suspended as thousands were herded towards the area just in front of Eleonore's detention center. Then, once the camp had been assembled, the Nazis brought out the revolutionaries who were bound in chains at their hands and feet. There were hundreds of these rebels, but Eleonore fumed when she noticed that the gallows had room for only two, and understood the Nazis' intentions: the executions were to be drawn out.

Yet for all her rage, Eleonore spotted something peculiar as the first man and woman were put in place at the gallows. Neither begged for their lives or prayed for mercy. Instead, they held their chins high and proud and Eleonore thought she could almost see a smile on their faces. They had carried out their mission and succeeded in destroying the crematoriums. Yes, they would be rebuilt, but the Jews had shown their oppressors their mettle and grit. They were a people whom God had created to despise a life absent of honor. However small the measure, they had reclaimed some of that valor.

The first two were elderly and, in many ways, reminded her of Ruth and Alex. Eleonore pressed herself against the window as she watched in horror. She wanted to look away, but her heart begged her to remain; there was something at work, something beyond the mortal realm being articulated before her very eyes.

As the executioner hung the noose around their necks, Eleonore saw the Commandant climb onto the gallows and stand triumphantly before his victims. Inspecting the woman, Rudolph looked her up and down, then moved on to the man and examined him in the same fashion. Then, turning to the crowd, he addressed them.

"Today we shall taste the sweetness of justice," he began as he projected his voice. "Before you are men and women who have acted like beasts: mere brutes. They have been deceived by one of your own into believing that the will of the Fuhrer can be overthrown. See where their deceptions have led them? See the fruit of their destructive labors?"

Eleonore shook her head in disbelief as she listened. How could he call them brutes for trying to stop the killing of their own people? Was he so disconnected from reality that he believed his own fabrication?

"Through our investigations," Rudolph continued as he threw his hands behind his back and paced, "we have discovered two ring leaders: Roza Robata, whom we accepted into our own household as a maid, and Ella Gartner, the great deceiver whom many of you know."

At this, Eleonore's blood boiled. She hated hearing Ella's name slandered. She looked out over the crowd, trying to study the faces of those she could see from her position. She watched as the inmates began to whisper excitedly to one another. It was then that Eleonore's heart felt fuller than she could ever remember: Ella was not the criminal that Rudolph had tried to paint her. She was their hero.

"Roza Robota will be the last to be executed today," Rudolph continued and looked up at Eleonore standing in the window, "and Ella Gartner will be the last to be executed tomorrow."

Seething with rage, Eleonore wiped away an angry tear and clenched her jaw as she grew hatred in her heart for Rudolph. How could he use Ella against her to gain an advantage? What a disgusting, wretched thing to do.

Nodding to the executioner, Rudolph climbed off the gallows, but held his gaze upon Eleonore. His twisted game had begun.

"Be strong and of good courage!" the male prisoner shouted.

The trap door swung open and the two prisoners dropped sharply. Their bound legs kicked wildly as they suffered, but within minutes it was over. Still, his last words reverberated through Eleonore's heart and she recalled that it was the encouragement of God to Joshua after the death of Moses. The prisoner had reminded his fellow Jews of their faith, and the insurmountable odds they had overcome throughout all of history.

Weeping, Eleonore watched as two more men were led up to the gallows. She wished she could turn away, but these were their last moments and how could she refuse them the honor of witnessing their victory? To say these revolutionaries had been defeated would be to ignore their triumph. Their bodies had been broken but their spirits remained unbent. What is courage if any man can summon it at will? What is valor if not bravery in the face of certain death? They sacrificed their lives knowing that some may be spared the gassings.

"Be strong and of good courage," the man's voice broke as he echoed the encouragement.

Again, the trap door fell out from under their feet and Eleonore watched them struggle until the end. The people forced to watch wept for the fallen, but these were not tears of disparity, but rather, of inspiration to face the insurmountable. They knew suffering and death awaited them, but after they passed through the veil they would be taken to a place where the Nazis could never reach; a place where neither rust nor moth can destroy.

The executions continued unimpeded as each pair pronounced, "Be strong and of good courage," before being dropped unto their death. Eleonore watched each one, weeping and wishing there was something she could do to stop the atrocity.

But sorrow swelled when Roza was led to the gallows. She was the last to be hung and had endured the torture of witnessing, time and again, what was to be her fate. Roza looked pale with tear-stained eyes which were wide and full of panic. Eleonore hated seeing someone who had been so kind to her in such a state of terror.

As the noose was placed around her neck, Roza tried to speak but the words wouldn't form. Stepping into place, she looked out over the crowd and then at her executioner, her eyes begging for more time.

"Be strong and of good courage," someone shouted from the crowd.

Roza's eyes welled as she looked out the one who had spoken, thanking them for saying what she was unable to pronounce.

"Be strong and of good courage," another shouted, and then another, and another.

Like a wave, the encouragement ran through the people and they became animated as they raised their fists and shouted the phrase over and over. The guards aimed their weapons at the crowd, but it did nothing to quell their support and they kept shouting. Only when the floor was opened underneath Roza did they watch with quiet reverence until the final seconds.

With intolerable fury, Eleonore glared at Rudolph, wishing she could enact justice. How she wanted to watch him hang from a rope for all to see. He, above any of those who had been executed, deserved such a fate.

The clock read 11:00 PM and Eleonore waited for Rudolph as she stood beside the bed, pen clutched tightly behind her back.

"What are you planning there, love?" Ruth spoke to Eleonore.

"I'm going to kill him," Eleonore whispered as she shook. The thought of carrying out the deed was terrible and, previously, she doubted she had the fortitude to carry it to completion. But watching him during the executions provided Eleonore with all the resolve she required.

"What about Ella?"

"You heard what Jung said," Eleonore wiped the sweat from her forehead, "Rudolph will kill her no matter what. Besides, it's time that I do my part for the resistance."

"They'll kill you too," Ruth warned.

"How can I cower any longer," Eleonore welled up, "after witnessing their courage? I promised Ella that I would prove where my priorities lay."

"*If that's the route you're going down,*" Ruth's voice echoed in her head, "*then make sure you strike true.*"

"I doubt he'll see it coming," Eleonore whispered to the fabrication of Ruth. "I have the advantage of surprise."

As expected, the keys jingled from outside the cell and in walked Rudolph. Tonight, however, he carried with him the look of defeat, presuming her answer.

"Good evening," Eleonore began, disguising the agitation in her voice.

Mumbling his greeting, Rudolph removed his shoes and hat and stumbled over to the bed, exhausted. Sitting down, he slumped over and sighed like a child seeking attention. With his neck exposed, Eleonore worked up the courage to strike and, with a quick inhale, raised her weapon.

"Hedwig knows," he rubbed his hand through his hair, catching Eleonore off guard.

"Knows what?" Eleonore panicked, and quickly hid the pen behind her back again.

"About the purpose of the crematoriums," Rudolph looked up at her and then back at his feet as he sulked. "She won't sleep with me anymore."

"Is she taking the kids?" Eleonore asked, but heard Ruth nagging at her to attack while she had the chance.

"What?" he looked up at her in surprise. "No, she's not leaving me. She detests me is all."

"Oh," Eleonore frowned, guessing the purpose of his game. *Men are pathetic,* she shook her head. *Is he really thinking that if he reveals his marital strains that I will somehow want to jump into his lap?*

"She has too much pride to seek a divorce," he continued. "Besides, she loves Auschwitz. It's perfect for the children. Anyways, have you reconsidered?" Rudolph stood and walked over to the writing desk where he turned over the picture of Ella and held it like he was looking at an endearing photo of a family member.

"I have," Eleonore spoke quietly.

"And?!" Rudolph looked at her anxiously.

"I will be your friend on one condition," Eleonore raised her finger.

"Anything," Rudolph shrugged.

"Liberation for Ella and myself," Eleonore spoke boldly. If Rudolph relented, she could lower his guard further and kill him when he was most vulnerable.

"Out of the question," Rudolph shook his head. "She's a criminal responsible for masterminding a revolt. If I released her, I might as well be signing my own death warrant."

"Then what can you offer?" Eleonore raised her eyebrows, unimpressed.

"Alleviation," Rudolph flinched his eye, unaccustomed to bartering with those below his station. "I can place her in the cell next to yours."

"It's been empty since Em was murdered," Eleonore spoke to herself. "It would be nice to have some company."

"Who?" Rudolph frowned, but then waved his hand when he decided that he didn't care. "Yes, yes, that can be arranged."

"Good," Eleonore sighed her satisfaction. "And when it has been 'arranged,' then we can become friends."

"No," Rudolph shook his head, "sleep with me first, then I shall bring Ella here."

If ever I felt like a prostitute, Eleonore squirmed at the awkwardness of the discussion. *If he gets what he wants, then he won't have to follow through with his promise.*

"If you believe I'm only after relations," Rudolph moved closer to her, but not in a threatening manner, "then you've misjudged me. I have affections for you. You're beautiful, bright, elegant, and something I feel I'm missing in my life. Please consider the possibilities: I could bring Ella to the cell tomorrow night, have my way with you, and then kill both of you the next day. In fact, I could've forced myself on you a long time ago, but I respect you, though I desire you fiercely."

"Do I have your word?" Eleonore closed her eyes as everything within her screamed that she was making a critical error.

"Of course," Rudolph smiled in his victory.

Nodding, Eleonore relaxed her shoulders and motioned for him to come closer: the deception required perfection. With an alluring gaze, Eleonore hinted that the attraction was mutual and, maybe, she had desired this all along. Then, with her free hand, she undid the top button of her outfit and pulled the shirt to the side, revealing her shoulder.

Standing mere inches away, Rudolph wrapped his arms around her with one, fluid motion and began kissing her bare shoulder. This was her chance, Rudolph had lowered his guard, and Eleonore knew she couldn't miss.

Lifting the pen, Eleonore eyed her mark and brought the weapon down with all her might. But it was of little consequence. Grabbing her wrist, Rudolph looked at her with marvel.

"What did you suppose was going to happen?" Rudolph wrung the pen free and threw it to the ground.

"I…" Eleonore shook.

"Everything you said, was that just a ruse?" Rudolph looked at her as though he was hurt.

"You're going to kill Ella no matter what I do," Eleonore looked at him bitterly, though still trembling.

"No, no," he shook his head and stepped back slightly. "I gave you my word. I can have you killed for making an attempt on my life."

"You can't kill me," Eleonore shook her head.

"How so?" Rudolph folded his hands.

"You'd publicly expose your own intentions with an inmate."

"Eleonore," Rudolph spoke patronizingly, "jurisprudence at Auschwitz is often muddled with falsities. While everything done here is legal, none question the orders relayed to them. It is within my legal right to kill you."

"Then take what you want and leave!" Eleonore bent over the desk.

"What are you doing?" Rudolph remained calm.

"Do it!" she shouted.

"Come here," Rudolph grabbed the back of her arm and stood her upright. "If that's what I wanted, I could go to the brothel."

"Then what do you want?" Eleonore fumed. She couldn't bear his presence any longer.

"To give yourself to me, body and soul," he squeezed her arms gently, "Just as I will give myself to you."

"I can't," Eleonore shook her head.

"Then you will never speak to Ella again," Rudolph's grip on her arms tightened as a warning.

Relinquishing her dignity, Eleonore sat on the edge of the bed as she let Rudolph kiss her neck. Absent of emotion, Eleonore lay on her back as Rudolph proceeded. A vacant vessel, a hollow soul, Eleonore had finally given the last of herself for the sake of another. She would be empty so that Ella could be whole.

Relations with another man had not occurred for many years, and Eleonore had forgotten much of what the experience felt like and, to be honest, how overrated it was. Rudolph was awkward and, although gentle, didn't take into consideration her needs.

Over nearly before it began, Rudolph sighed and rolled over as he laid in the bed beside her and seemed to almost fall asleep. While Eleonore was thankful the 'event' had been quick, the pace had left her feeling used, worthless. Yet she hoped that some good would come of it and that Ella's suffering would indeed be alleviated.

"There was a woman I met when I was rather young," Rudolph lit a cigarette. "I think, to a degree, you remind me of her. I was on campaign in the first great war, fighting near Jerusalem."

Interested, Eleonore turned on her side to look at him as he spoke. She had given her body, now he was after her soul and she had no choice but to play along. Besides, she loved to hear stories of the first war as her father rarely spoke of it. She wanted to know what it was like for him and maybe shed some light on his volatile moods.

"I was shot in the knee during the campaign. More painful than anything else I experienced," he continued with one hand behind his head as he stared at the ceiling. "I was taken to the hospital near Jaffa where I was put under the charge of a young nurse. Thankfully, she had affections for me; otherwise I don't think I would've survived. I contracted malaria as well, you see, and she would watch over me diligently to ensure I didn't harm myself during the fits or my fever didn't run too high. Eventually, I recovered and, when I was well enough to walk, she took me to a private place and introduced me to every stage of lovemaking. I was rather shy around the opposite sex and if she hadn't initiated, I doubt I would have summoned the courage."

Eleonore continued to watch him silently as she listened to him. Maybe there was some clue to his past that she could exploit for her advantage. She hated thinking in such a way, but against a man of his caliber, she would require every means at her disposal to not only save her life but that of Ella's as well.

"It was a wonderful experience, and I vowed to only engage in relations if it involved true warmth," Rudolph turned on his side to look at her.

"What was the war like?" Eleonore asked, pretending to enjoy his company.

"The best experience of my life," he returned to staring at the ceiling. "That's not to say I enjoyed it. I rather hated war, but I was a damn good soldier. I was part of the twenty-first Baden Regiment of Dragoons, the same cavalry regiment in which my father and grandfather served."

"Quite the honor," Eleonore lit her own cigarette and joined Rudolph in staring at the ceiling.

"Yes, well," he chuckled, "my mother didn't see it that way. It wasn't until we were en-route to the Middle East that I sent her a letter advising of my decision to join. I was only fifteen at the time and she had tried with endless patience and kindness to make me change my mind. Only when I took part in my first battle did I realize she was right."

"How so?"

"My unit was supporting the Turks against the British and, just as we had received orders, we were attacked by an Indian brigade under English command. I escaped the initial onslaught by jumping off my horse and hiding behind an ancient pillar, caking my uniform in the desert's yellow dust. I remember being surprised at just how loud it all was. Horses neighing, grenades exploding, shots firing, and wounded men shrieking. Even now, as I lay here, I can picture it perfectly: a man to my left falls dead and, turning to my right, my comrade is struck down with a head wound. I was overcome by a horror worse than I had ever known."

"How did you survive?" Eleonore continued to pretend she was genuinely interested in the story.

"I saw my captain, crouched behind a block just a few feet away, firing back at the enemy with discipline. His calmness encouraged me, and I remembered my duty. Not that I had much of a choice as the next moment I saw a tall, dark Indian with a full black beard charging towards me. His bayonet was fixed, his pace was rapid, and I was his target. Raising my rifle," Rudolph held his arms out to reenact the scene, "I aimed and shot. He fell down dead at my feet: my first kill."

"Must've been shocking."

"It was," he nodded, and a smile grew on his face, "but also liberating. The spell of fear broke, and I began to fire off shot after shot, killing rapidly. I could kill, efficiently and effectively, and I damn enjoyed it. Fortunately, my captain took notice and, throughout the campaign, became like a father to me. He made sure I was spared from the most dangerous of missions and watched over me. Oddly enough," Rudolph huffed, "I was much closer to him than my own father."

"Why's that?"

"Long story with that one. Anyways," Rudolph reached over and touched her hand, but she made no effort to return the affection, "I will leave you in peace. Tomorrow, I promise, Ella will be in the cell next to you and I will give the doctor orders to have her wounds tended to."

"Thank you," Eleonore whispered.

Glancing over his shoulder, Rudolph studied Eleonore for a moment and then left her alone in the darkness and isolation.

Placing her hands over her stomach, Elenore breathed in and out, feeling them rise and fall as she stared blankly at the ceiling above. *Rotten,* was the word that came to her mind as she felt an emptiness unlike any other.

Chapter Twenty-Four: Ti Amo

"If you're going through hell, keep going." – Winston Churchill

Sitting on the edge of her bed with excitement, Eleonore waited patiently for Ella to be placed in the cell next to her. She had been so thrilled that she tidied her bed, the books and writing instruments were neatly aligned, and even the cigarettes were hidden. She knew Ella wouldn't be able to see it, but still, she felt as though a long-lost relative was returning home.

The morning gong rang, and Eleonore looked outside the window to see the camp stirring into action. A lonely twinge irked within her and part of her wished she could be back within the barracks. She was happy to be without the cold and to have an actual bed to sleep on, but the days and nights were a bitterness of their own sort without the companionship of others. Rudolph only heightened the loneliness with his visits.

Then, Eleonore noticed that instead of the inmates lining up outside their assigned barracks, they were herded again towards the gallows. More prisoners due for execution were dragged out with chains binding their hands and feet.

Panicking that Rudolph had gone back on his word and that Ella was among them, Eleonore scanned the crowd of prisoners for any sight of her. She spotted Rudolph climbing onto the gallows but ignored him. Again, he began a speech, but Eleonore was too focused on searching for Ella that she didn't catch what he was saying, though she assumed it wasn't much different than the demonization of yesterday.

"Be strong and of good courage," the first pair shouted as they dropped to their death.

The next pair were put in position for execution, and Eleonore sighed her relief that neither were Ella. *If that bastard lied to me,* Eleonore began to imagine the possibilities but, as she was fuming, the cell door next to her opened.

Pressing herself against the thin wall, Eleonore listened to the commotion, but she could only hear the shuffling boots, likely from the soldiers.

"Be strong and of good courage," a female voice shouted from outside.

Running to the window, Eleonore rubbed away the fog to watch as two women dropped: neither were Ella. Returning to the wall, Eleonore pressed her ear against it as she listened.

"Just leave her," one of the guards panted.

"What if she suffocates?" the other guard replied.

"Not our problem."

"The Commandant ordered her here for a reason," the second persisted.

It must be Ella! Eleonore chewed her nails nervously.

"Then hurry up with it," the first grew annoyed.

Eleonore listened as the bed shifted under the weight of a body. The guard wheezed and puffed as he put the body into a better position.

"There," he breathed heavily and the two left the room.

"Ella?" Eleonore whispered but there was no reply.

"Ella?" she asked again and knocked lightly on the wall. Still, there was no answer.

Is she breathing? Eleonore listened intently.

"Be strong and of good courage," a male shouted from outside the window and he wept loudly before being silenced.

"I'm going to talk to you anyways," Eleonore whispered as she leaned her back against the wall. "I don't think I can stand another day hearing them being executed. Such a dreadful thing. I was brave yesterday and watched, but today I don't believe I have the courage. Odd thing to admit, when it's not you being executed, but it does take some nerve to watch without becoming desensitized."

The deafening silence continued as Eleonore leaned her head against the wall and listened to the occasional, yet triumphant shout from those being executed.

"I do hope they didn't hurt you too badly," Eleonore spoke again. "Though, to your credit, I think you put a right scare in them. I don't know if that was the extent of your plan, but well done nonetheless."

A groan.

"Ella?!" Eleonore spoke up. "Can you hear me?"

Huffing in impatience, Eleonore tapped her leg anxiously, wondering how she could pass the time. She didn't want to seem inconsiderate to those who were giving their lives but watching hanging upon hanging two days in a row would be nothing short of maddening.

Unable to think clearly, Eleonore paced about the room, checking on the executions ever so often to see if Ella was among them, wondering if it was indeed her in the next room.

"Stand beside the bed," a knock came to the door and the guard slid the peephole open and closed.

As usual, the guard walked into her cell with a tray of food, except today there was something different which caught Eleonore's eye. The meal, which was warm and fresh, had been prepared with care. The potatoes still held their form, the beef was tender and slightly red, and a garnishing of vegetables was arranged in a pleasing manner.

"Who's that for?" Eleonore asked in confusion.

"Who else?" the guard replied sarcastically and slammed the door on his way out.

Startled by his reaction, Eleonore was left mystified and watched the food enviously as it gave off steam, begging to be eaten and savored. Who more willing and appreciative than Eleonore? Still, she dared not touch it for fear it was reserved for someone of greater importance than herself.

Then, the keys jingled again, and Eleonore stood beside the bed, anticipating the peephole to be opened and the command given. *What now?* She wondered and glanced again at the food, wishing she had at least taken a bite.

But as Eleonore waited, she was surprised when her cell door didn't open. Instead, she heard the creak of Ella's door, and then hushed voices whispering to one another. Pressing her ear against the wall, Eleonore guessed that there were at least two men in Ella's cell, but couldn't make out what they were whispering to each other.

What is that sound? Eleonore squinted. *Is that water? Where is it coming from?*

A sudden splash and a gasp for air from Ella answered Eleonore's questions. The guards had awakened her rudely by pouring water over her. The bed squeaked under her frantic body, and Eleonore wondered if they had tied Ella to the bed or if they were holding her down. Either way, it was cruel.

"Again!" a guard shouted, and his request was met with another splash and a gasp for air from Ella.

"You stupid dog!" the other guard shouted and hit Ella with something which caused her to scream in agony.

"How long do you want this to continue?" they shouted. "You have the power to make this stop."

Thump! came another strike which produced another cry of agony, but no voice of discontent or begging for relief. In fact, Ella said nothing at all but only cried at their strikes.

"Look," said the first guard and Eleonore heard him light a match and take a deep puff, likely from a cigarette, "you may think I'm enjoying this, but I'm not. Truly. I take no pleasure in torturing beautiful women such as yourself."

"Now Dr. Mengele, on the other hand," the other guard interjected. "He doesn't have the same, um, what would you call it Herr Gehring?"

"Inhibitions," Gehring said with a hint of pleasure.

"Inhibitions, yes, that's the word," the guard chuckled. "I've seen him do things so inhumane that-"

"Get your rotten hands off me!" Ella barked.

That's my Ella, Eleonore couldn't help a smile. She wanted Ella to fight back, to overcome.

"Easy now," Gehring laughed. "I wasn't going to hurt you. Or is that what you prefer?"

"She didn't get this upset with anything else we've done," the other guard snickered.

"I prefer the batons over your wandering fingers," Ella spit. "What's the matter? Are you getting tired?"

"Watch it you shit," Gehring warned.

"Awe, did I upset you?" Ella patronized.

A swoosh went through the air and a hit landed firmly on Ella who screamed at the strike. Then another and another landed as Ella cursed loudly at them.

"Even I can hit harder," Ella mocked as she panted between breaths. "Don't hold back just because I'm a woman."

Enraged, the guards struck her harder and harder until, finally, the cell door swung open.

"Stop! She's provoking you!" Dr. Mengele spoke and halted the guards from their relentless attacks. "We need her alive."

"What's the point in saving any of them?" Gehring panted. "They'll all be sent to the gallows anyways."

"The point is," Dr. Mengele spoke condescendingly, "to find out if we rounded up the remaining resistance. We must drag that rotting house of dissension up from the roots. If not, then another revolt, the likes of which killed seventy of your comrades, will become a regular occurrence."

"That's what we're trying to do," Gehring defended.

"You're failing," Dr. Mengele said with a hushed rage. "She is a particular specimen: one who believes you can break the body, but not the soul. I intend to destroy both."

"What do you need us to do?" Gehring asked, still panting.

"Leave."

"I can't authori...yes, sir," Gehring agreed, and Eleonore could picture the look on the doctor's face which had so quickly brought the officer to heel. Two pairs of boots walked briskly out of the room and the door was closed behind them.

"Miss Gartner," Dr. Mengele took a deep breath and Eleonore heard a chair being dragged across the room.

"Are they done already?" Ella spoke with a lisp, indicating to Eleonore that her friend's face was already swelling.

"God has planted in the Jewish breast a soul with such a temperament as to abhor dishonor," Dr. Mengele began.

"You know the works of Josephus?" Ella asked.

"You're surprised?" Dr. Mengele boasted.

"I'm surprised you could read," Ella quipped, and Eleonore covered her mouth to stifle a laugh.

"I've read all about the Jewish general who became a slave and then rose to freedom. I've studied his defense of the Jewish fortress at Jotapata, and his recollection of the fall of Jerusalem."

"What's your point?" Ella grew annoyed.

"The Jews were defeated," Dr. Mengele spoke quickly. "Valiant? Yes. Courageous? Without a doubt. But for all their heroism, for all their zeal, the Jews still lost Jerusalem to the Romans and the Temple, the Holy of Holies, was burnt to the ground. Because of the nature which still resides within you, it has been nearly two thousand years in which the Jews have not had a country to call home. Again, your actions here with the crematoriums were valiant, but that won't stop us from eradicating every last Jew."

"You'll run out of bullets and gas before the world runs out of Jews."

"Then we'll use our bare hands," Dr. Mengele spoke with all the menace in his heart. "Resources, my dear, resources govern who rules and who is ruled. The Romans crushed the Jews, the Muslims enslaved you, and the Christians massacred your people. Now, the Fascists have the greatest resources this world has ever seen, and the Jews will be wiped from the face of the earth."

"Are you always this boring?" Ella sighed and, again, Eleonore had to stifle a laugh.

"You have an excellent gift for seeing another's weakness," Dr. Mengele chuckled. "With the guards, you implied that they were perverted. This is an area of depravation to which they have never stooped, and they pride themselves on it: the last piece of their morality. With me, you attack my intelligence and my ability to humor."

"I'm still failing to see the point," Ella sighed.

"Tell us the other names, and you can change the course of history. You can be the Jew on the right side: one who survives. Not for long, of course, your time will still come, but you can stretch those days out a little."

Ella snickered.

"Or," the doctor said slowly. "I can take away that glorious finale you're so anxiously awaiting. You won't be given your heroic death in front of the crowd. You won't be quoting Joshua. You'll be killed silently, right here, strapped down to this bed with a needle in your arm."

"That's what you keep forgetting," Ella whispered.

"What's that?"

"You're not my audience, and neither are they."

"I presume you mean God?" Dr. Mengele laughed. "You think he's watching? If he is, then he is cruel indeed. My dear, if the almighty exists, then it's the strong he favors."

"Must you be so temperamental?" Ella defended, and Eleonore detected a trace of fear in her voice. "God is eternal. This moment of suffering is but a breath of air. As for strength, God uses the weak things of this world to shame the strong, and the foolish to shame the wise. When this is over," Ella scoffed and began to chuckle, "you will be dragged before the judges of the world and made to account for your sins. The Nazi party and its ideals will be buried so deep it will never see the light again. Before the foolish democracies and the weak ideologies of the west, your strength will be put to shame for all eternity."

Silence. Eleonore listened closely with her ear pressed against the wall, her heart beating strongly, but there was no movement, no sound of any sort. Ella's words had found their mark.

"I have another trick to play," Dr. Mengele finally spoke, and Eleonore could hear his chair dragging away from the bed. "Before long, you will confess the other names."

"Go to hell!" Ella screamed as the cell door slammed shut.

"Ella!" Eleonore tapped the wall excitedly, but there was no reply.

"Ella?" Eleonore frowned.

"What do you want?" Ella replied coldly.

"I, um," Eleonore was stunned by the indifference, "I thought you'd be —"

"What? Happy?" Ella scoffed in frustration. "I was due to be executed today. Instead, I'm meant to suffer through these tortures. I'm tied to a bed with no ability to use the facilities, I haven't eaten in God knows how long, and I could've been released from these sorrows and already on my way to see my sweet husband again."

"I'm sorry," Eleonore shook her head as her eyes welled. "I will make sure you are fed and released from your bonds."

"Leave me out of your plans," Ella spoke through gritted teeth.

"But I saved you," Eleonore slumped back, confused as to how she had misled herself.

"From what?" Ella nearly shouted. "From seeing my family again? I wanted to die. Don't you understand? I wanted the Nazis to put that noose around my neck. Whatever you thought was a benefit for me is just a way for you to silence your conscience."

"But you —"

"Leave me in peace," Ella demanded.

You'll see, Eleonore thought as she relented. *I'll make this right. Whatever it costs.*

11:00 pm. As expected, Rudolph arrived and, feeling more than comfortable with this newfound habit, began to undress without so much as offering Eleonore a glance.

"What are you doing?!" Eleonore grew indignant.

"Aren't we friends?" Rudolph paused and looked at her in confusion.

"How dare you!"

"Whatever do you mean?" Rudolph frowned and nodded to the wall. "Was she not placed in the cell?"

"Yes, but I didn't ask that she be tortured!" Eleonore threw her hands onto her hips.

"Neither did I," Rudolph shrugged, "but she won't provide us with the names of the other conspirators. There was no choice."

"Then I have no choice, either," Eleonore crossed her arms, signaling her opposition to his desires.

"You are bold," Rudolph squinted and came to stand just across from her.

"The answer is no," Eleonore held firm. "Not until Ella is released from her bonds and treated properly."

"She's not within my jurisdiction," Rudolph shrugged. "I have no power over what happens to her."

"Then who?"

"Dr. Mengele."

"Maybe I should be sleeping with him then," Eleonore offered a steel glance.

"Are you trying to infuriate me?" Rudolph asked rhetorically. Then, after a moment of keeping his temper within check, continued, "You and Miss Gartner are close, yes?"

Eleonore nodded.

"Does she trust you?"

"I'm not about to report on my friend, if that's what you're asking."

"Think about it," Rudolph put his hands on Eleonore's arms which were still crossed. "She's too prideful to confess to us, but without her disclosure, her condition will not improve. If she confides in you, then I can provide the information to Dr. Mengele and we can see about making life more comfortable for this Jewess."

"And until then," Eleonore cleared her throat, "we will not be friends."

"It's best not to upset me," Rudolph warned.

Studying Rudolph for a moment, Eleonore weighed her options. Yet how could she give in? She had slept with Rudolph to alleviate Ella's condition which, as it turns out, only alienated her from Ella. Not that Rudolph had placed her in a position that offered much of a choice.

"Don't you see the advantage of our relationship?" Rudolph persisted.

"Help Ella," Eleonore demanded.

Clenching his jaw, Rudolph squeezed his hand into a fist. He was not accustomed to being denied, especially with his previous 'victory' the other night.

"I'll do what I can," he spoke at last, though still seething with contempt.

"Then I shall see you tomorrow," Eleonore turned away.

"I've already proven I'm a man of my word," Rudolph pressed.

"That you have," Eleonore caught the glimpse in his eye and knew that he was at the limit of his patience and to test him further would be catastrophic.

"Eleonore," Rudolph sat on the edge of the bed and looked up at her longingly while speaking softly, "you know how dangerous it is for me to be here. I'm risking everything: my marriage, my career, and likely my life just to come and see you. My desire for you grows with each passing moment. I need you and you need me."

"I don't need you," Eleonore spoke quietly.

"Then Ella shall remain in her discomfort!" Rudolph stood in a rush and bolted for the door.

"Alright," Eleonore raised her hand to stop him from leaving and she climbed under the sheets before undressing.

"I don't want it like this," Rudolph shook his head as he held his hand on the door. "I need you to want me."

"Does it matter?" Eleonore welled up.

"I suppose not," Rudolph slowly let go of the door and returned to the bed.

Again, the two were joined in unholy relations. He kissed her neck as she turned away, not allowing him near her lips; he ran his hands across her body while hers lay limp; he was enraptured in passion while she stared at the names written on the wall: *Filip, Abend, Josef, Blanc, Bittner.* She kept her gaze fixed on the wall towards Ella while Rudolph had his way, wondering if her friend knew the extent of what she had done. How she wished to trade places. Yet there was also the strange reminder as to how little she knew the woman. Why should she be sacrificing so much for someone she didn't truly know?

"I will speak with Dr. Mengele tomorrow," Rudolph spoke after they had finished and began dressing.

His mood had embittered significantly, and he carried the burden of regret. The event had become cheap, even for him, but Eleonore didn't care as her only concern was Ella.

What does it matter? Eleonore sighed. *It's given me a purpose, and without it, I would have lost my humanity a long time ago. Maybe it's because I admire her so much? She is brave in the face of torture while I'm rather timid and self-seeking. I wish I was more like her. Stay the course. Stay the course.* She thought repeatedly as she drifted off into a world far removed from the hell of this one.

Chapter Twenty-Five: Penance

"Faith is to believe what you do not see; the reward for faith is seeing what you believe."
St. Augustine

The morning gong rang, and Eleonore sprang to her feet. She had forgotten where she was and, in the darkness, assumed that she was back in the barracks. As recollection caught up with her, Eleonore placed her head in her hands as she sat back down on the bed, rubbing her pounding temples and tired eyes.

Ella! She recalled that her friend was but a wall away. She wanted to call out and talk to her, but then remembered the distaste Ella bore towards her. Besides, the sun had not yet risen, and it would be unkind of her to wake Ella in her state.

Turning on the lamp, Eleonore sat at her writing desk and, retrieving a piece of paper and a pen, stared blankly at the vacant page. She wanted to write, to allow for a creative outlet, but the empty page mocked her.

With a barren mind, Eleonore knew that she wouldn't give birth to anything useful, so she abandoned the pursuit and reached for a cigarette from the silver casing Jung had given her. Only, she fumbled in the low light and the case fell onto the floor, spilling its contents.

"Damn it!" Eleonore panicked as she felt around in the shadows beneath the desk.

Eventually, the cigarettes were accounted for and carefully returned. Grabbing the silver case off the floor, Eleonore was intrigued when her fingers ran across what felt like an inscription on the back. Turning it over, she examined it under the lamp to find an engravement which read: "My dearest husband, you really should stop smoking."

She was rather witty, Eleonore chuckled as she thought of Emily Jung. *But why would she buy her husband a case when she wanted him to stop? Unless she didn't purchase the case, but only had it engraved. When he spoke of her, Jung seemed to have a genuine affection for his wife, so why would he leave this case with me?*

Lighting her cigarette as she tried to unravel the mystery, Eleonore began smoking as she watched the sky brighten to the arrival of the sun. How she loved the perfection of a sunrise: the gradual incline of Apollo as he painted the sky in pinks and oranges that let one feel that they were partaking in something majestic. *I should design a bright, yellow sundress,* Eleonore exhaled her smoke and was about to set the pen to paper when a groan came from the other side of the wall.

"Ella?" Eleonore turned her ear to listen for a reply, but none was given.

She's probably still upset with me, Eleonore shook her head in annoyance.

"Eleonore?" a slow, exhausted call returned.

"I'm here," Eleonore stood quickly and moved closer to the wall, touching her fingers lightly against the thin metal. "Are you alright?"

"Yes," Ella answered slowly through swollen lips. "Well, as good as I can be, I suppose. They've untied me."

"Oh good," Eleonore sighed her relief.

"I assume you're responsible for my reprieve?"

"Indirectly," Eleonore shrugged.

"I want to be mad at you," Ella coughed, "but the numbness in my hands and feet is already subsiding. I think that I should rather thank you."

"Oh," Eleonore smiled shyly.

"But," Ella continued, "I sense there are some strings attached to my liberty."

"What do you mean?" Eleonore frowned.

"Conditions to be met, otherwise my bonds will return."

"The terms are mine to bear," Eleonore explained, reluctantly.

"Sleeping with the Commandant?" Ella laughed in mockery. "You think this means you also suffer?"

"I don't mean to compare grief," Eleonore defended, "but you're not the only one who has lost loved ones. I'm a prisoner, just like you."

"You're nothing like me," Ella continued in her stubbornness. "I would've never slept with him."

"You'd still be under torture if it weren't for me!" Eleonore defended. "Besides, I didn't exactly have a choice."

"There's always a choice," Ella spoke bitterly.

"That's not fair!" Eleonore grew indignant. *How dare she throw that in my face.* "I've sacrificed my dignity for your sake."

"Sacrificed?!" Ella scoffed. "Whose idea was it to bring me into this cell? Was it yours or the Commandant's?"

"It was my—" Eleonore paused as she replayed her conversation with Rudolph. "It was his," Eleonore sat with her back to the wall as the gravity of what had occurred weighed upon her shoulders.

"They were planning on putting me into this cell long before he made the proposition to you," Ella spoke, and Eleonore heard the creaking of springs as she sat up on her bed. "They thought I would trust you."

"How do you know this?" Eleonore turned her head.

"I heard the stupid one talking," Ella snickered.

"The stupid one?"

"Gehring," Ella explained. "The one who dragged you out of the barracks with his cruel game."

"I knew I recognized his voice," Eleonore fumed, remembering that the 'game' was, in fact, Jung's invention. "I heard what you did for me, by the way. I was angry at first, but Em enlightened me on why you stopped me from taking his gun."

No reply. The only sound was the clock ticking patiently.

"I'm a damned fool, Ella," Eleonore rubbed her eyes in disbelief. "I thought my sacrifice was—"

"You didn't sacrifice anything," Ella seethed with resentment. "You slept with the Commandant because you're a traitor to our cause. You've likely been on his payroll this whole time, learning whatever you can from me."

"How dare—"

"We've nothing left to discuss," Ella interrupted. "I won't converse with spies."

"I won't allow —"

"Shut up!"

With tears streaming, Eleonore hunched over as she wept silently. She had given herself to one of the most detestable men who had ever existed and received nothing in return. She could live with herself under the pretense that her submission was bringing alleviation to Ella, but now that this deception had reared its hideous head, Eleonore felt an emptiness unlike any other.

But the more she thought about his trickery, the more she became upset. A rage, a burning, fierce hatred for Rudolph grew within her. Clenching her fist, she brought it to her mouth and sank her teeth into her knuckles as she screamed her revulsion.

"You don't have to reply," Eleonore spoke angrily and quickly, "but I need to you to listen. I'll kill Rudolph for this. Somehow, someway, I'll kill the man who divided us."

A knock came to the door and Eleonore froze, hoping that whoever was on the other side had not heard her murderous declaration.

"Yes?" she replied and stood beside the bed.

"It's me," came the lieutenant's reply.

"Oh good," Eleonore whispered, relieved to hear his voice. Even if he had heard, it was unlikely he would report on her. "Come in."

Opening the cell door, Jung entered and, looking rather sheepish, removed his cap.

"What's the matter?" Eleonore studied him.

"I, uh," Jung fiddled with his cap and motioned towards the bed, requesting permission to sit.

"I'm your prisoner, not your host," Eleonore huffed. "Do as you please."

"Right," Jung stared at his feet as he continued to play with his cap awkwardly but didn't move.

"You're making me nervous," Eleonore grew cross.

"Sorry," he drew a deep breath, "I just wanted to be the first to inform you that your release is being prepared."

"Really?!" Eleonore clasped her hand over her mouth.

"Yes," Jung offered a shy smile.

"That's great news!" Eleonore wiped the tears from her eyes and ran her hands down her stomach as she looked about the room, not sure how to react. She wanted to jump into his arms and squeeze him with delight.

"There's just one issue," Jung swallowed.

"What?" Eleonore looked at him with wide eyes, wondering if she had fallen for the promise too soon.

"Dr. Mengele needs to sign the order," Jung cleared his throat.

"Of course," Eleonore closed her eyes as her arms slumped down by her sides.

"Don't give up hope," Jung glanced at her and then away.

"I didn't," Eleonore ran her hand over her forehead, "you took it from me."

Jung remained silent as he waited for her to continue.

"I know what the doctor requires of me," she nodded to the cell next to her. "You didn't give me hope, you simply offered a drowning woman a glass of water."

"Ella's not awake. I just checked on her. You can speak freely."

She must've fallen back asleep, Eleonore wondered. *I hope, at least, that she heard what I said about the Commandant.*

"How does she look?" Eleonore braced for the report.

"She's in rough condition, but you alone can alleviate her sorrows now."

"She won't listen to me," Eleonore whispered and fought back the tears. "And I don't blame her. I robbed her of her greatest desire."

"She won, you know," Jung shook his head in bewilderment.

"What do you mean?"

"The crematoriums aren't being rebuilt."

"I don't understand," Eleonore frowned.

"The Allies..." Jung looked over his shoulder then walked closer to Eleonore and whispered. "The Russians are making headway into German-occupied lands and Nazi power is beginning to succumb. The camp administration is in the process of destroying evidence, unless we are spared by some miracle."

If everything here is legal, then why are they destroying evidence? Eleonore wished she could say, but watched Jung in sheer amazement. Even if Rudolph and Dr. Mengele had their way to keep Eleonore as a permanent resident of Auschwitz, the Allies would soon arrive to liberate not only her but Ella as well.

"You need to get out," Jung continued to whisper. "They will liquidate the camp before our work here is discovered. Witnesses will be exterminated."

"How much time do we have?"

"It's impossible to say," Jung shrugged, "maybe a year, could be as little as a month. Depends on how well our soldiers resist the counter-invasion."

"And if I'm not able to secure my release, what happens then?" Eleonore asked.

"I'd rather not think about that," Jung looked at Eleonore with longing. He wanted to protect her, but there was little he could do.

"I'd like to have a backup plan to prepare for such an eventuality," Eleonore looked knowingly at Jung. *This is my one chance,* she thought, *he loves me and I can use that against him. Under the guise of self-protection, I'll get him to bring me something: poison, a gun, anything. Then I'll kill Rudolph and prove myself to Ella.*

"If you're asking what I think you're asking," Jung took a deep breath as he measured his reply, "then I'll see what I can do, but I can't promise anything."

"I don't mean to pry or sound ungrateful," Eleonore began nervously, "but why are you here?"

"Well—"

"Before you answer," Eleonore held up her hand and cleared her throat, "I recall your admission of affection for me, but is it not dangerous for us to be seen together? Especially considering the rumors that circulated about a relationship? If you still hold true to those feelings, then you will bring me what I desire. If the Russians arrive, well, I think you know what they'll do to me and I'd rather not endure that."

"As I was about to say," Jung looked at her with slight annoyance, "I'm assigned to review your work."

"What work?" Eleonore frowned.

"The death certificates," Jung pointed to the papers stacked neatly on her desk.

"I forgot about them entirely," Eleonore slapped her hand onto her forehead. The executions, Rudolph's involvement, Ella's indifference, and her anxiety had overridden any sense of urgency to complete her assigned duties.

"I assumed as much," Jung offered a limp smile.

"Are they going to kill me now?" Eleonore slunk down into her chair.

"Fortunately for you, the executions have provided the clerks with a rather busy workload, so your failure has gone unnoticed and unreported."

"That doesn't exactly make me feel all that relieved," Eleonore sighed. "I shouldn't be thankful that the hangings bought me some time."

"Regardless," Jung studied her, "time has been purchased. I'd advise you not to put it to waste. I'm a poor liar, Miss Hodys, and I won't be able to cover for you with much success should I be questioned."

"I'll get started," Eleonore shoved aside the blank paper and retrieved the death certificates.

"What were those papers for, anyways?" Jung asked curiously.

"I was thinking of designing a dress," Eleonore spoke bashfully, she was rather private with her creations, especially in the initial stages. She detested when anyone saw her unfinished projects.

"I'm sure my wife would've approved," Jung offered a slight chuckle.

"Speaking of your wife," Eleonore retrieved the silver case from the desk, "I wouldn't have accepted this if I had known the sentimental value."

"Keep it," Jung held up his hand and then replaced his cap, "it belongs to someone of greater quality than myself. I wish you the best of luck with your friend. I understand your moral dilemma, but if she talks, then it's likely that both of your lives will be spared."

"In the likely event that I can't bring these desires to fruition, I will need your assistance. Anything you can get your hands on, please, I beg of you."

"I'll see what I can do," Jung nodded as he left.

Lighting her cigarette as the cell door closed, Eleonore's mind buzzed with possibility. *If Jung doesn't bring me what I need, then I'm dead,* Eleonore sighed. *In the meantime, I really should get to these certificates. Don't think about what you're writing, just pen what they want and save yourself.*

"I'm a little early tonight," Rudolph explained to a surprised Eleonore who glanced at the clock which read 9:30 pm.

"Are the guards still on duty?" Eleonore glanced passed him out into the hallway but saw no one.

"I'm here on official camp business," Rudolph cleared his throat. "Besides, I dismissed the guards early. We won't be bothered."

"Should I be concerned?" Eleonore asked with resentment as she continued to smoke at her desk.

"Of course not," Rudolph smiled, but Eleonore didn't return the gesture. She understood that deception would be the key into luring Rudolph into trusting her so that she could avenge the betrayal, but found it impossible to rouse the required performance.

"Before I begin, I have something for you," Rudolph held up his finger as he dug into his coat pocket. "It seems you've made quite the impression on my little Heidetraud, and she speaks of you from time to time."

Eleonore watched Rudolph curiously as he procured a folded piece of paper with green and red crayon lines drawn incidentally on the corners. Setting it on the desk beside her, Rudolph stood back and waited anxiously for Eleonore to unfold the paper, but she refused to even acknowledge its presence.

"Here," Rudolph took it upon himself and opened the paper to reveal a rudimentary illustration.

"This is you," Rudolph tapped on a tall stick figure with curly hair, an exaggerated smile, and a large red square beside her.

"And I believe this is a dog," Rudolph tilted the drawing as he tried to determine the shape.

"It's a phoenix," Eleonore said dryly. "It's a drawing of the time your daughter sat with me at the Villa while I mended the carpet."

"Ah, yes," Rudolph clicked his tongue. "That would make more sense."

"Is this the official state business which has provided you with the opportunity to visit my 'chambers' during the day?" Eleonore spoke sarcastically.

"No," Rudolph folded the drawing back up and set it on the corner of the desk. "I just thought that it might please you."

"Then speak your peace and leave," Eleonore reached to grab another cigarette, but Rudolph swatted her hand and she looked up at him in surprise.

"Who do you think I am?!" Rudolph seized Eleonore's arm and stood her to her feet as he brought her face within inches of his. "I'm not some servant that you can dismiss! I'm the Commandant of this camp and you will show me the respect I deserve! I could have you killed for any reason I desire! You should be revering me for saving your life!"

"Empty threats!" Eleonore sneered as she tried to break his grip. "I'm not your whore that you can use night after night. Go on you coward, have me killed. Put the bullet through my head yourself if you can stomach it. Or are you going to watch as your men carry out the deed?"

"Is this how you thank me for assisting Ella?" Rudolph nodded to the wall with his grip still firm on her arms.

"I know what you did!" Eleonore glared at him. "I know how you deceived me."

"Deceived you?" Rudolph frowned as his grip loosened. "What are you talking about?"

"Ella wasn't placed in the cell because I slept with you. It was your plan all along. You used her to get to me, and I fell for it because I believed that I didn't have a choice. I believed what I had preached against for years, and now I'm no better than any of you."

"Who told you this nonsense?" Rudolph stood at a distance as he defended himself.

"Does it matter?" Eleonore shrugged. "I know the truth, and I know that you'll never release me. How could you relinquish your prize? But it's not you that I have to wait out, is it? All I need is to bide my time until the Russians arrive and liberate us."

"Russians?" Rudolph snickered. "The eastern front is well under our control. What would make you think otherwise?"

Staring at Rudolph, Eleonore couldn't decipher if he was listening to Nazi propaganda, or if Jung had led her astray? In this world of half-truths and blatant lies, who could tell the fact from fiction?

"Regardless," Rudolph waved his hand. "Sleeping with me did alleviate Ella's condition. The doctor has stopped torturing her, hasn't he? Well?"

"Yes," Eleonore gritted her teeth.

"Then what do you want? Ask for anything and I'll provide it."

"My release!" Eleonore half-shouted.

"It's in progress," Rudolph gave a warning look.

"I know what that means," Eleonore spoke under her breath.

"If there's nothing to request, then shall we?" Rudolph nodded to the bed.

"How dare you!?" Eleonore frowned her incredulity.

"Do you want flowers?" Rudolph spoke sarcastically. "We both know what this is."

"Don't patronize me!" Eleonore clenched her hands into fists.

"What more do you want?" Rudolph threw his hands into the air. "I put Ella in the cell beside you, I ordered her treatment to be improved, and you still keep me at a distance. Who is being used here?"

"You..." Eleonore glanced at the wall before continuing with a whisper, "...you put her there under a false pretense and expected me to inform on her."

"She's a Jew!" Rudolph shook his head. "And a traitor to the state, no less. She masterminded a plot that killed seventy of my men. Good men. Loyal men. The fact that you are protecting her makes you guilty by association. If I didn't love you, then you would've been killed a long time ago and your Jewess would still be suffering under the doctor's hands. I've seen his work. He's creative, to say the least, when it comes to methods of prolonging life under torment. Do you really want that for her?"

"Of course not," Eleonore rubbed her eyes as clarity began to flee.

"Then I'm the only one who can keep her from the doctor," Jung nodded to the bed.

"I need something in return," Eleonore couldn't believe what she was saying. "I can't simply give myself without assurance."

"I'm saving the life of a seditious inmate and sparing them from extreme pain," Rudolph spoke with warning. "Isn't that enough?"

"What am I worth?" Eleonore looked at him with sincerity.

"Pardon?" He shook his head in confusion.

"What am I worth to you?"

"Everything," Rudolph shrugged as if the answer was obvious.

"You'll help Ella?" Eleonore began to cry as sensed herself giving in. "You'll make sure that she's fed and fed well?"

"I promise," Rudolph spoke softly and moved closer to Eleonore who finally relented to him.

Eleonore knew that Ella would continue to hate her, but love, she grasped, went beyond what was reciprocated. She would sacrifice her dignity for Ella's comfort, despite her denunciation. Then, if Jung provided her with what she desired, she would kill Rudolph, despite the consequences.

Chapter Twenty-Six: Unplanned

"There are many devices in a man's heart; nevertheless the counsel of the LORD, that shall stand."

Proverbs 19:21

Days and weeks passed in much the same fashion, though Rudolph's visits became less frequent. The excuses were genuine, however, as Rudolph found himself busy entertaining Himmler or other state visitors. To pass the time, Eleonore increased her habit of smoking, reading the limited selection provided her, and Ella continued to ignore her. Not that Eleonore didn't try, but Ella refused her a single word.

Still, Eleonore didn't relent, and she used her position with Rudolph to make sure Ella was fed, was brought warm water with which to bathe, the opportunity to read and write, and that the beatings ceased. Despite this, Ella remained stubborn and harbored resentment against Eleonore, even refusing to eat the food brought from the Villa.

I believe it's been close to two months now, Eleonore wrote in her temporary journal. She had to dispose of her 'works' afterwards lest anyone read them and she be executed. But somehow, writing her experiences down helped transfer the trauma to the pages in front of her and let her sorrows anchor within another harbor. She liked to imagine that the fragments from the burnt pages found their way to Ruth and Alex and, in a way, she was writing to them.

I have yet to receive news of my release, though I ask daily. Rudolph has employed every excuse known to man, but none of them are satisfactory. I'm reminded of Jung's warning about the approaching Allies, but I've not heard any news regarding the Eastern front. The crematoriums, apart from one, have not been rebuilt, so he must be telling the truth. Still, I'm to be counted as fortunate. I'm not required to work in the labor fields, and the only thing occupying my days are the death certificates. Though, should I pay much attention to what is being written, I would weep from morning till dawn. I'm fed the same dishes as are prepared in the Villa, as well, and I must thank Sophie for allowing me to gain a few pounds. I'm back to my old weight, and then some. I'm getting a little tub around the corners. I wonder —

A sudden surge of pain arose in her stomach and Eleonore clutched her side as she doubled over. The pain was so severe and so immediate that her breath was stolen and she couldn't scream for help. Her face flushed red and she felt as though her eyes were about to burst out of her head.

Finally, the pain receded and, catching her breath, Eleonore waited anxiously to see if it would return.

Have I been poisoned? She wondered and looked at the empty tray of food near the door. She hadn't noticed anything peculiar about the taste but, she supposed, that would be why it was effective.

If I was poisoned, I suppose it wouldn't come and go like –

"Ugh!" She felt the pain rising again and fell to her knees as she grasped her stomach.

Oh no! she thought as she ran to the toilet just in time for the contents of her stomach to be neatly disposed of.

"Eleonore?" came a tap from the other side of the wall. "You alright?"

"I th—" Eleonore vomited again.

"I'll call for help!" Ella ran to her cell door and shouted out into the hallway.

"No!" Eleonore tried to call, but she wasn't loud enough. All she could think about was the letter on the desk. If anyone saw it, she would be killed without trial. Jung, too, would face grave circumstances for even being named.

Thankfully, the guards were ill concerned for the wellbeing of their inmates and Ella's calls fell flat.

"Eleonore?!" the knock came as Ella had returned to the wall. "Eleonore?!"

"I'm here," Eleonore spoke as her throat burned.

"I was so worried!" Ella sighed. "You sounded like you were dying."

"I'm glad to hear you're concerned," Eleonore spoke with a hint of resentment. The weeks of a cold-shouldering caused Eleonore to despise Ella, to a degree. She had given everything for Ella but had not received so much as a 'thank you'.

"I was thinking," Ella began but was interrupted by keys jingling from outside Eleonore's cell.

Watching the door curiously, Eleonore knew it wasn't a guard as the peephole was not customarily opened and the command to stand beside the bed was not given.

Instead, in walked Dr. Mengele and Eleonore's stomach felt the sickness of another sort. At his word, he could deem her unfit for life and, after a simple injection, murder her right then and there. She was at the mercy of a madman.

"You're unwell?" the doctor asked and dragged the chair away from the desk, paying no attention to the letter.

"It's nothing," Eleonore shook her head.

"Hm," the doctor continued as he sat down across from Eleonore who was sitting on the bed near the toilet. Crossing his legs, the doctor examined her, not with concern, but rather, with a judging gaze determining the weight of her life.

"Honestly," Eleonore wiped her mouth and sat up straight, proving she still contained utility. "I'm quite alright."

"Disease?" he tilted his head.

"I don't believe so," Eleonore glanced at the tray of food.

"Did you feel this way after eating?" the doctor noticed her gaze.

Eleonore nodded.

"May I examine you?" he asked rhetorically as he scooched his chair forward.

Ignoring the proximity of the mass-murdering psychopath, Eleonore tried her best to remain calm as he put his hands on her abdomen and back.

"I was wondering if it was gallstones," Eleonore broke the awkward silence.

"They don't grow in the womb," the doctor replied, and Eleonore shot him a horrified glance.

"You're pregnant," he continued without much reservation and moved his chair backwards.

"I'm what?" Eleonore shook her head, lost for words.

"Who's the father?" the doctor watched her, now entirely interested.

"I...well...there," Eleonore fumbled with her words. She thought they had been careful, and she had taken all the necessary precautions post intercourse.

"You're about eight weeks along," Dr. Mengele exhaled deeply. "Which means that you conceived sometime during your installment here. And, further puzzling, I don't remember any reports of you leaving this cell. The other inmates that were stationed with you were all women."

"Please," Eleonore whispered. "If you tell anyone, I'm dead."

"Tell me who the father is," the doctor shrugged, "and I'll consider discretion."

"You wouldn't believe me if I told you," Eleonore began to shake. "Just give me something to get rid of the child."

"If you don't tell me," Dr. Mengele stood, "then I'm unable to help you."

"Please," Eleonore pleaded as she continued to shake.

Studying Eleonore for a moment, the doctor jotted down some notes on his clipboard and left the cell, leaving her alone with her thoughts.

"Ella," Eleonore whispered to the wall, knowing she had heard everything.

"You'll be alright," Ella whispered back, her voice full of panic. "I promise."

"Rudolph will have me killed," Eleonore sat at the desk as she trembled.

"You're not the first to get pregnant at Auschwitz," Ella replied. "There are measures to be taken which can 'alleviate' your condition."

"You know of such procedures?" Eleonore asked, understanding that if she didn't terminate the pregnancy, both her and the child would be killed.

"I know enough. Our only issue is obtaining the materials."

"What do we require?"

"It's rudimentary," Ella paused.

"I don't care," Eleonore pressed. "Just tell me what I need."

"A long and thin needle, and then some soap to put inside," Ella answered quickly. "Can you get these from Jung?"

"He hasn't had reason to come by my cell in weeks," Eleonore sighed. "Not since I asked him for something with which to avoid capture by the Russians. If you understand what I mean."

"You were going to kill yourself?" Ella spoke slowly.

"Not myself, but Rudolph," Eleonore swallowed. Even the mention of his name reminded her of the gravity of her situation.

"I see," Ella drew a deep breath. "I...uh...I believe I owe you an apology."

"There's no need," Eleonore shook her head as the tears formed.

"No, there is. I was angry, and I took my rage out on you. I see now how wrong it was of me to assume you were disloyal," Ella cleared her throat. "I feel like I've wasted these past months ignoring you."

"I'm just happy to be friends at the end," Eleonore wiped the tears from her eyes.

"This is not the end," Ella spoke but lacked the conviction that Eleonore needed to hear.

"Then what is it?" Eleonore scoffed.

"When the Commandant visits tonight, can you ask him for the items without making him suspicious? Maybe tell him you need them for washing."

"I doubt it. Chances are the doctor already informed him," Eleonore spoke but suddenly grew enraged and pounded her palm against the desk. "I hate that man! What a wicked creature. And now his child is within me. How did I end up here?"

"How did any of us?" Ella quipped.

"Quite right," Eleonore calmed a little.

"For what it's worth," Ella tapped the wall lightly, "I'm glad that I met you."

"Likewise," Eleonore placed her hand on the wall and felt the heat where Ella's hand was. That was all she required to fill her heart: a moment of kindness to forget the months of animosity.

11:00 PM arrived with no sign of Rudolph and Eleonore's anxiety increased with each passing second. Grabbing the silver case, desperate for another smoke, Eleonore panicked when she noticed it was empty. In her distress, she had used her entire supply of cigarettes.

If I don't find a way to terminate this pregnancy, then I'm as good as dead, Eleonore placed her head in her hands as she sat at the desk. *He's still not here*, she glanced at the clock again, *which means Dr. Mengele must've told him.*

"You don't know that for sure," Eleonore heard Alex speak in his comforting way and carried the encouragement that she was desperate to receive. *"There have been other nights where he hasn't visited. You'll see. If he doesn't return tonight, then he'll be back tomorrow."*

"I'm sorry, Alex, I'm sorry that I've let you down. I've let you all down," Eleonore felt the extent of her shame.

"No," Alex spoke softly. *"You could never disappoint me, love. You were put in a difficult situation. You did what you had to for survival."*

"Why do you come to mind, rather than my father?" Eleonore wiped away a tear, but there was no answer. Alex was her imagination, and she was pulling reassurance from her projection of him. He was the last man who she looked up to and he was in her life later than her father was. Still, she felt the guilt for forgetting her papa.

Keys jingled outside the cell and Eleonore smiled her relief. *I worried about nothing.*

But fate wiped away her cheer as two large men entered her cell with flashlights and batons at the ready. These were not messengers, Eleonore understood, and their bruised knuckles revealed their violent disposition.

"What are you doing?!" Eleonore startled as they walked towards her.

"Seven Five Six Nine Three?" one of them asked, and Eleonore's heart sank when she recognized that the voice belonged to none other than Gehring.

"Yes?" Eleonore held her hand up to block the brightness.

"Come with us," Gehring replied.

"Where we are going?" Eleonore shook as she spoke.

Grabbing each of her arms, the guards dragged her out of the cell. She knew it was pointless to resist, but she was also petrified to the point of shock. It had been nearly three months since she had left that small cell, but now all that she wished for was its protective comfort.

With her legs going limp, the guards had to drag Eleonore through the bunker. Bursting through the main doors, they pulled Eleonore out into the cold without care that she should not be dressed adequately or that she was without shoes.

Then, Eleonore spotted the wall where the executions took place and vomited out of fear. This, however, was of little consequence to the guards and they kept their pace.

This is it, Eleonore closed her eyes as her heart raced. *Don't be afraid. It will be over in a minute.*

But when they didn't slow down or stop, Eleonore eventually opened her eyes to realize they had passed the wall. Yet her heart sank even further when she spotted their destination and she found herself wishing for the firing squad. She was being led to Cell Block 11.

"I," Eleonore looked up at Gehring, "I can't."

Still, Gehring did not listen.

"Please," Eleonore found her voice again and regained her strength as she straightened and planted her feet into the earth, "I can't go back there."

"C'mon," Gehring gripped her arm tighter and forced her along.

"No!" Eleonore tried to escape his grasp, but her strength paled in comparison.

"No!" she screamed. "No! No! No!"

"Shut up!" the other guard struck her in the chest.

Winded and gasping for breath, Eleonore was dragged back to the dungeon where Jung himself had taken her those many nights ago. The same two, young guards from her previous stay stood in front of the doors, only now their innocence had vanished from becoming desensitized. They didn't offer her the same worried expression as before, and Eleonore knew that she would be offered no mercy or clemency.

The guards opened the metal door with a terrible, heavy groan and at once, the screams and wailing soared up the stairs from a dark, lightless basement. Her previous stay had been so traumatizing that Eleonore had removed the memory altogether, but now the harrowing events came soaring back.

Gehring pushed her down into the dungeon and Eleonore passed by the cells as the clunking of metal against metal echoed from the inmates trapped within.

"Get in," Gehring pushed Eleonore inside her allocated tiny, dark cell. Slamming the doors behind her, they locked the doors and left, uncaring what should become of her.

Eleonore shivered and looked up at the tiny slit at the top of the cell where the cold, winter air was pouring in. There was to be no hope of warmth and already she could feel her feet and fingers stiffening.

Maybe if I kneel and huddle for warmth, Eleonore thought but, as she began to kneel, her arm bumped against something cold. At first, she figured it was just part of the wall, but then her breathing ceased when her hand brushed against what was unmistakable as human hair. While still kneeling, Eleonore turned her head slowly and, in the dim light, locked eyes with a dead man.

"Help!" Eleonore screamed while standing and pounding her fist against the cell door, pressing her body as far away from the corpse as possible.

"Help!" she pounded harder, yelling as loud as she was able. She could bear many things, but sharing a tiny cell with a dead body was not something to be endured.

"Quiet!" came an eventual reply and Gehring rattled his baton against the door.

"Please!" Eleonore ignored his demand. "There is a dead body in here."

No answer. Eleonore began to weep as she returned to pounding against the cell door, her skin crawling with disgust. Finally, the outer door swung open, startling Eleonore. Before her stood Gehring with such a detestable smile, she believed him to be a demon. In his hand was a bucket of water, and at once Eleonore understood his intentions.

"Please I—"

The ice-cold water smashed against her face and body and Eleonore inhaled sharply as her breath retreated. Shivering uncontrollably, Eleonore crossed her arms as Gehring shouted at her, but Eleonore was in such a state of shock she couldn't comprehend him. Yet from the vulgarity that she could hear, she doubted it was anything important as the door slammed shut.

Still, Eleonore wouldn't yield. With her stiff hands and arms, Eleonore could only offer an ill-timed pound against the cell door. Still, she was met with silence.

For what seemed like hours, Eleonore continued in her protest. She knew she had been placed in that cell to die. Whether that be from starvation, or hypothermia, or thirst, or exhaustion, she was doomed to death. All because she had become the mistress of Rudolph Hoess: the mistress of Auschwitz.

Pound, pound, pound, Eleonore's fist hit against the door. Though lessening in intensity, she continued nonetheless. She couldn't open her eyes or bear to think of the body beside her, but felt the cold legs rubbing against her naked feet. She tried to think of Ella or Ruth and Alex, but they were silent in her mind, just as frightened of the terrors of existence as she was.

Finally, a familiar voice called from outside the cell. *Jung!* Eleonore's eyes flew wide open and she screamed his name as she slammed both her open palms against the door, not caring that her hands should be bruised.

"Where?" came the muffled reply from Jung talking to the other guards.

The door swung open and Jung stood before Eleonore, looking at her with disinterest and smoking a cigarette. He had to appear indifferent, she understood, but she didn't care. She stared at him with a pleading expression, whispering his name in her delirium.

"What are you complaining about, you cow?" Jung took a puff of smoke as Gehring laughed.

"There is a body in here," Eleonore spoke through shivering. "Please, put me in another cell or take the body out."

"See," the Gehring chuckled, "she's nothing but a bleating goat."

"Let's put her in that cell," Jung pointed down the hall. "Just to shut her up."

"I suppose," Gehring agreed and, opening the iron bars, Eleonore nearly fell on her face as she burst out of the cell.

Grabbing her arm roughly, Jung dragged Eleonore along to another cell down the hallway. She looked up at him with begging eyes, but he refused to look at her. Putting the keys to the door of her new cell, Jung began to unlock it.

"Hold on, now," Gehring said with a smirk.

"What?" Eleonore looked at him with tired, red eyes.

"Your clothes," he bit his cheek as he smiled.

"What about them?" Eleonore glanced down.

"Much too wet," he clicked his tongue. "You can't go in like that."

Understanding his purpose, Eleonore bounded towards her cell, but he caught her arm. Trying to break free was useless, but she wasn't about to satisfy his depravations without a struggle. All Jung could do was stand by and watch, helplessly, but Eleonore wondered if he also was pleased by Gehring's shameless behavior.

Grabbing the back of her regulation outfit, Gehring gave a heave as he ripped the fabric while it pulled against her neck. She screamed her pain and rage, but he kept ripping at the seams until the clothes fell off her and she was naked before him. She covered her breasts with her arms and hunched over as she shivered and wept.

"Now, get in," Gehring ordered with a slap on her backside.

Eleonore looked to Jung for relief but knew he couldn't interfere. Still, she caught the hurt in his eyes and understood that this was not a pleasant experience for him.

Entering the cell, Eleonore winced at the cold concrete floor and the winter air pouring in from the slit above the cell.

"I need to question her," Jung stopped Gehring from closing the cell entirely.

"On whose authority?" Gehring looked at him suspiciously.

"I'm here on orders directly from the Commandant," Jung lowered his brow.

"Fine," Gehring threw his hands behind his back and stood to the side.

"Alone," Jung ordered.

Studying him for a minute, Gehring glanced at Eleonore naked in the cell, then back at Jung. He understood something foul was afoot, but he couldn't determine how, and he didn't have anything concrete to advise otherwise, so he left the two in peace.

"Here," Jung grabbed a loaf of bread from under his jacket and handed it to Eleonore who grabbed it immediately.

"Thank you," Eleonore covered herself with her arms as she held onto the food.

"I'll try to bring you as much as I can," Jung looked away to allow her some dignity. "The Commandant has ordered that you be starved to death, but I won't let that happen."

"Why would he order such a thing?" Eleonore shook her head, but she was well aware of his reasoning. If Rudolph was discovered to be the father, then he would be executed without delay.

"I'll be back as soon as I can," Jung whispered when Gehring returned. "I'm sorry about this, but hide the bread behind your back."

With that, Jung grabbed a bucket of cold water that was beside the cell and threw it at her legs as she gasped from the sharp cold splash.

"Dog!" Jung shouted as he slammed the cell door shut.

Shivering, Eleonore couldn't speak and, in the darkness, knelt to the ground as she pressed against the wall, wincing at the coldness, but trying to heat the steel to match her body temperature.

"Help!" a cry came out from another cell. "Please! Just a drop of water!"

"Shut up!" Jung could be heard hitting his baton against the cell door.

"Please!" the inmate persisted. "Anything! Please!"

But no reply came, and the inmate continued to beg and beg and beg. This was hell, Eleonore understood, and if her life was to be judged beyond the grave, then she feared not the life to come: she had paid her dues.

Chapter Twenty-Seven:
The Depths of Hell

"Wither shall I go from thy Spirit? Or wither shall I flee from thy presence? If I ascend up to heaven, thou art there; if I make my bed in hell, behold, thou art there."

Psalm 139:7-8

The weeks passed in torment, at least, Eleonore assumed it had been weeks as there was no accurate method of tracking the days. In the darkness, Eleonore was subject to a void in which time was held captive. Only the bitter begging from the other cells gave her a sense of how long she had been detained.

Fresh prisoners doomed to death by thirst lasted roughly three days; sometimes more and sometimes less. Those who were allowed water but denied food lasted a week, maybe more. It was likely they could've lasted longer, but their poor state of health and the horrid conditions didn't permit the suffering to endure.

New prisoners would be brought in, weeping and begging for relief until, eventually, the cries grew faint and their voices ceased. Eleonore hated being unable to alleviate their lamentations. Her guilt, too, plagued her conscience when Jung would sneak her a piece of bread or meat. She ate it heartily to quench her starvation, even amidst her fellow inmate's pleas for food. Still, a little substance and water every odd day was akin to nothing more than life support, a prolonging of the suffering.

Jung! Eleonore smiled as she heard footsteps approaching and knew she was about to receive nourishment. The lieutenant had a certain gate about his walk. Every third step seemed to speed up as if he had suddenly remembered his mission or needed to accomplish a task with the greatest possible efficiency.

The door opened, and an apple fell into her lap which Eleonore grabbed and began to devour. The crisp juices spilt into her mouth and her tongue seized from the shock to her taste buds.

After a few, large bites, Eleonore noticed that Jung had lingered. Usually, he would provide her with food and leave without a word. He had to be quick and time his 'visits' as his sustaining of Eleonore's life would be met with his own death should he be discovered.

"Water?" Eleonore asked, wondering if that was the reason for his delaying.

"Not today," Jung shook his head regrettably.

"It's been two days already," Eleonore felt the thirst in her dry mouth; the juices from the apple only stirred her body to beg for more liquid.

"I was here yesterday," Jung squinted as he watched her curiously.

"Oh. What is it, then?" Eleonore whispered, surprised by the coarseness of her own voice.

"Your comrade, Ella," Jung glanced away.

"What about her?" Eleonore frowned.

"She was executed today," Jung replied bluntly.

"I see," Eleonore looked down at her feet. She was exhausted and unable to comprehend the loss, at least not fully.

"I thought you should know."

"Thank you," Eleonore looked up at him. "Did she say it? The encouragement of Joshua?"

"She shouted it so loud," Jung leaned down, "that Hedwig heard it from the Villa."

"Of course she did," Eleonore beamed with pride, then felt the rush of emotions and began to weep for her friend. She recalled how they had held hands in the train car when they first arrived at the camp, and how her brightness had stirred her to love.

"You two were rather close, weren't you?" Jung looked at her with compassion.

"As close as sisters," Eleonore sobbed bitterly.

"She inquired of you often, asking how you were and if you were being taken care of."

"And what did you say?" Eleonore looked at him through tear-stained eyes.

"I lied a little," Jung raised his eyebrows.

"How so?" Eleonore frowned.

"I told her you were doing well, but I think she saw through my fabrication."

"She's rather adept at unveiling the truth," Eleonore wiped away her tears. "But I appreciate your attempts at lying on my behalf."

"I also have some good news," Jung straightened, and Eleonore waited anxiously. "Your release is being prepared.

Giving an ironic chuckle, Eleonore looked up at Jung in hopelessness, "I've heard that phrase so many times that it has lost all meaning."

"I don't blame you," Jung took his cap off briefly and scratched the top of his head nervously before replacing it.

"What aren't you telling me?" Eleonore watched him warily.

"You will be transported to Dachau. There, you will train in the SS hospital," Jung cleared his throat.

"Dachau?" Eleonore frowned as she searched her memory. "I've heard that name, but can't recall from where."

"Its another camp," Jung paused.

"I see," Eleonore watched him warily.

"Dachau's administration doesn't have the same stipulations that we have here," Jung swallowed as he continued. "They're rather barbaric in their approach."

Eleonore let out an incidental laugh at his portrayal. More barbaric than this? Was that possible?

"I understand how you'd find that amusing," Jung looked at his feet awkwardly, "but the Commandant has made Auschwitz free of the panic and unruly sites that inhabit the other camps."

"What should I expect from Dachau then?" Eleonore scoffed.

"I don't have the heart to tell you," Jung became solemn as he reflected.

Eleonore watched him with wonder. He was suffering from his memories and they had made him cold, callous. Yet the thought of someone he cared for being sent into further misery brought those fresh memories to surface.

"When am I set for Dachau?"

"Soon," Jung nodded before closing the door again. "The moment I have word, you'll be advised."

With that, the door shut and Eleonore reflected on Jung's forewarning. How could anything be worse than this? She had been locked in a cell so small there was no chance of lying down. Even as petite as she was, kneeling was her best chance of rest, yet her legs would become numb under her and she would have to shift positions constantly. Worst of all was the inability to use the facilities or wash oneself. She almost looked forward to when the crueler guards would throw ice-cold water on her.

While her head was crowned again with the glory of hair, there was no chance to clean the grease and she longed for the bathtub in her little flat. That's all she wanted now: a hot bath with the steam filling her lungs and a glass of tea in her hand. She wept at the reflection as she leaned her head against the wall, visualizing what it would be like to dip her dirty feet into the cleansing waters. She motioned the air towards her face, pretending to inhale a freshly poured cup of tea. She could almost smell it, too: that refreshing, striking scent which lured the senses into desire.

Then something unexpected occurred, something Eleonore had nearly forgotten about: movement in her womb. It wasn't much, just a twinge of the muscle, reminding Eleonore of her child's existence. Still, the movement triggered a feeling in Eleonore she didn't think possible: love.

"Hello little one," Eleonore placed her hands over her small, but swelling belly. "I nearly forgot you were there. It's nice not to feel so alone. I'm sorry I haven't thought of you much. This is, without a doubt, the strangest, most wonderful thing I have ever experienced. Are you a boy or a girl, I wonder? I always wanted a little girl, though I thought that when I passed thirty-five that such a chance was behind me. I should've spoken to you much earlier, but I suppose you've chosen now as your opportunity to introduce yourself. I'll keep you safe, I promise."

But as she reflected, Eleonore heard footsteps approaching. *That can't be Jung returning so soon,* Eleonore frowned. Then came another set of boots against the concrete floor, and another, and yet another. *There must be four in total,* Eleonore pressed her ear against the cell door, still holding her stomach.

The cell door across from her opened, and Eleonore listened intently. A shot fired, reverberating through the bunker and Eleonore recoiled from the ringing in her ear. Then, the cell beside her opened, and Eleonore tried to decipher the mumbled speech of the guards, but she was still partially deaf from the shot. There seemed to be an argument of sorts, but the context was hidden from her.

Whatever it was, they had sorted it out rather quickly and the footsteps approached Eleonore. Standing, Eleonore shook from weakness as her door was opened and she stood naked before four guards, including Gehring, who seemed almost shocked to see her.

"Seven Five Six Nine Three?" one of them asked as he looked at his clipboard but couldn't help glancing at her pregnant belly.

"Yes?" Eleonore replied without taking care to cover herself any longer. She had caught the shock in his eyes: her condition humanized her when they were determined to treat otherwise.

"Come out," the guard opened the iron-barred door.

"Where?" Eleonore took a step out of the cell, but her legs shook and she fell to her knees.

"Up!" Gehring demanded and reached for his baton.

"I haven't walked in some time," Eleonore trembled as she tried to stand.

Reaching up her hand, Eleonore requested assistance but Gehring turned a dreadful shade of white and looked at a loss for how to behave. But as swiftly as it had left, his cruel nature returned and he delivered a swift kick to the back of her leg. Eleonore's screams echoed throughout the dungeon as she held her leg, but the pain was so severe that she couldn't move.

"Up!" he clenched his fists, threatening further punishment.

When she didn't move, Gehring kicked her again in the same leg and Eleonore fell onto her back as she writhed in pain.

"That's enough!" another guard stopped Gehring from striking her a third time.

"Why?!" Gehring scoffed.

"What's going on?" Eleonore became cross as the other guard helped her to her feet.

"We were unaware of your condition," he explained and revealed his sympathy and even removed his cap. "Which makes what we have to do rather difficult."

"Then don't do it," Eleonore began to panic. She didn't know what they were eluding to, but it likely meant her death.

"If only there was a choice," the guard looked at her full of sorrow.

"There's always a choice," Eleonore pleaded. "Besides, I'm due to be released any day now. I'm expected at Dachau."

"Change of plans," the guard took a deep breath.

"Stop stalling," Gehring grew annoyed. "Let's get this over with."

"Here," the other guard removed his coat and draped it over her shoulders to cover her nakedness.

"Thank you," Eleonore looked at him in confusion. What was so terrible that he was behaving with such regret?

"Come," he placed his hand on her back and ushered her towards the main doors.

"Where are we going?" Eleonore looked at him.

"You're scheduled for processing," he said as he avoided looking at her.

"No," Eleonore shook her head. "There must be some mistake. Please, seek Lieutenant Jung, he will tell you himself."

"When did you see the Lieutenant?" Gehring squinted at the irregularity.

"When?" Eleonore asked, realizing she had inadvertently used Jung's name in her panic. If his visits were discovered, it would put his life in jeopardy.

"Answer!" Gehring's shout echoed through the dungeon as he watched her intently, gritting his teeth and seething with violent rage.

"When he first detained me here," Eleonore nodded back to her cell.

"Ah," Gehring nodded, satisfied with the answer. "Well, the officer is being sent to the front."

"Really?!" Eleonore shook her head as she wondered at the peculiarity. She had just seen him only minutes ago.

"Does it matter anyways?" Gehring opened the door to the outside world, flooding the dungeon with the white glow of the sun.

"Yes!" Eleonore continued her protest as she was led onwards.

"Our orders are final," the other guard shrugged.

"Then at least tell me how I am to die!" Eleonore shook from weakness as she limped along from the kicks to her leg.

The guard didn't reply but looked at her with all the sympathy he could muster.

"I can't believe this," Eleonore looked around as her eyes adjusted to the light. She was desperate for a glimpse of Jung or even Rudolph, but the camp was eerily quiet.

"This way," the guard called as he led her to a transport truck near the gates which was filled with other prisoners.

Most of the inmates were staring at their feet or looking straight ahead. There was a defeatism in their expressions, and they understood these were their final minutes. They had experienced more death in the camp than they had thought possible, and now they had been selected to go the way of all men.

"Please," Eleonore protested. "Please find Lieutenant Jung."

"I told you," the guard shook his head, "he's not here."

"I just saw him," Eleonore muttered under her breath.

"You did?" the guard frowned.

"He questioned me," Eleonore nodded.

"Odd," the guard replied but continued, determined in his duty. "I'll need this back," he apologized as he removed the jacket and returned her to her nakedness. It was strange, Eleonore knew, to be treated so cordially, especially when she had seen these same guards treat others with brutal rage. Her pregnancy, she understood, was the reason for such courtesy, yet it would still not save her from a premature death.

The guard stationed in the truck leaned down and offered his hand for Eleonore. Pulling her up into the truck, the guard sat her down beside him but did not show the same care for her condition as the previous guard. He simply smoked his cigarette and held his gun limply by his side.

Shivering as a gust of wind blew into the truck, Eleonore rubbed her arms and shook uncontrollably. How she longed for warmth, for clothes. Her previous existence as a seamstress seemed a cruel irony: she had designed some of the most beautiful dresses in Berlin, and now she was about to die naked.

Despite being nude, none in the truck looked at her as she was just another of the disenfranchised and doomed to death. The inmates instead were thinking of their loved ones, of their hatred for those who had taken them, their questioning of the divine and its absence, and the hope of what they would see beyond the grave.

Slapping the back of the truck, the guard who had escorted her signaled for it to move out. With a sputter, the truck engine roared to life and drove towards its hateful destination. Leaning over, Eleonore watched the other guard shrink into the distance but caught the tears in his eyes. She couldn't understand his behavior. For one so cruel, why had he changed his tone for her sake? She had seen thousands of children being marched towards the crematoriums before, why was her pregnancy on a different level?

Bouncing along, Eleonore sat on the wooden bench squished in between the guard and a frail man who was a mere skeleton. Then, Eleonore noticed an elderly woman sitting across from her and staring at her with the largest smile. Confused by the reaction, Eleonore didn't smile back but looked away, thinking the woman had gone mad.

"How far along?" the elderly woman pointed a delicate finger at her belly.

"I," Eleonore shook her head. "I don't know."

"I found the fourth to sixth months of my pregnancies to be the most difficult," she chuckled. "But don't worry, it gets easier and children are worth it. I just remember being so tired, especially near the end."

"You—" Eleonore wanted to correct her, but something caught her tongue. This woman was living in a fantasy which removed her from this hell. Why should she be corrected and reminded of the horror?

"I think it's a boy," Eleonore continued and offered a weak smile back.

"I agree with you there," the woman raised her eyebrows. "It's likely to be a male if you carry it a bit higher and…oh…dear you're naked! I wish I had something for you. My daughter is about your size."

"They took my clothes," Eleonore shrugged as she explained.

"Was it the one in the corner?" she whispered and gave a side nod to the guard beside Eleonore.

"No," Eleonore shook her head but, feeling faint, couldn't continue with the conversation.

Instead, she stared out the back of the truck, watching nature pass them by. The blue sky shone brightly behind scattered clouds as if the heavens were as happy to see Eleonore as she was to see the outside of her cell.

I wish you could see this, Eleonore spoke inwardly to the child in her belly. *The leaves are returning to crown the branches with a lush green after a bitter winter. You can smell spring in the air: that fresh scent of life re-awakening. All this beauty mixed in with all this wretched, heartless evil. Maybe it's best I don't bring you into the world, as harsh as that sounds. Maybe its best you don't see what has become of mankind. Though in the face of all this sorrow, I should still wish to see your face. I could've held your hand as you learned how to walk, heard your first words. I would've kept you safe.*

But as fate willed, the truck just so happened to slow down and Eleonore could hear shouting from the front of the vehicle. Taking a slight detour, the truck drove up onto the grass and then around a smaller military vehicle which had become stuck in the mud.

Jung?! Eleonore spotted him trying to push the vehicle out.

"Jung!" she shouted, surprised that she had enough strength, but he couldn't hear her.

"Jung!" she shouted again but the truck's engine was too loud.

Then, the guard who was with Jung, saw Eleonore becoming frantic and raised his rifle as he pointed in warning.

Surprised, Jung looked up to see the disturbance and caught site of Eleonore.

"Wait! Wait!" he shouted as he waved his arms frantically and bounded after the truck which, finally, came to a halt.

"What's going on?!" Jung asked the guard beside Eleonore as he leaned against the back of the vehicle, catching his breath.

"They're due for processing," the guard explained.

"That's a mistake," Jung waved for him to provide the documentation and the guard complied.

"She's not listed," Jung tapped the clipboard as he looked at the guard in confusion.

"No," the guard shook his head. "The order came from the Commandant himself."

"Ah," Jung sighed. "That explains it. Come," he offered his hand to Eleonore and, reaching forward, she climbed down.

"I have my orders!" the guard in the truck grew indignant.

"She's not on the list," Jung replied and handed the documents back to him. "She's due in Dachau."

"And when the Commandant asks?" the guard continued.

"He won't know the difference," Jung persisted.

"It's my neck you're risking," the guard shook his head.

"Then feel free to blame it on me," Jung gave the guard a look of warning and he finally relented.

Removing his jacket, Jung threw it over Eleonore's shoulders and signaled for the truck to continue. Sputtering its black exhaust, the transport vehicle returned to its path.

"I'll get you straight on the train to Dachau," Jung led Eleonore back to his vehicle. "The Allies are closing in," he whispered, "and believe me when I tell you it's much better for you to fall into the hands of the Americans than the Russians."

"What if they see I'm pregnant and kill me the minute I arrive?" Eleonore stopped in her tracks.

"C'mon!" Jung ignored the question and waved for her to hurry, but she didn't move.

"Admit it," Eleonore shook, "there's no chance for me, is there?"

Dropping his shoulders, Jung sighed, "All I know is that if you stay here then the Commandant will surely kill you. Dachau is the only way."

Eleonore searched his eyes carefully, wondering if she could trust him.

"We have to hurry," Jung grabbed her hand and led her back to his vehicle at a quick pace.

"They said you were being sent to the front," Eleonore looked at him curiously as they walked.

"Last minute orders. I would've told you had I known. They need every available man to defend from the invaders."

"Is this train like all the others?" Eleonore looked at him, bracing for the response.

"Yes," Jung cleared his throat.

"What if I don't survive the journey?" Eleonore glanced at her belly.

"It's not far from Auschwitz," Jung replied and glanced at the guard beside the stuck vehicle whose curiosity was increasing with every passing minute. "A day's journey, no longer."

"What about my release?" Eleonore shrugged. "You mentioned there was a release being prepared."

"When," Jung paused and took a deep breath, "when someone is released from Auschwitz, it means they are transferred to another camp, like Dachau. Then, when they are released from that camp, they go to another and another and another. There is no freedom."

"Then help me escape," Eleonore pleaded, unconcerned that the other guard should hear her.

"That's not possible," Jung shook his head with regret.

"I thought you had affection for me," Eleonore persisted.

"What's going on here?" the guard raised his voice.

"One moment," Jung held up his hand for the guard to yield.

"Think about it," Jung put his hands to his hips, "where would we go? We would be hunted down for all time. If we win the war, then we will be hunted by the Nazis. If the Allies win, then they will hunt me down. Your only hope is Dachau."

"This is treasonous!" the guard studied them.

"Shut up!" Jung broke off from Eleonore and put his hand to his pistol as he stood a mere foot from the guard.

"What is she to you?" the guard squinted.

"Everything!" Jung drew his pistol and held it by his side. "If anyone deserves to be spared the fate of Auschwitz, then it's Eleonore."

"I'm not taking the fall for you," the guard increased the grip on his rifle.

"I'm going to drop her off at the train, which lies directly on our route anyways, then we shall be on our way," Jung pleaded with his fellow guard.

"What's in it for me?" the guard released his grip, seeing an opportunity to barter.

"I don't shoot you," Jung cocked his pistol.

"I accept," the guard complied readily, sensing the passion in Jung's voice.

"Get in," Jung signaled to Eleonore as he holstered his weapon.

"The train is about to leave," the guard glanced at this watch.

"Then we'd better hurry," Jung hopped into the vehicle and tried to start it, but the engine turned and turned without success.

"You piece of trash!" Jung slammed his fist against the steering wheel as he tried again and again.

Finally, the vehicle roared to life and purred angrily like a beast being awoken from a deep sleep. Throwing the vehicle into reverse, Jung floored the gas and they burst out of the mud and back onto the road. Then, Jung sped along as they tried to make the train in time.

Yet Eleonore couldn't help wishing for the little drive to continue forever. She felt a peacefulness sitting in the back of the topless vehicle, feeling the wind rush through her returning hair and nature speeding by her view.

For now, I think I shall call you L, Eleonore spoke inwardly to her child. *If you're a girl, I'll name you Ella, after an incredibly brave woman. If you're a boy, I think I shall name you Levi, in recognition of the Jewish people which I have come to know and love.*

A train horn bellowed, and Eleonore sat up straight to see the engine, about two hundred yards away, begin its gradual and sluggish journey.

"Shit!" Jung slammed his fist against the steering wheel when he spotted the train moving.

"Take the road to your left," the guard pointed.

"Are you sure?" Jung held his gaze firm on the train.

"Yes!" the guard pointed rapidly for him to take the turn.

"Ah!" Jung spun the wheel sharply in frustration and they took the side road which ran perpendicular to the train's path.

"I grew up around these parts," the guard explained, "this road will lead you straight to a crossing which meets the train."

Speeding along, Jung went down the backroad, avoiding potholes and bumps as Eleonore clung to her seat while being jostled this way and that.

For her part, Eleonore couldn't imagine why she felt the urgency to board the train. She would have to stand, for hours on end, in a crowded car with other inmates pressing around her. With a pregnant belly and feet beginning to swell, her condition was not ideal for such a journey.

As promised, the road led to a crossing and they arrived well ahead of the train. Honking the horn, Jung and the other guard waved their caps to the conductor, signaling for the train to stop. Fortunately, the train hadn't built up the momentum to be moving at any quick pace and the wheels let off a hellish squeal as the train came to an eventual stop.

"Thank you!" Jung almost laughed in relief and helped Eleonore out of the car.

Rushing towards the train, Jung opened the train car while the guard with him aimed his rifle in warning at the 'passengers'.

"Take off your shirt," Jung pointed to one of the men who returned a confused look.

"Now!" Jung drew his pistol and the man quickly obeyed.

Grabbing the shirt, Jung handed it to Eleonore who gave him a thankful glance. Removing the lieutenant's jacket, who turned away to allow her dignity, Eleonore donned herself in the large, male regulation shirt which stretched down to her knees.

Helping her into the train as she squeezed in beside the other inmates, Jung looked at her intensely. It was likely the last time he would see her, and he wanted to remember every detail.

"I wish there was another way," Jung stood back with tears in his eyes, "but this is your best chance."

'Thank you,' Eleonore mouthed. She knew what he was doing was not easy. His love for her was strong enough that he could send her away to spare her life. He wished to protect her, but knew he was unable to prevent Rudolph's hatefulness.

With a nod, Jung closed the train car again and locked Eleonore inside. There was nothing else that could be said, at least not safely. He had compromised himself enough as it was.

With a heave and a shove, the train groaned as it began its trek again and Eleonore remembered her first train ride to Auschwitz. She looked around her, as best as she could anyways, and caught the same blank expressions as in the first 'ghost train'.

A hand brushed against hers and she looked at the host and, for a brief, cruel moment, thought that she had locked eyes with none other than Ella. While similar in appearance, the woman frowned her dislike of being stared at, and Eleonore turned away. How she wished to have her friend back, to reach out and take hold of her hand.

I'm glad I have you at least, Eleonore patted her belly with a love only a mother can understand, *you've had a rather exciting day.*

The world around her was cruel and death reigned supreme, but in her womb grew the future and she would make sure it was bright. She would raise the child in the way it should go, and they would live to see a world in which the Nazi regime had breathed its last breath.

As the hours passed, Eleonore felt herself becoming faint from exhaustion. With the coming of spring, the temperature had increased drastically and, coupled with the swelling body heat from the others beside her, Eleonore found breathing difficult. After weeks, maybe months, in a bitterly cold cell, Eleonore now wished to be rid of the overwhelming warmth.

Raising her head, she tried to breathe above them, but she was too short. Slowly, the world went dark around her and the last thing she remembered was the warning whistle of the train, announcing its arrival.

Chapter Twenty-Eight: Death

"Death is the wish of some, the relief of many, and the end of all."
Seneca

"Patient seven five six nine three is stabilized," a familiar voice spoke over Eleonore.

Opening her eyes slowly, Eleonore squinted as she peered through the bright, white light stemming from the ceiling above her. She tried to lift her hand to shield her eyes but couldn't move. As her consciousness returned, Eleonore noticed that her immobility was due to her confinement to a rudimentary bed in a hospital. Groans and moans echoed from every corner, nurses checked on their patients with indifference, and Kapos stood guard in front of two large, swinging doors.

What happened? Eleonore began to panic. *Am I still in Auschwitz?*

"Can you hear me?" the familiar voice spoke again.

Eleonore's terror intensified as she looked up and saw Ma'am standing over her while talking to a doctor who was frantically scribbling notes. Then, Eleonore winced at a sore on her stomach, and tried to look down, but her strength waned, and she could scarcely lift her head.

"Can you hear me?" Ma'am asked again, growing short on patience.

"Ya...yes," Eleonore answered groggily.

"Good," Ma'am stood straight and nodded to the doctor who then moved on to the next patient without so much as offering Eleonore a glance.

"Where am I?" Eleonore squeezed her eyes shut.

"Dachau," Ma'am replied with pride as the name rolled off her tongue and then began to unfasten Eleonore's restraints.

Right, Eleonore lifted her now free hand to rub her forehead. *That doesn't explain why I was restrained, though.*

"You're lucky to be alive," Ma'am spoke with resentment.

"What happened?" Eleonore struggled to keep her eyes open, still unclear as to the details.

"I saved your life. That's what happened," Ma'am crossed her arms as she looked down on Eleonore. "The doctor had orders to kill you, but I stopped him."

"Orders from who?" Eleonore frowned.

"Commandant Hoess," Ma'am nearly shouted his name and the very mention of him sent Eleonore into a near panic.

"How can you overrule the Commandant's orders?" Eleonore squinted. There was something in ma'am's expression which eluded to a hidden intent.

"The Americans are coming," Ma'am leaned in and whispered. "I spared your life, and in return you'll spare mine."

"And how exactly did you spare my —" A surge of pain in her belly stole Eleonore's breath.

My baby! Eleonore sat up with a start and grabbed her stomach.

"What have you done!" Eleonore glared at Ma'am with red, tired eyes.

"As I said, I saved your life!" Ma'am spoke coldly.

"You killed my child!" Eleonore laid back down and began to weep uncontrollably. She was tired, alone, suffering, and now the one thing which she had to cling to had been destroyed. It was a child brought on by sin, by lust, and by a man she despised, but she loved her child nonetheless, and was determined to correct the course.

"You ungrateful whore," Ma'am shook her head as she left Eleonore alone.

Laying on the bed as she wept, Eleonore placed her hands over her stomach and felt them rise and fall with each breath over a now empty womb. *I don't want to be here without my child,* Eleonore grew bitter. *Why couldn't my fate be attached to theirs?*

"I remember you," a comforting voice spoke, and a soft hand grabbed Eleonore's.

Startled, Eleonore looked up to see none other than Mrs. Felix, the woman who had given her the bowl, standing over her with a sympathetic smile. Lost for words, Eleonore studied Mrs. Felix as she welled up before bursting into tears.

"It's alright," Mrs. Felix patted her hand as she, too, welled up. "I heard what they did to you."

"What's the point," Eleonore spoke through sobs. "What's the point of continuing?"

"I can't promise it will get easier—"

"I've heard your speech before," Eleonore interrupted. "I don't mean to sound rude, but that won't work on me."

"Why's that?" Mrs. Felix looked at Eleonore with a stern kindness, donning the countenance from her previous vocation as a teacher.

"It's rehearsed," Eleonore wiped away the tear.

"Doesn't mean its untrue," Mrs. Felix shook her head.

"I've lost everyone," Eleonore spoke as the tears returned. "Ruth and Alex, Em, Ella, and now my child."

"We've all lost," Mrs. Felix squeezed Eleonore's hand.

"Then why do you carry on the way you do?" Eleonore looked at her with incredulity. "Why offer false hope?"

"Purpose," Mrs. Felix smiled as she reflected.

"What do you mean?"

"Purpose is the antidote to suffering."

"Then what's my purpose?" Eleonore studied her earnestly.

"Only you can answer that," Mrs. Felix smiled.

"There is no purpose," Eleonore shook her head. "If the Americans save us, what shall I do with my life? Go back to being a seamstress? Seems rather trivial upon reflection."

"And why is that such a shame?" Mrs. Felix tilted her head.

"Because it doesn't matter," Eleonore huffed.

"And how can you say that doesn't matter?"

"Because how would a dress help those I lost," Eleonore swallowed. "How can I return to that life with the horrors I've witnessed? To exist is to love, and I have no one left to love."

"Regardless, return you must," Mrs. Felix nodded firmly. "You'll carry this wound for the rest of your days. None will know or understand the pain you've endured, why you are peculiar in certain regards, and why you'll never heal."

"That doesn't sound promising," Eleonore grew solemn.

"No," Mrs. Felix shook her head. "I don't promise anything but sorrow. Still, if you can get through today, you might find that tomorrow is not as difficult. Some days will be challenging, but eventually you'll come to that clearing and see the sun above the dark clouds. You'll walk through this vale of tears alone, without any to help you, but you'll make it. You'll make it."

Watching Mrs. Felix intensely, Eleonore took a deep breath, "At the Villa, they called Hedwig the angel of Auschwitz, but I believe that title is better suited to someone else."

"Fallen angel, maybe," Mrs. Felix whispered as she slandered Hedwig and Eleonore chuckled slightly.

"By the way, how is it that I find you here?" Eleonore frowned. "How did you escape Auschwitz?"

"My daughter and I have been transported between a handful of camps and we arrived here about a week ago."

"Really? How many camps?"

"More than I can —"

Sirens blared followed by the shouting of frantic officers relaying orders. At this, the doctors and nurses burst out of the room, leaving behind anything that wasn't absolutely necessary.

"Remember," Ma'am returned to Eleonore's side before leaving, "remember that I saved your life."

"You're afraid," Eleonore squinted as she looked into Ma'am's panicked eyes.

"Promise that you'll remember," Ma'am took Eleonore's hand in hers as if they had been the dearest of friends.

"Oh, I'll remember," Eleonore threatened with a victorious smile.

With a violent huff, Ma'am let go of Eleonore's hand and hurried out of the room.

"What's going on?" one of the patients asked another who had stumbled over to the window to observe.

"A hundred men, maybe more, a couple hundred yards away from the camp," the patient at the window replied.

"What's their allegiance?" another called out.

"It's hard to say," the patient peered through the dirty window, but then started cheering. "Oh! Americans! They're Americans!"

An excited gasp resounded through the hospital room and Eleonore didn't believe she had ever been more relieved to hear a word. But there it was, 'Americans', bringing her the happiest of tears.

At once the room was a hive of activity as those who were able to walk rushed over to the window to get a glimpse of their liberators. Yet some, Eleonore noticed, seemed rather apprehensive as if they had believed the Nazi propaganda about how barbaric the 'Yankees' were.

"I can't believe this!" Mrs. Felix put her hand to her mouth as she wept tears of joy. "I'm going to find my daughter."

"I'll see you soon," Eleonore squeezed her hand before she departed.

"What's happening now?" Someone called from their bed.

"A single American," a watcher replied. "He's standing out in the field with a white flag of parlay."

"Just one?" Eleonore asked.

"As far as I can see," the watcher scanned the field for anyone else.

"What's he doing?" Eleonore asked.

"Waiting," he replied with a frown. "I think he wants to discuss terms."

A shot fired.

"Are they shooting at us?" a panicked cry arose.

"No," the watcher shook his head and raised his hand for them to calm down. "One of the inmates tried climbing the gates to get a glimpse. The guards shot him."

So close to liberation, Eleonore shook her head. *They couldn't stay their murderous hatred for one moment?*

More shots fired, this time it was undoubtedly from the Americans as the walls cracked and popped with the bullets. Eleonore turned on her side as she covered her head with her hands. Then, suddenly, they ceased fire, and a German officer could be heard shouting out at the Americans.

"We're surrendering!" the watcher called out and raised his hands in triumph and a cheer erupted around the room.

Tears of joy streamed, and strangers hugged each other knowing that their days of suffering were at an end. The Nazi regime was doomed, and they were about to be liberated – something none of them had dared to dream.

The steel bars from the main gates sang their heavy tune as they swung open: there would be no further resistance. This was the end of the camps, the end of the genocide, the downfall of hatred, and the dawning of a new era.

"They're coming!" the watcher stood back from the window and all waited expectantly for their liberators to burst through the door.

Shouting came from outside as the Allies ordered the Nazis to drop their weapons and surrender. The engine of a Jeep or two roared on into the camp which had become a chaotic scene of disarray.

Finally, a shout in English came from the other side of the hospital door. But when none answered, the shout came again, only louder and more aggressive. Eleonore struggled to recall her English, but her mind was still captive to exhaustion.

"We are patients of the hospital," one of the inmates shouted back in German.

A kick and the door burst open as two young men entered rapidly with their rifles raised and their fingers on the trigger. All inside raised their hands, unsure of what to expect from these terrified Americans.

But as the Americans looked about the room, they began to lower their guns as their eyes widened. Their rifles shook in their hands as they studied the nearly starved subjects in front of them. Glancing at each other, the soldiers were at a loss as to how to react.

Then, the Americans asked something in English, calmly, but none knew the language. Eleonore thought maybe they had asked what was wrong, but she couldn't quite fit the words together. Reading English was one thing, but hearing it was another altogether, especially with an abundance of accents.

Shouting, the Americans repeated the question as they raised their rifles and pointed at random about the room.

"Please," one patient raised his hands even higher, "English...I...uh...."

"That's enough," a voice spoke in German from behind the Americans and, entering the room briskly to quell the tension, an Allied officer put his hands on their rifles and lowered them slowly as he looked reassuringly at them.

The officer was tall with dark, piercing eyes. From his accent, Eleonore thought he was from near Berlin, but there was something not quite right about it, like it had been watered down to a degree.

"I'm looking for the patient numbered Seven Five Six Nine Three," the man read off a notepad. "Also known as Eleonore Hodys."

Frozen, Eleonore wondered if she had heard him correctly. Even if had called her name, should she answer? Could she trust this man? He had the look of honesty about him, but she didn't know anything about the Americans. It was likely they were just as brutal as her Nazi captors.

"Anyone have information on this prisoner?" the man asked again and looked about the room until his eyes locked with Eleonore's.

"Here," Eleonore raised her hand timidly.

Suddenly, more shots fired from outside and the Americans spun towards the door, raising their rifles. They shouted to their comrades outside and were answered with shouting amidst some more shooting. Screaming could be heard in the distance, and Eleonore thought it sounded like someone was being beaten.

"Don't worry," the tall officer turned towards those gathered in the hospital, "my American compatriots have discovered the purpose of this camp and are enraged by what they have witnessed. They're unleashing their violence upon your oppressors."

"Are we free?" one of the patients asked, unsure if they should dare allow themselves to believe.

"Yes, yes," the man nodded without showing much concern and continued dryly, "You will be fed and clothed."

A collective sigh of relief went through the hospital room; others turned their face to heaven as they thanked God. All knew that a visit to the hospital meant death and they had been expecting its swift arrival. Instead, they were not only being liberated, but would be finally able to eat, and eat substantially.

"Miss Hodys," the man looked again at her.

"Yes?"

"I need to speak with you, privately."

"Uh," Eleonore looked about the room.

"Can you walk?"

"I believe so," Eleonore sat up slowly and put her feet onto the cold floor.

"Good," he nodded. "Come with me."

"I will need something decent to wear," Eleonore cleared her throat.

"Decent?" the tall man scoffed.

"A dress of some sort," Eleonore persisted.

Looking about the room, the man spotted a pile of clothes and, stooping down, retrieved a navy-blue dress. There was a hole in the chest from a gunshot, and the man held it in horror.

"That'll do," Eleonore walked over slowly, holding her stomach and, without shame, changed in full view of everyone. She was aware her nakedness did not invoke lust, but rather, pity with surgical cuts all throughout her torso from where the doctors had performed a quick, rudimentary abortion. It was unnecessary for them to perform the operation in such a manner, but Eleonore assumed it was to ensure that she would never become pregnant again.

"Ready," Eleonore said as the man looked at her in shock. He had been able to hide his emotions with relative ease until he had seen the scarring on her swollen belly and understood what had transpired.

"Right," the man held the door open for her. "There is an officer's command we can use for the time being."

"I'm not sure what I've done to garner such interest?" Eleonore frowned as she was led out of the hospital room.

Some more shots fired, and Eleonore grabbed onto the man as they both ducked down. This was her first conscious experience of the camp and it was much as Jung had warned: barbaric. Bodies upon bodies were piled up in a mass grave without any care to hide the atrocity.

Then, a German officer burst out from a doorway about two feet from Eleonore. His face was bloodied from being beaten and his uniform was torn. Two Americans followed closely with their eyes red from rageful tears. Taking aim, one of the Americans intended to shoot the German as he ran away, but the man escorting Eleonore stopped him at the last moment.

The American shouted in English at the man and a heated exchange took place until the officer finally calmed the American down. Eventually, the American fell to his knees and wept as his star of David neckless dangled from his neck and Eleonore at once understood his reaction.

"Come on," the man waved for Eleonore to catch up with him as he continued deeper into the camp.

"Why did you save that Nazi?" Eleonore looked at him curiously.

"That's not your concern," the man shook his head, annoyed at her questioning.

Not my concern? Eleonore frowned at the curtness. *Is he a spy working for the Nazis?*

Finally, the two came to a smaller building near the center of the camp. It was the officer's building, or so she assumed, and inside the Americans were collecting as much intel as possible by throwing documents and files into whatever boxes they could find. It was clear to Eleonore that, when the Americans arrived, they were ill-prepared to deal with the extent of the camp. That is, if they knew about its existence at all.

Opening the door to a small interview room with large, clear windows, the man asked for her to sit at a plain, greenish-grey table. Even though he was rather abrupt and a little rude, Eleonore found herself trusting this man. Sitting at the table, Eleonore winced at the strain on her stomach and held her belly as she positioned herself on the chair.

Sitting across from her, the man threw his satchel onto the table and retrieved a black pen, a pad of paper which was heavily depreciated by wear and tear, and a pack of cigarettes. Lighting his cigarette, the man didn't offer one to Eleonore who half-expected the gesture to be customary.

"May I have one?" Eleonore asked with longing.

"No," the man shook his head quickly as he wrote hurriedly.

"What are you writing?" Eleonore grew annoyed, mostly by his refusal to offer her a cigarette.

Closing his eyes as he spoke to himself softly, the man struggled to remember something pertinent that was just beyond his recollection.

"Right," he nodded and continued writing, ignoring Eleonore's question and she sighed at the disregard.

"How do you know German so well?" Eleonore continued to pester him. "Your accent is rather familiar."

"My name is Hanns Alexander," Hanns finally replied and sat up straight as he looked at her without much interest. "I grew up in Germany but was forced to flee."

"You're a Jew?" Eleonore asked.

"I am. As were those American soldiers who wanted to kill the Nazi officer."

"Then why did you stop them?" Eleonore squinted.

"A dead Nazi can't talk," Hanns looked out the window at the Allies making themselves busy, "and the world needs to hear what has been done in the name of their ideology."

"I'm still confused why you need me," Eleonore shook her head. "What have I to do with all of this?"

"Vengeance," Hanns smiled slightly.

"I'm not much use when it comes to violence," Eleonore huffed.

"Rudolph Hoess," Hanns blurted the name and Eleonore froze in terror at the mention of him. "He was the father, wasn't he," he nodded to her belly.

Eleonore's eyes welled as she thought of her child. She tried to speak, but the words wouldn't form and instead she replied with a simple nod.

"The Commandant of Auschwitz has escaped, and I have been tasked with tracking him down," Hanns leaned in and folded his hands as he spoke quietly.

"Escaped?" Eleonore frowned.

"Yes," Hanns nodded quickly.

"I don't understand how this involves me?" Eleonore shook her head.

"Will you help me hunt him down and bring him to justice?"

TO BE CONTINUED...

Ella Gartner

**Rudolph
Hoess**

Roza Robota

Eleonore Hodys with the Hoess children

The Hoess Family

The gates of Auschwitz

Standing Cell in Block 11

<u>Auschwitz Barracks</u>

Women at Auschwitz after being shaved

CPSIA information can be obtained
at www.ICGtesting.com
Printed in the USA
LVHW111620050320
649104LV00003B/627

[4]